Praise for
The Waking Land

"Abducted when she was five, Elanna is raised to despise her heritage. But when she's falsely charged with murder and must run for her life, Elanna is forced to resort to her innate magical ability to save herself and the other people she's come to care for. *The Waking Land* is all about rising to challenges, and it succeeds wonderfully."
—Charlaine Harris

"Callie Bates has written an exciting and involving first book, and she is clearly a writer of real talent."
—Terry Brooks

"A heartbreaking, enchanting, edge-of-the-seat read that held me captive from start to finish!"
—Tamora Pierce

"A simmering tale of magic that builds to a raging inferno, and hits like a cross between Brandon Sanderson and Pierce Brown."
—Scott Sigler, author of *Alive*

"This superior novel blends passionate romance and sweeping magic. . . . Bates has a delicate, precise touch with human and superhuman relationships."
—*Publishers Weekly*

"The world Elanna inhabits combines fascinating pagan symbolism, Regency romance, and political intrigue, where nothing and no one are as they first appear. Even the lush and fecund landscape itself shifts and changes form, and is itself an ever-evolving character. . . . The strong characterizations and nature-inspired magic feels fresh and ripe for a sequel to further develop this ecofantasy."
—*Booklist*

"Bates deftly builds Elanna's character, transforming her from an overly naïve pawn into a confident woman growing into her powers as she allows herself to explore love. . . . Ideal for fans of romantic fantasy such as Naomi Novik's *Uprooted*."
—*Library Journal*

BY CALLIE BATES

The Waking Land
The Memory of Fire

The Memory of Fire

The Memory of Fire

CALLIE BATES

DEL REY
NEW YORK

2019 Del Rey Trade Paperback Edition

Copyright © 2018 by Callie Bates
Map copyright © 2018 by Laura Hartman Maestro
Excerpt from *The Soul of Power* by Callie Bates copyright © 2018 by Callie Bates

Originally published in hardcover in the United States by Del Rey, an imprint of Random House, a division of Penguin Random House LLC, in 2018.

This book contains an excerpt from the forthcoming book *The Soul of Power* by Callie Bates. This excerpt has been set for this edition only and may not reflect the final content of the forthcoming edition.

ISBN 978–0–399–17743–9
Ebook ISBN 978–0–399–17742–2

randomhousebooks.com

Book design by Diane Hobbing

For my parents

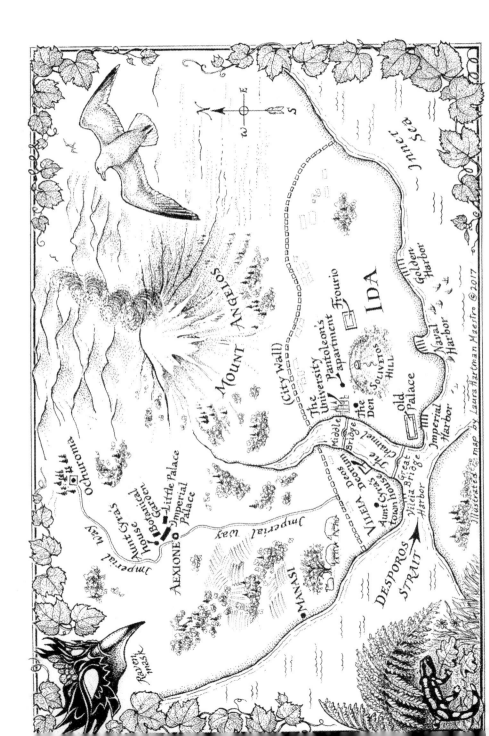

Illustrated map by Laura Hartman Maestro ©2017

THE ISMAE

Tundra

EMPIRE of AGRA

Chozat

Waset

Inner Sea

Hepsabah

PALADIS

Tsaritsa
Pontica

EDONIS

IDA

Desporos Strait

EMPIRE

Middle Sea

Pira
Britemnos Isles

TINAN

CAERIS

Laon

EREN

Tarican Strait

BAEDON

The Occident

Great Ocean

map by Laura Hartman Maestro © 2017

The Memory of Fire

PROLOGUE

Most of my childhood is torn into pieces, memories I've scraped together, guessing at the whole. But I remember waking up that afternoon, ten years old, on the stone table in Madiya's cave. I don't know why she never took the memory from me. Maybe, in the chaos, it was an accident. An omission.

I remember the taste of opium lingering bitter on my tongue. How cold my feet were. How the high, dark ceiling seemed like it could swallow me up. I couldn't remember what I'd had for breakfast. I couldn't remember coming down into the cave, or lying on the table. I couldn't remember waking up the *first* time, in my own bed, that morning. It was gone, all of it. The way it was almost every day. My memories ripped from my head by Madiya, sacrificed to make me the ideal sorcerer. *It's the patterns of your minds,* she told my brother Rayka and me. *If I can just rearrange them, I can make you the greatest sorcerers in the world. As great as Mantius of old.*

Tears burned my eyes. This once, I should have remembered. I should have resisted her. I should have spat up the laudanum—that bitter tincture of opium and alcohol Madiya fed us every day. But I hadn't, again. And again, no one had come to rescue me.

Cool fingers pressed my arm. I startled. Madiya leaned over me, a long trail of golden hair swinging over her shoulder. She smiled, gently, though it never reached her eyes. "There you are, Jahan. Let's try transforming again. I'm sure you can do it this time. Try just your arm." She leaned closer and said softly, "Think *feathers*. Think of Mantius."

Mantius. A tear ran, scalding, down my cheek. How did she know so well how to hurt me? Mantius was my comfort. My ancestor, the greatest sorcerer of his age, who had worn a cloak of black feathers. He had been able to transform himself into a raven. I would imagine him coming for me. Rescuing me. Materializing out of the past and sweeping down into the cave, gathering me up in his cloak, and carrying me far away from here, and my brothers, too. When my mother screamed at my father, saying he had no right to subject her children to Madiya's experiments, I imagined I was wrapped up in Mantius's black cloak, the feathers muffling my ears. I was warm there. Safe.

"Jahan," Madiya said, a hint of impatience coloring her voice. But when I looked at her, she smiled.

If I didn't do it, she'd drug me with more laudanum and tinker again with the patterns in my mind, and I'd wake up more muddled than ever. But if I cooperated, maybe she'd stop. And if I could get my arm to transform even slightly, she'd take me back to the house and tell my father how well I'd done. He'd puff up his chest and pontificate about how our family used to be sorcerers, back before our islands were conquered by the Paladisans, and how we'd destroy the witch hunters and reclaim our fortune. And later, I knew, I'd find my mother weeping. Saying Madiya was changing me. Saying she couldn't bear it.

Still, I was here now, with Madiya. I had no choice, even though I shrank from it. I sat up. I reached for the power from the earth, from the waterfall that surged through the cave. I thought *feathers*. I thought hollow bones and flight and the delights of eating worms. I was only ten and every day I forgot half of what I'd learned the day before. I didn't know much about birds. I thought *Mantius*.

But nothing happened. My arm stayed flesh and hair, wrist and bone and knuckles. Madiya was watching me, her mouth growing smaller and smaller. Shame dug through me. And even though I hated her with every fiber of my being, for some reason I still wanted her to like me. I tried to grin at her. "I guess I'm just bird-*brained* now!"

"You tried so hard," she said in a soothing voice, and I relaxed even though I knew I shouldn't. Madiya's kindnesses always preceded her greatest cruelties.

She walked away toward the shelves lining the cave wall and stopped before a row of shining bells. Not the bells! They were horrible, an endless ringing that left my ears aching and my mind twisted up on itself, even though she claimed they were necessary to protect me from the witch hunters. I scrambled down from the table. I had to think of something, fast, to distract her. "Let me try again to be a bird! Or maybe a badger! I know I can do it."

"Oh, Jahan." She ran her fingertips over one of the bells, her voice dispassionate now. "It's not your fault your mother made me damage you. Your brothers will always be better than you. But at least we can make you immune to the witch hunters' bells, so they don't send you mad before they kill you."

I felt myself shrink inward. Mother had interrupted one of Madiya's first experiments, when I was just a baby. Madiya had done something wrong; she claimed it had stunted me. And though she always said it wasn't my fault, it never seemed like she really meant it.

Her head came up. She tilted her chin as if she heard something— or *felt* it. She went still, and then she said in a hard, commanding voice I'd never heard before, "Jahan, stay here."

She ran for the stone steps. I hesitated. If something was scary enough to frighten Madiya, then it must be terrifying indeed. But something that frightened Madiya might also be enough to redeem my world. I raced after her, up the steps into the blinding sunlight.

I paused at the top, my eyes watering. Somewhere, a bell rang— a bright, shivery sound. A shudder ran through me. I didn't see how there could be a bell, because Madiya couldn't endure the sound outside the safety of her cave—but if there was, then it meant my brothers might be in danger, and I needed to save them. The air smelled of orange blossoms and, squinting, I saw Madiya running through the trees toward her neat white cottage. I pounded after her.

At the cottage wall, she stopped dead. I slowed, and then I saw them, just beyond Madiya. My mother and a strange man, walking down the path. I almost didn't recognize my mother; she hadn't been out of the house in weeks. She was dressed in a real gown today, and had put up her hair. She kept touching the man's arm, in a way she never did with my father. And the man . . .

I couldn't breathe. Everything flared white inside me.

He was facing my mother, his black hat tilted toward her. But even with his back to me, I recognized his blue uniform, strapped with a bandolier covered in clear stones. Even from a distance, even though Madiya insisted she had rendered us immune to their noise, I heard their hum. I knew what the man must be. A witch hunter, here. In Pira. At Madiya's cottage.

And he had my mother.

"Jahan!" It was my father, standing at the garden gate behind the cottage, my baby brother clutched squirming in his arms. He beckoned me toward him. I hesitated, swinging back to Madiya, who stood frozen, watching Mother and the witch hunter. But then the baby let out a wail and Father snapped, *"Jahan!"*

I ran to him. He shoved the baby into my arms and yanked my other brother, Rayka, out from behind the hedge. "Go! Take care of them, hide! Go!"

On the other side of the cottage, the bell rang again. Fear split through me, liquid and hot. I ran—*just the wind in the branches*—back toward the cave. Lathiel cried. Rayka bounded past me down the stairs. I spared a last backward glance for the witch hunter, but I couldn't see him beyond the trees.

We stumbled down into the cave. Lathiel hiccuped with sobs. I rocked and whispered to him while Rayka fumbled for candles and muttered at them to light themselves, even though Madiya already had two tapers burning. I tried not to be jealous at the ease with which my younger brother lit them. It cost him so little—just a flicker of deeper chill in the already cold cave. If I weren't damaged, it could have been me.

"Is it really witch hunters?" Rayka whispered. The candlelight flickered madly over his face. "What are they going to do?"

"You know what they're going to do," I said. My teeth kept chattering, but I knew it would be much colder than this in the Ochuroma—the great big prison where they kept sorcerers, the prison where Madiya had been chained for five long years, where they had leached away her magic and tried to send her mad, leaving her with only the stuff that could manipulate our minds, until finally she escaped and found refuge with Father. The witch hunters would take *us* to that prison, drain our magic and send us mad—and then kill us. Lathiel must have sensed my fear, because although he'd stopped screaming he kept crawling over my shoulder, as if he was trying to get away.

I had to be the big brother. I had to be strong for Lathiel and Rayka—and for my mother, too. I would never let the witch hunters take them.

"It'll be all right." I forced a smile at Rayka. "We're missing half our memories. We're halfway to madness already!"

He didn't smile back, and the sick, aching feeling in my stomach didn't go away. Madiya had always promised she would never let the witch hunters find us. She'd said she would die before she let them touch us—her handiwork, the boys whom she was perfecting to exact her revenge. To be the greatest sorcerers the world had ever seen, and destroy the people who'd tried to destroy her.

But the witch hunters were here, and we were alone in the cave. *Hiding.* And Mother was in danger. I stood up, my legs wobbling. My brothers would be safe here, I told myself. I handed Lathiel to Rayka and collected my courage. I might be damaged, but I was strong enough. Madiya claimed she'd made us immune to the witch hunters. So I would go back up there and save Mother.

I started toward the steps, bravery pumping hot through me. I didn't hear the footsteps at first. Didn't see the shadow of someone descending into the cave.

I looked up and my fear pulsed away into sudden warmth. *Relief.* I felt *relief.*

And then, nothing.

A BLANKNESS, LIKE nighttime, dulled by opium.

I woke in my own bed in our family villa, evening light purple on the coverlet and a scraping in my throat, like I'd screamed. I'd been dreaming of Mantius in his feathered cloak. I flailed upright. *The witch hunter.* But I was entirely alone. Not even servants made noise in the hall.

A pressure throbbed behind my right ear. I reached up a tentative hand and gasped. Pain caught me in the chest. I couldn't get my breath. I grasped at the shreds of my memory, thought I glimpsed a face, thought I saw crimson droplets on a knife. Then it was gone.

I was alone with a bandage encircling my head. I dug my fingers under it, and they came away covered with crimson grit. Dried blood. Four gentle lumps sewed up my skin—stitches.

I swallowed hard, sick with a nameless terror. Had someone attacked me? Madiya must have stolen my memories, again. Which meant she wasn't imprisoned or dead. If someone had assaulted me, why couldn't they have done better and gotten her instead?

Unless *she* attacked me. Unless this was her punishment for something I'd done, that I didn't remember.

Something thumped in the room below me—my mother's rooms. Terror plastered me to the bed, but Mother needed me. She had no one else to help her.

I picked myself up and tiptoed through the fabric of the wall itself into Rayka's room. The particles of plaster buzzed in my skin, then I stopped with a gasp. My brother lay fast asleep in his bed. A bandage swathed his chest, white against his olive skin. So someone had attacked him, too. The witch hunter? Had Rayka attacked him? Was that why Madiya was still alive? Had he—had he *killed* him?

Or had I?

I stared down at my hands. They trembled. Even the fingernails were clean, but that meant nothing. I might have done anything in the last hours, and not remember it.

I bolted for the stairs, as if, this one time, my mother could save me, though she never had before.

She woke as I flung myself into her room. I scrambled onto her bed and burrowed down beside her, pressing my face into the coverlet. Her fingernails caught in my hair. A gentle gesture—a tentative one.

"Who's this?" she said.

I lifted my head, ready to grin. I thought she was teasing.

Then I saw her face. The line between her eyebrows, the vagueness of her eyes. How her hand reached toward me but stopped, as if she was unsure whether to touch me or not.

"Mama?" Dread pulsed through me, so ferocious I called her by the name I hadn't used in several years. "What happened?"

She looked surprised, as if she hadn't expected to be called anyone's mother. Her hands brushed at her cheeks. She stared doubtfully around the room. "Where's Cyra?"

I blinked. She meant her sister. Aunt Cyra had never come to the Britemnos Isles; I'd never met her. My father burned all the letters my mother wrote to her, because each one revealed that her children were being experimented upon by a cruel sorceress.

I was shaking, but somewhere in myself I found a grin. "Did you invite her to visit?"

My mother stared at me, her lips parted, as if each word I spoke were foreign. Then she brushed her hands through her hair. "I'm . . . I'm tired. I was having a little dream. I can't remember what your papa and I called you . . . darling. Isn't that silly?"

Darling. My mother never called me darling. She called me by my name.

"Mama!" I tried to find a laugh inside me, but I couldn't. My throat kept trying to close.

She just stared at me, utterly blank.

"I'm Jahan," I whispered. I could hardly speak. "Papa wanted to name me Mantius, for our ancestor, the great sorcerer. The one he admires so much. But you talked him into naming me Jahan, after Grandpapa. Remember?"

She just stared at me, uncomprehending. And I began to cry.

Footsteps stirred behind me. I whirled, my heart lurching so hard I thought I'd throw up. Madiya stood there, silhouetted by the window. I didn't know how long she'd been watching us.

Her face was cold. And I knew, then, that she'd done it. This wasn't one of my mother's episodes. Madiya had taken away her memories—not just the ones of breakfast or what she'd done that morning. *Years* of memories.

I was supposed to save her, and I'd failed. Failed so completely I couldn't even comprehend it.

Madiya strode over to the bed. I backed away, falling off onto the tiles and smacking against the wall. I didn't have any weapons to defend myself, and my magic was a failure. Madiya had taught me everything I knew. I couldn't fool her. This time, she would take away my entire mind, just like she'd taken my mother's.

Maybe she *had* stabbed me. Maybe this time, she hadn't been careful when she rummaged around in our brains. Or in Rayka's case, in our hearts. Or maybe this was what she'd been doing to us all along, after she drugged us with the opium. Maybe there were other scars I'd never found. She'd taught us, after all, how to heal ourselves.

She put her hand on Mother's forehead. My mother gave her a placid, lamblike smile and fell instantly asleep.

A shiver ran up my body. This was all wrong. Mother would never let Madiya touch her.

"It's a mercy for her, forgetting," Madiya said. "She's suffered a great deal."

"N-no!" I stammered. "I know what you did! You stole her—you *took* her—"

"Jahan," she snapped, and I fell silent, shaking. "*She* summoned the witch hunter. She put us all in danger."

I stopped. That couldn't be right. Mother wouldn't have summoned a witch hunter to capture Madiya, because capturing her meant capturing *us*.

"It's safe now," Madiya said, impatient. "The witch hunter's gone. We got rid of him. Go back to bed."

We. I looked down at my clean hands. I tried to stare into the empty hole in my memory, but there was nothing. Nothing but a kind of ache. A nameless grief.

Madiya was ignoring me now. She collected her book from the night table and tucked it under her arm. Then, without a backward glance, she walked from the room.

I huddled there for a long time, between the bed and the wall. Waiting for her to come back and force the laudanum down my throat. To scar me again. To take all my memories, even the ones of my mother.

But she didn't come back.

And I didn't forget.

CHAPTER ONE

I still hear her voice. Even in Eren, an entire sea away, Madiya's whisper flickers into my mind. *Jahan.* My own name, digging like a hook into my head, *insisting* that I follow its lead. Demanding an answer. Demanding that I return to her.

Doesn't the woman have anything better to do? I ran away from home when I was fifteen. It's been six years since my mother died. Since I fled. Yet even as I try to brush her away, even as I tell myself I'm hundreds of miles from her, that I'm safe, her whisper comes again, more demanding. *Jahan!* Maybe I should answer. She's still got Lathiel—something might have happened to him. If it has, I'll never forgive myself.

Jahan—

"Jahan?"

Not Madiya's voice. Elanna's.

El's hand on my wrist, her fingers warm and slightly damp. I see her, now—bundled in a coat, her chestnut-brown hair curling loose from its knot beneath her black felt hat—as I didn't see her before. Cold terror pulses through me. How long was I oblivious to anything but Madiya's voice? I shouldn't succumb so completely. I've grown practiced at pushing Madiya away—or so I thought. After she finally let Rayka come to me, two years ago, her whispers quieted. I thought perhaps she was loosening her grip. That maybe, if I bided my time, I could pressure her into freeing Lathiel, too. I thought . . .

"Jahan." El's eyes widen meaningfully. "Are you all right?"

Oh, *damn* the gods. We're standing outside a coach on the edge of a winter field. A group of townspeople and farmers have tramped out to meet us, a cluster of brown coats and worried looks. They're warmly dressed, even though it's late in the month of Noumion and that ought to translate to spring in southern Eren. But the winter has been cruel—crueler, the people claim, than in other years. El says the land is trying to regain its rhythm after being woken, but some Ereni claim that the *Caveadear,* rather than bringing the land to life, has irrevocably distorted its natural rhythm. They've been taught to distrust magic for centuries, after all.

So El and I came out here at the crack of dawn, all the way to the border with Tinan, to prove that the *Caveadear*'s magic can and will help them. We're supposed to be reassuring them that they won't starve; that the Tinani won't cross the river behind us and destroy them.

Instead we've stopped dead, and I've been staring into space like a lunatic. Reassuring, indeed.

El shakes my wrist, eyebrows lifted, her eyes widening further. She's getting nervous, though surely her heart isn't ricocheting quite as madly as mine. *She* doesn't hear Madiya. She casts a pointed look at the coach boy, who's coming around to see what's the matter.

"Isn't this marvelous!" I say brightly, ignoring the fact that my shirt is soaked with rapidly cooling sweat. I'll finally catch my death in this abysmal Ereni winter, even though I'm already bundled in twice as many clothes as the locals. "Look at the view!"

Elanna stares from the farm fields, a flat and unrelieved white, to the charcoal smear of trees on the ridge above our coach. The sky lies gray and flat. Nearby, the wide river Ard mutters over rocks. Her eyes narrow. "Indeed."

She doesn't believe me—and she's irritated that I'm lying to her—but she's not going to berate me in front of these strangers. She releases me and strides away toward the gathered farmers.

I flex my hands and swing my arms. If I freeze to death, or fail to hear Tinani charging over the river, it'll be Madiya's damned fault. *Jahan,* she whispers, and I shiver all over. All the same, I manage a grin at the coach driver. "Sorry you volunteered to leave so early, eh?"

The boy, bright-eyed and eager to impress, visibly stiffens. "No, sir. I'm honored to serve the *Caveadear.*"

I stifle a sigh. Once again, I've said the wrong thing—and these Ereni take themselves too damned seriously. Those who aren't grumbling about the crown changing hands follow El with a fervor bordering on worship.

No, I reflect as I tramp after Elanna through knee-high snow, it's me no one particularly cares for. When I first arrived with Finn, the people here seemed to think me a kind of exotic legend come to life. I kept my role in the rebellion largely secret, not wanting to advertise my sorcery and put my brothers in danger. And now, on the brink of war with the empire of Paladis, I'm the resident Paladisan. I'm the face of the enemy. It doesn't seem to matter that Elanna and the new queen, Sophy, trust me. I can always see the moment these people register my accent, my foreign manners. I can see them wondering what I'm doing here. What I want. Whether, and when, I'm going to betray them.

Maybe they're right. Maybe I don't belong here. But I fought for their freedom. My friend Finn gave his life for their cause. If I belong anywhere, it should be in Eren.

And yet . . . What good am I doing here? Thanks to the stone circles, my power comes with astonishing ease here—nothing like the effort it takes in Paladis—but my magics are still small. I advise Sophy on relations with the empire—much good though it's done. I welcome the small stream of refugees to Eren, translating misunderstandings, trying to put the haunted-eyed Idaean and Baedoni and Tinani sorcerers at ease. But the emperor is still poised to declare war. The Tinani are still attacking our eastern border. The refugees would survive without my help.

And my brothers aren't here. From here, I can't get my lawyers to pry Lathiel out of Father's and Madiya's clutches. And even though Rayka's safe at his military academy, every day I'm apart from him I worry that Madiya has found him again. That he's succumbed to her.

Ahead of me, Elanna's gesturing enthusiastically at the farmers. Her voice drifts across the snow, bright with the power of the land. ". . . and I will bring you the wheat you need!"

No, Elanna Valtai doesn't really need my help. She tells me she loves me—and the tenderness that swamps me when I look at her must be love, too. But love isn't the same as *need*.

Jahan. Madiya's voice whispers again into my mind.

I almost want to laugh, even though my palms are sweating again and my heart beats faster. Of course Madiya thinks she needs me—to use the sorcery she gave me to carry out her plan to destroy the witch hunters. Even though she spent my entire childhood telling me how inadequate I was.

But if I don't respond, does it put Lathiel in danger? Something could have happened. She could have gone too far in an experiment. She could have overdosed him with opium.

I tell myself I'm making things up. But her voice follows me, insidious, as I come up behind Elanna and the farmers. And the ache in my chest doesn't go away.

El stands apart from the group, her hands outstretched. The locals mutter among themselves. A murmur drifts toward me: ". . . can she?" one of the farmers is saying.

I look at them, gathered together in their somber coats. Except for a few daring glances, they all ignore me. Many faces are gaunt from the long winter's privations. A girl child leans against her mother's leg, shivering in a too-thin coat. Guilt stings me. How can I complain about the cold when these people struggle to stay alive? If I need another coat, I merely have to commission it. That's not a luxury they have.

The little girl sees me watching her. Her gaze flickers from me to Elanna to her mother, who seems oblivious to our interaction. I crouch, gesturing the girl closer. She approaches on hesitant legs. I unwrap one of my three scarves and whisper a little magic into the thick wool. *Keep her warm.* The power floods through my fingers, buoyant and eager, with an immediacy that still surprises me. It's as if the magic in Eren is yearning to be used, as if the land has so much to give it's overflowing.

The girl, casting an uncertain look back at her mother, takes the scarf from me. She frowns a little; it feels like ordinary wool. I gesture for her to wrap it around her neck. She does, and her eyes widen. Its warmth will be heating her now—but no one else, not even her mother, will feel it.

I put a finger to my lips and wink at her. She gulps and darts back to the safety of the adults.

The wind shifts through the stalks of dead wheat, mingling with people's whispers. Elanna still stands there, her legs braced. She looks small, unremarkable, under their eyes, dwarfed by the great-coat she always wears. Unease shifts through me. This is taking too long. In the first few days and weeks after she woke the land, she hardly had to snap her fingers and a plant would spring to life. But now, two months on, the power that made forests walk and rivers change course is less quick to come. The mountain people tell her she's simply exhausting herself—and the earth. But the need to provide her people with food, and protect them from the war dogging our borders, has required El to use her power again and again. She's wearing thin, and if she continues in this way I'm afraid she'll deplete herself entirely.

And the locals have noticed. I see their glances. *This* is the steward of the land? they ask each other, unspoken. This girl, hardly twenty, who looks so slight in her too-large coat? This isn't the magnificent personage the stories promised them. This is a human girl, and she's tired.

Come on, El, I think. But nothing happens.

Just as I'm wondering whether I'll have to try some magic of my own, however, the whispering wind grows louder. The dead wheat stalks flush a brilliant green, shocking against the whiteness of the snow. They begin to grow, climbing higher and higher, verdant in the winter field.

I let out a breath. It's working. The green ripples out through the fields, until the land is a brilliant carpet. The snow begins to melt as the ground warms.

The locals exclaim. One actually laughs in amazement. A man rushes past me, past Elanna, out into the sprouting wheat.

El glances over her shoulder and catches my eye. I can feel her worry even from here. Maybe the magic worked this time, but what about the next town, the next farm field, the next battle with Tinan? If El can't make an entire field of wheat grow from frozen ground, will the people think she's failed, when all she really needs is rest? What will come of the whispers against her, those who say the Eyrlais should never have been toppled by the Caerisians with their savage magic?

I shake my head slightly, trying to tell her she can't let the worry overcome her, not now. These people need to see a confident *Caveadear*. We can worry about the future later.

I waggle my hands, trying to make her smile. "I can hardly feel my fingertips!"

She rolls her eyes. But when one of the farmers approaches to clasp her hand, she manages to smile at him. I wait while she talks to everyone who demands her attention, the slush growing softer under my feet. At last the farmers scatter, tramping back along the road toward the village. I offer El my arm, though she scrambles through the slush more nimbly than me. "Where to next, milady?"

"Gourdon, I think. I can do the same thing there."

But there's a weariness in her voice. I look down at her. She's frowning into the distance. As gently as I can, I say, "You don't have to make *every* wheat field sprout green, you know. Besides, it's not terribly exciting. Watching wheat grow . . ."

"But if I do one, I have to do them all," she says, with an edge of panic. "I can't just leave one village to starve because I'm—I'm *tired.*"

All of Eren and Caeris will starve if she exhausts herself and the land, I think, and then we'll be even more vulnerable. "It doesn't have to be today, though. It must be, what, ten miles to Gourdon? We can make the journey last a bit longer, find somewhere to stay the night . . . I know ways to entertain you."

She sighs. "The ride there will be time enough."

I raise an eyebrow. "I'm not sure the coach boy is *that* obtuse."

She blinks, and a laugh gurgles out of her as she realizes my meaning. I grin. El grabs the lapel of my coat and pulls herself up to whisper in my ear. "Jahan Korakides, when we have a chance, I'm going to show you a thing or two!"

"Well," I say, smiling into her eyes, "I shall look forward to that very much ind—"

An explosion of noise interrupts me. *Gunfire.* It blasts through the trees, down from the cliff above the coach. Sparks flare. I shove Elanna behind me, protecting her with my own body. Who the hell is firing at us? I scrabble for the guns with my mind, reaching for the stocks—

The coach boy runs out, waving an old musket. The shots catch him. His body jerks. The old musket flies up into the air. No, damn it, no! I'm running toward him like an idiot. A shot wings toward me. I let it dissolve through my chest and out the other side, leaving the sour taste of burning on the back of my tongue. I pump my arms, but the poor, brave fool is already lying there, his eyes wide, blood gurgling through his lips. Above us, the shots have ceased. Smoke hangs on the air.

I crouch beside the boy. The soul's gone; his eyes are empty and open. He shouldn't be dead—not now, not like this.

I look up. Movement rustles through the trees above me. Whoever's there must be reloading their guns. I reach up to break them, glancing back at the same moment for Elanna. She's unscathed, thank the gods. But she's frowning—not up at the ridge, but toward the left, where the forest trails down into the farm field. Someone's coming through the trees. I catch the glimpse of a sky-blue coat.

A bell *tings*.

I freeze. The first bell is joined by another, and another—a cacophony rising over the fields, buzzing into the earth. Burrowing into Elanna's mind. Sliding around mine.

Witch hunters.

I *knew* it wasn't safe to come so close to the border—

A voice barks an order. A *Paladisan* voice. It's my people on the ridge, firing at us—and my people in the woods. Shots ring out above us, again. I scramble for their guns, clenching my fists, reaching for power. It floods up through the earth into my feet, washing through my body. Slower, perhaps, than when El first woke the land, when healing myself took scarcely minutes. My heartbeat races in my ears, then slows. My veins flush cold as I pour out magic, but at the same time Eren's power hums through me, vibrant and alive and eager to be used. I catch as many shots as I can with my mind. They stutter and go out, falling to the earth, nothing more than dust.

Behind me, the ground trembles—Elanna's doing. She's standing there, arms outstretched, her face pale with strain. One of the shots must have caught her. Blood trickles down her cheek.

But the trees don't fling their roots from the earth and walk. The witch hunters are sliding out through them, a contingent of three walking toward us in formation, their bells ringing. Elanna grunts. The bastards are stopping her magic. Toying with her mind.

I reach for the clappers on the bells, but my power slides off, as if I've pushed a finger against glass. The witch hunters continue to advance. I try persuasion. *Go,* I think at them, *you're not wanted here. We're not who you're looking for.* But again, nothing. My legs prickle, and I swallow hard against the fear rooting me to the ground. I've never attempted magic on a witch hunter—not that I remember, at any rate—and now I know why. It doesn't work.

And if I can't work magic on them . . .

They're advancing. El's fallen to her knees, her eyes scrunched with the effort of pushing her sorcery back against the witch stones and bells. There's a rustle in the trees—more soldiers sweeping in behind the witch hunters. The ones on the ridge must still be there. By now they'll again be reloading their weapons.

Maybe Elanna and I can't fight the witch hunters with magic, but the fools are proceeding toward us, unarmed, across the field.

I reach for the muskets up on the ridge and *command* them with all the power in my body. *Come.*

Startled cries rise from the ridge. The muskets come sailing overhead. One backfires in midair, sparks flying over the empty field. So does a second. But I catch two in my hands. I toss one to El, who catches it. Without hesitation, she trains it on the approaching witch hunters. So do I.

All three men stop. Funny how that works.

"Go back to Paladis!" I shout at them in Idaean. "Scram!"

They mutter among themselves. Their hands are up, the bells no longer ringing. The word *Korakos* carries over the field. My nickname, for the raven crest of my family. I've been recognized. They don't know, of course, that the name really belongs to the great sorcerer I'm descended from.

My palms are sweating. It's strange to be looking at my own people down the length of a musket. Even if they are witch hunters.

One takes a hesitant step forward. "Stop," I shout, "or we'll shoot!"

He halts. The other two are looking at Elanna—of course it's her they're here for. They've crossed the border to capture her, to drag her back to Paladis with a sack over her head, so they can send her mad in the Ochuroma and execute her before the entire empire. Because that is what my people, the guardians of civilization, do.

Well, not this time. I'm not letting them take El any more than I let them take my brothers when I was a boy. No matter the consequences.

"You're on the wrong side of this war, Korakos!" the witch hunter calls.

I studiously aim the musket at him. The damned thing is growing heavy in my arms, and I don't know if I can actually shoot a fellow Paladisan, even a witch hunter. I'd certainly never be welcome back in Ida again if I did. But he shuts his mouth.

The earth trembles. Maybe it's the silenced bells, but Elanna is working around the witch hunters somehow. Within the forest, a tree stretches. It pulls one root, then another, ponderously from the ground. A man cries out, high-pitched. Another tree is moving, and another. The witch hunters swing around to stare. One rings his bell frantically.

Elanna fires at him. The shot goes wide, but my ears whine and the witch hunter throws down the bell as if it's burned him. I feel myself grin. The trees are advancing now, their roots kneading the earth. In the forest, the soldiers have already dissolved into chaos. *You're terrified,* I tell them, insisting with all my might. *You've never seen anything so frightening. Run!* Splashes echo as they scramble down the slope to the river.

One witch hunter, the one who threw down his bell, turns and races into the forest. The other two hesitate.

I sigh. It's so damned tempting to fire at them. So I do.

I aim wide but magnify the sound. The witch hunters turn tail and run. The trees sway after them, menacing.

Elanna glances at me. The trickle of blood has reached her jaw, and my body starts instinctually toward her to see if she's all right. But I force myself to wait, listening to the distant sounds of men crashing through the river, their shouts barely audible now. Elanna's staring at the corpse of our coach boy, crumpled on the grass a little distance from us.

"Jahan," she says quietly. Her nostrils are flared. "How are we going to stop them?"

I crack a grin, though performing so much sorcery leaves me feeling hollowed out. Thin. "We'll make the emperor legalize sorcery and recognize you as steward of the land."

Of course she doesn't return the smile, and I wonder if I've said the wrong thing. But the truth is that the emperor won't stop sending the witch hunters until El's dead, or he is. She knows this as well as I do. The Paladisan emperors built their empire on the subjugation of sorcerers; they're not going to stop just because we've asked nicely. Soon they'll send the black ships to bully us into surrendering. Even with Elanna's magic, even with mine, I don't know how we'll defeat a navy that's famously invincible.

Unless . . . The idea hits me squarely in the chest and I have to catch my breath. "El," I begin, but she's walking in tight strides to the coach boy, kneeling beside him to whisper the Caerisian benediction to the dead. Her hand trembles as she pushes his eyelids shut.

I follow. A whisper worms into my mind—Madiya's voice. *Jahan. Not* now.

I shove her aside and kneel beside Elanna, touching her jaw lightly so she faces me. Unshed tears gather, luminous, in her eyes. Tugging out my handkerchief, I blot away the blood that stains her cheek. There doesn't seem to be a larger wound—one of the shots must have just grazed her.

"We *won*," she's saying, her voice a furious whisper. "We defeated the Eyrlais. We claimed Eren and Caeris. But our people are still dying."

I swallow hard. My own eyes itch. It's impossible not to think of Finn, dead on the floor of that bakery. The prince, my friend, who brought me here in the first place. The one who was supposed to be king, even though he never wanted it. The revolution was his way of proving himself to his father, his way of saying, *I am the son you want me to be.* I came along for the magic, for the whispers about the legendary *Caveadear,* the steward of the land. I wanted such a person to exist. I wanted her to do what I couldn't: wield such an unimaginable magic that it would render an entire land untouchable by the witch hunters who believe sorcery to be anathema.

But even though I found her, even though she kneels beside me, even though she woke the land, the witch hunters are still coming for us. Eren isn't untouchable. It's vulnerable, and isolated. We defeated the Eyrlais, but now we're open to a far more dangerous foe: the empire of Paladis itself. Not to mention all of Eren's neighbors, especially Baedon and Tinan, which have already descended on us like eager dogs.

And now another boy lies dead on the ground. For nothing.

Elanna rubs her cheeks. She shifts closer, and her forehead bumps my jaw. I look down at her, her face shadowed between our bodies. She looks both angry and soft, with her hair curling out from beneath her cap, her chin set, the stain of blood lingering on her cheek. The privations of this winter have created hollows in her cheeks I want to fill, and tension in her strong, slender frame that I can't loosen. Her love is such an uncomplicated thing—a fact that she holds up as irrefutable, that she's unafraid to show. While I cringe when people see us touching; while I hide our relationship from the world. Because if anyone sees how much Elanna matters to me, she will be taken from me, just as my mother was. I know this in my bones, even though it jars against all logic.

But I won't let Emperor Alakaseus take her. It's that simple. And I know what I need to do. Even if she doesn't like it.

She's leaning back, wiping her eyes. "We should go find the coach. See where the horses went . . ."

"I have—" I begin.

But El's head snaps up, her gaze moving behind me. "Someone's coming!"

"—an idea," I finish, unheard. She's already on her feet. I suppose it'll wait—and I'm not ready for her disappointment. Not yet.

I won't leave her until I have to.

I scramble to my feet to see who's come to find us.

CHAPTER TWO

A party of riders on horseback are barreling down the road, past the shoots of new wheat. The soldiers' uniforms still bear the colors of the deposed Eyrlai monarchs, but a woman in a red coat rides at the head of the line, her yellow hair bare and bright under the clouded sky.

"Sophy?" Elanna calls out. She bursts into a run. I force myself to a trot after her, though I still don't feel quite myself. The hollowed-out feeling takes a long time to pass. But at least it no longer leaves me completely crippled, the way it did after I escaped Madiya.

She's whispering again at the back of my mind. *Jahan.*

No, I think at her, even though a treacherous part of me begins to answer. What if Lathiel needs me? What if I'm failing him, again?

Ahead, the riders rein in. Sophy Dunbarron, the queen of Eren and Caeris, flings herself off her horse, her pale cheeks bright red from the cold. She runs toward us and grips Elanna's arms. "El, what happened? The villagers said they heard gunshots—"

"A party from Tinan. Witch hunters. We stopped them."

"You heard it from the villagers?" I ask Sophy. Curious that they didn't send help. I glance at Elanna, who gives her head a quick shake. She's not going to risk incurring anyone's wrath by accusing the villagers or their friends of letting witch hunters across the border. I suppose the Paladisans might have found the ford with Tinani help. But still, I don't like it.

El shakes Sophy's arms. "What are you *doing* here? I thought you'd gone north, to the Butcher!"

"That's what I had planned to do." Sophy wets her lips and fumbles a small bundle of papers from her pocket. She can't seem to look at either of us. She seems, suddenly, terribly young and overburdened. She thrusts one of the letters at me. "This came for you, Jahan."

A letter for me? I glance at the script. Clear, elegant letters spell out my full name. It's Aunt Cyra's handwriting. I move instinctively to break the seal, a kind of hopeless dread tightening my chest. It must be news about Lathiel. Our lawyers must have failed, again, to prevail on my father to hand over guardianship of my youngest brother. We always knew that, when he finally agreed to send Rayka, Father didn't consider it a concession but a trade. We could have Rayka, but he'd keep Lathiel. At least, until Madiya tired of him. Which, so far, she hasn't. My gut already twists, ugly with sickness.

Maybe I *should* answer Madiya's summons. For Lathiel's sake.

Sophy bursts through my thoughts. "Our contact in Ida sent news. The fleet the emperor has been assembling—he's announced plans to send it. Here. To our shores."

I stare at her. She's looking into the distance between Elanna and me, her mouth tight, the paper crumpled between her hands. Even though we knew it was coming, this can't be the future Sophy longed for, any more than El did. She must have hoped that once she'd won, all the conflict would end. That she would be queen, and that would be that. But it's so far from reality that it's almost laughable.

Her throat works. "Ad—Admiral Moreau says we have less than half the forces Paladis is assembling. Especially if they combine their navy with Baedon."

"We have magic," Elanna begins. She falters. "The land . . ."

She doesn't say what we're all thinking. That she's exhausting her power, and in order to grow strong again she needs rest, but cannot afford it. That the Tinani on the land border have persisted despite floods and wandering forests. And even if she were at full strength, her magic still might not be enough against the might of the Paladisan fleet, the sheer number of men and weapons and vessels they can throw against us. They conquered Eren once before without magic. If the black ships land on Ereni soil, we are in danger of losing everything we've fought for. Our own lives are the least of it.

I look at Sophy. "How much time do we have? Before the black ships set sail?"

She gives me a blank stare, but rustles the paper. "A week, maybe two. The seas are a bit rough yet. That's the only thing delaying them."

A week is enough. I can work with that.

"I have a plan," I say. "I can go to Ida. I'll treat with the emperor for peace."

"What?" El says. "No, Jahan—"

I shake my head. Sophy's listening, her breath held in. "We're on the brink of war. But I can try to persuade His Imperial Majesty that fighting Eren isn't in his interests. I could try to procure an alliance."

"But they know you're a sorcerer!" Elanna exclaims. "You just summoned *muskets* through the *air* against *witch hunters*."

"They won't be sure what happened. It was fast. It might have been me, or you, or someone they didn't see." I pause. El's eyes are large, angry; she twists the seal ring furiously on her finger. But Sophy is staring at me as if I've offered her water in the desert. "Look. I know everyone at court, and everyone knows me." Unlike the Ereni, who see only a distrustful foreigner. "I stand a better chance of persuading the emperor than anyone else in Eren. It may not succeed, but I can try."

"It makes sense," Sophy says, too fast. Elanna glares at her.

"El," I say. Maybe I'm making a hash of this. I'm terrible at love, or whatever I'm supposed to call what's between us. I meet her eyes, willing her to see my thoughts. "Please, let me do this for you."

Her nostrils flare. "It's too dangerous. If you stay here, we can fight together."

"But if I go to Paladis, I can fight *for* you." And if there's anything I know, if there's any place I truly belong, it's at the imperial court in Aexione. She has to understand that. Even if Prince Leontius hasn't sent me a single letter since I left, I know him. He'll help us. "I can use my friendship with Leontius, my reputation—everything—to save us. And even if some rumor about my magic follows me back . . ." I glance between them, hesitant to share this secret. But El won't believe me if I don't. "I can *persuade* people that I'm not a sorcerer."

"But it's a *lie*, Jahan," Elanna bursts out. "Don't you—how can you—" She shakes her head.

I grin at her. "It's the perfect trick, don't you see? Using magic to save magic, *secretly*—" I throw up my hands. "You hid your magic for years! So did I."

"But we fought so that we don't *have* to hide it anymore. The refugees are coming here so *they* don't have to hide it! And yet you are returning to Ida on the pretense that you have nothing to hide. If they find out . . ."

I start toward her. I want to put my hands on her shoulders, fit my thumbs into the grooves of her collarbone. But Sophy is here, and unlike Elanna I can't bear for anyone else to see us touch. I don't want anyone to see where I put my heart, not even Sophy Dunbarron. So I cough and pull myself up. "They're not going to find out."

"Aren't you tired of holding on to secrets?"

I blink. *No,* I think. My secrets are as comfortable to me as a second skin. But that's not the way it is for Elanna, who holds up truth like a banner. She won't understand, even if I try to explain. So I say quietly, "For you, I'll hold on to them a little longer."

Her eyes brighten, but then she presses her lips together. "*I* don't need you to hold on to any secrets. I don't need you to go to Ida. You could stay right here. With me."

I look at her, slim and quivering in her old greatcoat, her chestnut hair tumbling over her collar, and my throat tightens. She's right. I can't go, not with her looking at me like this. Not if it means losing her.

And yet . . . It's not as if she needs me here. It's not as if my small magics do any good, especially against her great land magic. She has to see that, and if she doesn't now, she will one day. One day she'll realize she's given her heart to a damaged sorcerer who's little more than a charlatan, who's such a coward he's never been able to tell her the whole truth about himself.

Sophy utters a sigh. "Listen, El, this isn't about you! He's offering to save our nation. Our people. We have to let him try." She turns back to the riders and beckons a soldier for pen and ink. "I'll write you papers, Jahan, authorizing you as ambassador royal under my name and seal."

"Ambassador royal?" I almost laugh; it's not as if I've pledged fealty to Sophy. "What will Ida's wits say? I left Idaean and am coming back Ereni."

Sophy, busy negotiating with her inkwell, doesn't answer. Elanna strides away into the wheat, her shoulders hunched. I hesitate, but though it feels safer to linger beside Sophy, I follow El.

Some distance out into the field, she stops. The clouds are clearing; we stand alone in a patch of sunshine, boots sinking into the sodden ground. Alone, for the moment.

"I'm coming back to you," I say to her back. "You know that."

She turns, and I see tears have left marks down her cheeks. "No, Jahan, I don't know that. You don't tell me everything. You go off into your head, and something different comes out of your mouth. You keep telling me this is for the good of Eren and Caeris. So maybe you won't come back, if that's 'for the good of Eren and Caeris,' too. Maybe you think you're better off without me."

"No, I—" I offer a weak laugh. "You're probably better off without *me*."

She folds her arms, looking at me. I want to distract her with a joke or a kiss. I don't want to be seen like this, so open-eyed. But instead I return her look. The trace of freckles around her nose, a shade darker than her tawny skin; the golden brown of her irises. The way she studies me like she's trying to see the framework of my being. How strands of her hair are always falling out of their practical knot. Her fierceness; her determined courage. She's open where I hide, and brave when I'm merely charming. The scent of earth and growing things rises off her skin; there's a wildness about her. A vastness. This woman holds all of Eren and Caeris in herself. She's the land and the land is her.

And I am the one Madiya damaged. The weakest of the three brothers. The one who charmed his way into a position of power when he didn't merely trick people with sorcery. I'm no match, not truly, for Elanna Valtai.

She sighs. "Jahan . . ."

But even as she says it, another voice repeats my name at the same moment.

Jahan!

It's not Madiya's voice. It's young, and male, and desperate.

Rayka.

"What's wrong?" El's saying, but I can't find the breath to answer. I'm digging in my pockets for something, anything, that might reflect my face. Cold metal hits my fingers. A coin. I hold it up. It's recently minted—with the late Antoine Eyrlai's profile on it—and my reflection is nothing more than a dim smudge. But it should still work.

"Rayka?" I say. "Rayka!"

I can't see whether my reflection transforms into his. But his voice echoes into my head. *Did she find you?*

Cold white terror washes up my legs. I can hardly speak. No. Madiya can't have Rayka again, not after everything I did to free him from her. I fumble for words. "Does she have you? I'm fine. I'm in Eren. Where's Lathiel? Do you have news? Rayka?"

But he doesn't answer. His connection's been cut.

I stare at the coin in my fingers. My skin feels numb. Something's happened. My brother has never contacted me of his own volition before.

"Jahan?" El says. She's touching my elbow, but I don't feel it.

"I—my brothers—" Sophy gave me a letter from Aunt Cyra. I've been holding it all this time. I break the seal, though my fingers are shaking so badly I almost rip the paper. The letter begins with the usual greetings, but my gaze drops straight to the second paragraph.

I trust that Rayka found you in Eren. That is, I presume that's where he's gone. He ran away from the Akademia *last week— you should have seen the commotion those military folk made, looking for him. If he is there, give him my regards, and remind him he won't be granted a second try on his exams.*

A pressure is rising in my ears, swelling my head. Aunt Cyra knows Rayka wouldn't just disappear, not from the military academy he loves. This isn't simple concern.

It must have been Madiya. She must have summoned him. She must have spoken his name—her voice sibilant, commanding, insistent, even if her magic is weak. He must have heard her just the way I do. And he must have finally been unable to resist.

That, or the witch hunters discovered his secret.

"Jahan," Elanna is saying. She's gripping my wrist; I didn't even feel it until she spoke.

"I have to go," I say. My mind is spinning. It's two days by sea to the Britemnos Isles. I can get to Roquelle, the port, today. But all the gods, what if Madiya has a new plan? What if she's not only experimenting on Rayka but doing something even more dangerous with Lathiel, too?

Elanna's leaning over my shoulder, reading the letter. Softly, she says, "She doesn't say he's been taken by witch hunters . . ."

I shake my head. It's possible, I suppose. But if that's the case, they'd have a warrant out for my arrest. Sophy's contact in Ida would have told us that. At least, I think so.

El lowers her voice. "You'd know if . . . the sorceress . . . took him, wouldn't you?"

I shake my head, mute as the street performers in Ida. I fumble for words. "How would I know? I don't know what she's done to him. If she . . ."

I stop. Madiya took my mother's memories. She erased them utterly. She's taken my memories, and Rayka's, and Lathiel's—maybe not as a whole, but in bits and pieces. Neither she nor my father wanted Rayka to go to Ida. If she's angry with him, what will she take from him this time? What will be the cost of me trying to save him? Will she punish Lathiel, too?

"Rayka," I say aloud. *"Rayka!"*

But there's nothing. Maybe my will isn't strong enough. After all, Madiya called me her failure. And I ran away from home when I was fifteen. I kept the knowledge I learned, but I've spent six years avoiding its practice. Six years hiding what I am.

If I have to stop Madiya, will I even know how?

Elanna's gripping both my hands. "This Madiya is only a woman. You told me she has hardly any sorcery of her own. She has no *power*, Jahan."

"You don't understand. She—she—" I stare down into El's face. If I go back to Pira, Madiya could seize me, too. She could steal my memories. She could take the knowledge of Elanna away from me. She could take everything, just as she did to my mother.

"If you don't hear from me," I say, "don't send anyone after. There may not be anything left of me to salvage."

"Yes, there will." She's holding me fiercely. "There has to be! Your brother probably ran away because he was worried about failing his exam."

I shake my head. She doesn't know Rayka at all—any more than I know him, really. He's far too stubborn to give up on the exams. He *wanted* the blasted military academy. He begged to join it. He didn't want to laugh with me or talk about the years without me. The years I abandoned him. He didn't want to say what Madiya taught him, or what she took from him. He just wanted to read about ancient battles and biographies of conquerors. He didn't even have the knack for making friends with the other students, who'd sneered at his accent and intellectual interests. He wanted to wall himself away from the world. The one time I got him to laugh was when I offered to challenge some of his rivals to a duel. "We could do them in," he said, and I don't think he was joking.

He's stubborn. An unpleasant bastard, half the time. But he's my brother, and I can't leave him to Madiya. Not when she still has Lathiel. I can't leave both my brothers with her.

And to find him—to save them both—I have to go home.

"All right," Elanna says softly. I focus on her face. "You're going to talk to me every evening. At nine o'clock. Or I'll think you've been imprisoned for lying to everyone."

Her tone is gently teasing. I force a smile. "It's an hour different in Ida. And . . . Pira."

"Then you'll talk to me at ten o'clock." She pauses. "Do you promise?"

"I . . ." How can I make a promise, not knowing whether my mind will even remain my own? I look into her eyes. I need to remember them as long as I can, but I already know how the memories will slip and fade. I know what it's like to wake up on that stone table, with nothing but the certainty of loss. Maybe I should have told Elanna everything while I had the chance—about Madiya, and my mother, and how I've survived. How I used magic everywhere but here, even if it made her push me away. But it's too late now. There's no time.

She must see some of this in my face, because she lowers her head and gathers my hands in hers. "Let's make a different promise, then. I promise to love you. I will always make that promise, no matter what."

My throat closes. *Say it,* I tell myself. But what if Madiya takes even this away from me, the memory of love? She'll take everything from me if she can, and Elanna most of all. She would hate to have herself replaced by anyone else.

Yet Elanna's eyes are bright. Her grip is tight on my hands. She's afraid, too. Afraid of losing me.

"I promise the same," I whisper. My throat tries to close, but I force the words out. They're thin. Inadequate. "My love. To you, always."

Her lips tighten. When she kisses me gently, lightly, I think I can taste the bittersweet tang of tears on her lips. Or maybe the tears are my own. I gather her tight against me, feeling the outline of her body against mine, even through the bulk of our clothes. I close my eyes. I have to remember this moment for as long as I can.

"You will come back to me, Jahan Korakides," she whispers. "You *will*."

I nod. But I'm not sure either of us is convinced.

CHAPTER THREE

Two days from Eren, at high noon, the Britemnos Isles form out of the sun-hazed horizon. I stop pacing the quarterdeck. My hands fall to the railing. The sun pounds, too hot, on my bare head. Six months ago, on my way to Eren with Finn, we passed near the islands. Finn asked if I wanted to stop, but I couldn't. I told myself our lawyers would rescue Lathiel, the way they had finally rescued Rayka. I told myself I couldn't abandon Finn to lead a rebellion on his own. But I should have stopped then. I shouldn't have given in to my fear. Maybe I could have saved both my brothers, then.

"Rayka," I whisper. "Lathiel."

But it's Madiya's voice that drifts into my head. *Jahan. Jahan.*

Raw panic squeezes my chest. Around me the sailors whistle and chatter. I feel for the ridged scar behind my ear, the scar I have no memory of receiving. The old, ugly grief claws at me. If this is what Madiya did to me as a child, how much worse will my punishment be now?

But I can't surrender to that fear. I'll strike her before I let her touch me. She's got Lathiel. And now, again, Rayka. I already know I'm too late. They're the ones in danger. I have to save them. I can't run this time.

Behind me, the sailors shout and point. A school of dolphins flashes past the *Celeritas*'s stern. The sailors dredge up stories I left behind years ago, about the Britemnosi prince who fell in love with the dolphin-maiden and begged the gods to transform him into a dolphin so they could swim together eternally. Maybe the poor bastard just found Pira as unbearable as I did.

"You've heard the story of Kyros, haven't you?" one of the sailors calls to the others. I smother a groan. Maybe I should have commandeered an Ereni ship, not the Paladisan vessel I sailed over on. The Ereni wouldn't know all these damned stories. But then we wouldn't be able to sail into the harbor unquestioned. I rub my face. I'd almost rather a sea battle than this nonsense about my most shameful ancestor.

"Kyros Korakides was a Britemnosi lord!" the sailor is saying. "A great hero! He defeated those wicked old demagogues and claimed the Britemnos Isles for Paladis . . ."

Yes, he did. By betraying everyone. He stationed the Paladisan army, in secret, outside the walls of our senate house. When the senators took their seats inside, the Paladisan soldiers fell upon them, surrounded them, and slaughtered them. That is how Paladius the First took the Britemnos Isles, which until then had held out against him with their superior navy. By treachery and betrayal. The sailor doesn't know the part of the story in which, after Paladius left Britemnos, Kyros was in turn murdered by an unknown assassin. A Paladisan agent, perhaps, or a fellow Britemnosi seeking revenge. So Kyros got none of the riches and titles Paladius had promised him—and neither did his children.

And that, my father would say, *is how we've come to be what we are. Disenfranchised. Disgraced. A shame to Mantius's glorious legacy.*

Mantius, whom I used to imagine picking me up and carrying me away from Pira, wrapped in his black-feathered cloak. How desperate I must have been. Mantius made whole cities vanish and reappear, crossed endless deserts in a day, defeated enemy armies with their own nightmares come to life, but he never returned from the dead. He died in Paladius the First's siege of Ida, along with too many other sorcerers to count. The Paladisans have spent a long time trying to eradicate us.

Now we're rounding the southern tip of Pira, the principal island, and the city comes into view, shining white and ocher in the sun, rows of buildings clinging to the steep hill that plunges into the harbor. Smaller than I remember, but dazzling after the gray stone cities of Eren and Caeris. A thrumming begins beneath my breastbone. This time, I'm going to confront Madiya. I'm going to save both my brothers.

Jahan, Madiya whispers into my head. I shudder.

The ship's captain, Sannas, speaks at my elbow, and I nearly jump out of my skin. "Will we stay the night, sir?"

I swallow. If I succumb to Madiya, it's not as if I'll be returning to the ship. But I can at least hope I'll succeed. And if I do, I'm hardly going to spend the night in familial comfort with my father. "We'll set sail when I return—tonight."

"This is where your family lives, isn't it?" he says, too casually. Of course they all know I'm from Pira. In the songs extolling my bravery saving Prince Leontius's life, they still had to work in jokes about my Britemnosi accent.

"Some of them," I say, in a tone that ends the conversation. The captain looks as if he wants to question me further—or demand that we stay the night—but then he shrugs and walks off, calling orders to the crew.

I sag against the railing. *All the gods, let me resist Madiya. Let me be back here, tonight, with Lathiel and Rayka.*

The ship sets anchor, and sailors row me to shore. Their boisterous conversation sets my teeth on edge. They're glad to be back under the imperial flag, making for Pira's bustling harbor, to taverns where they can commandeer beer and flirtations in their own language. I stare at the great ships we pass. They're merchant vessels, mostly, bringing goods from all over the world, some of which will remain in Pira. But little wealth will go up the hill to my father's house. He claims he can't turn Mother's inheritance over to me, despite the terms placed in her will, because of his unrelenting poverty. His lawyer asserts that he can hardly afford to repair leaks in the roof or prune the apricot trees in the courtyard.

We'll see about that. I'll find Madiya, and then I'll find him.

We dock. No one on the crowded wharves seems to notice that Ghesar Korakides's eldest son has returned. I stride past knots of merchants and naval officers. Ahead of me, a bell rings.

I stiffen. I look closely enough to see a blue uniform, and a bandolier strapped around a man's back.

I dive for the narrow street of honey-colored stone angling up between the bright, whitewashed buildings. I don't dare to pause, even though the witch hunters can't be here looking for *me*. Word can't have traveled that quickly from Eren. Unless they've finally discovered the truth about us. Perhaps *that's* why Rayka and Madiya have both called me.

I run up the steps beneath a curtain of wisteria, forcing my sea-sluggish legs to action. I haven't thought about this street in six years, but my body knows the way. My heartbeat jogs in my ears. I used to race Rayka and Lathiel to the harbor to watch the ships come in. We'd count masts and sails and try to name what types of vessels they were. Rayka always declared he was right even when I could prove him wrong. Sometimes there would be post for us on a ship from Ida—addressed to my mother, in her sister Cyra's elegant script. I could never work out why Aunt Cyra still sent letters when Mother was never allowed to reply. Father used to burn them all.

After she lost her memories, I smuggled the letters past Father and read them aloud to her. I thought they might bring something back to her. Aunt Cyra would tell her about the gardens at Aexione, and some understanding would light Mother's face at those words. But then it would be gone as quickly as it came.

I pause, looking back, my breath coming hard. No witch hunters pursue me.

I climb through the upper market. After Mother died, when I was fifteen, I stole money from Father and came here. I bought an astrolabe, compass, and maps. We had just put my mother in the ground, and the vendors had looked at me with silent pity, the child of the poor, broken woman who'd fallen off the cliffs to her death. They didn't know I'd lost my mother years before that. Or that my father had finally given me the key to freedom: a sailboat. I kept it in a little harbor beneath our villa, reached by a path rendered precarious by darkness. Twice, as I ran, I slipped. But I didn't fall, and my boat was waiting for me, tucked up on some rocks below the gate. With each scrape as I pushed it into the water, I was sure someone would hear me. Father and Madiya would find and stop me. Rayka would tell on me; he'd refused to come. He was too afraid of what Father and Madiya would do to him, if they found out.

But they didn't find out. Or perhaps they simply didn't care.

Between maps and sorcery, I made the crossing from the Britemnos Isles to the mainland, and worked my way over to Aexione. By then I was a shaking, trembling shell of a boy, deep in withdrawal from the opium Madiya had forced on me for most of my life. But Aunt Cyra took me in and brought me back to health. And though I think of my brothers every day, I've never dared to come back. Until now.

Perspiration slicks my spine as I climb to the crest of the hill overlooking the city. Behind me, Pira drowses in the cradle of sky and sea, the facet of a blue jewel. The street's grand houses are interspersed by riotous gardens and the occasional vineyard. A bird trills. A group of well-dressed servants hurries past me, talking and laughing, and some distance ahead there's a man being carried in a sedan chair. Another Britemnosi lord, wealthier than my father.

Who would guess, in such a tranquil place, what Madiya has done?

The road curves onto a rise, and I swallow hard at the sight of my father's villa. It's at the end of the road, where the hillside crumbles to the sea. Beyond the villa is the blue lip of water, where my mother fell to her death. To the right lies the green smear of the holly oak forest. The shoulder of Mount Leda, where Madiya's cottage lies.

As I stand there, a whisper of silence comes up behind me. It's strange. Concentrated. *Alert.*

I swing around. Hope pounds bright through my veins. Is it—?

But no boy stands behind me on the road. I see no one. Yet I can still *feel* someone there. A small, intent presence.

"Lathiel?" I whisper.

The silence evaporates. I'm alone, sweating, heart pounding, on the road to my father's villa. I scared him away.

Jahan, Madiya murmurs into my mind.

I hesitate a moment longer. But Lathiel is so completely gone that I wonder if I invented his presence.

I swallow hard. It's time to find her. I've stopped by the track that cuts away from the main road, toward the holly oaks. I can't seem to move forward. But then I think of what Elanna said, about Madiya being only a woman. She's right; Madiya's power was clipped and cauterized by the witch hunters long ago. One of the few abilities she had left was the power to give *us* magic. So why are my hands still shaking?

I duck onto the track, passing along the vine-creeped wall to where the old olive tree still hunches over the crumbling stones. I swing over the wall and onto the holly oak path. The stillness is absolute: a green, tranquil warmth beneath the leaves. It smells just the way I remember. Dry. Sweet. Like home.

It shouldn't comfort me, but it does.

I pass through the holly oaks to the stream that rushes down from Mount Leda, splashing from stone to stone in a pattern my body recalls exactly.

Jahan, she whispers.

I slow. There, just beyond the swaying branches, are the terra-cotta tiles of Madiya's cottage.

I let instinct take over: *I am the wind among the trees. A hoopoe, flitting between branches.* Let her look out and see nothing, even if she already knows I'm coming. Has Lathiel warned her?

I don't feel the silence. I don't feel anything but my pounding heart.

Jahan.

Rage bursts through me. I won't creep into her house, like a petty thief, to steal Rayka and Lathiel from her. She gave me the power to confront her, so I'm going to use it. I stride through the trees, toward the blue door. The upper balcony sits empty, but her voice echoes in my head. *Jahan.*

She won't stop me this time. She won't twist what I've done. She won't guess how my chest thrums or how terror makes my mind white.

I don't knock. It's locked—Madiya always locks it—but I throw back the latch with my mind. The door bursts open.

I stride in. My anger is bigger than me: a force unto itself. I let it throw open all the windows in the house, and the back door to the herb garden. I could knock the roof off. I could make the chimney explode.

But I don't. Because the house is empty.

Jahan, she whispers.

But she's not here. Dust lingers on the counters. Pots and pans hang tidily in the kitchen. A tremor runs through my legs. What could drive Madiya to abandon her cottage, her fortress against the world? I walk, unsteady, up the stairs. The sitting room holds the books I remember—the sorcerous texts Madiya spent years smuggling here. In the next room, the coverlet is pulled tight over her bed. The back garden is overgrown, weeds strangling the basil.

Where *is* she? And where is Rayka?

Madiya can't be gone. She never leaves the island. Rarely leaves the acre on which her cottage sits, even to come to the villa, in case a stray rumor of her existence reaches the witch hunters, in case they come for her again and lock her once more in the Ochuroma.

Jahan, she whispers.

I know where she must be.

All the feeling rushes out of my legs. I sway against the wall. She must be waiting for me in the cave. Of course.

My brothers, I remind myself. I'm here for my brothers. For them, one last time, I can walk down those stone steps. I can face Madiya. Strike her, if I have to. Smash all those bottles of laudanum, and burn her notebooks.

Before I can think more about it, I stride out of the house and through the orchard. The sweet scent of the orange blossoms makes me nauseous. Ahead of me, tucked into the hillside, the cave mouth opens, a dark gash in the green earth.

I fumble for the lantern Madiya used to leave at the entrance—still hanging on its rusty nail. My hands are shaking so badly I almost drop it. I reach for the memory of fire in the candlewick. Nothing happens. I'm no longer in Eren; I'm back home, where the slightest magic takes backbreaking effort. I can feel the flame, its heat just out of reach. I reach for one of the orange trees and tug the energy out of the nearest branch, funneling it through myself into the wick. A blue glow touches it. Reluctantly, the glow transforms into flame . . . and the orange branch crashes to the ground, charred to a husk. Startled bees swarm from the tree's still-living flowers. I wince. I'm glad El isn't here to see this.

The lantern aglow, I enter the cave.

The darkness swallows me up. I hiss at the sudden cold. The steps descend, an uneven, twisting flurry. I'm shaking so hard I miss a step and nearly twist my ankle. Nearby, the waterfall roars, deafening me. All I feel is terror, and the nameless ache that seems to consume my entire body.

But I force myself down the rest of the steps, into the cave.

It's empty.

The stone table sits, smaller than I remember, abandoned. The waterfall froths into an ink-black pool. Madiya's shelves sag against the cave wall, poorly constructed, laudanum bottles shoved up against moldering notebooks. Candle wax coats the small, rotting worktable.

It's just an empty cave. Hard to imagine this is what has shaped a lifetime of fear. Yet even now, the ceiling seems to press down on me.

Jahan.

I startle, swinging the lantern wildly, but her voice is only in my head.

She *has* to be here. Madiya wouldn't give up. And now that I think about it, I realize where she must be. My mother's been dead for years, and Madiya must have moved up to the house, now, to be closer to my father. Closer to Lathiel.

I charge up the steps, desperate to get out of here, dropping the lantern at the top. The flame gutters out. I race back to the holly oaks. As if I can outrace my past. As if running will get me there fast enough. As if she hasn't already done the damage to my brothers, long ago.

I RUN TO the house by the route I always used: through the holly oaks to the back wall of the villa, where the crumbling, never-finished tower overlooks the sea. Rayka and I used to dare each other to climb out on the tower's treacherous rafters. There's a gate inset beside it; by my command, it flies open as I approach.

Coming inside, I feel as if I might be sick, though I don't know whether from fear or fury. The garden is smaller than I remember. Paint peeling off the statues. Leaves fallen in the reflecting pool. Tiles cracked. The place looks run-down. Neglected. Maybe my father's lawyer wasn't lying when he blustered about Father's poverty. Somehow it makes me angrier than before. What has Father been doing with Mother's inheritance—using it to buy food and pay the servants while he huddles in his study reading arcane texts? Or using it to support whatever experiments he and Madiya have planned?

"Madiya!" I shout. *"Madiya!"*

Jahan, she whispers.

But she doesn't appear. The balconies sit empty. No woman rushes from the house, her golden hair a preoccupied tangle.

Where in the name of all the gods is she?

A knot of silence edges toward me, unspooling from the tower.

"Madiya!" I shout again.

This time a door does open. A man peers out. It's the steward of the house; I recognize him. "An intruder!" he calls behind him, just loud enough for me to hear.

Abruptly, I feel a fool for standing in the middle of my father's garden courtyard, calling Madiya's name like a child. I take my fists off my hips and approach the door. "Kemal! Don't you know me? It's Jahan."

The man stares. "Master Jahan?" He begins to laugh. "After all these years, you still haven't learned to use the front door?"

I force a grin. "I wouldn't want to shock you by coming in the expected way."

He shepherds me into the house. I'm embraced and kissed on either cheek by the old servants and the cook. Even my former tutor, Master Tavanius, comes down so we can bow to each other. He teaches Lathiel now.

There is no sign of Madiya. Not even her scent lingers in the house.

Why haven't I come back before now, the servants are asking, why did I never write? Unspoken: Why did I never send my poor father money when I had the crown prince of Paladis for my dearest friend? Why have I, instead, dragged him into legal arguments over the terms of my mother's will? Why did I never bestow any favors on the people I left at home?

"Is my father here?" I ask, at last. "And Lathiel? Rayka?"

They all grow quieter. "We heard that Master Rayka left the *Akademia*," Kemal says. "Did he not find you in Eren?"

My hands go cold. He has to be here. What has she done with him? "I thought he had come here."

"No. We haven't seen him in two years."

I rub my scar. They don't seem to be lying—and why would they?

Madiya hasn't come out to gloat over my return. If she hasn't appeared, and neither has Rayka—and Lathiel remains stubbornly invisible—then there's only one person left to turn to.

The steward seems to have reached the same conclusion. "Your father is in his study. I'll take you to him."

My gut tight, I follow him up the staircase, noticing the frayed carpets, the worn cloth on the walls. Father has always wanted to live in a princely manner, but our family—as he never fails to remind us—has been robbed of its rightful wealth and prestige by our Paladisan overlords. Our own ancestor betrayed us. Not only this, but the singular Britemnosi god has been supplanted with multiple Idaean ones. Even the Britemnosi language is now subservient to that of our rulers.

The thing is, I agree with him about the latter. Our people shouldn't have been forced to denigrate our own beliefs or our words. And we shouldn't still be secondary citizens of Paladis, denied full citizenship unless we apply for it. But as a boy, I didn't miss the wealth or prestige I never had, and which, for all I know, our family had never really possessed. And I can't say I admired my father's plan to regain it.

Kemal pauses before the doors. I gather my breath. But I shouldn't have bothered, because as soon as I walk in I feel like I'm fifteen again. The study looks smaller than I recall. Shabbier. My father, seated behind his desk, looks grayer. Spectacles pinch the end of his nose. He flicks a glance toward the door and keeps reading.

My hands curl into fists. He always did this to me—always forced me to speak first, so that I was the one making trouble and he could be the one to punish me for it. This time, I'm not falling for it.

The silence at my back shrinks against the cold silence in the room.

"I'll bring tea," Kemal says, and backs out.

My father still doesn't set down his book. "Should I summon my lawyer?"

Hatred socks me in the stomach, old and ugly. It takes me a moment to recover. "Yes. You can add abduction to your list of offenses."

At that, he looks up. His brows knit; he's puzzled. Genuinely, it seems.

"Rayka," I elaborate for him, unable to suppress my sarcasm. "Surely you noticed that he came back?"

My father looks annoyed. "Why would he come back? I told him not to return if he left."

Of course he did. I look at his phlegmatic, careless face. It's hard not to want to punch it. "Where is . . . *she*?"

"Madiya?" His gaze flickers toward the door. He's always been a bad liar. "She's . . . visiting a friend."

"A *friend*?" A snort of laughter escapes me. "Madiya doesn't have friends. She has experiments." I pause, eyeing him. I've always wondered just what kind of relationship he and Madiya enjoyed in their long hours alone—reading arcane texts, supposedly. "And . . . benefactors."

He doesn't even have the grace to look chagrined. He just shrugs.

I bite down on my impatience. "Is this friend in Pira? You could give me the address."

"So you can harangue her? I think not."

"Maybe I'll go door-to-door. Or stand in the street shouting her name."

Now he shifts, uncomfortable, and fiddles with the chain of his pocket watch. The fear of discovery has always motivated him. "That won't work. You'll only embarrass yourself."

"So she's not in Pira," I say. "Is she on one of the islands?"

Again, he shrugs. "I'm not privy to her whereabouts."

A bold-faced lie. I fold my arms, fixing him with a stare. He and Madiya always shared everything. I can't imagine that has changed. "Is she even on the Britemnos Isles? When is she coming back?"

He doesn't answer, but the shifting of his gaze tells me I've guessed the truth. She's gone—off the islands entirely. Or at least he believes she is. But if Madiya isn't here, then how can she be calling me? Even now her voice murmurs at the back of my mind, lifting the hairs on my neck. She's never left Pira since she took refuge here twenty-five years ago. I don't see any reason for her to leave now. And where would she go? Nowhere is safe for someone like her. Both her and Rayka disappearing is too coincidental. She might be here, hiding, waiting to spring on me.

The silence behind my shoulders shifts away toward the door.

"Where's Lathiel?" I ask, curious to see if my father can sense him. Despite his obsession with it, Father's never exactly had a bloodhound's sense for magic.

He makes a disinterested gesture. "Here, somewhere."

"You're not concerned he might have disappeared like Rayka?" I ask drily. It's comforting, in a way, to know that my father's preferred son is of slightly less interest to him than his book.

"Lathiel isn't—" he begins, then bites off the words. I've irritated him, at least. He purses his lips, then says, as if it is slightly distasteful but must be offered, "Stay to dinner. Stay the night. You can see him then. And we can talk about your recent exploits in Eren. This *Caveadear* waking the land."

I stiffen. I should have known he'd be curious about Elanna. She's done what he and Madiya always dreamed of, bringing sorcery back into the world, to be practiced openly. At least Elanna never declared a desire to destroy the witch hunters, or Madiya would probably have descended on Eren and Caeris like an eager parasite. Now I see that the book he's reading is *Legends of the Great Theurges*. There's a story about Caeris in there. I know, because I've read every story in that book. I had most of them memorized before I ran away.

He's noticed my discomfort. A small, pleased smile tugs at his lips. Now he says, "We thought you'd turned your back on us, Jahan. We didn't think you had it in you, bringing sorcery back. Destroying the witch hunters."

I recoil in spite of myself. This is all he wants, all he's ever wanted: our family's prestige back. Our family, the descendants of Mantius.

"I am *not*," I begin, unable to stop myself, "here to further your delusions of grandeur. Stopping the witch hunters isn't a personal favor to you and Madiya."

He's actually smiling, now that he's gotten a reaction out of me. "Would you leave your Elanna Valtai to suffer? To be captured and tortured, her mind destroyed? For six years, you've been mere miles from the Ochuroma. Think of all those sorcerers tormented and suffering inside! Yet you've done nothing to help them. I thought we raised you to do better, Jahan. I thought we raised you to think of others."

My hands have tightened into fists. This is what he always did to me, the way he always made me feel, as if I had to apologize for my existence. My eyes seem to be clouding over. I want to scream at him, the way I did as a child. But I can already hear his cool, detached response.

I stuff my rage back down, even though my throat is burning. "You're wrong, Father." I force my mouth into a grin. I refuse to let him see how much he's gotten to me. "I do think of others. I think of how I'm sparing them from you and Madiya."

Without waiting for his answer, I stride out, past the silence lingering by the door. I don't know where I'm going—I can't even think straight—but my feet carry me through the house, to the opposite wing, up another flight of stairs. Two doors. Our old bedrooms. I lean against Rayka's door, breathing hard. For once, I wish he was here. He might just glower at me, but he also understands our father the way no one else does.

Father was lying about *something*. Maybe Rayka *is* here—or maybe he passed through. Maybe Madiya's taken him somewhere. I throw his door open, my chest tight with a kind of terrible hope.

But it's dusty and abandoned inside. The bookshelves have been emptied, the shutters closed. There's no sign of his presence. I feel myself sag. I should be relieved. But if Rayka's not here, where is he?

Silence occupies the threshold behind me. I try to gather my wits, but it's ancient habit that takes me out and around to the other door. Into my old bedroom. I expect it to be the same, only emptier.

It's not. Books sprawl open on the carpet. A cup of half-drunk tea perches on the windowsill. A plate holding crumbs braces open a map of Eren and Caeris. The bed lies rumpled, unmade.

Is *Lathiel* staying here? A strange feeling crawls over me. I don't know whether I should be flattered, or whether I should take it as a sign of how very little I matter to them. Perhaps, despite the stream of alternately threatening and cajoling letters Father wrote to me, despite Madiya's whisper worming into my mind, they never actually expected me to come back.

I glance at the silence behind me, but it doesn't speak.

I want to drop to the bed and rub my hands over my face, but I can feel the silence watching me. I don't want to scare him off. I still can't believe Madiya isn't here, that she wasn't waiting for me in the cave with opium and a smile. I can't believe I'm standing, whole, my mind unscathed.

Then it occurs to me: There is one last place to look for the truth. I go downstairs, the silence ghosting behind me, to the two double doors below our rooms. They're unlocked. I almost expect my mother's things to be sitting around, gathering dust. But the rooms stand empty, the bed stripped of clothes, the vanity bare of brushes and pots and creams, the writing desk naked of paper, ink, and pens.

She may as well not have existed.

This time I do drop onto the bed. I rub my eyes; they're dry, but they ache. The last time I visited this room, my mother's corpse lay on this mattress. Her skin was flat, her hands folded over a bunch of flowers at her chest. The maids had dressed her in a white gown. I couldn't cry then, either. Couldn't think, except that it was time for me to escape the island at last. I held Mother's cold hand while Rayka sobbed into the coverlet and Lathiel wept in his nurse's arms. He was only six. I don't know if he even understood what had happened.

I don't open my eyes, but I can sense the silence standing before the vanity. "Do you remember her?" My voice is rough. It's hard to speak.

My youngest brother doesn't answer.

"I suppose you don't," I say eventually. A nurse raised him. After what happened, Mother wasn't competent to look after a child. Besides, most of the time she forgot he was even hers. I wonder what poison Father and Madiya have fed him about me.

But then I hear a footstep. Clothing rustles.

I lower my hands.

There's a boy in front of me. Twelve years old. Slight, with a flop of dark hair. Shoulders canted forward. Evasive eyes. As if he's trying to tell the world there's nothing here to see.

"There you are," I say. My face feels warm. I'm smiling, stupid with relief.

Lathiel's gaze lifts to mine, reluctant. Resentful. "Why are you here?"

I don't know why I thought he might be glad to see me. I have the feeling I need to catch my breath.

"Oh," I say, "you know. Making sure you and Rayka didn't burn the place down after I left."

His eyes narrow, as if I'm quite mad. No doubt Father and Madiya have fed him a diet starved of humor. But I shift, uncomfortable. Maybe I've just proved my inadequacy. I can't ask him what I really want to know: if he's suffocating here, what Madiya has done to him, how Father has tormented him. I can't put words around it.

And now I find myself saying, unable to corral my sarcasm, "When did Madiya make friends?"

A shrug. Clearly being around Father has rubbed off on him.

"And you don't know where she is," I say, in a more temperate tone. "Rayka never came back."

He just blinks at me, owlish.

I study him. I recognize the sallowness of his skin. The faint tremor in his hands, the hollows around his eyes. I feel sick. "Is Father still giving you laudanum, with her gone?"

"No." So much disdain, forced into one word. He's angry at me, clearly. But also, maybe just a bit, angry at the entire world. And also afraid of it.

I rub my forehead. Father probably doesn't even notice anything's wrong. I don't need to be a physician to know he's like me, like Rayka. When I take him from here, away from the opium, he'll fall apart.

Guilt chokes me. I left him here to turn into this. Why the hell didn't I grab him the night I ran away? Why didn't I sneak into his bedroom and haul him out, whether or not he screamed?

Because he loved Madiya with a child's blindness. He didn't want to leave her. He would have summoned her, and I would never have been able to get him, or myself, away. I would never have made it to Aunt Cyra's, never have eventually been able to get Rayka out. I wouldn't be standing here, like this, now.

But that doesn't excuse me. It doesn't make this better.

"Look," I say, "let's go get your things. Don't worry about Father; I'll take care of him. I'm getting you on a ship to Eren. I have an errand to run in Ida, but I'll be back as soon as I can, and Elanna—"

"You're going to Ida?" There's a jittery hope in his eyes.

I hesitate. Ida's not safe, but the gods know it's safer than here. I would be able to keep an eye on him, then. Look after him as the tremors and cravings get worse. Keep him away from Madiya. "Of course. My ship is in the harbor. The *Celeritas*. I'll take you with me, wherever you want to go."

"Oh." He twists his fingers together. Another question bursts out of him, high and breathless. Scared. "Do you know how to kill a man without touching him?"

This isn't the question I expected. Slowly, I say, "Why would you want to do that?"

He just stares at me. It's damned unnerving.

"Lathiel," I begin, "if you want—"

A *thud* sounds elsewhere in the house. We both go still. There's a clatter, like a bell. My pulse thunders into my ears.

Lathiel bolts from the bedroom. I leap onto my feet, following before I can even think. He's forgotten to be invisible. He races for the foyer, straight for the ringing bells and the distant, fuzzy hum of witch stones.

I forgot about the witch hunters in the harbor. They must really be here for me. For *us*.

There are two of them, standing on the worn carpet. Kemal is there, making apologetic gestures with his hands. But the witch hunters look right past him, to Lathiel. To me.

"Jahan Korakides?" one of them says, his tone doubtful. He's short and wiry, with a peremptory curl to his lip.

I can't seem to get my mouth to work. My whole body feels numb. Witch hunters came here once before, when I was ten, the day we ran to the cave. They left a scar behind my ear and a deep, aching grief I can't put words to.

The stairs squeak: Father appears, a book tucked under his arm. He stares down at the witch hunters, then at me. Accusatory. As if perhaps, single-handedly, I've brought them here.

"I am Inquisitor Quentin, sent here in the emperor's name!" the short witch hunter declares, as if our attention has been taken from him for too long. "You will cooperate with me and Inquisitor Faverus! Are you Jahan Korakides?"

I clear my throat. "Guilty as charged."

Both witch hunters stare. They obviously don't recognize me. I seem to have forgotten to shave, and I'm still wearing an Ereni coat of tightly woven tweed. Then again, I've never had the pleasure of their acquaintance before.

"Since you seem concerned," I say, "here's my seal ring." I hold out my hand so they can admire the flying raven. Mantius's symbol.

Inquisitor Quentin glances up at Father and murmurs to his tall, broad-shouldered companion—Faverus, apparently. He's going to say they've been looking at their records. I know it in my bones. They've realized a witch hunter once disappeared here. They're here to investigate a murder, eleven years old.

"Lord Jahan," Quentin says, "you brought a ship from Eren to the docks. All ships from Eren must be searched and quarantined while we examine them for sorcery, and yours is no exception."

I seem to fall back into my body. Of course this isn't about whatever happened when I was a child. This is about Elanna—and, if I'm spectacularly unlucky, about the witch hunters I attacked in Eren a few days ago.

"I'm sure that's not necessary," I say with a smile I don't feel. "It's not as if we're smuggling sorcerers *into* the empire; that would be quite foolish. I've returned to Paladis to negotiate an alliance with Eren . . ." I dig in my pocket for Sophy's papers. Behind me, Lathiel is peering wide-eyed at the witch hunters. He seems too frightened to make himself invisible. I want to pass him some reassurance, but anything I say will be hollow.

The witch hunters look at each other. Faverus says, doubtful, to Quentin, "Isn't he a subject of His Imperial Majesty?"

"I represent Queen Sophy's and *Caveadear* Elanna's interests as well as Emperor Alakaseus's," I say genially, pretending they were talking to me. "I don't believe the two to be mutually exclusive."

Now everyone seems to be staring at me, my father included. Maybe I've made a mistake.

Quentin clears his throat. "There is also a warrant for your arrest."

I'm so shocked I laugh. "My *arrest*? I'm no criminal!"

The witch hunters exchange a glance, obviously uneasy, though I'm not sure why. Perhaps it's my reputation; they're nervous about arresting Prince Leontius's dear friend. "We've been dispatched to bring you back to Ida with us. You're charged with aiding and abetting the Witch of Eren," Quentin says. "And your brother Rayka Korakides evaded an attempt by our people to examine him for sorcery."

Rayka. The fool. I should never have left him alone in Aexione. This must be why he fled the *Akademia*.

Leaning down from his height, Faverus murmurs to Quentin, just loud enough for me to hear, "Perhaps we should search the house, too, and the father and the boy."

I draw in a breath. My legs seem numb. I could let them search the house. It's the opportunity I've always wanted, presented in the most unexpected way: Father and Madiya stopped. They'll find his library full of magical works, and the punishment will be an exorbitant fine, at the very least. He'll be left destitute.

But if the witch hunters discover Lathiel or I have used sorcery . . .

I glance back at my brother. He's trembling visibly.

If it were just my father receiving his comeuppance at last, perhaps I could leave him to it. But I can't let this happen to my little brother.

My little brother, who just asked me if I know how to kill a man. More than anything, I can't risk him murdering a witch hunter on our doorstep.

Which means I have to submit to them. Let them take me to prison, or wherever it is I'm going. And once again, I can't take him with me. I want to sink into the floor. How completely I've failed him, again.

But I plaster on my most charming smile and hold up my wrists. "That won't be necessary, gentlemen. I have nothing to hide! I surrender fully to His Imperial Majesty's will. Lock me in irons if you must and take me back to Ida. We'll get this all sorted out quickly, I'm quite certain."

Lathiel quivers at my back, silent, but my sudden acquiescence confuses them. "Just come with us," Quentin says.

"With pleasure," I lie. But maybe there is still a way to save Lathiel, if we are both bold enough to take the chance. If he will even take the hint. I firm up my voice, making the words almost a command. "Don't forget to tell the *Celeritas* that they must sail to Ida without me. And send any possessions I left aboard to my aunt." My father frowns at the words. He's always despised Aunt Cyra— and feared her revealing our secrets to the world. But perhaps Lathiel doesn't share his distrust. "How long do you expect the ship to be delayed?"

"Depends on what we find aboard, sir," Quentin says, with a sharp look.

I force my airiest smile. "I assure you, there was nothing on board from Eren save me and some bottles of whiskey. Though there are a few more . . . fashionable coats I'd be loath to lose."

I gesture to my uncivilized attire, and Inquisitor Quentin relents— fractionally. "Then no more than a day," he says.

"Thank you."

I follow them outside, glancing back just once at my father and youngest brother. Father has already turned his back on us, hurrying away up the steps, no doubt to safeguard his library. But Lathiel remains, his eyes wide and frightened. He takes a hesitant step toward me. I manage to nod at him before the door slams in my face. I can only hope he understands the plan I'm offering him.

CHAPTER FOUR

Despite the witch hunters' claim that I will remain unharmed, I can't stop shaking as I'm bundled into a coach and taken back to the wharves. I keep thinking about Lathiel's wide eyes, and how my father's first concern was for his damned books. I can only hope that my brother will follow my advice. And that we both won't live to regret it. He's only twelve, and I've just ordered him, alone, to follow me to the largest city in the world . . .

The coach is close and hot. Prim Quentin seems mostly annoyed that I haven't followed protocol, while large Faverus eyes me with something between awe and wariness. Sweat pools under my arms. The bells on their uniforms clink softly, but my mind is still my own.

Except for Madiya whispering into my head, *Jahan.* I wince.

"Aren't you planning to examine me?" I ask to distract myself. "I might be a wicked sorcerer, after all."

Faverus looks alarmed, while Quentin sniffs. "The warrant says you're to be examined by Grand Inquisitor Doukas."

I flinch and try to cover it by scratching my head. They're saving me for the grand inquisitor himself? "Business must be slow these days. Doesn't he have anything better to do?"

Quentin just sniffs, and Faverus stares at me and then away. They're not exactly forthcoming, but at least neither of them has mentioned that I fired a musket at some of their fellow witch hunters. Word must not have reached them yet.

No irons appear at the wharves. The witch hunters bundle me

onto their brig. The last thing I see before the witch hunters prod me belowdecks and stuff me into a solitary cabin is a swarm of their fellows boarding the *Celeritas*. A latch clanks on the door, but they still haven't shackled me.

I pace the small confines. Am I a prisoner, or a disgraced lord headed for a scolding? The comfortable cabin suggests the latter: There's a narrow bunk, a desk, a window. Nothing to keep me here except the locked door.

And a bell. I startle as it clanks. It hangs from the doorframe by a leather rope. A witch hunter's bell.

I back away so fast my legs hit the bunk and I stumble. I rip off my neckcloth, ready to stuff it around the damned clapper, when I realize I'm being a fool. If I silence the bell, they *will* believe I'm a sorcerer.

It's annoying, I decide, not disturbing.

I stretch out on the bunk. All I can see now is my father and Lathiel. Where in the gods' names is Madiya? She's still hounding me: *Jahan, Jahan*. And Rayka—what's become of him?

And what am I headed toward in Ida?

By nine o'clock, long after a tray of dinner arrived and was taken away, I'm so restless I could eat my shoes. Instead I climb up on the desk and wedge a candle between myself and the window. I listen hard, but I don't hear anything from the cabins on either side. I tug on my own energy to muffle the walls with quiet. Only, every time the bell clanks, it rips through my sorcery as if it could puncture it. And I have no idea whether the witch hunters can somehow detect magic being used.

I'll have to be fast, or I'll get caught, not to mention drained. I put my hand to the cool window glass and conjure Elanna's face in my mind's eye. I whisper her name. When I open my eyes, her dim image wavers in the glass. But even the poor quality can't hide the intensity of her gaze. I feel myself smiling. I murmur, "Hello, there."

Did you find out she's only a woman? El says.

I wince. "I still remember the taste of your lips, don't fear."

She rolls her eyes. *What happened, Jahan?*

"She wasn't there. Neither was Rayka." I pause. "Some witch hunters found me. Or rather, they were alerted to the presence of the *Celeritas,* and the captain directed them to me. So much for loyalty."

But you're not in chains, El says.

"No." I decide not to mention I'm due for a heart-to-heart with the grand inquisitor. El has enough to worry about. "Where are you?"

North, near Tavistock. The Tinani have been concentrating their regiments here. She pauses. *Sophy thinks I need to make a show of force.*

By which she means, of course, magic. "Will it . . . be enough?" Or will it leave her exhausted and drained, and still not terrify the Tinani into backing down?

She rubs her eyes. *It will have to be.*

Behind me, the bell clanks. I startle. I realize the warm protection of my muffling magic has dissipated, just as a knock rattles the door. "Who are you talking to in there?"

"Myself!" I shout back. "I'm a very lively conversationalist!"

"Well, keep it down."

The speaker moves away and I remember to breathe. Damn. The bell really does rip apart my sorcery, even if it leaves my mind intact. I've grown too complacent in Eren and Caeris. I'll have to be more careful.

I turn back to Elanna, ready to make my excuses, but her image has already vanished. Only my own face looks back at me, smeared and broken by the glass and the darkened sea.

QUENTIN AND FAVERUS unlock my door two days later. Two days of sweltering in my cramped cabin; two days not daring to converse with Elanna; two days of endless waiting that dulls my mind and senses.

"We've arrived," Quentin says, without ceremony. He gestures me forward, then sniffs the air with some disgust. They permitted me to shave this morning—under observation—but it's been days since I had anything like a bath.

"It's a new scent," I say. "The perfumers will call it *Friends of Eren.*"

They herd me onto the upper deck. Sunlight glitters off the water, dazzling me. We've already sailed into the Desporos Strait, where the water narrows between the Middle and Inner seas. We're almost to Ida. I lean against the rail, trying to appear casual, though my heart lurches. Now that I'm here, staring at the snow-crowned bulk of Mount Angelos looming over the city, I feel completely unprepared. I'm still wearing Caerisian tweed, for pity's sake. I've been locked in a cabin for two days; my mind and body are both sluggish. And I've been arrested by witch hunters. Will the grand inquisitor see through Madiya's immunity?

Beneath the mountain, the sun winks off golden domes and gilded spires, gleaming white walls and the glow of white sails on black ships, the great cracked dome of the temple on the top of Solivetos Hill. Ida, the shining city. Even after everything, even with two witch hunters at either shoulder, when I see it I think *home.* I watch the shore approach, pretending I don't feel this strange surge of hope and fear. Our ship angles among merchant vessels, fishing boats, and pleasure barges. Faverus and Quentin mutter to each other. Ahead, a sheer promontory rises over the water, crowned by the craggy bulk of the Old Palace. I wait for us to maneuver to Vileia Harbor, though I look much too disreputable for its aristocratic patrons, or east to the mercantile Golden Harbor. Or even, most likely, Naval Harbor, a suitable place for a disgraced nobleman to disembark.

But we keep on sailing toward the Old Palace. Soon we'll pass through the breakwater that surrounds it, into the deep azure water beneath the crag.

"Imperial Harbor?" I say at last. "You honor me, gentlemen."

The witch hunters exchange a glance. Quentin clears his throat. Neither of them says anything.

Not an honor, then. Tension creeps into my shoulders. Of all Ida's ports, the Imperial Harbor is reserved exclusively for use by the imperial family and their closest associates. I've sailed into it many times—at Leontius's side. But I know in my gut that the crown prince isn't waiting for me on the pier. Instead my welcome will be witch hunters and the imperial guard. This is by far the most heavily guarded harbor in Ida, and sailing into it is not the privilege it appears, despite the excited murmurs that spread through the ship. "Maybe we'll see the empress!" one of the younger sailors exclaims, loud enough to be heard on the quarterdeck. "Out on her pleasure barge, with all her ladies, taking in the sun! I'd love to see the Idaean Rose!"

I suppress a snort. Empress Firmina always sails from Vileia. It's prettier, and there's less chance of colliding with a warship. In any case, the imperial family is rarely in residence here, since Antonius the Second moved his seat of rule, along with the entire court, out to the then-village of Aexione. He complained of Ida's crowds and smell, but everyone knows he just wanted his courtiers where he could keep an eye on them. But the wink of muskets and cannons high on the ramparts reveals that the Old Palace is far from unoccupied.

I don't like how small it makes me feel. I knew this wasn't going to be easy. Or *feel* easy.

But I like a challenge. I do.

The ship rocks slightly as the sailors put down anchor. The witch hunters nudge me down the plank to the wharves, where a coach-and-four waits, outfitted in plain black. It appears my arrival is to be kept secret.

I stretch my legs, glancing around the high walls surrounding the wharves. I can't see the city, or even hear the sound of it. It's suffocating, even with the water behind me and gulls crying overhead.

Quentin gestures me into the coach. It's warm and musty and claustrophobic. The witch hunters climb in, and the horses begin to move. A bell *clink*s from the roof, and a hammering starts in my chest. I fight the urge to run. Instead I reach for the crank to lower the window. Maybe some air will make me feel more myself.

"Sit back."

I stare at Quentin, who watches me with displeasure. Faverus shifts. I look at him. A sweat has broken out on his forehead.

Is it the heat in the coach, or is he worried about something? Quentin seems even more tense than usual.

I sit back. I don't want them to close the shade, depriving me of any view at all. Am I supposed to remain unseen, or is there something *I'm* not supposed to see?

"I'm so looking forward to this interview with your grand inquisitor," I remark. "Will it be here, in the palace?"

Quentin looks uncomfortable.

"Aexione," Faverus says. "We have to get you to Aexione."

So they *are* bringing me to the emperor—if the grand inquisitor doesn't declare me a sorcerer first. But to judge by Faverus's sweat, it's either the journey there that frightens him, or what we'll find when we arrive. I've heard rumors about the grand inquisitor's casual cruelty. He's been known to mutilate people accused of sorcery, to unhinge them with simple torture, even when they're later found innocent. Perhaps even his own men are afraid of him.

Abruptly, we rattle into darkness. We're beneath the Old Palace now, in a series of tunnels hewn into the rock by some ancient, enterprising laborers. They connect to the equally labyrinthine passages leading up into the palace complex itself. We seem to rattle forever through the dark, broken only by the occasional torch or lantern outside the coach.

Out of nowhere, I'm assailed by the visceral memory of Madiya's cave. Of lying there on the stone table, my memories torn away, longing for Mantius to sweep in and carry me away in his feathered cloak. All the gods, I hope I haven't abandoned Lathiel to that, again. I hope he followed the lead I gave him. And I've lost Rayka. It seems as if no matter how hard I try to help my brothers, I can never save them.

And now, as if I've summoned her, Madiya's voice slips into my mind. *Jahan.*

I grip the cushioned seat. I can't afford to hear her in my head. Not here, not now.

Jahan.

No, I think. *No, no.* She has no right to do this to me—to violate my mind like this. But she keeps on whispering. I want to scream at her, but it won't do any good. I don't know how to stop her. I never have.

Light lances through the coach. I gulp a breath. I'm cold with sweat. Her voice still echoes on, but somehow, in the light, it seems more endurable.

The coach slows—so that we can be released through the gates, presumably—and Faverus shifts to look out the window. As we pick up speed, his face contorts.

Shouting hits us like a wave, voices echoing outside the coach. I straighten, forgetting Madiya. Faverus's eyes flick to me. Sweat gleams below his cap. Quentin just stares me down, as if daring me to look outside or ask them what's going on.

The roar resolves into a single word: *"Korakos!"*

The whole coach shakes. A face appears in the window—there and gone—as if a mass of people are throwing themselves at us. Clearly someone spread word of my arrival.

We burst forward. I glimpse hats and raised fists. A throng fills the space between the grand buildings of Pompeia Boulevard. It's nothing like the usual jaded citizens who populate Ida's streets. I've never seen anything like it here.

"Justice!" they're shouting.

"Sorcery!" they're shouting.

"Bread!"

"Equality!"

Someone leaps close and thrusts his fist at the closed window, then tumbles off, leaving a paper in the window's edge. It flaps as the coach gathers speed. I crane my neck to look behind us, ignoring Quentin's protest. What's going on? Has Ida completely transformed in my absence?

We pull free of the crowd, dashing through the busy streets. Here no one shouts except to protest when the coach nearly collides with them. I glimpse honey-colored stones, decorative cornices over windows. Ida. The driver is aiming for the Great Bridge, which links the Old Palace to the exclusive, aristocratic neighborhood of Vileia on the other side of the Channel.

I eye Quentin, who's seething, and Faverus, still sweating. No wonder they wanted to keep me away from the windows. The emperor isn't going to like this. "That was quite the welcome! It looks like someone's glad to see me."

Quentin just mutters something. Faverus mops his brow with a handkerchief.

Past the flapping paper, an expanse of blue gleams out the window. The Channel. We're on the soaring arch of the Great Bridge now, one of Ida's most monumental feats of engineering.

I lean back. "I couldn't tell if they wanted to kiss me or kill me. Kiss me, I think."

At this, Quentin erupts. "They're traitors! They want you to bring that Ereni witch to Ida. They want sorcery."

Sorcery? Ida's cynics want *sorcery*? I can't say I'm complaining, but it's not quite the response I expected. "What would they *do* with sorcery?"

"They want to change the government." Quentin sneers. "They want to bring back the Glorious Republic and they think your witch can help them do it. Because there was *magic* in the Glorious Republic."

"How ambitious," I say neutrally, trying to hide the hope that pounds into me. If Ida's people want sorcery, then Emperor Alakaseus will have to do a good deal more to suppress it than declare war on Eren. No wonder he's bringing me to Aexione by an unmarked coach. If the fervor for revolution that's swept Eren has arrived in Paladis, then it's not only sorcery the emperor has to fear, but the loss of his throne.

He's not going to be happy to see me. On the one hand, if his control is wavering, I may have an advantage in our negotiations. But on the other . . . Alakaseus Saranon has been emperor for nearly thirty years. He's accustomed to having his way. He won't want to listen to an upstart from the Britemnos Isles.

No wonder I'm being sent straight to the grand inquisitor.

"They're disloyal," Quentin grouses. "They've been Paladisans for more than two hundred years now. Why don't they want to be part of our glorious empire?"

"Maybe because they're treated as secondary citizens?" I suggest. I was. Aunt Cyra pressed the emperor to grant me full citizenship, but before that I was just like most of the empire: a citizen without full rights.

Quentin just rolls his eyes.

The paper jammed in the window is chattering. I can't quite make out the words on the back. With an angry sigh, Quentin opens the window and snatches the paper before it can blow away. He shakes it at Faverus. "Another call to arms by 'the People's Party.' I knew it."

He makes as if to throw it out, but I reach for the sheet. With a dark look, he lets me have it.

The People's Party. That's Lucius Argyros, a man I've heard speak many times in the university's lecture halls. And Pantoleon. My friend: a lawyer, an intellectual, a dreamer.

I read the heading. *Brothers and sisters of Ida & All Paladisan States!* it proclaims. *Self-governance is your birthright! Sorcery is in your blood! Rise up together, today and every day, against the tyrants who would impose their laws on us!* I feel myself wince; it is rather loaded with hyperbole.

My gaze catches a paragraph at the bottom of the sheet and the breath stills in my lungs.

The Paladisan emperors made sorcery anathema. Paladius the First never received a mandate from the gods, but acted out of his own lust for power! Sorcery is a skill like any other, a talent anyone may possess. Our brothers and sisters in Eren have shown us how it may be used. Now it is time to show them that we've heard their cry for freedom! Let us answer them and bring magic back to Ida and Paladis, where it belongs!

No wonder the people were waiting for me at the gates. Everyone in Ida must know how Elanna woke the land and threw off the Eyrlais. They're rising to *our* revolution.

The emperor really isn't going to be happy to see me.

Dislodging him will be far harder than deposing the Eyrlais. But I didn't come here to fight the Saranons; I'm here to broker an alliance. And I know the cost of revolution. I've already lost one friend.

Besides, I know who wrote this pamphlet, and I'm not sure I like it. Its words bring back the visceral smell of the university archives, the old scuffed wood and the soft musty scent of books. The cramps in my legs from sitting too long hunched over age-spotted pages. Pantoleon, grinning up from a passage he'd found—triumphant at first, but the grin sliding away as he read to me what was written there. The bald facts of how the witch hunters oppressed Ida's sorcerers, how they systematically slaughtered and subdued all resistance to Paladius the First's new order.

"You see the vitriol they're writing," Quentin says, from the other side of the paper. "It's grown worse since what happened in Eren."

Since what I did in Eren, he means. I'm trying to find my breath. There it is; I can breathe again.

Pantoleon and I spent three years sifting through the archives, hunting for the truth—as if understanding the past would be enough to mitigate the grief of the present. As if it could bring back my mother, his father. Sorcery orphaned us both, in different ways.

And we both know the consequences of being caught. What on earth is Pantoleon doing, writing our secrets on public flyers? Revolutionary fervor must be upsetting his common sense.

I fold the paper in half. I have an interview to survive, and an emperor to negotiate with. I don't have the luxury of telling Quentin my true opinion. "It is unfortunate," I hear myself saying. "The people can be so excitable."

Quentin looks dubious, but Faverus nods vigorously. "They've been agitating throughout the city. Talking about how the government needs to change, and the emperor's ministers need to be elected by the people, and His Imperial Majesty himself is a tyrant. It's *treason*! They should be arrested, but the city watch is too soft to do it. Of course, they're secondary citizens, too . . ."

I make noises of agreement as they talk. Neither of them seems to notice me slip the paper into my pocket.

Pantoleon and I are going to have words about this.

IT'S TEN MILES to Aexione—plenty of time to forget my tentative hope at the sight of the crowd and the flyer, and remember I'm being taken to be examined by Alcibiades Doukas himself. I can't let Quentin and Faverus see my mounting fear, so I stare out at the countryside as if my life depends on it. Outside the city, the landscape turns impossibly bucolic, young vineyards green under a staring blue sky, dusty olive groves, lambs bleating on rocky outcroppings. This side of the Idaean peninsula, west of Mount Angelos, is far greener than the land to the east, which becomes abruptly arid in the mountain's rain shadow. The mountain itself looks no more troublesome than a high-piled cloud. It's hard to imagine that this is what periodically shakes the ground from Aexione clear to Ida and beyond.

"It's been talking lately," Quentin says, evidently noticing where I'm looking.

Faverus stares down at the cards he's shuffling. "People in Ida are saying it's the gods," he mutters. "They're angry with the Saranons."

Quentin smacks his knee. "Maybe the gods are warning them to be silent!"

I watch Faverus. He hasn't looked up from the cards, which must be quite well shuffled by now. He's frowning. Does he not approve of the rebellious Idaeans, or is it Quentin who bothers him? For the first time in my life, I wonder how someone like Faverus becomes a witch hunter. What would make a young man hate sorcery so much that he wants to hunt down witches? Or does it just sound like a noble thing to do?

"All the gods, Fav, are you going to deal?" Quentin demands. Faverus startles and passes out the cards. None for me, of course. I may be a well-treated prisoner, but I'm not invited to join the game.

Just as well; I don't want them to see how damp my hands are. I stare back out the window. I need to make a plan, but so far all I can think is *survival*. The bells will fray any magic I attempt to work. I'll have to rely on my wits, and Madiya's claim that she rendered me immune. It's not entirely reassuring.

We draw into Aexione through a purpling dusk. The sprawling palace, larger than most towns, seems to float in the growing darkness. Torches blaze against its white marble colonnades, throwing the friezes on the lintels into relief and deepening the shadows of the courtyards. I feel gritty and anonymous in my Caerisian tweed. Our coach wades through a chaos of carriages and phaetons and berlines, past shouting footmen and cross drivers. Courtiers lean from their conveyances to harangue their servants and laugh at one another. The racket seems to rise in a wave against my ears. I'm careful not to lean forward; Quentin is watching me. The courtiers are still wearing the styles I set: the short hair, loosened cravats, unbuttoned coats, long trousers. Strange to think Finn and I were once mocked for wearing such things. From this distance, I can't recognize anyone. I wonder where Leontius is. I wonder if he even knows I'm coming. If he'll even speak to me, if he does.

Our coach swerves through an archway into the open courtyard that serves the palace's eastern wing. We're surrounded now by the barracks and training yards and rooms that house the imperial guard. The emperor's chambers are on the other side, reached through a long, well-guarded corridor.

Heat is building in my chest and on the back of my neck. If the grand inquisitor finds me guilty, I'll die in this place or in the Frourio, the emperor's prison in Ida. Or they'll take me to the Ochuroma, where Madiya suffered for all those years. They'll torture me; they'll destroy my mind. Imagining Mantius coming to save me won't be enough. Nothing will.

Maybe my father was right. Maybe I should have used the opportunity I had to destroy their damned order.

And grant Father and Madiya the satisfaction of seeing their work done for them? Not likely.

We stop. Quentin leans forward, pleased. But Faverus is perspiring again. I don't understand it. The door flies open, pulled from outside by imperial guards. There are two of them—no, four—six— eight. They wear elaborate, old-fashioned costumes and plumed hats. But the bayonets slung around their shoulders prove they're not merely decorative.

Someone else waits behind them—a light-haired man wearing a bandolier of stones. A bell quivers between his outstretched fingers.

My stomach has gone cold. My chest, too. It's Alcibiades Doukas.

I remember the girl they took, the one they brought before the emperor. The witch stones had unhinged her mind. She was barefoot, her gown crumpled and dirty, her matted hair crawling with lice, judging by the way she kept scratching it. Her eyes held a vacancy that showed she saw something the rest of us didn't, something that wasn't really there. She didn't seem to see us or even recognize the emperor except as a backdrop to whatever was playing out in her mind. We were meant to laugh at her, but I couldn't make myself. Neither could Leontius, it seemed. He just grimaced and swallowed and, as soon as he could, strode out of the Hall of Glass. I followed, and when I glanced back over my shoulder, the witch hunters were tormenting her with their bells, making her cry out.

Now that is going to be me. And then they're going to kill me.

But no. I think of my ancestor in his feathered cloak, the greatest hero of his age. Mantius wouldn't be cowed by these people. I can't let the witch hunters see anything but an irritated nobleman, shocked he's being treated with such indignity.

Quentin slides out into the evening. "Sir! We brought you the Korakos."

I'm not sure I like how pleased he sounds. Faverus, meanwhile, just gestures me forward. I get out of the coach, ignoring the tremors in my legs. The grand inquisitor, Alcibiades Doukas, looks thoughtfully at me. He's a slight man, with a dimpled chin and a narrow smile. With his light, fading hair, he must be from one of the northern provinces, or had a parent who was; either way, he didn't grow up a full citizen, even with his Idaean name. His uniform is cut from silk velvet, and gems wink on his fingers. Did he ring the bell? I didn't even hear it.

I decide to pretend I don't even know who he is. "Gentlemen, I must object." I pitch my voice in the most laughingly aggravated manner I can, inspired largely by Zollus Katabares, one of Leontius's Companions. "I'm innocent of any crime! Unless coming back to Aexione after so long is a crime? Has the length of my absence offended someone?"

"We're merely taking precautions, Lord Jahan," Alcibiades Doukas says, his narrow smile deepening. His voice is surprisingly modulated—a courtier's. "Follow me, if you will."

His smile unnerves me. My mouth goes so dry I can't do anything but grunt.

I have no choice but to follow him into the palace, trailed by Quentin and Faverus. The guards stop at a small, narrow room. It's unfurnished except for a plain wooden chair in the middle. One of the legs is cracked. A single lantern hangs from the ceiling.

Alcibiades flicks his fingers. The guards go out, bolting the door, but Quentin and Faverus remain. Quentin stands with his shoulders back, as proud as if he's on parade. Faverus casts surreptitious glances at Alcibiades. Is he afraid of the grand inquisitor, or what he does?

With a courtier's grace, Alcibiades gestures to the chair. "Lord Jahan, please sit."

He can't tell that I'm a sorcerer. Madiya saw to that. I *know* it. This is just a demonstration of force. It's the emperor trying to intimidate me. Trying to remind me that he has more power than I ever will.

But I've never had a witch hunter examine me before. Not alone in a room. Not like this.

I try to muster a laugh, a modicum of disdain, but all I feel is the quivering in my legs. "Surely you don't think *I* . . ." I can't finish.

Alcibiades cocks an eyebrow, but merely gestures again to the chair.

I sit.

"There's nothing to fear," he says mildly, coming to stand in front of me, the bell pinched in his fingers. Then, with a mirthless smile, "Unless you really are a sorcerer."

I manage to crack a grin, but I feel it slide off my mouth the moment he rings his bell.

I plaster that damned grin back on even as my heartbeat surges into my ears.

And I'm aware, like a slap to the face, of Madiya's voice ringing out. *Jahan!*

All the gods, not *now*. I gulp in air.

Alcibiades Doukas raises an eyebrow. "I promise, Lord Jahan, this is quite painless."

Jahan, Madiya whispers.

Shut up, I think. My pulse is wild. I have to stay calm.

I grind my teeth together. Alcibiades has begun to ring the bell in a figure-eight pattern. But, I realize, nothing has actually happened. I'm light-headed from the terror pumping into my brain, from Madiya's voice, not from the bell racking my mind.

But . . . even if I'm not proven a sorcerer, Alcibiades could lie. According to rumor, he's more than capable of torturing innocents. It would be an easy way to remove my inconvenient presence from court. An easy way to stoke the warmongering against Eren and Caeris. The emperor has never been particularly fond of me, even though I saved his son's life. He once said to me, "Korakides, someday your irreverence is going to get you killed." Which I suppose it might. By him.

Jahan, Madiya whispers.

She always wanted us to use our power to destroy the witch hunters. But how can I use magic against Alcibiades, if it slides right off the bells and stones?

Now he's taking some stones from his bandolier and placing them in a circle around me, with one at each of my feet. In a conversational tone, he says, "I heard you're from Pira on the Britemnos Isles, Lord Jahan."

"Yes," I manage. Every fool in Aexione has spent the last two years gossiping about it.

With a delicate touch, Alcibiades turns my hands over and sets a stone in each of my palms. "I was there once," he remarks. "Years ago, now."

I stare at him. His head is bent. I can't tell if he's threatening me, or inexplicably making conversation. And all at once I think of the witch hunter who came to our villa that morning when I was ten. I never saw that man's face; never thought he might have colleagues, friends, family who would come looking for him.

Perhaps I *am* going to be charged with murder. The witch stones hum gently in my palms, a half-heard thing. Not enough to drive me mad, unless perhaps I listened to it for the rest of my life.

Alcibiades rings a bell directly in my ear, and I wince.

He pats my shoulder. "Just making sure you're in there."

"I may be deaf now," I grumble.

He chuckles, then comes around and peers into my face. Again, one eyebrow rises.

I'm sweating as much as Faverus, but I wet my lips and begin, "The emperor can't truly believe I'm a sorcerer . . ."

"It is one possible explanation for your recent behavior." He pauses. "And your brother's."

"Rayka?" All the gods, did they find him after all? Have they taken him to the Ochuroma? But Quentin told me he'd evaded their attempts to examine him. My pulse has lurched back into my ears, but I force a grin. "Rayka's always been trouble. I apologize if he's been giving you the runaround."

Alcibiades chuckles again as he takes the witch stones from my palms.

I flex my hands. "I don't know what would possess him to run away from the *Akademia*. Maybe he thought he wouldn't pass the exam. It's strange, isn't it, how we understand our own families less well than other people, sometimes?"

This would be the moment for Alcibiades to confess that they've hauled Rayka away to prison. Instead he just says, "You show no signs of sorcery, Lord Jahan. We won't detain you further."

I stand. Quentin utters a disgusted sigh, but I don't miss the relief on Faverus's face. Perhaps the torture they subject sorcerers to disturbs him. It's strange; he should have been bullied out of it by now.

"We seem to have wasted your time, sir," Quentin says crossly.

"Not at all," Alcibiades replies with a cool smile. He glances at me. "It was a pleasure, Lord Jahan."

A pleasure? Well, I'm not about to refuse my freedom. I practically bolt out into the corridor. But if I was hoping for a reprieve, perhaps a hot bath and supper, I don't have such luck. A guard leads me down a flight of stairs and up another, to a filigreed door set unobtrusively into the wall. A footman in imperial livery—purple and gold—stands to one side of it. He bows to me. "His Imperial Majesty will see you now."

ALAKASEUS SARANON, the ninth emperor of Paladis, waits for me in a gilded armchair beside the fireplace. He must have come from the public supper he takes almost every night; he's dressed in a lavishly embroidered suit, lace cascading at his chin and gemstones winking in his ears. His face, however, is a good deal more sober.

I was right. He's *not* pleased to see me. Disdain pinches his face.

I'm starkly aware of the fact that I haven't bathed, and that my Caerisian tweed is rough with road dust, salt, and sweat. The emperor won't be charmed into thinking I'm setting a new fashion. The dog lying by his feet thumps its tail on the carpet, but lays its head down when its master doesn't react.

I lower my head. I make a bow from the doorway, pace forward ten feet and make another. I'm not sure of the protocol here. Footmen and guards occupy the two doorways, but otherwise the emperor of Paladis and I are alone.

I have never been alone with Alakaseus Saranon. It's not exactly something I dreamed of.

He's watching me like a hawk. Or a snake. And although I would love to be like Elanna and boldly stare him in the face, I drop to one knee and lower my head. It feels like capitulation.

I don't speak. The emperor must do that first.

He says nothing. Somewhere, a clock ticks.

Finally he shifts in his chair, an expensive shuffle of silk. "I am eager to hear exactly what you think you've been doing." He does not, however, sound eager at all.

I lift my head. His eyes are narrowed. One bejeweled royal finger taps the arm of his chair. A pulse of hilarity bubbles up in me. I want to say, *I was taking a holiday. The air is very fresh in Caeris, you know.* Instead I do my best to look honest. The emperor values sincerity, as men who are frequently lied to often do.

"I went to Eren to help the Dromahair family reclaim the throne of Caeris," I say, which is of course true.

"Yet Euan Dromahair is still in Aexione," the emperor says, "his son Finn is dead, and his bastard daughter stole the throne. I did not encourage this endeavor."

My teeth lock together. He has no right to throw Finn's death in my face. None. It's not as if Finn mattered to Alakaseus Saranon—not as the son of a crownless king living off Alakaseus's charity. I'm surprised the emperor even remembers his name.

And it's difficult not to point out that he was in the business of funneling us funds and munitions when Elanna woke the land.

I force my jaw to release. "Your Imperial Majesty, the Eyrlais were no great friends of yours. We believed we acted with your approbation."

He drums his fingers on the silk-padded arm of his chair. "You must have known your rebel friends planned to use sorcery."

"There have always been such rumors about Caeris," I say, "but it was hard to credit them."

"Until that witch made the land move."

"The Eyrlais drove us to great desperation. The *Caveadear* did what she had to." It's hard to keep my voice even. "Without her sorcery, we would never have succeeded."

The emperor looks at me again. The clock ticks. I refuse to look away, though the angle strains my neck. At last he says, "And you've had the audacity to return. Why?"

"I . . ."

A door creaks open behind me. The emperor's head jerks up and—just for a moment—his face softens. I tuck in my chin as a woman passes me in a whisper of soft-soled slippers and jasmine perfume.

"Jahan Korakides," she says in her bright, laughing voice. "What sort of trouble have you gotten yourself into now?"

It's impossible not to smile when I look up. Even the emperor snorts, amused. She's standing at his side—our empress, the Idaean Rose, Firmina Triciphes. The first empress from the city of Ida in more than two hundred years. The first in history not born of noble blood. One of her hands grasps Alakaseus Saranon's shoulder. She's leaning into him the way a lover does, though they are twenty years apart in age. She must have come from the public supper, too, though she dresses more simply than her conservative predecessor, the mother of the emperor's children Leontius, Augustus, and Phaedra. She's smiling at me, her golden eyes lively.

"I was just asking him why he's troubled to return to Aexione," the emperor is saying, though less forbiddingly than before.

"Oh?" Firmina Triciphes says. "It must have been the Ereni food. Was it very dreadful? Do they really eat sheep's brains? And do they truly never bathe?"

"Not sheep's *brains*. But the worst was the weather," I say with a responding grin. "We were assailed by *snow* this winter, followed by an interminable rain."

"How cruel of the gods!" Firmina exclaims. "No Idaean can survive under such conditions."

Though I know she didn't intend to, this only serves to remind me that I'm not truly Idaean, or Paladisan. But Firmina Triciphes is an outsider herself—the common daughter of an Idaean financier. She persuaded the emperor to wed her rather than install her as his latest mistress, though Leontius insists she tricked Alakaseus with her feminine wiles. But I've always thought Firmina was clever. Even the courtiers who initially despised her common birth have been won over by her charm. Idaeans love her: one of their own, raised up to the imperial dais. It's a victory for those who don't possess full Paladisan citizenship, though the emperor pretends to ignore this.

And he doesn't appreciate our levity. "We can only presume it's the Ereni's abominable witchery that's driven him home."

"In fact, Your Imperial Majesty," I say with a smile, because one should never *appear* to contradict the emperor, "I have come on behalf of Queen Sophy and *Caveadear* Elanna, to sue for peace between Eren and Paladis." I pull out my papers. "You'll see in these documents I am named ambassador royal."

He snatches them from me, casting off his wife's hand. "Are you indeed? I seem to recall you begged to be named *my* ambassador *to* Eren."

I say mildly, "The kingdom of Eren no longer exists quite as we knew it then. Now it is the united countries of Eren and Caeris. I imagined that my post terminated when Loyce Eyrlai was deposed."

"So," the emperor says, his voice cold, "you've come back here on behalf of a bastard girl?"

"Queen Sophy has been elected by her people." Unlike him. "Your Imperial Majesty, forgive me, but there is no practical reason to go to war against people whom, six months ago, we considered allies. Believe me, Queen Sophy holds no animosity toward you, only a desire for peace."

He stares at me, then shrugs. "The black ships will make quick work of them. We'll get rid of this bastard girl and her witch and place Euan on the throne, as he's always wanted. Then things will be as they should."

"That may be less easy than it seems," I say. "The *Caveadear* is heavily guarded—and she's beloved by her people. Your Imperial Majesty, as I said, we don't have to fight a war. You may negotiate with Queen Sophy instead—through me. Why should Paladis waste its resources, its funds, its men, because of the actions of one woman?" He looks at me, and I hurry on before he can interrupt: "The *Caveadear* may be a sorceress, but not in the way you imagine. She isn't like the sorcerers of old whom Paladius the First destroyed." This may be the largest lie I have told in my life. "She is a humble girl who desires nothing more than to bring freedom to her people. You know how poor Caeris is. With so few resources at their disposal, how could they not turn to the one thing guaranteed to set them free? How could she not take action, even knowing how you and the other great powers would punish her for it? She *had* to act, against the dictates of her own conscience, because not to do so would have left Eren and Caeris in the grip of a tyrant. So she used her magic, though she loathes it. And now she humbly begs your forgiveness. She hopes that you will overlook this one action to see the larger advantage of an alliance with her nation."

The emperor folds his arms.

I wet my lips. He looks far less persuaded than I'd hoped, but at least he hasn't summoned the imperial guard to haul me away again. Yet. It's a good thing Elanna isn't here; she would hate the portrait I'm painting of her. But it's the only thing I can think of to dissuade the emperor from war—making him believe that Elanna Valtai, despite her great magic, is truly harmless. That she's only acting this way out of dire necessity.

"What would happen," I ask, "if Paladis allied with Eren, instead? We needn't condone sorcery. And Paladis is allied with other nations that practice far worse things for far less worthy reasons."

But the emperor is unmoved. "I will not make a *precedent* of this witch. I will not invite further riots in the streets. Riots," he adds, "taking place in *your* name."

I wince. "I would never incite anyone against Your Majesty. But the riots might stop if you made Queen Sophy—and by extension Elanna Valtai—your allies. If Paladis cooperated with Eren, there would be nothing to riot against."

Alakaseus Saranon gathers himself to speak, but Firmina strokes his shoulder. "He makes a good point, my darling. It would confuse the rioters' ambitions."

He looks up at her. "Condone one witch, and you condone them all."

"You're right, of course, but Eren is our ally, not our subject. We cannot impose our laws on a nation we don't rule! As Jahan said— quite thoughtfully—we condone far worse things than sorcery. Consider how we allied with the Czars of the Ismae after they slaughtered their own people in the Winter Uprising!"

"The Czars have a standing army I am loath to fight," the emperor retorts.

"But, darling, it is the same! The Ereni witch defeated the Eyrlais. What if she defeats us? The Ismae Czars have not done that, because we were wise enough not to give them the chance."

The emperor's scowl grows more pronounced. Over his head, Firmina gives me a small smile.

I'm fighting down a smile of my own—one of pure relief. Firmina Triciphes's support was not something I had ever thought to hope for.

And with her support, maybe we can succeed.

"I will give this consideration," Emperor Alakaseus pronounces, flapping Sophy's papers. "I must speak to the ministers. We'll meet again, Korakides. You may not have done as poorly as it first appeared. Though," he adds, "it would have been better if you had done something about the witch before you left Eren."

I force a laugh. "How could I, Your Imperial Majesty? She's only a girl fighting for freedom."

"Only a girl?" The emperor snorts. "By all accounts, you are quite well acquainted with her."

I feel a flush burn into my face. So they know about Elanna and me—and now my entire argument is crumbling under the emperor's knowing smile.

"Nothing more than vicious rumors, I'm certain," Empress Firmina says. Her gaze passes over me, amused. "Who would take a wild Ereni girl for a lover, after sampling the rose garden of Aexione?"

"Indeed!" I feign a shudder. Thank all the gods for the empress. "Ereni ladies have none of our women's grace."

The emperor sighs heavily, as if we've denied him personal pleasure in bringing me down. "Ah, well. Get out of here, Korakides. I need to get back to my supper."

I rise—my knees protest after so long on the Agran carpet—and make another bow. The empress is smiling. "So much trouble, Jahan Korakides," she says with a laugh.

The emperor laughs, too, though without kindness.

"My only hope," I say devoutly, "is that the trouble benefits our great empire." And I bow my way out.

CHAPTER FIVE

In the corridor outside the emperor's chambers, I draw in a breath. I want to sag against one of the brocaded walls. We have a chance. We have Firmina's support. It's more than I ever expected. I'll have to write her a note expressing my gratitude.

There's a whisper behind me—silk slippers on the parquet floor. I spin around just before Augustus Saranon's silver-tipped cane can whack me between the shoulder blades. It taps my chest instead.

I stare at Leontius's younger brother. He smiles back at me.

"What a charming greeting," I say. "Have you taken to jumping courtiers and hitting them like a highwayman?"

He shakes his glossy hair. Augustus received all the good looks and charm Leontius didn't, and he never passes up an opportunity to show them off. "You aren't a courtier, Korakides, you're a parasite. What did you say to my father?"

I bare my teeth in a grin. "We exchanged some pleasantries about the weather, mainly."

Augustus's eyes narrow. His smile slips. He looks sullen now, which suits him better. It's hard to imagine why he was their mother's favorite. I'm glad I never met her; she clearly had terrible taste.

"Well," I say, "delightful as this has been—"

The cane swings back up, pinning me in place. I pretend not to feel the servants' gazes on my back, staring. "Not so fast," Augustus says. "I know your game, Korakides."

I find myself laughing, even though I know I shouldn't. The gods alone know what Augustus thinks he knows, though if he suspects the truth of my sorcery and duplicity, he'll have my liver pickled and set out for wolves to dine on. "That's not difficult to discover. You might ask anyone at all. Cross-and-circle has always been my favorite game."

He visibly grinds his teeth. "You know what I mean. You've been holed up with that witch in Eren. You probably plotted to kill Finn Dromahair together."

What? My mouth falls open; I wonder what sort of stories Augustus Saranon has been bandying about in my absence. Lightly, I say, "Finn was my friend, which is far more than you can say about him. I'm surprised you even know his name. In any case, everyone knows I went to Eren to teach the Eyrlais a lesson for your father."

That catches him off guard. He lowers his cane with a frown, and I take the opportunity to step away.

"My father didn't deputize you to proliferate sorcery!" he splutters.

"He deputized me to depose the Eyrlais. Which I did. Great fun, rebellions. All the running about, waving pistols and shouting for liberty." I glance behind him. The corridor looks empty, but I know better than to trust the Saranons. "What a shame your sister didn't join us."

Augustus glowers at me, which I take to mean Phaedra is otherwise occupied. Small mercies. He says, "If you're back here to bolster my brother's miserable public image, think again. All of Paladis knows he's unfit to rule. He's proved that amply in your absence."

I halt my attempt to edge away down the corridor. What has Leontius done now? But I'm not fool enough to ask Augustus that question and give him the opportunity to gloat.

"Not at all," I say instead. "I've come back for the food, mostly. The cuisine in Eren—"

Augustus interrupts me, smug now. "He hasn't written to you, has he?"

I'll be damned if I'll tell Augustus that Leontius hasn't sent me a single note. "In fact, I'm going to see him just now. I'm sure he can tell me anything he left out of our communications—"

Augustus sticks up a finger. "He hasn't participated in a single public dinner in six months. Father offered him a commission to restore the naval defenses at Kasia Harbor. He refused." Another finger. "During Father's birthday celebration last month, he said not one word. All the work has been left up to Phaedra and me. *We* gave speeches. The people love us."

I suppress a snort, even though this news makes me uneasy. The people don't love Augustus. They love the *stories* about him; his drunken escapades and titanic love affairs with half the women in court always make the gossip papers. The people love Augustus the way they love to see a mansion in flames: It delights them to see the dissolution of all that wealth and privilege.

And Phaedra is even less lovable, if that's possible. She's a paragon of the dubious Paladisan virtues of purity and reserve; she has never taken a lover or set a foot wrong. A marble statue has more warmth. Yet, for whatever reason, Augustus adores her.

"How gratifying it must be to know the people love you," I say. "It must make up for knowing you'll never ascend the throne."

Augustus draws himself up, as cold and angry as Phaedra. "I know what you did, Korakides. Remember that. And I have power you can't even imagine."

He turns to stalk away. I call after him, "I *believe* you've invented some fiction about me. I hope it gives you much pleasure."

He just holds up his hand, shaking the cane at me. I turn the other direction, rolling my eyes. The gods alone know why Augustus thinks he has the right to make up stories about me.

But what he said about Leontius does worry me. I knew Leontius wasn't happy when I left—he put his back to me and refused to speak—but I didn't think it would lead to a public demonstration. Augustus relished telling me that story far too much.

I need to find Lees. Now.

*

EVEN AT THIS late hour, the palace's gleaming corridors are filled with laughter and courtiers drunk on champagne and intrigue. I slip past the knots of conversation and whispers in alcoves. I might as well be as invisible as Lathiel for all the notice they take of me. You'd think someone would have something snide to say about my Caerisian tweed, but if a single glance follows me, they disguise it quickly.

Maybe I shouldn't have come this way. I walk faster. I know plenty of these people. A few months ago, they would have called out to me, either to joke or to curry favor with Leontius, or both. Perhaps, in my foreign clothes, missing a barber for too long, they simply don't recognize me.

Once, I wouldn't have minded. But after that conversation with Augustus, it makes me uneasy.

Leontius isn't among them, of course. Nor will he be in the garden this time of night, and he certainly won't be gambling over cards in the grand salons or flirting with the exquisitely mannered daughters and sons of Aexione's nobility. If I know Leontius—and after two years of nearly indivisible friendship, I do—he's tucked away in his own chambers, probably poring over a treatise on irrigation designs or *The Journal of Botanical Studies*. Will it comfort him to know that, across the water in Eren, Elanna also reads the latter? She and I have discussed it almost as comprehensively as I have with him.

Finally I reach the grand staircase leading down to the ground floor, where Leontius's apartments face the Palm Garden. A man is just coming out of the crown prince's chambers, the candles glaring off the diamonds scattered through his hair and sewn into his velvet suit. He seems preoccupied; the line of his mouth is too long. But then he sees me and all that vanishes into genteel astonishment. He lifts his eyebrows. "Jahan?"

I find myself matching his tone. "Zollus."

His gaze sweeps me up and down. "*What* are you wearing?"

I shake out my arms. "This? It's the height of fashion in Eren and Caeris." I try a smile, but he doesn't return it.

"We didn't know you were back," he says, almost accusatory. Zollus Katabares has never really approved of me. He's a true Paladisan blue blood, from the signet ring on his smallest finger to his languorous pronunciation of everything. His family has served the empire as Dukes of Paphlonia for generations, since Paladius the First stormed out of Edonis. Zollus himself is one of Leontius's Companions, the age-mates assigned to him practically from birth. Leontius shook most of the others after Chozat, but Zollus hung on like a barnacle. My departure probably made him ecstatic—finally, Leontius wouldn't have been able to shelter behind his friendship with me, but would have been forced to deal with Zollus directly. Although if Augustus is right, Leontius hasn't done much to bolster anyone's reputation, least of all his own.

"I was in disgrace," I say mildly.

"*Was?*" Zollus arches an eyebrow. "Did His Imperial Majesty change his mind?"

"He's deciding." I pause, wondering just how much to scandalize Zollus. "Eren's sent me here to secure an alliance. I'm benefiting everyone now, really."

Zollus draws himself up, shocked. "You swore allegiance to the bastard queen? Have you lost your mind?"

"Oh, no," I say cheerfully. "I'm still a loyal Paladisan subject."

"Korakides"—he draws out the syllables of my surname as if this might encourage me to listen—"that doesn't make a damned bit of sense. You can't represent both."

I smile. "Why not?"

He stares at me, his disapproval pressed as sharply as the cravat he wears. The desire to be anything other than a Paladisan courtier must be so far outside his realm of comprehension it resembles lunacy.

"Well, it's been a pleasure." I take a step forward. "I'm sure Leontius—"

"He's asleep," Zollus retorts. He doesn't move aside. The footmen on either side of the door stare at us and away.

I'm so close to Zollus now that I can smell his orange-and-ambergris cologne. One of us has to move, and unless I persuade him with magic, it's got to be me. But Leontius isn't asleep at this hour. What makes Zollus think he has the right to block my access to my friend?

Then I remember how Leontius put his back to me. His unrelenting silence over the last months. Maybe he *wants* Zollus to keep me away. I swallow hard.

"You must be sleeping with the witch," Zollus says abruptly. "There's no other conceivable reason why you would remain in that backward country. Look at you. You've gone savage."

A laugh bursts from me. *"Savage?"*

"You'd have done better to take up with that Dromahair boy," Zollus says. "He was pretty enough. But he was such a *bore . . .*"

I feel as though I've been kicked. "His name was Finn. And he's dead, Zollus."

He makes a face. "A shame, for his looks. No great loss, for his conversation."

Heat burns up the back of my neck. I shouldn't let Zollus get under my skin; he talks this way about everyone—except, of course, Leontius. But I'm tired of having Finn's death thrown in my face. "You have no right to say such things. You barely even knew him!"

"Oh, well, the gods will absolve me this once."

His tone finally registers with me: not vicious, but *angry*. He's affronted that I went off and chose an Ereni rebellion over the tedious peccadilloes of Aexione. He *resents* it. He's even angry that I chose Elanna rather than Finn, because Finn at least grew up in Paladis and had, therefore, the veneer of respectability. Even though Zollus hardly deigned to speak to Finn because he wasn't a full Paladisan citizen.

Quietly, I say, "Has it occurred to you that Finn and I went to Eren because it was the right thing to do?"

"Don't lecture *me* about right and wrong!"

I feel abruptly weary down to my bones. Zollus isn't going to move from the door, and if Leontius doesn't want to see me, so be it. "Fine," I say. "I'm going to bed."

Zollus snorts, but he doesn't say anything. He just folds his arms. I feel him watching me walk away.

I must see Leontius, but it will just have to wait for morning. I'll find him in the garden. He's more likely to talk to me with his feet in the soil. Now I can have a bath and supper, and sleep in my own bed.

I climb up to the second floor, to a pair of doors covered in filigreed vines. A footman stands outside them, watching me approach. I don't recognize him. Did Aunt Cyra reassign him in Basil's place, or did Leontius replace my man with someone new?

"How long have you been waiting here?" I joke with him. "Six months?"

The footman just stares at me. He makes no move to open the door, so I reach for the handle myself.

"Sir!" he exclaims. "These apartments belong to the Count and Countess of Lamea."

But I've already pushed open the door. The sitting room is bright with candles, and a startled maid rises from a pile of mending.

"Sir!" the footman protests again.

I slam the door shut. Why is someone else—a *maid?*—in my rooms? It has to be a mistake. But a look at the footman's aghast expression tells me it's not.

They've given away my rooms.

They might as well have put a sign on the door saying JAHAN KORAKIDES IS IN DISGRACE. Courtiers vie to have apartments in the palace; the Baron of Policastro fell down in a fit when he lost his. Leontius fought to secure these rooms for me after we came back from the campaign in Chozat. Even though I'd saved his life and people were writing songs about it, nobody wanted to give some provincial Britemnosi a three-room apartment in the palace of Aexione. But Leontius prevailed. It's been my home for two years.

No wonder Zollus snorted when I said I was going to bed. He knew exactly what awaited me here. What on earth have I done to make Leontius publicly demote me? Is he that angry with me for going to Eren? Angry enough to send the message this way, instead of to my face?

Maybe he never expected me to come back.

The footman is still gaping at me. But what can I do? I can't demand my rooms back. In the end, we're all just servants of the imperial family and their whims. I've always known that my privileges could be taken away at a snap of Leontius's fingers.

"Please convey my apologies to the maid," I say to the footman, and then I walk away.

THEY MUST HAVE sent my things to Aunt Cyra's house. I'll go there. And with any luck, Lathiel will soon arrive with my luggage from the *Celeritas*. Yet I can't help feeling, as I descend another staircase into the Argent Court, that I've been kicked out. Discarded, the way all the courtiers said I would be, sooner or later. It's not the welcome I envisioned. I thought the rejection would come from the emperor and his ministers, not from the prince who so stubbornly claimed me as his friend.

Jahan, Madiya whispers, and coldness burns up my spine.

No. But I almost wonder if I should answer her. I need to find her. I have to stop her from ever harming my brothers again. And if I find her, perhaps I can find Rayka. I hope Lathiel took the risk I offered him and is on his way here, but if not . . .

I cross the courtyard, making for the arched exit to the Avenue of Oranges. After the brightly lit palace, the archway is little more than a pit of darkness.

Jahan.

But even if I find her, how will I stop her? Would I strangle the last magic out of her, to keep her from whispering into my head? I don't want to physically harm her. The idea revolts me. I don't even know if I can take her magic away. But if I could, that would make me no better than the witch hunters. And yet, if there was a way, if it would protect my brothers . . .

I hesitate. The darkness under the arch blinds me. It's odd—torches should be blazing here, too—

The blow catches me in the jaw. Pain shocks my face. I stagger backward, gasping, into a pair of waiting hands. Another blow pounds my gut. I thrash, but the man behind me keeps a hard grip on my shoulders. The first assailant kicks my legs. I push back, only to get another punch to my nose. My head snaps back. Blood leaks, bitter, into my mouth. What the hell is this? Who would jump me in the Argent Court?

More blows rain into my stomach, my ribs. I'm groaning, the pain spreading, trying to keep upright, trying to wrestle myself away from the man holding me. I jam an elbow back into his ribs. He grunts but holds on to me.

Let me go, I demand, pushing at him with all the persuasion I can. His grip loosens just a fraction. I swivel and bring my fist up under his chin, just as the other fellow strikes me in the back. *Nothing but shadows.* I try to slide away, but one of them catches me all the same. I go flying onto the cobblestones. Another blow strikes the back of my head.

"Hey!" a man shouts. Running footsteps echo across the Argent Court. Light flares.

One assailant plants a final kick in my gut. Then they run.

I push myself onto my elbows. My entire body is screaming with pain. I should go after them, work some magic, figure out who the hell they are, but I don't think I can move. As if I needed a more thorough removal from the court.

My rescuer crouches in front of me. Through tearing eyes, I glimpse a striped silk coat and the knife-edge of an Idaean profile.

"Korakides?" he says. "Is that you?"

I don't recognize the voice, but I feel myself grinning like a lunatic. "To the life."

"All the gods, you're a bloody disaster. Who . . . ?" He's looking after the assailants. If they have any wits, they're long gone by now. "Where are the guards?"

I sit up, spitting a gob of blood. "That's a . . . fair question." I can't seem to get my breath; my diaphragm is sharp with a splintered pain. Those bastards must have cracked one of my ribs. I reach for the power to heal myself, but, as with the lantern I struggled to light on Pira, nothing happens. Eren's abundant magic made me complacent. Now I'll have to steal energy from a plant—or a person—but I'm not about to attempt that in front of my erstwhile rescuer. If he had the faintest inkling . . .

"They doused the torches, too." The fellow is holding a guttering taper. He must have snatched it from a candelabra somewhere. Now he digs a handkerchief from his pocket and thrusts it at me. "You make enemies awfully fast, you know."

Now that I'm sitting more or less upright, the rush of blood from my nose slowing, I recognize him with a kind of stupefied relief. "Bardas . . . Triciphes?" I can't stop wheezing. The empress's cousin is the last person I expected to see, especially after the emperor dismissed him from court for espousing radical views and throwing scandalous parties at his palace in Ida. "Thought they . . . kicked you out . . . of here."

He flashes a reflexive grin. "Oh, that's all over. His Imperial Majesty forgave me some weeks ago. We had the most touching scene in the Hall of Glass, where he nodded once to me in the crowd and I bowed deeply." He pats my shoulder. "Shall I fetch a doctor?"

"No . . . no." I try to push myself upright. My head swims. Bardas grabs me, steadying my arm around his shoulders. I test my legs gingerly. I'll have some nasty bruises tomorrow.

"Anything broken?" Bardas asks.

I shake my head, making it spin slightly again. But I manage to take one step forward, then another. Out on the avenue, a group of people pass us, laughing and talking.

Bardas tracks my gaze. "You must have offended someone."

I can only grunt. It doesn't take a genius to recognize Augustus Saranon's handiwork. Who else has the authority to call off the imperial guards and douse torches that should otherwise be lit? He must have summoned his thugs the moment he left me.

Did he act alone? Or does the emperor know? I can't imagine

Emperor Alakaseus condoning this petty violence, but . . . he wasn't very happy to see me.

It takes far more effort than it should to reach the street, and once there, I have to stop and wheeze. As soon as I'm alone at Aunt Cyra's, I can heal this damnable rib, but it's going to be a long walk there.

"Thank you," I manage, trying to reclaim my arm. "I'll let you . . . enjoy . . . your evening."

"I'm not letting you walk alone!" he exclaims with genuine horror. "I doubt you'd make it half a block without collapsing like a drunk. And I've no desire to rescue your dead body from the gutter if those thugs come back for more. Besides, it seems as if you could use a friend."

I grunt a laugh, but I'm touched. It seems like more kindness than anyone has shown me in a while. Bardas and I have always been cordial, even if Leontius views him as a nuisance. We ought to have been good friends: two boys who didn't fit into the court, both interested in reform politics. But saving Leontius's life swept me away from all that—from what, I've often thought, I really am.

"I could call a chair, or a coach," he offers, but I shake my head. Walking will be faster. Bardas shrugs, awkward with my weight on his shoulder. We start walking again. "Everyone thought you were quite heroic leading the rebellion in Eren, until the stories about your Ereni sorceress started crossing the sea." He begins to laugh. "Really, Jahan? A sorceress? Is she seven feet tall, as they claim, with a crown of fire?"

I just grin, though it makes the blood crack beneath my nose. A carriage rushes past us, but otherwise the night is cool and quiet. It makes the pounding in my head bearable.

"I was sorry to hear about Finn Dromahair's death," Bardas says. "Couldn't your sorceress have done something to save him?"

I shake my head. "Battle . . . accident." But this is far more kindness than the emperor, Augustus, or Zollus bothered to offer toward Finn's memory, and it surprises me. "Didn't think . . . you knew him."

"Only by sight, but I think it's a great shame when people must die in the name of the cause they fight for. It makes the victory—well—is it bittersweet, or harder-earned? I suppose you're the one who would know."

"Both," I manage. I tell myself the dampness in my eyes is from pain.

We hobble past a house, its high, shadowed gables more massive than anything in Eren or Caeris. My clogged nose is clearing enough to smell winter roses and woodsmoke and orange blossoms. It's everything I've missed, but I didn't think I would come back to so little.

"Listen," Bardas says. "It would be disingenuous to pretend I can't guess who set those brigands on you tonight. He's no friend of mine, either, you know. Neither of them is."

"I . . . know." Augustus and Phaedra despise their stepmother as a second-class social climber and, by extension, Bardas. They're always digging for gossip to discredit her. Last year a rumor circulated that they commissioned an artist to create lewd drawings of Firmina; before that, she was supposedly stealing jewelry from courtiers like a petty thief. The emperor seems completely oblivious to the fact that his own children want to destroy her.

Bardas nods. "If you need a friend, you know where to find me."

"Thank you." After the last few days, I feel more touched than my inadequate words can say.

Aunt Cyra's house comes into view on the corner, lit up like a midwinter tree. Silhouettes move across the windows in the dining room. I groan. It's just my luck she's hosting a dinner party.

"Ah," Bardas says, noting the people and the noise, too. "Perhaps the back?"

We make our way around to the alley, where the rattling of dishes and pans in Aunt Cyra's kitchen sets up a din. Both of us have to pound on the door before we're heard, and then the maidservant who answers screams at the sight of me. The cook comes running and gasps. "Lord Jahan! You're back! What on earth happened to you?"

"He fell afoul of Aexione," Bardas explains. "It happens to us all, sooner or later."

The cook just blinks at him, but she and the maidservant help wrangle me upstairs to the bedchamber that used to be mine. The maidservant goes running for hot water and washcloths, while the cook returns to the kitchen to alert the household to my return, as if they haven't already witnessed the commotion.

"I'll send for a doctor," Bardas tells me. "You look peaked."

I wave a hand, though every movement stabs pain through my upper torso. "No . . . need."

He frowns at me, then shrugs. He glances at the door. "Look, Korakides, I doubt you'll be in any state to attend, but . . . I'm throwing a party the night after tomorrow, at the Deos Deorum."

I wheeze, trying not to laugh. "I've heard . . . about your . . . parties."

"Oh, don't be like that!" he protests. "They're not for the nobles. They're for people like *us*. And I have an orator coming whom you may know. Lucius Argyros."

I go still. I'm aware of, like a sudden heat, the paper stuck in my pocket, beneath the gore and grime.

How does Bardas Triciphes know that I know Lucius Argyros? Maybe he asked someone about the courses I took at the University of Ida. Maybe he knows that I sat in Argyros's lecture hall, watching him fix his spectacles on the end of his nose and speak more eloquently than anyone I had ever heard about the rights we all deserve.

He's watching my reaction. "You have more friends in Ida than you know. Pantoleon Chrysales, for instance, will be quite eager to see you."

I don't trust the reassurance I feel. It makes me wheeze harder. "You know . . . Pantoleon?"

"Oh, I make it my business to know everyone worth knowing. And Pantoleon most definitely is. Remember, two nights hence. Come at ten, if you can."

There's a noise in the hallway—an entire army of servants, from the sound of it. Without another word, Bardas ducks out and I'm left to wonder who he knows, and what he wants.

THE SERVANTS REFUSE to leave me alone. First the maid insists on dabbing away the blood under my nose—though my hands still work perfectly well—and then I'm dragged down to the bathing chamber and unceremoniously ordered out of my filthy clothes. The hot water feels shockingly good, though I have to bite my lip against groaning at the pain of my cracked rib. Clusters of potted green plants sit about the tiled bathing chamber. When the manservants finally leave me to soak in peace, I reach for the living energy of the plants. *Knit together, smooth and snug,* I whisper at my rib. At first it's sluggish, so I tug harder at the green power, letting it run through my veins. With a sick *snap,* the rib clicks together. I ignore the tears pricking my eyes. The pain pales to a dull ache.

I open my eyes and flinch. Two of the plants have withered. The others don't look so good, either.

If Elanna knew this is how I use my sorcery, at least anywhere save Eren . . . I shake off the thought, but the guilt lingers. I don't know how I'll explain the plants' demise. Perhaps Aunt Cyra, ever efficient, can make them disappear without anyone suspecting a thing.

A mirror glints on the wall across from me. I sit up, though I'd rather linger in the copper tub. But it's late, and I need to contact Elanna before she starts to worry.

A knock raps at the door before I can lever myself up. "Jahan?"

It's my aunt, and she sounds concerned. Next thing I know, the manservants have invaded the bathing chamber again. I'm helped out of the tub, wincing at the bruises starting to mottle my torso. I must have only had enough power to heal the rib, not the bruises. A towel is thrust into my hands, followed by a shirt, loose trousers, banyan robe and slippers. I cast a last glance at the mirror, but while I might be able to duck away from the manservants, there's no evading my aunt.

She's pacing in the corridor like a small, vigorous brigantine at full sail, her silver-streaked coiffure towering and her silk skirts billowing. One look sends the manservants scuttling back to clean up the bathing chamber. I slink toward her. I feel as though I'm fifteen again, come to Aexione from the Britemnos Isles with little but the clothes on my back, sick and begging her to take me in.

She jerks her chin at the sitting room. I limp inside. The room is dark, save for two thin tapers on the sideboard. Aunt Cyra busies herself lighting more candles. I pour us each sherry from the cut-glass decanter; I know what's good for me.

But my aunt doesn't claim her drink. She closes her eyes and explodes a breath. "Who did it?"

"I didn't get their names. We didn't really have the chance for conversation."

Aunt Cyra fixes me with a bright, black-eyed stare, and I feel myself quail just as I did the first time I met her. She terrified me then; I was certain she'd summon witch hunters and dust her hands of me. She didn't, of course—though I suppose there's nothing to prevent her doing so now if I thoroughly irritate her.

I hunch a shoulder in a shrug. She deserves the truth, and she'd suss it out fast enough on her own anyway. "Our dear friend Augustus Saranon sent them to say hello."

"Augustus," she mutters, her nostrils flaring with disgust. Then she points at the velvet settee. "Holy Aera, sit down! You look ready to collapse."

I sit with relief, my body aching. I'm still holding both sherry glasses; I sip out of one.

She sighs, then pulls up a footstool and sits in front of me, rubbing a hand over her cheek. She smells of food and drink, and I remember the supper party I interrupted.

"Auntie, your guests must be missing you," I begin. "I can take rooms elsewhere—"

She flaps a hand. "Nonsense. They can manage well enough without me. You're not going anywhere." She pauses, looking at me. "But you shouldn't have come back."

I wince. "Yes, that's been a popular opinion today."

"Oh, darling, I'm glad to see you, of course." She pats my knee. "But these riots in Ida—pro-sorcery, anti-sorcery, everything. Have you not heard? The witch hunters are cracking down. This is not . . ." She doesn't say the word *safe*. "This is not being careful."

She's right, of course. I think of the day I came here, fifteen years old, shaking from opium withdrawal and terror. When the servants left us, my aunt grasped my wrist and asked baldly if I had come to Ida by sorcery. A bit, I told her, because part of what had driven my sailboat wasn't ordinary wind. Her grip on my wrist had tightened. She brought her face close to mine, so that I couldn't look anywhere but into her eyes. *I will shelter you,* she whispered. *But do you understand what will happen if anyone guesses what you are? If you use what you have been taught?*

I understood; Madiya had seen to that.

Now I know better than ever. And I know what will happen to her, this upstanding paragon of Aexione society, if my secrets are revealed.

"Oh, Auntie." I smile at her. "Am I ever careful?"

"*Often,*" she says. "You are *usually* careful." She leans back with a sigh. "I told you what would happen if you left."

She did. My aunt didn't want me to go to Eren; she thought it was a fool's venture. *You'll lose your standing. You'll lose everything you've gained. Do you want that?*

In a way, maybe I did.

Her hands move restlessly over her skirt, smoothing the embroidered silk. "The witch hunters went looking for your brother. The fool gave them the slip. The gods alone know where he's hidden himself, but now they'll suspect you."

"Oh," I say, "I've already made the acquaintance of two of them. They provided me escort back to Aexione."

Aunt Cyra's gaze snaps to my face.

"The grand inquisitor himself examined me, and pronounced me clean." I can't quite meet her eyes. Guilt digs through me. Even if Alcibiades Doukas has acknowledged my innocence, I'm still putting Aunt Cyra at risk. I clearly don't have Leontius's protection. Augustus's thugs could come here. The emperor agreed to treat with me, but for how long? I can't risk my aunt after everything she's done for me. I fumble for the right words. "I had to come back. It's the only way I can see to prevent war with Eren."

My aunt goes very still. Slowly, she says, "Jahan Korakides, do you mean to tell me you're here representing *a foreign nation?*"

I offer her a grin. "The emperor accepted it, more or less."

"Because you talked circles around him, no doubt." She snorts. "Does your Ereni sorceress actually believe you have this kind of influence? Are you really her only hope?"

My gaze drops back to the sherry. The liquid quivers. I want to disappear into it.

"Surely you've discovered Leontius has forsaken you? He gave away your apartments—"

"Yes. I'm in disgrace."

She nods. "You've lost your influence with him. I don't know who else will back you."

"Lees and I are friends," I snap. "Friends forgive each other."

Her expression tells me I'm being a fool. "He has the melancholy. He's spent weeks talking to no one at all but his gardeners. He won't forgive you for choosing an Ereni witch over him."

I swallow. Guilt seems to dig in around my sore ribs. "Contrary to rumors, he's not in love with me." At least, I've never seen real evidence of it. But Leontius is so reserved—what do I know?

"How does a young man, who's never had a real friend before, react when his first true friend abandons him? A prince, at that? Now you're back, but you've come to use your influence—with *him.* Why should he think you care for him at all?"

I stare back at the sherry, swallowing hard. I want to tell her she's wrong. I want to laugh it off. But in my gut, I'm afraid she's right.

"Then," she continues relentlessly, "there are the riots in Ida—"

"Oh, yes," I interrupt. "They met us at Imperial Harbor. They seemed to be the only people glad to see me."

My aunt purses her lips. "There's an—*ugliness* about those people. You haven't seen them as I have." She jerks her chin downstairs, toward her dinner guests. "The Kourtunes are taking their possessions and retreating to their country estate."

I sit up straight. "They're leaving Aexione?" No self-respecting courtier leaves Aexione voluntarily.

"Melisandra whispered to me that they may even take ship for Agra, or Baedon. Somewhere outside the empire's boundaries. There was a Paladisan lord lynched on his own estate a few weeks ago, by his own field-workers. They said he had never paid his taxes, but had taxed so much of their income they could no longer eat the food they grew." She shudders. "I've ordered meetings with the overseers and the field-workers at our Tyana Pontica estate. But I might have to go myself, to make sure they're dealing with matters as they should."

I must be staring. My aunt hasn't gone to Tyana Pontica, where the Potazes wheat and barley are grown, in years.

"You see?" she says. "In Aexione, it's as if none of the rest is happening. Matters go on as they always have. The court. The dancing. The gambling. The *money*. In Ida, people are starving, and here Emperor Alakaseus built that miniature palace for Firmina Triciphes. Your reformer friends keep writing about it in their pamphlets, saying we need a revolution like the one in Eren. I don't think they know what they're inciting."

"Hmm." I can see why this alarms my aunt, who depends on the blind subservience of the common people for her wealth and way of life. The Tyana Pontica estate alone makes her one of the richest independent women in the empire, not counting her investments in trade and banking. But I wonder how different Paladis's rebels are from the ones in Eren who spoke out against King Antoine. Quentin claimed we'd inspired Ida's reformers, after all.

Aunt Cyra sighs. "I can tell I've failed to suitably impress you with the difficulty."

"I'm here to sue for peace. A rebellion within Paladis might force it to happen."

"Don't be so sure. There's nothing like a good, self-righteous war to take people's minds off revolt."

"True." I pause. Maybe my friendship with Leontius is in danger, and I don't enjoy the influence I once did. I do have one advantage, though. "But Elanna's magic is extraordinary. If anyone can defeat the black ships, it's her."

My aunt eyes me. "Are you in love with her?"

I laugh. "I should have known that rumor would precede me." But I can't bring myself to acknowledge the truth, even to Aunt Cyra. I want to say that Elanna is courageous and fierce and brilliant; I want to tell her about El's magic and how much I miss her. But perhaps Cyra is right. Perhaps I *did* mislead El in telling her that my influence could stop war. Perhaps I've run back to Paladis simply to avoid telling her all my secrets. I think of how she looked at me when I left, as if she didn't truly believe I would come back to her. Perhaps El isn't the one I've been deluding; perhaps it's myself.

Aunt Cyra's gaze seems to mark too many of my thoughts. "It's not too late to go back to Eren."

"And put Elanna through war if I could end it?"

The look on her face tells me what she thinks of my odds. "In Eren," she says, "you would be able to protect her."

"She doesn't need my protection. She needs this alliance, if I can achieve it."

She gives me a long stare—so long I start to fidget underneath it. "I know I'm putting you at risk," I begin, fumbling with the words, "so I'll go, if that's better—"

"Absolutely not," my aunt says. "You are staying right here. I'll do what I can to help. But if things get bad, I'm fleeing to Eren with you."

I smile, though it feels forced. "I may have to impose further on your generosity. Lathiel . . ." I pause. Even after six years together, I feel small and strange when I tell her that Madiya whispers into my head. That it feels like a violation I can't resist, and yet at the same time I feel I should answer it.

But hope has brightened her face. "Is there news of him?"

"I went home—looking for Rayka—but the witch hunters found

me there. I'm hoping Lathiel hid himself on my ship and followed us here."

Aunt Cyra's lips twitch. "You encouraged your youngest brother to become a stowaway?"

I laugh. "I suppose I did." At least, unlike most stowaways, he can make himself invisible.

"Of course I'll welcome him." She shakes her head at me. "Isn't that what our lawyers have been fighting for all these years? Come along, enough pitying yourself. You need rest."

"Thank you." I follow her to the door. "Aunt . . ."

She looks inquiringly at me.

I gesture toward the bathing chamber. "I'm afraid some of your hothouse plants met with a rather . . . abrupt demise."

Her lips press together, but then she simply sighs. "I'll see to it. Good night, Jahan."

I LIMP BACK to my bedchamber. Some industrious servants have put a fire in the grate, and a platter of food and tea sits on the table. Carefully, I close the door. It's strange to be back in this house; I was fifteen when I last stayed here for any length of time. I was hollow inside when I came, sick and trembling, racked with guilt that I'd left my brothers. Aunt Cyra nursed me back to health and, once I looked less gray at the edges, introduced me to everyone she knew. Many people remembered my mother, and I couldn't stand their condescension. Their polite concern. I escaped to Ida as soon as my aunt let me, to study at the university. There, no one had known my mother; no one pitied me for being raised in the Britemnos Isles, far from civilization. No one asked after my father, or my brothers. Sixteen-year-olds aren't commonly admitted to the university, but Aunt Cyra knows nothing if not how to pull strings. I got in.

I still miss attending lectures and digging through the university archives with Pantoleon, drinking beer in the student watering holes, and soaking up all their ideals for changing the world.

All that changed once I went away to my military duty. Once Leontius decided we were the best of friends.

I stir sugar into my tea. Once more, I have to lean on my aunt's generosity, this time in the face of the emperor's ambivalence and Leontius's anger. But there is nowhere else to go.

A clock ticks on the mantel. It's long past ten. Elanna will be waiting for me at a mirror somewhere in Eren, irritated and worried that I haven't contacted her in days, since the bells ended our first contact aboard the ship.

I quiet the bedchamber walls, even though it leaves me feeling thin, and approach the great gilded mirror hanging between two swagged curtains. I touch the glass. "El."

There's no answer. The mirror shows only my own, rather haggard, reflection, my skin a paler olive than usual from the Ereni winter and the days in the belly of the ship. A bruise darkens my jaw. Some ambassador I make. I look like I got in a bar fight, and I feel exhausted into the marrow of my bones.

"El." I insist this time. *"Elanna."*

But there's still no response.

I push aside the worry tightening my shoulders. Anything might have happened. She might have been called to a different camp on the Tinani front and forgotten her hand mirror. She might be exhausted from traveling. It might be any one of any number of things.

Still, I don't like it.

There's another name I need to try. I sigh. "Rayka."

But of course he doesn't reply, either.

Only Madiya's voice whispers into my mind, as if from a great distance. *Jahan.*

CHAPTER SIX

"Look at this," Aunt Cyra says when I enter the breakfast room, lit by late-morning sun. We've both slept till nearly noon; my body still aches from the pummeling I took yesterday. Perhaps I could heal better out in the garden, but I wince at the thought of draining the plants of life. How El would despise me.

My aunt tosses a newspaper down on the table before me. Whatever it is, her chin is tucked in with disapproval. "Here."

I pour myself a thick jet of hot black coffee—the coffee in Eren is a weak, disappointing thing—and lift the newspaper. The headline catches me like a blow to the chest.

Jahan Korakides: Hero or Traitor?

"Evidently your friends Phaedra and Augustus Saranon made quick work of your return," Aunt Cyra remarks.

I drop numbly into a chair, unable to stop myself from skimming the article.

Jahan Korakides ("the Korakos") returned yesterday from his sojourn across the sea, where he forsook our glorious empire for the infamous Witch of Eren. Witch hunters escorted him from the Britemnos Isles and, though he now walks free among us, he was seen to be examined by the Grand Inquisitor Alcibiades Doukas, surely on charges of consorting with witches . . .

"The *Witch of Eren*?" I say drily. "Can there only be one?"

Aunt Cyra shrugs. "It's a nice piece of vitriol. Everyone at court should have read it by now. Someone delivered it to our door. So thoughtful."

But I hardly hear her. The article confides:

Most tellingly, Lord Korakides was seen by multiple parties to be rebuffed from Crown Prince Leontius's chambers last night. It would seem the romance is over. Perhaps this explains His Imperial Highness's recent melancholia; as we all know, a spurned lover may become bitter and impotent indeed, until the whole empire feels his pain.

The bastards. Leontius is going to see this—even if he doesn't, his siblings will make sure he hears about it. Maybe it was even Zollus Katabares who told them. Of course, Zollus may have affairs with anyone he likes and no one will raise an eyebrow, but since Leontius is the emperor's heir apparent, tongues wag over his slightest indication of interest in any man or woman. Not only that, they've accused him of being unfit to wear the diadem. He'll be utterly humiliated.

And he won't stand up to them. Sometimes I think he doesn't even know how. Instead he'll retreat even further, until he doesn't even appear in public anymore. And they'll win.

"Jahan!" Aunt Cyra exclaims.

I startle. My cup has exploded, spraying coffee-flecked shards across the pristine tablecloth. I stare at my hand, where I thought I still held the cup. I must have made it explode—with only the power of my anger? I never lose control like this.

Jahan, Madiya whispers, a mocking echo of my aunt.

"You're bleeding!" Aunt Cyra bustles over, wiping the remaining shards off my fingers with a clean napkin, and pressing it down over the gash on my thumb. She glares down at me, but doesn't say anything. Two maidservants have already come running. One cleans up the shards, while the other fetches me a fresh cup of coffee. Perhaps they think I threw the cup down in a rage. Aunt Cyra remains magisterially at my side, pressing down the napkin, until the two women depart.

"What are you thinking?" she whispers furiously. "You're lucky no one came in and saw that!"

"I don't know, Auntie, I just—I—" I stop. I have to calm down.

No. I have to find Leontius. I can't let him weather this alone—or with only Zollus Katabares to comfort him. Zollus is probably gloating.

I try to get up, but Aunt Cyra pushes me back down. "You're staying right here until you eat something."

My stomach feels flat as dust, but I take a breakfast roll and some stuffed dates. Aunt Cyra releases me—my thumb has stopped bleeding—and returns to her seat with a mutter of "Holy Aera!"

I look at my aunt. The skin beneath her eyes is soft, and the few strands of silver in her hair seem more pronounced. Guilt eats at me. I've done this to her. I brought this overwhelming worry on her by coming here in the first place, aged fifteen, and now I've made it far worse by returning from Eren.

I have to make this right. Now, before the gossip spreads further. And before—I dearly hope—my youngest brother arrives with my luggage and mires us in even more trouble.

I wolf down the rest of my breakfast, the coffee burning my stomach. My aunt scowls when I get up and make for the door. "You haven't shaved!" she calls after me. "And that suit is out of fashion!"

But I wave away her warnings and stride out into the bright day. I might not be able to unprint those words from the newspaper, but at least I can prove them false by reconciling with my friend.

OUTSIDE AUNT CYRA'S house, the street is busy with pedestrians and sedan chairs, carriages and horse riders. I cross into the relative tranquility of the imperial park, where courting couples linger beside the reflecting pools and a knot of state ministers hold conference in the marble arcade. But my feet are taking me toward a high gate planted with tall exotic bushes and ferns: the imperial botanical garden. Leontius's favorite place in the world. I've spent hours in there with him, digging in the dirt to plant this bulb or that, trimming branches, collecting specimens. It's one of the things that drew me to Elanna. When I first met her, she wanted nothing more than an introduction to Markarades, the emperor's chief botanist. I think she would have dug herself a bed under a myrtle bush and slept in the gardens if she could have. And she was so suspicious when I told her I knew Markarades. She had no idea who I was.

I duck inside. It smells as it always does, sweetly, of climbing roses. Bees drone. A salamander darts past my foot. Leontius will be here somewhere, probably discussing tree grafting with one of the many workers.

But he's not anywhere among the blooming flowers. Sweat starts to build on the back of my neck. He comes here every morning, as predictable as the sunrise. This isn't right.

One of the gardeners recognizes me. "Prince Lees isn't here, sir. He's been coming less the last few months."

"Thank you," I say automatically. Have I done this to my friend, somehow, driven him out of his favorite place? Several of the other gardeners have gathered on the other side of the tulip bed, whispering and glancing at me. Apparently Aunt Cyra and I aren't the only ones who read the newspaper this morning.

Maybe Leontius did, too. Maybe that's why he's not here.

I walk swiftly out. He won't be in the pleasure gardens—the chance of meeting courtiers he dislikes would be too high—so he must be either out riding or still in his chambers. These are the only things I've ever known Leontius to do on his own; he's a creature of habit. He hates risking anything out of the ordinary.

I hurry across the drowsy garden paths, staying as far as I can from the palace's grand veranda, where courtiers lunch beneath parasols and striped awning. I don't need to give rise to further rumors.

As I skirt along the park bordering the gardens, I hear a rumble of hoofbeats. A rider trots through the parkland, too distant for me to see his face. But I recognize him all the same—short and hunched forward in his saddle. Zollus Katabares. He's making for the palace's western wing, where Leontius keeps his rooms.

Zollus is the last person I want to see. But I follow him anyway. He draws closer to the gardens, but our paths diverge near the palace itself. He continues around the building, while I make straight through the Palm Garden for Leontius's windows. I trot down the shallow stairs to a sunken garden bordering the crown prince's chambers. Leontius's windows overlook a perfectly round pond and a tangle of rosebushes.

I stop short. There's a man among the rosebushes, wearing a floppy hat. He seems to be digging in the earth. It's Leontius, of course.

What am I doing here? I can already see how he'll put his back to me. I already hear his silence.

But I have to talk to him. I want him to hear about the newspaper story from me, if Augustus hasn't already rubbed it in his face.

And I *want* to see him. My own urgency surprises me, because I never shared much of my true self with Leontius. I never offered him any of my secrets. Yet he has, in his way, been as true a friend as he could be, these last two years. I can't believe he's really angry with me.

And maybe some part of me feels sorry for running off to Eren without him.

Leontius straightens as I watch, pulling off his wide-brimmed hat and running a hand through his short black hair. The combination of sweat and pomade leaves it rumpled up. I must make some noise. He turns quickly, hauling himself onto his feet.

I feel a smile warming my face. "Finding some treasures in the dirt?"

Leontius frowns. For a moment I think he's angry because I spoke first, when he's the crown prince of Paladis—even in his grubby gardening clothes with dirt smeared on his knees and forehead. But then I think of my reassigned apartments, and Zollus's smugness last night. Maybe it's true: Maybe Leontius wants nothing to do with me. He looks wearier than he used to, almost less solid, as if he wants to be overlooked even more than usual.

"What are you doing here?" He doesn't really look at me, even though his tone demands an answer.

"I—" I must ask him about the newspaper. But for some reason, my idiot tongue says, "I just got in yesterday. Thought I'd take a walk. It's too lovely to remain indoors."

Leontius keeps looking at the shrubs. "It's a nice day."

"We had few enough of those in Eren. You've never seen so much snow—and the cold *seeps* into your bones." I'm babbling, and Leontius still is not looking at me. "I swear, I've eaten better in the last day than I have in six months!" Mostly because we were running out of stores this winter, and our neighbors refused to trade with us. "The Caerisians have a saying—*We only eat well under a southern wind*. The joke is there's never a southern wind in Caeris. And this winter . . ." Why am I still talking? I can't seem to stop. "The harvest was poor, of course. But Elanna . . ." No, I can't tell him how she helped to grow wheat for our survival. "It's a different sort of place. Not like here."

Now Leontius is looking at me. "Did Finn find what he wanted there?"

He might as well have punched me in the face. Leontius never seemed to like Finn. A few times I dragged them both to a tavern in Aexione or out riding to the Horn, thinking it might do Lees good to have more than one real friend. But Leontius always retreated into himself more than ever. Because I'd known Finn since we were both fifteen, awkward outsiders in Aexione's high society, and we shared jokes and knowledge Leontius didn't? Damned if I ever knew. He certainly didn't seem to give a care about Finn's crown and our revolution when I left. Maybe this is his way of reminding me of my failure.

"He tried," I say, unable to force any warmth into my tone.

We both stand there for a long moment, not looking at each other.

Then, from the open windows above us, I hear Zollus Katabares calling, "Leontius!"

I swallow hard. It's now or never. Leontius is frowning at the window, as if wondering whether he can escape—or maybe that's just my imagination.

"I'm not really out enjoying the weather." Why does the truth stick so much in my throat? "My aunt—we saw a story in the newspaper. One that reflected poorly on you. And me. I wanted . . ."

I falter. Leontius is staring steadily at me now. Waiting for me to finish.

"Lees!" Zollus calls from above, impatient. He hasn't realized we're in the garden yet.

Impulsively, I say, "We could go riding together. Out to the Horn, by the main road, so everyone could see us. That would silence Augustus and Phaedra's gossip, or at least . . . make it easier to bear."

If I expected him to offer me his shy, thankful smile, he doesn't. He just blinks. Then he says flatly, "I'm not interested in gossip."

"Well, gossip is interested in you. Let me make this right, Lees—"

At the nickname, he jerks. His nostrils flare. "You do not have permission to address me with such familiarity," he says in the cold tone he uses with courtiers he dislikes. "Excuse me. As it happens, I'm already meeting some friends for a ride."

He strides away to the steps leading up to his room, abandoning the hoe—and me. I stare after him. There's a flicker of movement in the windows above. Zollus Katabares looks out at me, his eyes narrowed.

I turn away. He doesn't need to be concerned; Leontius already dismissed me more effectively than anyone else ever could.

CHAPTER SEVEN

I stumble back into the pleasure gardens, feeling mildly stunned. This time, I'm not careful enough; I almost plow into a cluster of young courtiers gossiping by the Naiad Pool. They recognize me with a collective gasp and all turn away at the same time.

I'm too sick with myself to care. Zollus told me the truth, and so did Aunt Cyra. Leontius *is* angry with me—a cold, long-running anger. But I don't understand it. Does he so profoundly disapprove of sorcery? Does he think I've come back merely to use him?

The worst part is that it does make my mission here harder. It's not only Leontius I'm sick for, it's Elanna. It's everyone in Eren and Caeris.

Jahan, Madiya whispers in my head.

All the gods, this woman! What is she doing, hiding somewhere whispering my name every spare moment? She's never tried to summon me this consistently before. What does she *want*?

I stride faster through the gardens, as if I can outpace her voice. But my hand has already gone to the scar behind my ear. The hot blurring memory of pain runs through me, and a sense of shock so bitter I can taste it. What did she do to me that day when I was ten? What did she make me do? What did she do to Rayka, and Lathiel?

Jahan, she whispers.

Maybe it's because I feel suddenly so alone. I dive down a side path between clustering cypresses, into the half-hidden grotto dedicated to the goddess Astarea. Among the green trees, with the waterfall muttering over the old green rocks, I could almost be back in Eren. I lean over the pool until I see my own reflection wavering back at me. I draw in a breath and whisper, "Rayka."

I wait, but there's no answer. Not even Madiya's voice whispers in my mind. I rub my forehead, and my reflection looks perplexed and mildly lunatic. I really must be desperate, to call on my impossible brother. Where is he? He wouldn't have gone to her—would he? But then I don't know where Madiya is. Father was quite cagey on the subject, and so was Lathiel. She might be anywhere, and Rayka might have succumbed to her.

No, I won't believe that. Not yet. Maybe he's taken refuge in Ida. He could have looked up Pantoleon and asked for help. I told him Pantoleon would help him if he ever needed a friend. Of course, at the time, Rayka only rolled his eyes and said *he* would never need to ask for anyone's help.

But maybe he has now. Maybe, for once in his life, Rayka did the sensible thing. If I go to Bardas Triciphes's party tomorrow . . .

"Lord Jahan?"

I rear upright. Someone else has come into Astarea's Grotto. Did they hear me whispering over the water? I turn warily. A woman in a white gown has paused between the cypresses, watching me, along with a severe man in military dress.

All the gods, I'm making a fool of myself in front of the empress. I clamber onto my feet and sweep a low bow. "Your Imperial Majesty."

"Were you communing with the waters?" Firmina Triciphes asks, her voice bright with laughter. "Is it something you learned from your Ereni witch?"

The empress's companion snorts. I feel a smile tug my mouth; I bend down and pluck a flower from among the stones. "Alas, my lady, I was merely offering my respects to the goddess. But this foxglove has a lovely scent." I hold the flower out to her, but she doesn't take it. She leans close to me, instead, so I feel the brush of air from her delicate skirts, and inhales deeply.

"Mmm," she says, looking up at me with unmistakable mischief. "That is lovely."

I feel my smile grow fixed. As if I'm not in enough trouble already. If anyone witnesses Empress Firmina flirting with me, the emperor will probably have me beheaded—*after* my reputation is thoroughly dragged through the muck by Aexione's industrious gossips.

"Although," she adds in a murmur, "foxglove has no scent. I thought your sorceress would have taught you that much. Or Leontius. Anyone, really."

Heat burns up my neck, but I force a laugh. "You've caught me out!"

With a little knowing smile, Firmina steps back and takes her companion's arm. "Jahan, you know Captain-General Horatius Bucellanus, do you not?"

Of course, now that I look at him, I know the minister of war, though he's the last person I expected to be touring the gardens with Empress Firmina. He nods to me; I nod back. I've only spoken personally to the general once, after we returned from Chozat and he presented me with a medal for saving Leontius's life. He asked me the most direct question anyone did: *How did you know?* I told him that I hadn't known anything about the Getai attack; I simply reacted. He said, "I see," but his eyes said he didn't entirely believe me, that no one could have done what I did without prior knowledge.

Now, however, he's nothing but cordial. "Lord Jahan, you are to be commended for your success in Eren."

"Indeed?" I say. His approbation is the last thing I expected.

"Success is success, no matter the method by which it is achieved."

I glance at the empress, who simply smiles. She holds the captain-general's arm with the affection of a friend, though I can't imagine what they have to converse about.

The captain-general looks at me. "You've returned to secure peace, I understand."

I laugh. "I suppose peace is antithetical to your occupation."

To my complete astonishment, he gives me a fatherly smile. "Peace, war." He waves a hand. "Nothing more than words. There is always conflict. The question is, where are our resources best spent? The Ereni revolt has inflamed some incendiaries in Paladis, true. But their fires were already burning. I don't see the point in policing an independent nation when we've already fought our battle there, and won."

"Elanna Valtai's use of sorcery doesn't trouble you?" I'm so surprised I ask the question outright.

He shrugs. "Do I care for it? No. But it's a waste of my—*our*—resources to make an example of Eren when there are riots in Ida's streets. Let the Tinani and the Baedoni fight this war. Let them send in witch hunters to take the sorceress. Let them . . . take care of her. We must look first to our subject states. I need to garrison troops in Seleuca and Istria. I need to strengthen the border with Agra, because if there is insurrection within the empire, our neighbors will be the first to fall on us."

The empress leans forward. "My husband claims the war with Eren distracts from the fires at home."

"So he has been telling me, repeatedly." Horatius seems to stop himself from rolling his eyes. "As I said, the fires are already burning. And between ourselves and the wind, there's word that many refugees—sorcerers—have fled from Paladis to Eren. Once word about that gets out . . ." He shakes his head. "Better to ally with Sophy of Eren. Maintain neutrality about how the sorceress defeated the Eyrlais. Meanwhile, we scour our own streets. Send out all the witch hunters. Station imperial guards around Ida. Suppress the riots as efficiently as we can."

My mouth is open. I close it. So Horatius doesn't mind sorcery as long as it happens at a safe distance. That doesn't make him an ally, exactly, though if he can persuade the emperor to his thinking, it would obviously benefit Eren.

But the idea of more witch hunters on Ida's streets—the idea of the military, not just the city watch, overseeing the riots—makes the skin on the back of my neck tighten. I came here to win peace for Eren, but not at the price of my friends in Ida.

"I somehow doubt Emperor Alakaseus will agree," I say faintly.

Horatius checks his pocket watch. "I'll find out for certain in a quarter of an hour, when I meet with His Imperial Majesty and my fellow ministers." Again, the paternal smile. "Your mission hasn't failed yet, Lord Jahan."

I feel heat rise in my chest. This is so far from what I expected that I can't trust the reassurance I feel.

"I am curious," Empress Firmina says, tapping the general's arm. "Do you mean to decriminalize sorcery in Eren, then? Would you change Paladisan law so that witch hunters have jurisdiction only in the empire?"

Horatius raises his brows, echoing my thoughts. "That would be quite a change."

"Or perhaps," the empress says reflectively, "we should consider sorcery a nuisance, not an abomination. After all, is it truly an offense to the gods? Elanna Valtai has not yet been smitten to the earth."

She smiles at me, and I realize I'm staring. I cough into my fist, trying to recover my thoughts. Does she really mean this? I find myself saying, with a kind of strangled hope, "You're right, my lady—sorcery isn't anathema. Our witch hunts were founded on a false premise. The truth is that no sorcerers would cooperate with Paladius the First's overweening ambitions—in fact, they allied against him, and nearly destroyed him. Sorcery was only declared an 'abomination' because Paladius could not bend the sorcerers to his will."

Firmina Triciphes blinks at me. I realize, too late, that I've said too much.

Then Captain-General Horatius chuckles. "You've been reading the nonsense proliferated by the People's Party, Lord Jahan. It's a good story, but not based in any fact, so far as I can see."

"*History* is a fact," I reply, but I force myself to stop. If I admit that the research behind the People's Party's claims belongs to me, that Pantoleon and I spent years digging through the university archives . . . Studying the history of sorcery is undoubtedly as criminal as practicing it.

I'm going to kill Pantoleon when I see him.

I turn to the empress. "My point is that the oppression of sorcerers has less to do with their natural wickedness than with political expediency."

She nods. "And by all standards of human decency, our methods of oppression are somewhat . . . outmoded. Barbaric."

The captain-general checks his pocket watch again. "Your sensitivity does you credit, madam. Would that the people responded to such gentle measures. It would make my occupation a good deal easier."

Empress Firmina's responding smile is faint. "Would that I did not see their struggle so clearly." Her gaze flickers to me. Of course both of us see the people's struggle in a way the captain-general and even my aunt never could: We've both come to Aexione from the other side of the gate, so to speak.

"Well," Horatius says, tucking away his pocket watch, "if you'll excuse me, my meeting is due to begin." He kisses the empress's hand and nods at me. "Your Imperial Majesty. Lord Jahan."

Together, Firmina and I watch him walk away between the trees. I feel slightly dazed. After being rejected by Leontius and the vitriol in the newspaper, hope is the last thing I expected to feel.

The empress holds out her arm. "Walk with me, Lord Jahan."

I have little choice but to comply. Her fingers tuck around my elbow, warm and delicate, steering me out of the grotto. We stroll in silence past the arcade and along the tree-lined path toward the Little Palace. We've left behind most of the courtiers and even the ubiquitous gardeners. Only a squirrel rustles in the high branches of the plane trees.

And Madiya whispers, *Jahan.*

As if my skin weren't prickling enough with the danger of being seen alone with the empress. Well, what's another slur on my reputation? But the emperor can be a jealous man. It's the insecure corollary, I suppose, of marrying a woman twenty years his junior. I just don't want my life to be a consequence of it.

Firmina sighs. "I must apologize, Jahan. I'm afraid Captain-General Horatius and I have misled you."

For a moment, I imagine she's leading me straight to a band of witch hunters who will spirit me to the Ochuroma. I clear my throat. "Have you?"

"Yes." Her footsteps slow; she looks at me. "Horatius and I were talking of our hopes, as reasonable people. My husband . . ." She lowers her voice. We're standing so close I can see the swift flutter of her pulse above her collarbone. "My husband is not a reasonable man. He doesn't believe in changing policies that have served Paladis for two centuries, regarding either sorcery or anything else."

I wince. I knew this, of course, but it's crushing to hear.

"Our main hope," she continues, "is that Horatius can persuade the other ministers to agree with him. That may put enough pressure on Alakaseus to relent against Eren."

"Ah," I say. I know the ministers well enough; though some of them can think for themselves, most will simply follow the official imperial line. "I won't raise my hopes, then."

Firmina's grip tightens on my sleeve. "I heard you were assaulted on your way home last night. I trust the brigands didn't do any serious damage."

I manage a smile. "Not at all. Fortunately, your cousin came to my rescue."

"It's lucky he happened to see it." She pauses. "Jahan, you must be careful. It isn't only my husband who propounds these intolerant policies."

"Oh, I know. I had quite an illuminating conversation with Augustus."

Her lips thin. "We must both take care. If he and Phaedra know we're in agreement, they'll know where to set their next traps."

"It seems to me they've already succeeded moderately well at that."

"The paper was vicious, it's true. But . . ." She looks at me. "You must know Leontius wouldn't have been able to help you much in any case. He's in Alakaseus's confidence less than ever."

I say nothing. I suppose I did know that, but I still want my friend back.

Firmina sighs again. "Do you know why I married His Imperial Majesty? I wanted to change things. I wanted to make a difference for my people, the ordinary Idaean people, from the second-highest seat in the land. I thought perhaps his willingness to wed me suggested that such changes *were* afoot. But I find myself silenced time and again—told to sit down and be quiet. Mind my manners. Be beautiful, but have no true intelligence. No thoughts. No plans." She turns to me, her anger fierce around her. "You know what I'm talking about, surely. You've experienced the same thing yourself."

As Leontius's friend, she means. There is so much I could have tried to accomplish, so many changes I could have tried to bring about. But Leontius doesn't have the influence or the means, and I have been too afraid of being found out for what I truly am.

So instead I ran away to Eren and Caeris, to make change happen there.

"Yes," I say drily. "If only our last names were Saranon."

"But soon that won't be the case." She grasps my hand. "Changes are happening in Ida—the people are demanding it. And my husband, his ministers, his courtiers, are all too blind to see it for what it is. To understand what it means. That *they* must change."

I stare down at our joined hands, then up into her eyes. She's smiling, showing small perfect teeth, and I can smell her jasmine perfume and feel the warmth beating off her. We're alone on the slope beside the Little Palace. Anything might happen here, with a woman like Firmina Triciphes. Maybe the emperor's right to be jealous.

But I promised Elanna I would return to her. I'm keeping that promise.

And if I lean any closer to Firmina, I have a feeling El won't take me back.

I step back, or try to. The empress's eyes crinkle; she doesn't let go of my hand or release her lock on my gaze. "Please know," she says softly, "that you can trust me. You can trust Bardas, too. *We* are your allies, Jahan. And if you go to the Deos Deorum tomorrow, you'll see how much we believe the same things."

Bardas's party—the one he claimed Pantoleon would attend. I stare at her. Maybe this isn't just sentiment. Maybe she and Bardas *are* planning something—and maybe they can help me.

But what do they want in return? Nobody gives something for nothing.

With a smile, Firmina releases me. She puts a finger to her lips. "I trust you'll speak of this meeting to no one."

"Your secret is safe with me," I say, even though the words make me uneasy. I'm not certain what I'm agreeing to. But she's already walking away, her skirts bobbing, to the fanciful steps of the Little Palace, leaving me behind.

A PILE OF LUGGAGE awaits me at Aunt Cyra's: two large chests of clothing and two smaller ones of books. They sit in a lonely pile at the center of my bedchamber.

Hope pounds in my ribs. "Lathiel?" I swing around in a circle, staring at the curtains and even crouching to peer beneath the bed. But I don't feel a concentrated, boy-shaped silence. The room feels undisturbed.

A whisper of sound sends me spinning toward the door, breathless.

Aunt Cyra watches me, gripping the doorjamb. Her mouth is grave. "Jahan, I don't think he's here. If he is, he's hidden so well we can't find him."

But I saw the longing on Lathiel's face. He wanted to come with me. I *know* it.

I fling open the nearest trunk, casting out coats and trousers and shirts. But there's no boy cocooned in the bottom of this trunk, or the other one. I sink, at last, to the ground between the piles of silk and linen, burying my face in my hands. He must have stayed home with Father. When it came down to it, he must have been too afraid to come.

I want to commandeer a ship and go back for him, but I can't do that. Not yet. Instead I'm left here with a mound of clothing I don't care about, and the knowledge that, once again, I've failed my brothers.

CHAPTER EIGHT

"El," I whisper. *"Elanna."*

But the gilded mirror stubbornly reflects my own face. I rub my forehead. I'm growing hoarse from whispering—I've been in here for an hour, in Aunt Cyra's Ida townhouse, stealing time before Bardas's party.

There's been no answer tonight. And nothing the two nights before. Something's wrong.

I have no other way of reaching her, though, and I can't remain here whispering. I've silenced the doors and walls with magic, but I can already imagine the servants saying I'm being misanthropic. I hardly need another rumor circulating now. And I need to get to the party. Firmina and Bardas are the only people who've really offered help, and I need to find Pantoleon.

So, with a sigh, I fix the mask on my face and go out. A faint tremble runs through the floorboards. I shorten my stride instinctively, but keep walking. The tremor is only nearby Mount Angelos, talking to itself. It hasn't erupted in centuries, and it's hard to believe the stories that it once leveled all of Ida and smothered people in cloying ash so thick even sorcerers couldn't save them all.

A servant shakes his head as I pass out the front door. "The gods aren't happy."

I raise an eyebrow. "Who can blame them?"

Outside, the nighttime streets of Ida are aglow. I'm too restless to trouble with a coach. Though it's going on eleven, the aristocratic quarter of Vileia is a riot of carriages and sedan chairs and pedestrians like me, all going to or from the opera or dinner parties or lovers' assignations, all laughing and gossiping and shouting cheerful insults. The vibrancy of it electrifies me. It's not like the cold, staid cities in Eren and Caeris, which are asleep by this hour, or even Aexione, which sets its clock to the emperor's routine. There is nowhere else quite like Ida.

Aunt Cyra, who remained in Aexione, wanted me to bring a chaperone—"one of the footmen, at least, so no one leaves you to die in a ditch if Augustus Saranon's people find you."

I pointed out that I would be in disguise: a mask that leaves only my mouth and chin exposed, along with the slits for my eyes.

She was unimpressed. "A gray-eyed raven? No one will ever guess. Even Augustus isn't that dense . . . No wonder you're wearing that black suit like Brother Death."

"And here I thought I looked rather dashing."

"Of course you do, darling, but you hardly need me to tell you that, do you?"

But maybe she was right about the footman. The anonymity of the crowd comforts me on the one hand—and makes me uneasy on the other. If I wear a mask to Bardas's party, who's to say Augustus and his cohorts won't, too? I tell myself I'm granting Augustus and Phaedra too much power—and prescience.

I move downhill to the cul-de-sac where the Deos Deorum towers over the sluggish black Channel, its walls palatial. The emperor couldn't have given his wife's cousin a larger house if he tried. I pass through the open gallery, following a party of young girls in low-cut gowns and flimsy masks—where are *their* chaperones?—into a cavernous courtyard. In its midst, a fountain spews not water, but champagne. People cluster around it, laughing as they fill glasses.

Jahan, Madiya whispers.

Be quiet, I think.

I push inside to a grand atrium. It's brightly lit by a massive chandelier hanging from the vaulted glass ceiling, so high it's difficult to imagine how the servants light the myriad candles. The colonnades are lost to shadow; stairs wind up to a second-floor ballroom. Party-goers cluster along the mezzanine, looking down over us on the floor.

I glance at the people around me, all busily filling space. For the first time in days, no one recognizes me. No one flinches away or whispers behind their hands. I'm simply another Idaean in the crowd.

A tightness unravels in my shoulders. *This* is the Paladis where I belong—not at Aexione, with its endless rules and intrigues, but in the unruly, vibrant city. This is the world I called home, before duty and Leontius dragged me back to the court. I claim a flute of effervescent wine from a tray and make for the stairs. Bardas is bound to be here somewhere, at least. Perhaps I can find Pantoleon before Argyros's speech begins.

And maybe someone will carry rumors about Ida's sorcerers. Or about a black-haired eighteen-year-old boy with a sullen mouth who's run away from military school. I may have lost my opportunity to save Lathiel, but I can at least try to find Rayka.

The ballroom is hot and packed. Not everyone wears a mask. I come in behind two men talking in hushed tones about Eren and the steward of the land.

"It's what we need," one is murmuring, just loud enough that I can hear. "Sorcery. To change things."

I startle. It's still strange to hear them speaking of sorcery aloud. Something really has changed in the six months I was gone.

"Have you *met* a sorcerer?" His companion lowers his voice. "What's to stop them being just another kind of tyrant?"

They both glance back at me, as if sensing my attention. Clearly I'm too eager for these rumors to eavesdrop successfully. I slip away from them, making a tour of the ballroom's perimeter, and decline offers to dance from three ladies and one gentleman. So far—unsurprisingly—this doesn't seem like the den of infamy the court makes it out to be, though perhaps other rooms hide the courtesans and the drugs and the shady deals. The doors stand open to a balcony overlooking the Channel, carrying a cool breeze and the faint scent of marsh. When I step out, I find some couples trysting among the potted plants, and a cluster of fellows talking politics.

". . . the right of the people to determine our laws," one of the political fellows is saying. "Not to be bound by arcane conventions. Not to make alterations only at the emperor's whim! What gives Alakaseus Saranon the right to determine our laws, anyway? Does he have a university degree? No!"

They all laugh. I sip my drink and drift closer, unable to suppress a smile. I know that voice.

"When you write your next essay, make sure to mention it," one of the others says. "Maybe he'll pen a response."

"What could his defense possibly be?" the first speaker says. "That it's the will of the gods that he rules, so a knowledge of law is unnecessary?"

"I'd leave him be on law if he had better sense on foreign policy," another fellow says. "Starting a war against *Eren*? No one's ever heard of the place."

"They send us timber," someone else points out. "And lead."

"But have they ever exported any *ideas*?"

More laughter.

"It's the magic," Pantoleon says with contempt. "The emperor wants the world to know he can squash even the grandest displays of sorcery."

Someone else pipes up, "I heard Jahan Korakides is back, and he's come to make peace!"

One of the others snorts. "Korakides is representing the Ereni queen now. His loyalties shift faster than the tide. He doesn't seem to believe in anything but himself. It's not as if the powers that be will listen to him. I wouldn't trust him to do anything but make trouble."

I wait for Pantoleon to defend me. He doesn't. Instead his shoulders rise in a shrug.

I take a step back; two, three. None of them have noticed me.

I should be inured to such criticism. But instead anger pulses, hot, into my head. I want to stride forward and defend myself—but of course I can't do that.

I do believe in something more than myself. I *do*. Pantoleon knows it. After I started at the university, I dragged Finn down from court to attend lectures with me; he was my only friend in all Paladis at first. Then we met Pantoleon in Argyros's lecture hall, and the three of us decided we were going to start our own revolution. We were going to tell the truth about sorcery and change the face of Ida. We penned pamphlets, cut our hair, loosened our cravats, pushed up our sleeves.

But then we turned nineteen. I might have gotten out of my military duty with Aunt Cyra's help, but Finn's father refused to let his son evade service—and I refused to let Finn endure the military alone. So we left Pantoleon. We trained. We went to Chozat. And then the Getai swarmed out of the woods, materializing seemingly from nowhere, and I used my illicit magic to save Leontius's life. I had to whisper so much persuasion to make everyone look the other way. I learned how to lie better, then, than I ever had in my life— even to Leontius, who so desperately wanted a friend.

When we came back, it wasn't to Ida but to Aexione and the court. I worked persuasion on everyone, from the emperor to the stableboys, to make them look the other way about the Getai. I saw Pantoleon only a handful of times. It was as if I had erased the boy I had been. I went to Eren and Caeris to find him again—to find *myself* again—but it killed Finn, and it might very well kill Elanna, too, if the world has its way, and all the Caerisians and Ereni I struggled alongside.

And now I'm back here, trying to assume the role that doesn't fit me anymore, struggling to button myself back into this shrunken, false version of me, and I can't breathe.

I'm back in the mansion; I've stumbled into a room adjacent to the ballroom. I take a fresh glass of wine and drink it down as a bell begins to sound. As one, the people in the room start shuffling toward the door, and I let myself get swept up in the crowd. "What is this?" I ask a woman beside me.

She looks at me as if I'm a complete fool. "The midnight oration."

Of course. And Argyros is speaking.

In the atrium, we find a crowd already gathered on the mezzanine. The third floor is brightly lit, and Bardas stands at the railing up there, scanning the crowd with a smile.

". . . sorcery," someone whispers near my elbow. It's one of the girls I followed into the party, flushed behind her flimsy mask.

I've been pushed toward the stairs, my view of Bardas partially blocked. I clamber onto the bottom step to get a better view, and startle. I'm standing three steps below a familiar figure with thick, curly black hair and night-dark skin. The university scholars are lined up on the steps, waiting eagerly for Argyros's speech to begin.

I push up to the step below Pantoleon.

"Hey, stop crowding m—" He sees my mask and stops dead. Then he begins to smile.

I put a finger to my lips. I don't need his friends sneering at me.

He punches me in the arm, grinning broadly now. "You idiot," he whispers. "Why didn't you tell me you were coming?"

"When did I have the chance? Was I supposed to write you a letter?"

He laughs. "You've missed these midnight orations. They're the latest thing. Instead of shouting to be heard in the city square, our speeches are being hosted by Bardas Triciphes. At midnight, every Enydia."

"Isn't the emperor annoyed?"

Again, he laughs. "That's probably why Bardas is doing it." Quietly: "You should see the funds he's donating to us, Jahan. He's sponsored the printing of thousands of posters and pamphlets, and distributed them around the city, and—"

"Shh!" the other scholars hiss.

On the third floor, Bardas has lifted his hands. "Greetings and salutations, citizens of Ida and the world! Welcome, welcome!" He seems to smile right at me. I smile back. It's easier to see him now without blood gushing from my nose: His smile is boisterous and welcoming. "You may have heard of tonight's orator—Lucius Argyros. But in case you've been living, I don't know, in the *cisterns*—"

The crowd obediently laughs.

Bardas grins. "For decades he's tirelessly given speeches and written treatises pointing to the iniquities of Idaean society, the absurdities of Aexione, the injustices that continue unchecked, the tyranny of rule by a few over many. He has been imprisoned. Exiled. But tonight, he is venerated. Welcome, Lucius Argyros!"

The man who steps up to the railing is shorter than Bardas, his hair tidy in an old-fashioned queue, his clothes impeccable. He adjusts the spectacles on the end of his nose. He looks far less like a rabble-rousing radical than a lawyer about to deliver an address. And he is a lawyer: a professor of law at the university, where Finn, Pantoleon, and I used to sit through his lectures in utter silence, absorbing his every word. Even now I feel the magnetism of his presence: the way he gazes down from the railing and seems to acknowledge each person in the audience.

I draw in a breath. Absurdly, I feel the same trepidation I used to feel in the lecture hall when I feared he might call on me and my answers would be inadequate. Pantoleon thumps my shoulder. My friend's face is turned up with a kind of triumph.

"Citizens," Argyros says. His voice, as always, is somewhat quiet, so the entire atrium seems to be leaning forward, taut with anticipation. "Tonight I want to talk about magic."

I actually startle. My whole body buckles, ready to bolt. Pantoleon grabs my elbow and keeps me there, locked in beside him.

Argyros's voice carries through the atrium. "You've all heard about the extraordinary events in Eren these last months. Whether or not the stories are true—though I have reason to believe they are—is immaterial. Indeed, these stories serve to *remind* us of what truly matters." He scans the crowd, gathering us all into his pause.

"They remind us that sorcery was once the provenance of all Idae-ans."

A murmur rustles through the crowd.

It's not the revelation that shocks me. I've known this fact too long. No, I'm shocked that Lucius Argyros is making these state-ments in a public place. In the Deos Deorum, which the emperor has given to Bardas Triciphes. The witch hunters have eyes everywhere. Bardas must know that; Argyros certainly does. He might print these claims on a piece of paper, but to stand there and proclaim it to the world? How do they know they won't be seized and ar-rested?

"It's true," Argyros is saying. "You may have forgotten, but the historical annals have not. Magic was the birthright of your ances-tors. And what have our emperors, the successors of Paladius the First, done? They have taken away our rights. Just the way they took away our rights to elect the members of our senate and district representatives, our right to vote and our right to full citizenship and all its benefits. They took away our right to practice sorcery just as they took away our government, just as they claimed our gods and our language for their own. And what were the Paladisan em-perors three centuries ago, when Ida was a shining beacon of civili-zation? They were *shepherds*! Goatherds! Edonis was so poor these men didn't even own cattle. So they had to come steal someone else's—and thus became thieves. And conquerors. They conquered us. They claimed Ida as their own, but it's not. And it never has been."

I should not be so rapt, I tell myself. I know this story as well as anyone else. Yet I can't help but listen. I can't stop myself from nod-ding, because Argyros is expressing a truth no one else dares to.

And I can't deny the longing that seizes me.

"You may ask where sorcery enters the picture," he's saying. "Let me explain. In those days, three centuries past, sorcerers were com-mon the world over. Some were itinerant; some earned their keep working for kings and queens. Ida was renowned for its theurges, as they termed themselves—men who not only practiced sorcery but also studied the workings of it. They were philosophers as much as magicians, and their school, the Academy, rivaled the University of Ida for attendance. For greatness.

"Were there sorcerers in Edonis? Perhaps, but they were the magicians of goatherds. What did they know of the great magics being worked in Ida? Little enough. But Paladius knew. Paladius's ambition was large enough to consume the world, and he believed that any similarly ambitious sorcerer would want a position at his court. He invited all the greatest theurges to join him and assist him in conquering Ida. And after that, the world."

I glance at Pantoleon. This is the history I know. It's the history the two of us pieced together over long months in the archives, dust in our noses, our spines aching from being bent over books.

"But sorcerers are cantankerous. None of them wanted to ally with Paladius, this vainglorious man from a brutal and unknown country. And what did Paladius do, when word of their refusal reached him?" He looks down into the crowd. "If no sorcerers would join him, he decided that he didn't need them. He would take Ida without their help, in defiance of their power. And he did."

"No!" someone in the crowd shouts.

Argyros smiles, rather sadly. "Paladius the First was a great tactician—not only of wars, but of minds. He besieged Ida for three years, and in the end he claimed her. He defeated the greatest magicians of the age—Theofanes, Diotima, the inimitable Mantius—not by sorcery, but by murder. After he won, many lesser sorcerers fled, taking refuge in places that should have been safe. Like the Britemnos Isles."

I freeze.

"But Paladius had a long reach, and even the safe havens fell to him eventually. Some fell through treachery, like Britemnos, where the people were betrayed by the great sorcerer Mantius's own son, Kyros."

He pauses for effect, and I look at Pantoleon. My friend stands unmoving, enraptured. It can't be coincidence that Argyros used the example of Kyros. That he's exposing my shame. But Pantoleon refuses to acknowledge my stare.

Argyros has continued; I missed some of what he said. ". . . some sorcerers remained in Ida. These allied against Paladius in secret and plotted to overthrow him. If he were a lesser man, they might have succeeded. They tried to send him mad, but even in his incipient madness, Paladius knew what was going on. He rooted out the sorcerers and killed them. He hung them from scaffolds. He burned them. He drowned them. And then, in punishment for what they did, he set out to systematically eliminate the practice of magic throughout the world. He began the witch hunts, which grew to their heights under his successor, Paladius the Second."

My jaw is tight. Yes, this is the story we uncovered, Pantoleon and I. The truth we so painstakingly put together.

It's obvious he must have told Argyros—and not just an abbreviated version, but all of it.

"The emperors created the witch hunters," Argyros is saying, "but the witch hunters could not erase all magic. They couldn't remove it from the frozen tundra of the Ismae, or from the Occident. They couldn't destroy it in the small nations south of Waset, or in Sindh or Tianxia. They tried to spread their reach that far—and they claim that those countries do not practice sorcery. But they do. And now magic is coming back to the lands that belong to the empire of Paladis." He seems to look directly at me. "The witch hunters are dwindling—they are less than a fifth of what they once were—and magic is surging back to life."

I swallow.

He smiles, and again I have the sense he's recognized me. "Now, you may be thinking that you are not sorcerers. But any one of you may have talent for it, if you only try. It is our birthright, given to us by our gods—the Idaean gods we worshipped before the Paladisans claimed them, the great beings who brought sorcery into the world so humans could use it. Let us show Emperor Alakaseus that this is one thing he may not claim for us—our divinely given right and ability to practice magic!"

The crowd erupts with cheers.

I feel ill. Argyros is going to get arrested for this. He must know that.

Around me, people begin to move. I realize belatedly that Pantoleon is climbing the stairs. I hurry after him and, as we reach the top, seize the back of his coat and drag him into the shadows of the mezzanine despite his greater height.

"What did you tell him?" I demand in a whisper.

He grins. He's so excited he doesn't seem to register my anger. "The truth, Jahan. I told him the truth. About my father, about you, about the histories we'd uncovered—"

A light seems to explode inside my head. "You told him about *me?*"

The smile slides off Pantoleon's face. Slowly, he says, "You've been in Eren these six months, winning a rebellion for your sorceress. And you're still hiding what you are?"

"Who did you tell?" I demand.

Pantoleon recoils. "Only Argyros. The secret's safe with him."

"It's *my* secret, not yours!" I almost shout, and Pantoleon stares at me. I don't think I've ever shouted at him before. I don't shout at anyone, let alone my closest and most sensible friend. The only friend who's ever understood how to really keep a secret. And now look what he's done.

He's getting angry. "At least I'm telling the truth, not spending my life sitting on secrets I'm too afraid to let out!"

I'm vibrating with rage now, and by the looks of it so is he. "I've done what I had to. How else am I supposed to return to court and win peace?"

Pantoleon's nostrils flare. Quietly, he says, "You could have come to *me.*"

"Oh? What would you have done, written a treatise?"

"I mean," Pantoleon says, an edge in his voice, "you could have come to *us,* the reformers. It wouldn't have taken much intelligence for your Ereni to realize we're organizing to do what they did. I thought that's why you were here tonight. I thought you'd come to help us." He snorts. "I should have known better."

My teeth grind together. I can't stand this disdain from Pantoleon of all people, who won't even practice the smallest magics. I lower my voice. "Is that what Rayka did? Have you suborned him into helping you?"

Pantoleon blinks at me, and I see him realize what I mean. "No, Jahan. I . . ."

"You what? *What did you do?*"

My friend's jaw bunches. Quietly, he says, "Nothing. I haven't seen your idiot brother in months."

"Then where is he? Hiding with the sorcerers here in Ida?"

Pantoleon is shaking his head. "I don't know. I haven't heard anything about him. I don't know where he is."

I swing away, clenching my fists at my temples. All the gods, where the hell is my brother? I simply can't believe he'd have allowed himself to be taken by witch hunters, and I don't think Alcibiades lied to me. Which means he's either run somewhere very far indeed—or he's gone back to Madiya. Where is she? What if, in my failure to bring Lathiel to Ida, she reclaimed him, too? If she has both my brothers again, I don't think I can bear it.

Her whisper floats into my head. *Jahan.*

Not *now.* I groan aloud. Pantoleon—the damned traitor—has backed up a step, watching me warily. Now his gaze flickers behind me.

I spin around. Bardas Triciphes is approaching with a smile. He claps his hands. "Lord Jahan! I'm so glad you joined us tonight. Does this mean—"

I look past him. Argyros is also approaching, eyebrows raised above his spectacles. He, too, smiles.

The truth smacks me in the face: This is what they want. Revolution. That's why Bardas asked me here; that's why Empress Firmina encouraged me to come. They want to change Paladis, and they want to do it with sorcery. All the gods—how much does the empress know? Has Pantoleon told them all, even her, what I really am? I can't believe he would betray my trust that fully.

So they—Pantoleon and Argyros, at least—want me to publicly declare myself a sorcerer. I can see it in Argyros's anticipatory expression. Pantoleon has told him the truth, almost certainly.

Bardas is talking to me, but I can't seem to hear him. There's a rushing in my ears. I think of Alcibiades Doukas and the witch he drove mad. Of how Faverus sweated at the idea of torturing a sorcerer. Of Madiya, refusing to even go into Pira town. I feel all the holes in my memory, and I know that's what they would do to me. They would turn my mind into one gaping blankness.

I came here to win peace for Elanna. I didn't come here to lead a revolt—not one doomed to failure. There's no way these reformers can stand up against the power of the emperor, his ministers, and his army.

"No," I say aloud. Bardas jerks back with a startled "Sorry?"

But I'm already striding away, practically running through the crowd. My heart beats an uneven tattoo. At the bottom of the atrium, I glance back. I thought Pantoleon would follow me; I almost wish he would. But he's still standing up there, beside Bardas and Argyros, looking down at me amid the crowd.

I don't owe them anything, not even an explanation.

I push away through the crowd, out into the night. The city throbs around me; laughter and shouts echo over the Channel behind the Deos Deorum. The air, thick with the scents of perfume and brine and excrement, tastes sour in my mouth. I can't stay here a minute longer.

I commandeer my horse from the Potazes townhouse and ride out, compressing space along the road, tugging space back like a curtain so I can move faster, faster. By the time I return to Aunt Cyra's house in Aexione, it's deep in the night. The gelding and I ghost through the silent town. I rub the horse down and set him up in his stall, careful not to wake the stableboy, then go into the still house.

I halt in front of the mirror in my bedchamber, staring into my own silhouetted reflection. I call Elanna's face into my mind's eye, seeing the riot of her wind-tousled hair, the brilliance of her smile, the way her eyes crinkle. "Elanna," I say aloud.

There's no answer. "Rayka," I say. *"Rayka!"*

Nothing.

Softly, I venture, "Lathiel?"

He doesn't answer. I don't know why I thought he might trust me enough to follow me here.

I drop my forehead against the cool glass. I whisper, "El. *El.*"

But no reply comes through the darkness, not even Madiya's incessant whisper. I'm alone with the echo of my own voice, my forehead smearing the empty glass.

CHAPTER NINE

A pounding fist on the door wakes me. "Lord Jahan!"

I fumble upright. I don't remember getting into bed. I fell asleep fully dressed, the raven mask digging into the back of my head. Golden bars of sunlight stripe the coverlet, and the clock on the mantel chimes twelve times.

A manservant sticks his head around the door. "Sir, you're wanted at the palace."

"Wonderful." I rub my forehead. It's probably the empress, ready to take me to task for refusing Bardas's offer of help. I snort. Some kind of help. I *knew* their generosity wouldn't come without strings attached.

Yet I suppose I can't simply ignore the summons. After all, in storming out of the Deos Deorum last night, I cast aside the one option left to me. Now no one at all will offer me—and Eren—aid.

I drag myself off the bed. Perhaps the reformers and I can come to an agreement, particularly if Pantoleon and Argyros keep their mouths shut about my secrets. But I'm not going to race over to the palace in my rumpled black suit. They don't need to know how desperate I am.

I order a bath, but have hardly lowered myself into the steaming water when a fist bangs on the bathing chamber door. "Jahan!" Aunt Cyra says. "Don't ignore the emperor's summons!"

The emperor? I slosh upright. Clearly I jumped to the wrong conclusion; it's not Firmina who summoned me, but her husband. What does Alakaseus Saranon want from me? My arrest, probably.

Or maybe he's decided to negotiate. Maybe Firmina and Horatius prevailed on him.

I take the fastest bath of my life. Aunt Cyra's waiting in the corridor, tapping her foot, when I emerge. "Finally," she says. "I won't ask what possessed you to ride back to Aexione through the dark, but it's as well that you did. The emperor sent a message more than an hour ago." She glances pointedly at the clock. "He wants you to attend him at once."

"You didn't wake me . . ."

"I thought you were still in Ida! Then the staff told me you'd returned and trailed dust all the way into your bedchamber." She snaps her fingers at me. "Eat something and get dressed."

"Do we know what he wants?"

She shrugs. "His page didn't deign to provide that information. Quick! The carriage is waiting."

I hurry into a fresh suit, not even arguing with the manservant over its screaming peacock-blue color, and seize a cup of spiced tea and a date-studded roll on the way out the door. As Aunt Cyra promised, a carriage is waiting. I jump inside. It lurches forward so fast I'm thrown back against the cushioned seat. The tea sloshes everywhere. I'm now nearly two hours late to my summons, and milky-brown flecks stain my coat's embroidered lapels. I mop them up with my handkerchief. I'll just have to be presentable enough.

If the emperor knew about my visit to Ida last night, I'd have been woken by witch hunters this morning, or the imperial guard. He must be summoning me to negotiate.

A footman meets my coach at the palace's inner gate. I dive after him into the perfumed corridors, winding up a back staircase to avoid the crowds. He deposits me at the Salon of Meres. I straighten my coat cuffs, trying to ignore the pounding of my heart. More footmen open the doors.

I step within. The emperor's dog barks, then settles with a resigned air. Emperor Alakaseus, along with Augustus, Captain-General Horatius, the minister of state, and several others make an industrious tableau around a massive oak table.

I make my bows, but the emperor and his colleagues are too busy with papers and pens to take any notice. I start to clear my throat when a flash of pale silk velvet catches my eye.

Phaedra Saranon raises an eyebrow at me. She's seated by the fireplace, though the room isn't cold, drinking a cup of chocolate. It leaves a faint mustache on her upper lip. She's fairer than her brother, probably because she abhors the sunshine. "Well, if it isn't the Korakos," she says frostily. "*Poor* you. I heard some thugs beat you up. What a good thing darling Stepmother's cousin was there to save you! The one useful thing he's ever done."

"Yes," I say, "Bardas was quite heroic. I can't imagine who sent those people."

She dabs the chocolate off her lip with a napkin. "I heard you were in Ida last night at one of his nasty little gatherings. Oh, don't look surprised. You're a very recognizable figure, even in a mask."

I pretend this doesn't send a jolt of fear through me. So Phaedra Saranon has decided it's worth her while to have me observed—so she can find some way to ruin me, presumably. Why can't she find a more productive hobby?

"Perhaps you should go sometime," I say. "You might learn a thing or two."

She sniffs, but I'm spared a response because the emperor finally notices I've arrived.

"Korakides!" Emperor Alakaseus claps his hands twice while I make another bow. "Come, join us." He's positively garrulous. "Planning to attend the public court this afternoon?"

I pause. Captain-General Horatius shoots me a look. Clearly there's something I don't know—Augustus is smirking, and so is Phaedra—though I can't imagine why the emperor wants me to attend the public court he holds every Atrydia. I used to have to go with Leontius, every second time it was held. It's always phenomenally tedious—or, if the emperor decides to make a statement, excruciating. Like the time the witch hunters brought in that sorceress they'd sent mad.

A flush runs all over my body. Maybe that's what the emperor's planning to do, again. Maybe the witch hunters have found new blood. It could be my idiot brother.

Or Elanna.

"Well?" the emperor says, and Augustus laughs. Phaedra sends him a small smile.

I realize I've let the silence lapse. Hastily, I bow. "Naturally, I will attend, if it pleases Your Imperial Majesty."

The emperor positively beams. "Oh, it does. Now." He gestures me closer. "We were just discussing the terms of our peace accord with Eren."

My footsteps slow. Horatius flickers another glance at me and shakes his head. His plan must have failed. How is Alakaseus Saranon planning an accord, then?

"Peace?" I say. "Terrifying witch and all?"

"Peace is the natural state of civilized nations," the emperor replies winningly.

My neckcloth is too tight; it's smothering my breath. I try to shove down the suspicion rising in me. If they had captured Elanna, I would know, wouldn't I? Somehow she would be able to tell me, wouldn't she?

But she hasn't answered my calls through the mirror for five days. And the emperor of Paladis would not be so pleased with himself if Elanna still posed a threat. Either she's been wounded on the Tinani border, or they've captured her.

I need to control myself. Emperor Alakaseus is talking, but the rushing in my head drowned out some of his words.

"We've been drafting a list of terms," the emperor is saying, gesturing at a secretary scribbling furiously. "You will want to discuss these with your queen, of course. Or rather, with Eren's current reigning monarch. Lord Euan, what do you wish to do about the girl?"

My head jerks up. I didn't see him when I came in, but he's standing right there, on the other side of the table. Sophy's father, and Finn's. Euan Dromahair. The would-be king of Caeris. The king, as El says, of air.

"I shall adopt her as my heir, since fate has robbed me of my son." Euan Dromahair, tall and dour and saturnine, doesn't even really look at me. "If, of course, she proves suitable."

I clear my throat, trying to ignore the pulsing under my ribs. "Am I correct in understanding that your terms demand Queen Sophy cedes her throne to . . ." I can't call him her father. Ruadan Valtai was a father to her, not this man. "Lord Euan?"

The emperor just smiles.

The room seems too close. I'm sweating. Phaedra Saranon is watching me with a tiny curl of her lips. This isn't a negotiation. These aren't terms, they're demands. *Requirements.* Something must have happened to Elanna. Otherwise they'd never think they could just go in and install Euan Dromahair on the throne.

"But," I say. I may have said it once already. "You would loathe Caeris and Eren, Lord Euan. You don't know what it's like. It's exceedingly cold, and the food is terrible, and no one bathes, and the people . . . you would not find the people to your liking. They do not live in the Idaean style."

Finn's father merely looks at me, his long bloodhound's face dour. If I wondered whether he blames me for his son's death, I know now.

The minister of state intervenes. "Sophy Dunbarron is a bastard child, Lord Jahan. She was not raised to a throne. It is only right to let her father rule—he is, after all, the true king."

The true king? I want to laugh. Euan Dromahair has spent his life living on the charity of the Paladisan emperors, complaining about how he should be king of Caeris. Sophy Dunbarron was raised by Ruadan Valtai—and if anyone ever ruled Caeris, it was him. "Perhaps we can compromise. The people have elected Queen Sophy in the traditional way. It is, after all, what they fought for."

The minister of state pushes up his spectacles. "Elected? Indeed?" He looks amused. So do several others.

The emperor does not. His face is cold.

Captain-General Horatius is watching me with interest.

It galls me, the arrogance of these men's beliefs that they have the right to determine who controls lands and nations and lives. I want to demand what they've done with Elanna, or what they know. But if I play my hand too obviously—if they completely dismiss me as a witch-lover—we risk losing everything.

And yet looking at their well-fed, self-satisfied faces, I remember why I fought beside the Caerisians and Ereni in the first place.

"Yes, elected." I look at the emperor when I say it. "Not all nations conduct their business in the Paladisan manner. You may want to consider the consequences of imposing your laws and customs on a people who govern themselves differently. How much more land does Paladis need to accrue? How much more resentment from the people you've conquered? The people of Eren and Caeris rose up against the Eyrlais. What makes you think they won't fight to keep the freedom they've won for themselves? What makes you think you won't face another insurrection?"

There's a silence. The emperor's face is flushed. They all seem shocked by my boldness, and I am a little, too. Six months ago, I would never have spoken this way in the emperor's presence—or, indeed, anywhere he might hear of it.

But I'm tired of placating this short, querulous man who happened to be born into the right family and lived to inherit a throne he did nothing to deserve. I'm tired of him thinking he can do what he wants, because he wears the imperial diadem, because he commands the black ships, because he oversees the witch hunters.

And I refuse to let Eren and Caeris be a consequence of his entitlement.

Nevertheless, I did come here to achieve peace. Eren and Caeris can't afford for this war to escalate because Queen Sophy's ambassador antagonized the emperor and his ministers.

"Lord Euan," I say, more moderately. "Perhaps you would be more satisfied serving Queen Sophy as her ambassador here in Ida. You wouldn't have to endure Eren, then. And as everyone knows, one's foreign ministers determine policy as much as a monarch."

"We can discuss this," he says, in such a way that he implies sitting down to a table with me would be utterly distasteful.

Why does he even want to go back? I suppose it's the only purpose to which he's ever put his life. The way he defines himself: the rightful king of Caeris.

But that doesn't entitle him to a crown.

The emperor snorts. "You will not discuss any such thing." He waves a hand at me. "Paladis does not recognize you as Eren's ambassador royal, Lord Jahan. You have no authority in this discussion."

"*What?*" I feel as if I've been socked in the gut. Phaedra and Augustus exchange little smiles.

"Paladis doesn't recognize your 'queen' as the true ruler of Eren," the emperor explains, slowing down his words as if educating a child. "Therefore we do not recognize your position as ambassador royal."

"But I have papers—"

"From a bastard daughter." The emperor chuckles. "A bastard queen!"

Everyone else laughs obediently, except for Euan Dromahair, who just looks dourly at us all.

I grind my teeth. "If you think she will stand for this—or that Elanna Valtai will—"

Augustus laughs aloud. "I don't think you'll find *she* has the authority for much of anything, anymore!"

No, no, no. I fight to breathe; to stay calm. What's happened to her? I can't make myself ask. I won't put myself at their mercy.

The emperor is watching me, bright-eyed, taking in the panic I can't conceal any longer. "Well, Korakides, as it turns out we don't need you after all! Off you go. But"—he wags a finger—"don't miss the public court."

The public court. That has to be his plan. He's going to send a message—and it must be that he's captured Elanna.

I manage a smile and a bow. I can feel Euan Dromahair watching me; the hair stands up on the back of my neck. Phaedra takes his arm. "I am quite sure Lord Jahan did not intend for Finn to die," she murmurs, pitching her voice just loud enough for me—and everyone else—to hear. But the tone of her voice, the look in her eyes, says the opposite. That I am callous and careless. That I let Finn's life slip through my fingers as casually as dust.

My chest burns. Euan Dromahair fixes me with a look that says he knows just how despicable I truly am. But we both know perfectly well how much affection he held for his dead son. It's not Finn he mourns, but the loss of his own rightful crown.

And why the hell does Phaedra care to console him?

I tear my gaze away from them. The emperor is watching me, too, smug, nearly smirking.

Of course, he thinks he's won.

He hasn't. Not if I have anything to do with it.

CHAPTER TEN

I retreat through the doors, perfectly obsequious despite the panic pounding through me. But once I'm in the corridor, I stand frozen. Maybe I should have sacrificed my pride to demand what they're doing with Elanna, because now I don't know where to look for her. The public court isn't happening for another hour—is it? I rustle through my waistcoat, but my pocket watch isn't there. The corridor is empty of clocks, but full of footmen and guards, all watching me.

I pick a direction and stride away from them as fast as I can. Is El here, being held prisoner? Or still on her way to Aexione? All I know is I need to find her before they parade her before the court. Before the witch hunters can completely unhinge her mind.

I've come blindly to the formal staircase, which leads to the Grand Court. My mind keeps stuttering. If I haven't talked to her in five days—it's three days or more from Eren to Ida by ship—they won't have brought her in *before* this morning's meeting, will they—?

Maybe I can meet them yet on the road and make a plan as I go. I need a horse. The imperial stables won't supply me anymore, so I'll have to go back to Aunt Cyra's and get a mount. Make some reasonable excuse for racing out onto the road when I only just returned. The failure of my alliance should be enough. I'll tell my aunt I'm going back to Eren—which, I realize, is what I must do. If I can save El, we have no choice. It's abundantly clear we can't stay here.

We'll return to Sophy and the others and fight the war there, like I should have from the beginning.

If I can find El. If we can commandeer a ship. If the witch stones haven't ruined her mind.

I run out into the sunlit day. The Grand Court is thronged with people, a practical river of humanity I have to shove against. Not just courtiers, but shopkeepers and restaurateurs and innkeepers and maids, all dressed in their finest for the public court. All the gods, it must be happening sooner than I thought. If I can get through the palace gates, perhaps I can stop them in Aexione town or just outside it. With a little more room, I can befuddle the witch hunters, compress space, break El's chains, free her—

Snatches of conversation fly past me as I push toward the main gates.

"—the emperor holding court—"

"—a special guest—"

"—*special*, all right! I heard—"

I stop. The movement of the crowd shoves me backward. I stumble, almost fall. I can't seem to catch my breath.

"That sorceress—"

"Elanna Valtai," someone says at my left elbow.

I stare toward the speaker, but they've already been jostled away from me. But I don't need to find them. The courtyard is full of her name, now that I pause to hear it. *Elanna Valtai. The witch. The sorceress.*

They all know. The emperor's made it public knowledge. While I slept, word must have spread through town.

But maybe there's still time. *Hang on, El.*

I fling myself forward again like a stunned salmon who doesn't know any better than to swim upstream. My heart is beating too fast, the air shallow in my chest. I'm almost to the gates. The crowd is, if anything, packed tighter still here. It's not every day the good people of Aexione witness a renegade sorceress brought to her knees.

The gate rises, mere feet away, but I bounce off the crowd. A woman yells at me to mind my manners.

And then, over the din, I hear it. The rattle of bells. A man's voice shouting, "Make way! Make way in the emperor's name!"

The crowd slowly parts. I'm pressed back against the wrought iron of the gate even as I struggle to push myself forward. I whisper for people to move, but they're too preoccupied by the spectacle even to respond to my magic.

I elbow my way through, fighting for the gates' opening, just as horsemen come pounding through. Imperial guardsmen, their colors bright, their faces impassive. Twenty of them, at least.

The clamoring bells draw closer. Then a coach bursts through the gate. It's black, reinforced with iron bars, and the small square windows are dark.

"Elanna!" I shout, and then I clap a hand over my mouth. I meant to cry out only with my mind. So many guards—they'll hear me, seize me—and with the mood of the people—

But no one seems to have heard me. The crowd has already started chanting, "Witch! Witch! Witch!"

Now a cavalcade of witch hunters follow the coach through, ten of them on horseback, more than I've ever seen in one place. Yet more imperial militia ride in their wake. So many men bringing one young woman to "justice."

I already know I'm too late to stop them.

There's a gap behind them. I break from the crowd, running after the horses, but everyone else seems to have the same idea. I'm rapidly surrounded, jostled by shoulders and arms. More imperial guards await us at the palace entrance. If I could get closer . . .

What would I do? I can't spirit El away from here by magic. I can't let all these people—all of Aexione, then all of Ida, all of Paladis—know I'm a sorcerer. If the emperor won't treat with me, I have to at least maintain my secret until I find both my brothers and take them to safety.

The coach stops. So do the horsemen. The crowd eddies. I rise up on the balls of my feet. All the gods—

There she is. The witch hunters are pulling her from the coach. She looks small. Her hair is bare and matted. Manacles clank at her wrists and ankles. She *shuffles.* My *Caveadear* shuffles onto the shining marble flagstones like a common criminal.

El! I shout, with my mind this time. But she gives no sign of hearing me. The witch hunters close ranks around her, and I can no longer see her shape.

The crowd shouts with renewed vigor, "Witch! Witch!"

The witch hunters are moving toward the palace. Toward the audience chamber, the Hall of Glass. I'll never catch them.

A thought strikes me. If I can move through walls, why can I not move through people?

It sounds unpleasant. Dangerous. But I have to be there. I have to save Elanna.

There's a man in front of me, square and heavyset. A cook, judging from the stains on his apron. He's next to another man, almost shoulder-to-shoulder. If I pick the point between them . . .

I launch myself forward. *I pass through.* The buzzing particles of skin and bones and blood part for me in a hot rush. Fabric snags at me. If either man notices someone just walked through him, I'm already too far ahead to hear their astonishment. But I'm betting they don't even know I did it.

I pass through the crowd, through wrists and elbows and shoulders, hats and gowns and coats. I'm trying to run. My breath is so ragged. My foot hits the lowest step into the palace. The witch hunters are halfway up the grand staircase, Elanna invisible in their midst.

I race up the steps, ordinarily now, pushing aside courtiers and fishmongers. At the top of the stairs, I burst through a door into largely empty antechambers, and then through a side entrance into the Hall of Glass. Courtiers stand packed in silk and velvet, their bodies heating the room to stifling. I push through them, not daring to use magic. No one's chanting in here, but the room practically hums with whispers of anticipation.

Then the herald shouts, "The criminal Elanna Valtai, so-called *Caveadear* of Eren and Caeris!"

I shove past two last courtiers, and I see her.

She shuffles down the long, long carpet toward Emperor Alaka-seus, seated on his throne at the opposite end of the room. Her face seems hollowed out. She's filthy, her Ereni coat and trousers crusted with dried mud and even a spot of congealed gore. Is it hers? She seems uninjured. But her gaze is dark and empty. Her lips are cracked.

It takes all of my power not to lunge onto the carpet and seize her. But what would I do? I can't sweep her away like a prince in a fairy tale. Not in front of the entire imperial court. Not with all the witch stones and bells.

And Alcibiades Doukas is leading her—by a chain attached to a manacle at her throat. Like a dog. Her witch stone, the one she transformed in Caeris, the one that protected her, is gone.

My hands curl into fists.

The grand inquisitor sees me. His eyebrows lift slightly in recognition.

I glance to my left. I'm in the middle of the vast chamber, surrounded by courtiers whom I know too well. The emperor's gaze has marked me. He looks much too pleased. Beside him, Empress Firmina's eyes are wide, but there's a blankness to her expression. Maybe I should have agreed to her offer of help. Maybe I shouldn't have thrown off Pantoleon, and Bardas.

But it's too late for that now. The entire chamber seems to be fixed on me. I realize I'm obvious—sweating like a pig, my chest heaving, my gaze no doubt wild. I've even, unconsciously, taken a step forward, out of the crowd, toward Elanna. Phaedra and Augustus are whispering, flashing their twin daggerlike smiles. Across from me, buried in the crowd by the window, Aunt Cyra watches me with her fingertips pressed to her lips.

Only Leontius, seated beside his siblings, doesn't look at me. His gaze skims over Elanna's head, bored, as if he's thinking about irrigation plans, not sorcery and treachery. Not us, here and now.

I must compose myself. I wipe a hand over my forehead, trying to dry the sweat. I take a step back.

Elanna's seen me now. Her lips part. Her mind must still be her own, somewhat; there's recognition in her gaze.

"Jahan," she whispers.

To hell with composing myself. The fear in her eyes sends a spike of pure rage through me—and fright.

What have they done to her?

The bells ring and ring. They must be deafening her, driving her mad.

But not me. I draw in a breath. Maybe there's still something I can do. One last thing to try.

I reach with my mind, fumbling for the chain binding El's throat. The witch hunters have embedded humming stones in the shackles at her wrists and ankles. I can try to break them off her, but even if I succeed, to do so will be obvious. Everyone will know a sorcerer is working magic, and if they don't suspect me, they'll suspect El. Of course, she already stands accused. Not only accused, damned.

Yet if I can break the witch stones' grip on her, she can perform her magic. She can wake the earth and terrify Alakaseus Saranon and his miserable court into submission.

No witch stones hum in her collar. I take it in my mind and find the weak point where it fastens. Perhaps my plan will work.

I press down. The collar snaps and slides off El's neck, thudding to the floor.

The crowd gasps. Alcibiades looks back in surprise. El's gaze flashes to mine.

Wood, I think at her. For all the gilt in this hall, it's made of wood! Like the scaffold in Caeris that she transformed—*wood!*

But I can't project thoughts so clearly into her mind. She doesn't understand—or doesn't agree. She shakes her head minutely.

Alcibiades's gaze flashes to me. It seems, in fact, that the entire court is staring at the sweat trickling down my neck.

Then Alcibiades seizes Elanna by the shoulder and pushes her down the carpet. They approach the emperor; he nudges her to her knees. I hear her slight gasp, as if in pain.

My ears start to throb. They'll pay for this.

Emperor Alakaseus is considering Elanna with calm, infuriating satisfaction. "Witness a sorceress, a witch, brought low by the might of Paladisan justice," he proclaims. "A criminal who flouted our laws, now to be rightfully punished."

I'm holding my breath, scrambling for the fastenings on her wrists and ankles. Elanna's power is immense; the small, spitting witch stones shouldn't be enough to stop her. *Now, El.* Reach into the earth now. Take the wood of his dais and imprison him in the cage of his own throne.

But again, she does nothing.

Only her voice rises, faint and hoarse. "I am the *Caveadear* of Eren and Caeris. Your laws do not govern my nation. I have been unlawfully abducted and I demand you release—"

"We did not grant you permission to speak!" the emperor thunders.

Silence stretches taut in the room. My fingertips are pulsing now. The emperor and Elanna have locked eyes.

Then, with slow, deliberate malice, Alakaseus Saranon says, "The criminal Elanna Valtai must be made an example of. Our glorious empire does not tolerate the abomination of sorcery. So this criminal will be sentenced to death tomorrow morning, in the Grand Court."

"No!"

I don't realize I've shouted aloud until people turn to stare at me. Whispers rustle through the court. I've moved, too, unconsciously, out onto the carpet. I'm panting. I need to control myself. I need moderation. Charm. Poise. I need to make them laugh.

But the only thing in me is this pulsing rage.

"Lord Jahan, we did not invite your opinion," the emperor begins.

I interrupt him. "As envoy from Queen Sophy of Eren—whether you recognize her or not—I demand to be heard. Elanna Valtai is not a Paladisan subject. You have no right to sentence her to death."

I stop, my chest heaving. People are staring. The whispers are growing. I interrupted Alakaseus Saranon, emperor of Paladis. I *reprimanded* him.

"As the greatest empire in the Two Seas, it is Paladis's obligation to be the arbiter of justice on this occasion," the emperor says coolly. But a certain triumph lingers in his eyes.

"Eren objects." Now I've started, I can't seem to stop. "Eren is governed by its own laws, and Paladis has no right to enforce *their* laws on an independent nation."

"But, Korakides, your loyalty is not to Eren," Emperor Alakaseus says calmly. "You are a subject of Paladis. A subject who has defected from its own laws by playing both sides. You are a traitor to our empire." He smirks. "A man who fired a gun on his own people."

I freeze. Word finally reached court, then, of how I shot at the witch hunters in Eren.

The emperor snaps his fingers. "Guards, seize this man!"

I remain there, stunned, even as the guards come running.

He planned all this. From the moment he summoned me this morning. He wasn't just rubbing my face into my own failure; he was playing with me. He's been planning to arrest me all along. He was just waiting for the right moment.

Hands seize my elbows, my shoulders. I don't throw them off. I can't seem to move. Phaedra is openly smirking. She whispers something to Augustus, who laughs. Empress Firmina stares, wide-eyed. I can't see Aunt Cyra, though surely she's trying to blend into the wall coverings.

But it's Leontius whose gaze I seek.

He doesn't look at me. He stares at the ceiling, his face as blank as a wooden post.

"Jahan isn't a traitor! He's been trying to accomplish *peace*!" Elanna shouts.

"Silence her," the emperor orders.

Alcibiades slaps El across the face. I flinch as if the blow struck my own skin.

Silence echoes in the Hall of Glass. No one speaks out in protest. No one tries to stop this, or even passes me a kind glance as the imperial guards march first Elanna, then me, from the room.

We are entirely alone.

CHAPTER ELEVEN

They lock us up in an attic in the east wing, depositing Elanna and me at opposite ends of a cramped hallway. We're above the quarters where the imperial guards are barracked; Aexione doesn't contain anything as distasteful as a prison. I step into the room and the door slams shut behind me. Guards murmur on the other side.

I stand in the stuffy dampness of the storage closet, my ears ringing in the sudden quiet. My heart still pounds.

El's at the other end of the hall. I could walk through the walls to her.

No. I need to be clever about this. I don't know what—or who—occupies the rooms between us. I don't know if she's alone. This is Aexione; there could be a spyhole anywhere. And I need a plan—a way to get not only out of Aexione, but out of the empire. Back to Eren and Caeris, which now seems our only recourse.

It *is* our only recourse—because I failed to secure an alliance. I should have known the emperor was never going to cooperate. He was never going to listen to me. I saw that, but I still stupidly persisted.

Elanna deserves better than this. She deserves someone who would remain by her side and fight with her against witch hunters and black ships and Tinani guns. Someone with the courage to stay, not go.

But I had to come back. For Rayka, and Lathiel.

A racket at the door startles me. I turn. I don't know how long I've been standing here. Male voices rumble outside—the guards—but a woman murmurs under them. I scrub my hands over my face, trying to wake my dulled brain, just as the door flies open.

"Go on," a guardsman says.

A maid edges into the room, clutching a tray full of food and a swaddled pot of tea. She eyes me dubiously and props the tray atop a stack of paintings, as far from me as she can get, as if my treachery might contaminate her.

"Compliments of Her Imperial Majesty," she says, bobbing a curtsy. Then she flees.

The guard tramps in and examines the tray, lifting the lid off the tureen of soup and peering underneath the teapot.

"What an unexpected kindness," I say drily. "Empress Firmina doesn't wish me to faint en route to the scaffold."

He just eyes me, as if speech might associate him too closely with me. Then he tramps back out.

I wait until the door is securely closed before approaching the tray. The celery soup smells divine, and the bread and meat cuts are fresh. But even though my stomach rumbles, I pick everything apart first, starting with the lid of the teapot. The guard was right to be suspicious; I can't imagine the empress sent this merely from the goodness of her heart.

Finally, I find the note, tucked neatly between two slices of ham. It's greasy, but legible. It contains a single word:

Midnight.

Is it a promise of rescue? Or a warning that the imperial guards will come for us then, instead of waiting until morning?

I eat everything on the tray, and by the time I'm done, I decide the note must mean rescue. Surely Firmina wouldn't have gone to the trouble of sending it just to tell me my hour of death.

So, clutching a cup of tea like a thin hope, I settle down to wait for midnight. Alone, for once, in the silence of my own thoughts, without Madiya's incessant whisper. Maybe I've waited her out—maybe she's gone for good. Maybe I will be that lucky.

*

THROUGH THE WALLS, I listen to the distant clock tower chime nine. Then ten. Eleven. Finally, twelve.

Nothing happens. Even Madiya remains silent.

I sit, listening, hardly daring to breathe. There's a thump down the corridor. The guards mutter to each other. Footsteps creak. Surely this is them. I stand up, electrified, ready.

But the footsteps fade. Everything goes quiet again.

I wait, though each passing minute seems to detonate a small firework in my chest. At last, the distant bell chimes, just once.

Perhaps they've been delayed. It's tempting to stay put. To wait for someone else to solve this.

But perhaps they're not coming at all. Perhaps they've been discovered.

If they have, El and I might be dragged out of here at any time. And while we are taken to our execution, the emperor will put Euan Dromahair on a ship. He'll sail to Eren. He'll claim it again as a subject state for Paladis, naming himself vassal king. He'll destroy Sophy and Rhia and Alistar and Victoire. He'll end everything we fought for, with the massive sweep of Paladis's power. The refugee sorcerers in Eren and Caeris won't be enough to stop them, once they get a handhold. And they will.

Finn will have died for nothing. And so will Elanna's father, and so many others. I will have lost my friends, my home, my place, for nothing. I will have put my aunt, who gave me so much, at risk for nothing at all. I will have failed both my brothers, for no reason.

I don't have a choice. Not really. Not if I want to live, and Elanna to live.

I blanket the room in silence, shield my candle, and step through the particles composing the wall. *Only a mouse.* But there's no need for my heart to pound. The next room holds nothing but piles of rolled-up carpets. I pause, listening, but the guards in the corridor are quiet. Bored, most likely, perhaps dozing on their feet. It's past one o'clock now.

I pick my way across the carpets to the next wall. The chamber beyond holds piles of furniture; it reeks of damp wood and dust and mouse droppings. I successfully avoid toppling anything over, then slip into the next room. It, too, contains stacked chairs and tables and footstools.

I stop at the wall. The next room holds Elanna. I can feel the witch stones gently humming.

I swallow. The candle flame wavers. I pull in my breath and listen. Nothing. The guards shuffle in the hallway, then go quiet.

I press my ear to the wall. I can't hear El.

Pressure swells in my chest. Carefully, I walk through the plaster.

This room contains chests and trunks. I stagger over one and nearly stub my toe, but I catch a curse before it can slip out. I peer around. At first my candle illuminates nothing but the trunks' hard edges. Then I make out a shuttered window. And below it, the shape of a woman huddled on her side, her long curling hair spilling onto a rough blanket.

I crouch beside her. She's sound asleep, breathing deeply. She won't like being startled awake. I reach gently for her shoulder. "El."

It takes her a long minute to come to. She doesn't exclaim or swear or even whisper my name. She says nothing at all.

"What have they done to you?" I murmur. I help her turn over and sit up. For some reason, she's wearing only a chemise, but there are no obvious bruises on her skin. No sign of pain inflicted or endured. But she just blinks at me, slowly, emptily.

"Elanna, it's Jahan," I say. I don't know why I'm hoping. I know what happens to us at their hands.

She doesn't even react.

Her mind can't be gone this quickly. She shouted at Alakaseus in the audience chamber, cogent and ferocious as ever. Whatever they've done to her—and I hear the hum of witch stones, placed on the chests around us—I'll find a way to restore her to herself. I will. I have to.

I stand, pulling off my coat. There don't seem to be any other clothes—I can't think about why they might have undressed her, not now—so I tug her into it. Her limbs are listless. Even her smell is wrong. She never looks me in the eyes.

At least she's moving.

"Let's get out of here." I take her hand. Her fingers don't curl around mine. She stands, though, unsteadily.

There's a noise at the door. I freeze. Have I not been careful enough? Did the guards hear something?

The door explodes inward, nearly ripping off its hinges. I dive instinctively in front of Elanna. Men pour into the room: witch hunters, followed by guards with bayonets at the ready. A racket of bells mingles with the cocking of the guns.

"In the emperor's name, stand down!"

It's Alcibiades Doukas. For a frozen moment, we both stare at each other.

"Jahan Korakides," he says slowly. And then, terrifyingly, he smiles. "Well, well. It seems our little experiment proved fruitful, gentlemen. A sorcerer who isn't sensitive to the bells and stones, is that it?"

I feel the muscles of my mouth push into a reflexive smile. "That's my secret." Still squeezing El's limp hand, I take one step back, toward the shuttered window.

"Stand down, Lord Jahan." Alcibiades sounds amused. "Don't you think we have ways of dealing with sorcerers like you? Don't force these men to shoot."

I could let them arrest me—again. But this time they would probably take me straight to the scaffold, and Elanna, too. Alcibiades might tell me to halt, but the truth is, we're already dead.

I take another step back, pushing El behind me.

"Lord Jahan!" Alcibiades barks.

I smile and shrug. One more step.

A guardsman cocks his bayonet and fires straight at me.

I fling up my hand. *Stop.* The gunshot *halts* in the air. A hundred thousand motes of powder spin like dust.

The particles fall to the floor.

The other guards make to shoot, but I'm faster, dragging the life force from everything I can—from the witch hunters themselves, from me, from El. Even though my power slides off the stones and bells, there's enough other power in the room to use. The guns *crack* as they break. The witch hunters ring their bells frantically. All except Alcibiades. He's just watching me.

I throw my candle to the floor and command the fire to burn.

Then I seize Elanna, throwing her over my shoulder—her weight is horrifyingly light—and leap through the fabric of the shutters and the bars beyond them into the open night air.

WE FALL. EL'S face is jammed between my shoulder blades; the wind stings my eyes. The rosebushes rear up below through the dark. At least we're on the garden side of the palace.

"Thicken!" I try to shout the word, but my voice is lost in the wind ripping through my mouth.

But the air obeys. It grows dense—but not dense enough. We're still falling. *String out!* I command with my mind, and the particles that make up our bodies, like the particles that made up the gunshot, spread loose and light. The dense air carries us over the rosebushes. My feet skim the top of a reflecting pool, spraying droplets. Elanna's almost weightless. The thought breaks my concentration, and suddenly the air becomes light again and our bodies become dense. We slam to the ground in a patch of tulips, startling a sleeping bird. I wheeze; the wind's knocked out of my lungs. My body feels strange and squeezed and strained.

El rolls off me and lies there among the flowers. Slowly, I push myself upright.

Shouts echo from the attic. I think I see a faint smudge of smoke, black on the night air, curling out of the window. We need to go—*now*. I scramble onto my knees.

Yet Elanna doesn't move. In the darkness, her hair mingles with the flowers, her limbs long and motionless. Too long. I reach for her shoulder but my hand only closes over empty cloth. I grasp her other shoulder—but it, too, is nothing more than cloth.

My heartbeat spikes into the back of my mouth.

Carefully, I turn the empty pile of clothes over. No—not entirely empty. Nestled within the coat and chemise is a long, slender tree branch topped with a bundle of rustling leaves. And wrapped around the branch, where El's face was, is a thick twist of knotted human hair.

Elanna's hair.

The stick and coat fall from my hands, flopping back onto the ground.

She was never anything more than a simulacrum. The appearance of a person, without the weight.

No wonder she was so light in my arms.

But this is impossible. Elanna was captured by witch hunters; she was herself mere hours ago. The witch hunters wouldn't have made a simulacrum of her. They can't have used magic . . . unless they did it to try to capture me. Unless they forced a sorcerer to make this magic for them.

Or unless this was Firmina's plan—if she and Bardas are in favor of sorcery, they must know sorcerers. Pantoleon does. Maybe this is what they were trying to do, make simulacra of El and me both, then make us disappear.

But they never came for me. Did Alcibiades find them out, or did the guards just hear a noise within Elanna's room and send for the witch hunters? Did I leave my room too soon—was the plan delayed somehow? Would they have come if I'd waited? Maybe I've made a huge mistake.

I stare back at the bulk of the palace. Is Elanna, the real one, still in there? Did the empress spirit her away to safety, or have they both been caught?

Somewhere inside the building, a bell is ringing. An alarm. A call to arms.

Should I go back? I scramble onto my feet, clutching the mess of stick and hair and clothing. But I don't know what's happened. It could already be too late. I don't do any good to anyone captured or dead. And if the empress and Bardas used their connections with Ida's sorcerers, Pantoleon will know.

Lights flare in a doorway, jogging as witch hunters and guards run out onto the lawn.

I gather myself. There are too many to fight. I already feel hollowed out from escaping. I could break into the empress's chambers, but if they've already found her out, it will be a trap.

I launch myself onto my feet, compressing the folds of space. I practically fly across the gardens. By the time the pursuit registers my presence, erupting with shouts, I'm already gone.

CHAPTER TWELVE

What have I done?

I used sorcery before a roomful of witch hunters and imperial guards. I threw myself out a window—*through* the shutters. The entire palace will be after me now. Soon all of Paladis will know that Jahan Korakides is a sorcerer.

The *emperor* will know I'm a sorcerer.

There's no chance of peace now. Maybe there never was.

I stop deep in a vineyard, my chest heaving. My body aches from the impact of hitting the ground—everything feels bruised—and with each step my muscles seem to tighten further. I feel thin, shaky, the way I always do now after using so much magic, the consequence of Madiya's damned laudanum.

I don't trust the main roads to be safe, so I've been sticking to the back ones. The bulk of Mount Angelos glows, snowcapped, to my left. A faint, purring rumble stirs the ground under my feet. It's the mountain talking, as everyone likes to say, the gods making their feelings known. Though whether they're voicing approval or fury is hard to say.

I drop the bundle of clothing to the ground; I've been carrying it too long and I need to lighten my load. But still, it feels strange to leave it there, as if I'm abandoning Elanna herself. *I'm not,* I want to tell her, but she's not anywhere to hear me.

I rub my face. Maybe she's already dead.

But I can't think that way—not if I hope to continue on.

Somewhere in the distance, a hound bays.

I throw down the stick, tuck the chemise like a scarf around my neck, and run.

My route takes me along rutted farming roads—I nearly break my ankle twice stumbling into potholes—and time drags on. Finally the city comes into view, draped like a behemoth over the hills. The walls funnel the city's glow up into the sky. But the sluggish gleam of the Channel separates me from them. I wasn't thinking when I picked this route; the only bridge will be on the imperial road. Have the witch hunters reached the city yet?

If I can compress space on land, I should be able to compress it over water, even if I feel hollow and spent. I loosen my stride, running down the final slope to the Channel, and then grab space like a curtain. I pull it back with the green power of the last vineyard I ran through. My feet crash against the water. I can't get a purchase—I'm going to fall—then the momentum of the magic carries me across. I stumble onto the far bank, breathing hard. My shoes are soaked through. A tremor runs through my body.

I'm among humped shadows—fishing boats. I don't know where the fishermen's gate is. I glance up at the wall. No one visible, but I still find myself whispering, *I am a coyote slinking among the boats. A strange reflection of the moonlight. The breeze off Mount Angelos.*

I approach the wall, then hesitate. I don't know what's on the other side here. But more than that, I don't know what sort of reception Pantoleon will give me. I don't know if he'll even help. If I enter Ida, I don't know if I'll ever get out again.

It's the risk I have to take. What choice do I have?

I walk through. It's not a thick wall, and I emerge quickly into the dead space behind a row of sleeping houses. I creep over garden walls, trying not to stumble on children's hoops and outdoor ovens, until I reach an alley to a street.

I look up and down. It's deserted. Eerily so, but that might have something to do with the hour. Dawn can't be far away. Neither can witch hunters and the imperial guard, if they've had the sense to guess I'd make for Ida. Since I went on foot and they have horses, even with my magic they might already be here.

I shake away the thought and hurry along the quiet streets until I find a familiar boulevard. I keep to the shadows, staying frozen in place when a night watchman passes by. The smell of baking bread rises from a bakery I pass. It's close to dawn, then. The shoulder of Solivetos Hill nudges over the rooftops ahead of me. I duck down onto a winding street that brings me, at length, to Pantoleon's street.

His house sits in the middle of the block; he rents upper rooms from a widow. With a concentration of magic, I jump up to his rickety balcony. Not quite as light as a cat: I bark my knees hard against the wood. The thump reverberates through the quiet street. I fling myself facedown on the balcony, trying to slow my heaving breath.

Silence.

I crawl into Pantoleon's rooms, passing through the slatted balcony doors. The main room is a dim muddle of strewn books and paper and empty unwashed cups that his landlady would, no doubt, find mildly horrifying. I push myself upright. Every inch of me aches.

Pantoleon snores quietly in the closet-sized bedchamber, separated from the living area by nothing more than a curtain. I tug it aside.

Faint light seeps through the bedroom window, illuminating Pantoleon's rumpled shape. I whisper his name and then, when he doesn't wake, I whisper it directly into his mind.

He startles at that. He wakes up with a soft, muttered curse.

Then he registers my presence in the doorway. "What are you doing here?"

This is somewhat less enthusiasm than I had hoped for. The tension thickens between us. Perhaps I should apologize for what I said the other night. But perhaps it's Pantoleon who should, for airing our secrets to the world.

So I just say, "I'm looking for Elanna."

"Elanna?" He sits up, apparently muddled. "Your witch? They brought her from Eren yesterday."

"Yes. And one of your sorcerer friends replaced her with a stick. A simulacrum, in fact. It was fairly clever." Or it would have been, if I hadn't fallen for the trick myself. And if I knew where Elanna was, and what happened at Aexione.

He rubs his forehead. "Jahan . . . Why the hell do you think I have friends who could do something like that?"

"You've made friends with Bardas Triciphes! You told Argyros all our secrets. Bardas and Empress Firmina are planning something, and you can't pretend you don't have even the slightest idea."

He stares at me, openmouthed, then smacks the coverlet. "You have no right to be angry! You ran off to Eren and started a revolution so magic could be practiced openly. We're sending our refugees to *you*—"

"But *I* am here. Trying to achieve peace."

His mouth closes. The light has brightened: He takes in my torn, dirty clothes, the riot of my hair. "And look how well that's working out for you. His Imperial Majesty took the opportunity to reaffirm his intent to annex Eren, I assume?"

He has no right to throw this in my face. "I had to at least try—"

"No. You didn't. You could have joined us. Sent us supplies and help from Eren. Come back here and looked *me* up. It couldn't have taken too much intelligence for your Ereni to discern what we're trying to do. But instead you waltz back to Aexione as if nothing's ever happened!" He's shouting now. "What did you *think* Alakaseus Saranon would do, Jahan? The man's not stupid."

"Oh, as I suppose I am?"

"In this matter, yes! Your damned secrets matter more to you than logic or even doing what's right!"

He stops, breathing hard. My hands are fisted against my chest. We stare at each other across the small room.

Several thumps sound below. We both startle.

"And now you've woken my landlady," Pantoleon says darkly.

"I wasn't the one shouting." She must have heard us despite the magic I put in place—or maybe I forgot entirely to muffle the sound of our voices. I run my hands through my hair. I'm losing so much control. I need to stop; I need to think.

And out of nowhere, Madiya's voice breathes into my mind. *Jahan.*

All the gods! Why won't the woman leave me alone? It's as if she knows I'm fraying. That soon I'll have no friends left, no allies, no recourse except her.

I will *never* answer her summons.

"What's the matter with you?" Pantoleon demands. "Did the bells and stones send you mad?"

"I'm sorry." I put my back to him. "I won't impose on your hospitality—such as it is—any longer."

"Damn it, Jahan!" he exclaims, exasperated, and I hear him throw back the blankets and follow me out of the room, floorboards squeaking. "That's not what I meant. Where the hell are you going?"

"To beg pity of the gods," I say sourly. "Unless they, too, have decided I'm not worth their notice."

Pantoleon explodes a sigh. "*Need* we be so melodramatic? Look. I'll ask the people I know about your sorceress."

"I'll come with you."

He stares up from stoking the brazier. "No. I'm sorry, but you haven't earned that right."

I'm so astonished that I laugh. "The right to meet your *friends*? Are you embarrassed by me?"

"Rather," he says frankly. Then, with painful gravity: "They are sorcerers who have spent their lives in hiding. But now, because of what you did in Eren, they're ready to fight for the rights they deserve. And what have you done? Come back here and pretended that none of it really happened."

"To save Elanna," I retort. "To save Eren."

"No," he says, "to save your own reputation. To keep your damned secrets. So yes, I'll ask about your sorceress. But I won't let you meet anyone. Because as far as they're concerned, you've betrayed us all."

WHEN PANTOLEON GOES OUT, I follow him. Neither of us speaks, or has spoken since he accused me of being a traitor. I don't see what there is to say. If that's what he and his sorcerer friends think of me, then that's what they think. I've been maligned far worse.

And yet I can't tamp down the guilt following on the heels of this thought. What if they're right?

At Nero Street, Pantoleon turns without a farewell toward the university. I continue on, toward the café on the next corner, burrowing my hands in the pockets of the overcoat I borrowed from Pantoleon. It's too big, and the elbows are worn thin with use. With the floppy wool hat favored by students hiding my hair, I hope I look just like any other wastrel spending his parents' money on obscure courses and late nights in academic arguments over beer. Besides, I've never been to this café, so I doubt I'll be recognized.

I pause at the stand on the street to buy a newspaper—this, too, with money borrowed from Pantoleon. I ran from Aexione with empty pockets. So this is another favor I owe my friend. Another debt I don't know whether I can repay.

"Big doings up at the emperor's palace yesterday," the vendor says, pocketing the coins I hand him. "They caught that Ereni witch."

"You see it?" I ask in my most careless student voice.

"Nah. Hard to get out of the city." A wistful look steals across his face. "I'd like to see me a real sorceress, though. I reckon she doesn't look like us ordinary mortals."

I smile, careful not to show my relief. He didn't bring up the Korakos. So my sorcery—and El's disappearance—hasn't hit the news yet. It would have happened too late last night to make the papers, and the morning is early. "Somewhere between us and the gods."

"Aye," the vendor says, patting the stack of newspapers thoughtfully. "It must have been something, to see the sorcery she wrought in Eren."

Someone else comes up behind me, and I tuck the newspaper under my arm and make for the café. I need to craft a plan before the whole city wakes up in search of me.

The warmth inside envelops me with a lover's tenderness, and I'm reminded that I've scarcely slept recently. Perhaps I ought to have remained at Pantoleon's apartment. But who needs rest? I'll soldier on, gritty-eyed and undaunted.

I surreptitiously check the café's corners for familiar faces as I approach the counter. But there's no one I know. An elderly couple sip tea while they read their newspapers, a woman marks notes on a stack of papers, and a group of young men cluster busily near the fireplace. Students, no doubt, judging by their matching black hats. Probably getting ready to save the world.

Much good may that do them.

I order a coffee—again with my borrowed money—and settle into a table beside the wall, where I should go unnoticed. I spread out the newspaper with a sigh, inhaling the heady aroma of roasting coffee beans and baking sugar from the kitchen. I have a little time, as I thought. My very bones seem to relax. I adjust my hat. Time, and a disguise. All I need.

Then I hear the youths at the next table, talking.

"If we needed any further proof of his tyranny, this is it!" The speaker, an excitable fellow with a pencil tucked behind his ear, shakes a copy of the newspaper.

The others shush him, but I see their grins. I have never been that young.

One of them sees me looking. Too late, I pretend to find something fascinating in my newspaper. My eye lands on a passage squarely in the middle: THE WITCH OF EREN EXECUTED BEFORE DAWN.

My fingers go numb. I nearly drop the newspaper. No, it can't be true. It must be a lie. El wasn't really in that room—they had no one to execute, not even a simulacrum.

Unless they *did* have Elanna. Unless the witch hunters did torture some poor sorcerer into crafting the simulacrum as a trap.

Or unless the empress betrayed me. Maybe this has all been an elaborate trap to make me reveal my sorcery.

"Come join us, friend!" the young man calls, and I startle. "Join the cause of liberty!"

I tear my eyes away from the newspaper and the bold, unrelenting headline. The paper's quivering; my hands are trembling. Maybe if I wasn't so shaken I wouldn't say it, but it comes out anyway. "Already done that, thanks. Once was enough."

He blinks, and I force a bland smile onto my face. Now his forehead puckers with confusion. Several of the others look over.

Damn, damn, damn. I had one thing to do—go unnoticed. I let loose a little persuasion: *Nothing to fuss about here. Just another student reading the paper.* They mutter a bit but return to their plotting.

I open the newspaper and pretend to be engaged with another article, but I can't stop seeing the first. El, dead? Is it really true? Even though I saw the bald words, even though I stood in the Hall of Glass yesterday when the emperor proclaimed her sentence, it still seems impossible. Elanna Valtai, with her quick laugh and fierce temper and extraordinary magic, can't be dead. The whole earth would be mourning. Wouldn't it?

"The revolution in Eren!" one of the students exclaims.

I flinch and peer up. The young men are all hunched forward, the tassels on their black hats quivering. The one with the pencil is now using it to write an eager diatribe, which the others dictate to him.

Once again, I'm noticed. Damn. Maybe my exhaustion is catching up with me, upsetting my talent for persuasion.

Or maybe it's the grief. But no. I can't believe she's dead. I *won't*. I need to go. I need some proof before I'll ever believe this.

I start to get up—but a young man swaggers over and stops dead in front of me. He's a scruffy type, his black coat worn at the elbows. He's smirking a lot for someone so short, but there's wariness, too, in his narrow dark eyes. I try to edge around him, but he mirrors my movements, blocking me. I glance from him to his friends. They're all staring me down.

"You like the emperor?" he asks me.

They must think I'm a member of the city watch in disguise, here to report them to the crown. And they're not going to let me go unless I give them a satisfying answer. I clutch the newspaper with its damning headline against my chest. "I can't say he's a particular friend of mine."

The young man barks a laugh. I eye him. If he decides I'm a threat, I can get out of here—but it would be hard to do it without causing a terrible stir.

"I like you," he announces, and pulls something from his pocket. "Here."

He shoves a leaflet at me. I scan the title. THE SARANON REGIME: CORRUPT, ANTIQUATED . . .

I have no desire to read this castigation, even if the Saranons can die off any damned time and I'll celebrate. I smile, though it feels like I'm pushing up the sides of my mouth by force of will. "Looks like good reading. I always enjoy revolutionary tracts."

Again, he laughs. Then he sticks out his hand. "Felix Tzemines."

I shake his hand, trying not to stare past him at the door. "Do you greet everyone in the manner of the Old Republic?"

"It's more honest than bowing," he says. "It lets you test a man's strength."

Ah. I squeeze his hand a bit harder—he hides a wince—and then release it. "I'll remember that the next time I'm planning to wrestle someone."

He gestures at the pamphlet. "If you like what you read, join us at the Den on Aeodia. Dinner hour. You know the Den?"

I nod, though it's not as if I'm going to join them. The Den is the university's most popular watering hole. Pantoleon, Finn, and I spent long hours there, years ago now, dreaming about the future.

"Tell the barkeep the New Republic sent you." He winks.

All the gods, they even have a name for themselves. I fold the newspaper into my pocket and step around Felix. A vibration is running through my body, but I tell myself again that Elanna can't be dead. In any case, it's time to get out of here. Felix Tzemines has gotten much too close a look at my face.

"I'll be there," I say lightly, "as long as I can get one of those black caps."

Felix guffaws, and then the rest of "the New Republic" joins in. So reassuring to know they've been listening to our entire conversation. With a liberal grin, I stride past Felix to the door, trying to keep my stride measured, even though every step seems to say *El, El, El.*

The door bursts open just as I approach. A tall woman in a red turban, with tawny skin and an academic hunch to her shoulders, rushes past me.

"Tullea?" Felix says.

"They're patrolling the streets!" she cries out. "Something's happened—the Korakos escaped from custody—and the Korakos is really a s—"

The door slams on her final, damning word. I bolt into the street, hurrying back the way I came, nearly running straight into the newspaper stand.

But the cobblestones are eerily quiet. My footsteps slow. A flower seller eyes me from the safety of her bouquets. Other faces peer out from shop windows.

Then I hear it. Behind me, coming down the street.

A bell, ringing.

My heartbeat spikes into my ears. But I don't run, though my body thrums with the need to. Instead I pace slowly, deliberately to the nearest storefront. Behind me, another bell joins the first. I hear horse hooves crunching.

Then I'm inside, and the sound fades. Two startled booksellers stare at me from behind a counter.

I pull out Felix's pamphlet as though it's a shopping list. "Histories of the Old Republic," I mutter, and dive between the shelves. Because of course this is a bookshop, one I used to frequent with Pantoleon. I haven't been here in years—and hope to all the gods no one recognizes me.

They haven't moved the history section. Another fellow stands in front of the shelves, pretending to examine a tome, though judging by his utter stillness he's also listening for the sounds from the street.

I retreat past him, deeper into the shop, and pull down a volume at random. Poetry by Cleïs. As if the pressure in my chest isn't tight enough already. I hope no one is near enough to see my hand shaking as I turn the page.

I should have known *they're patrolling the streets* would mean witch hunters. But how are they in the university district already? Why would they even assume I'd be here? I should have stayed in that café—or never gone at all.

I need to calm down. I try to read the first line of a poem, but all I can think is that Elanna really must be dead. They put out a call for me alone.

Someone calls from the front of the shop, "They've gone past!" The man behind me slams his book back onto the shelf with palpable relief.

But I can't seem to move. My heart is somehow too full and too empty. Everything seems distant. Beyond the echoing in my head, the shop bell jangles as its temporary patrons flood back into the street. I become aware of sweat dampening my back. I'm roasting in Pantoleon's greatcoat. But it's little to bear compared with what's happened to El.

I need to find a mirror. But even if I called for her, how could she answer? She's either been slaughtered by the emperor, or—and I have to admit to myself that this is unlikely—she's been taken to the Ochuroma and surrounded by witch stones.

Words march across the page I'm holding open. *The moon has set, and the seven sisters. The hours stack upon each other, and I am alone.*

Just a few words, but my eyes are burning.

The shop bell jangles again. I startle. A woman says wearily, "What's this, now?"

"City watch. They said to look for a young man, six feet, dark-haired, gray eyes, wearing a peacock-blue suit."

I freeze.

"I'd be happy to find a man like that," the woman says, and someone else laughs.

"You think you could snag Jahan Korakides? Because he's the one they're looking for."

With cold hands, I replace the book on the shelf and quietly step toward the back doorway. At the shop's front, everyone is exclaiming. Cushioning silence around my feet, I ease out the back exit, into an alley filled with some refuse and several stray dogs digging through it. I hurry down the alley, merging back onto the main street—

Just behind two city watchmen. They've accosted several university students and are delivering a lecture on criminal sorcerers, as well as, apparently, the dangers of thinking too much.

I swing past them with every shred of confidence I possess. *Nothing to see here.*

My shoulders tense. But the men don't shout after me, or follow.

I don't dare to break into a run. All the same I'm breathless by the time I reach Wisteria Street. It's quiet. I let out a breath.

Then I see the two men standing in front of Pantoleon's house. The landlady hesitates on the threshold, holding a broom to her bosom as if it can defend her. A bell clinks softly as one of the men shifts.

A hand captures my sleeve. I'm dragged backward into a cramped space between two houses, hardly enough to be a passage. Pantoleon clamps his other hand over my mouth.

I shake him off. His eyes widen so I see the whites of them. And how angry he is. How afraid. The combination swallows up all the space in the alley, leaving precious little for me.

"*Witch hunters* are at my house, Jahan!" he whispers furiously. "You didn't tell me they'd executed your sorceress, or that they've realized you're a *sorcerer*—"

I swallow. I wish I could fade through the walls surrounding us, but I don't. "I may have left out a few salient details."

"A *few*?" He stares at me. "If I'd been home a few minutes earlier, I'd be under arrest."

I can't meet his eyes. With a noise of disgust, Pantoleon turns back to the alley's entrance, ignoring me now. I say nothing.

I've brought this danger on him. On Pantoleon, whose father was dragged away with a sack over his head when my friend was ten years old. No one could believe that Pantoleon's mother didn't know his father was a sorcerer. She lost her job, a well-paid one as a no-tary. They lost their house. She moved the children to the country outside Hepsabah, to work the barley fields. And Pantoleon learned to hide his magic, to bury it deep, so that by the time he was of age to enter an essay contest for a position at the university of Ida, most people had forgotten the scandal surrounding his father. But there is still magic in him, even if he refuses to use it.

The witch hunters would destroy him. The way they did Elanna.

But how did they even come to be here? I suppose someone might know that Pantoleon and I are friends, yet no one in Aexione has even met him—except Aunt Cyra. She wouldn't betray me, or him. Someone might have found his name by searching through old let-ters of mine, but surely that would take hours, and presence of mind.

Unless someone saw us talking at the Deos Deorum . . . one of Phaedra's spies. I could easily believe that Leontius's sister has iden-tified all my friends, their homes, their professions, and their lovers—anything she could use against me, when the opportunity suited her.

Pantoleon peers into the street and bangs his palm against the wall. "She let them inside."

"Then we can get out of here," I point out. I got Pantoleon into this mess. I'll get him out even if it means sacrificing myself.

But the thought catches me. *Would* I sacrifice myself? I've always been able to talk myself out of anything. Heal any wound that needs healing. Whisper any persuasion. Remove any memories.

Except now the world knows what I really am. The rules have changed, and I don't know how to play the game.

"Come on." Pantoleon grabs my elbow. I let him drag me out into the street, hurrying around the corner. I call persuasion around us—*only students, late to class.* The way Pantoleon's going, a blind man could see we're criminals. Above the rooftops, Solivetos Hill rises. I can see the abandoned temple, its old dome half shattered like a cracked egg. The soft morning light makes it glow.

Pantoleon drags me around a final corner, and I realize the hill is our destination. The temple sits at the end of the street, its pillared entryway opening like a maw into the steep, wooded hill. Stairs angle down from the summit of the hill, where the dome seems to float over the treetops.

I slow. "Are we supplicating the gods?"

Pantoleon just grunts. He glances about furtively at the houses abutting the hill. The front balconies are deserted, though voices carry over from the back gardens.

I pull the persuasion tighter around us. "No one sees us."

He scowls. "How can you be so certain?" But then he strides off into the shadow of the portico without waiting for an answer.

I follow him. The columns tower over us. I thought that we might find beggars camped out under the dry roof, but the portico and vestibule are empty. Our footsteps echo in the massive round chamber; an oculus stares down from the high, domed ceiling. The floors are patterned in a mosaic lost to the dim light, and the walls are studded with pearls and shells, but no furniture remains. Even the ashes are absent from the hearth.

"Tirisero," I mutter. The abandoned temple is dedicated to the god of failure. It seems appropriate. Paladisans no longer worship him, of course; Paladius the First forbade his veneration since it might imply he wasn't invincible.

Pantoleon strides on, as if he's seen it all before. I sigh and pursue him through a high doorway. The corridor is pitch black, but we emerge quickly to the bottom of the stairs. I crane my head back to see the top of the hill. The staircase looks steep enough to put a god out of breath.

My friend has already started up, oblivious.

"What are we doing here?" I call after him. My voice sounds too loud, even though the place is deserted.

Reluctantly, he turns. "It's one of our safe places. Where we hide sorcerers."

Then he continues on without another word. I close my mouth and follow. It's a long slog. By the time we reach the top, my thighs are burning and my lungs feel like they've been stomped on.

Pantoleon bends over, wheezing. With an effort, he says, "Your sorceress . . ."

"Elanna?" I say. Hope electrifies me. I grab his arm. "What? Tell me! What did you find out?"

He shakes his head. The pity in his gaze is jarring after all his anger. "Jahan . . . they executed her before dawn."

"That's what the newspapers said." Hot fury seems to explode behind my eyes. "Did you even ask your sorcerer friends? Did you even try to find them, or did you just—"

"You have *no right*," Pantoleon flares, "to talk to me this way. After everything I've done for you! Of course I found my friends. I asked everyone I know. None of them had anything to do with it. None of them even knew she'd been caught. None of them saved her. She's dead, Jahan, and that's all there is to it."

CHAPTER THIRTEEN

Is Elanna dead? I refuse to believe it. I'm going to march up to Aexione now. I'll use all my power, now that the whole damned world knows I'm a sorcerer. I'll bring the walls of the emperor's palace down around him.

I'm going to destroy that man. Single-handedly, if I must.

But then a laugh falls out of me. I've staggered into the domed building, blinded by rage. My hands are fisted in my hair, as if by yanking it out I can pull free some of this burning anger. Except my anger's no use. *I'm* no use. I can't march up to Aexione and level the palace. I'm Madiya's damaged goods, and I don't have that kind of power. Perhaps I could, eventually, level the palace, but it would take hours. Days. They'd shoot me dead long before that.

Elanna *can't* be gone. She can't just *die*. Not on a scaffold. Not by the emperor's will. It's not right. It's not what's supposed to happen. We were supposed to escape together, back to Eren and Caeris. Fight together. Survive together.

And now they've killed her.

I stare around the empty temple. Part of the ceiling has toppled inward, felled by an earthquake. The tiles lie shattered upon the floor mosaic. The shells embedded in the walls hold jagged shadows, like knives. I can't breathe properly; my heart raps an uneven rhythm.

Jahan. Madiya's voice whispers in my mind.

Not her. Not now. I dig my fingers into my scalp. I want to claw at the holes in my memory, rip them open so I can see, at last, what she made me do. I want to tear her voice out of my head. I want to take away *her* memories, the way she stole mine, and my brothers', and my mother's—but I want to leave her aware that I did it.

Except I don't know how to stop her. I don't know how to fix things, or how to save my brothers. I can't even bring Elanna back from the dead. I'm digging at the roots of my hair like a lunatic.

Perhaps this is why I was never able to give El the commitment she wants, the honesty she deserves. Because I am not a whole person, and I never will be. Madiya took that from me, but somehow I can't shake the feeling that it's my fault. That I did something to deserve it.

I'm going to take this empire apart, starting with the top. With Alakaseus Saranon himself. Then I'll find Rayka. And together we'll destroy Madiya.

My head feels clear. Bright. I have a purpose. I'm going to find El's body and give it a proper burial. I'm going to take Aexione apart. Brick. By. Brick. Even if it means they shoot me. I can heal myself. I can survive it, and I have to, because I'm coming for Madiya. And this time, she won't be able to stop me.

I storm back outside. Pantoleon is closing his satchel, squinting down the long steps to the city below.

"You're going back down there." My shock makes it a statement, not a question.

He doesn't look at me. "You hardly need me to watch over you."

The rage blooms again, swelling my head. "There are witch hunters in your apartment, Pantoleon! They know who you are. They've gone through your things!"

"I'm not a sorcerer."

I stare at him. And he accuses *me* of being willfully blind? "It wouldn't matter if you could turn rocks into gold bullion. The witch stones still affect you. The bells—"

"I can withstand them. I won't have my life—my career—compromised. I have a lecture on civil law to deliver this afternoon, and I'm damned well going to be there. My students depend on me."

"And you accuse *me* of denying what I really am and living a lie? This is hypocrisy, Pantoleon, and it's going to get you killed. Imprisoned, at the very least."

We stare at each other for a long moment, the anger taut between us.

"I am not living a lie," he says quietly. "I am teaching students about the laws they should rightfully understand and use. I am helping those who would bring a revolution to Paladis like the one you began in Eren. We are completely different. I have no desire to be a sorcerer. You are one, and you insist on hiding it. You insist on hiding everything about yourself. You claim you're helping Eren but really you're only helping yourself maintain this ridiculous charade—"

"Stop. It." I grind the words through my teeth.

He raises his eyebrows. "Good. You're angry. For once in your life you didn't turn what I said into a joke."

I clench my hands into fists. "I—"

"Maybe you'll finally realize all this isn't a joke," he interrupts. "Our rights. Our freedom. Our lives. Maybe you'll finally do something that makes me proud to call you my friend."

He might as well have punched me. And while I stand reeling, he marches away toward the steps. "I'll be back after nightfall," he calls over his shoulder. "If it's safe."

My legs carry me forward after him, but he glares back at me. I stop myself. I can't let him go into this much danger. But if I go with him, I put him into even more danger.

And he doesn't want me. He doesn't want my help.

In the end I simply put my back to his retreating figure and stare across the open hill. Wind kicks up over the bald rock, carrying the briny scent of the sea. The sun gilds the masts of distant ships in Naval Harbor.

I'm alone. The realization hits me for the first time. I've lost Elanna. Leontius won't speak to me. I put Aunt Cyra in mortal danger. Rayka has disappeared without a word because he has such little regard for me. Lathiel didn't follow me to Aexione. Firmina and Bardas proved that they can't help me despite their goodwill. Now Pantoleon is only helping me because he feels obligated to, thanks to our friendship.

Pantoleon despises me.

I walk back into the great temple, out of the wind, and I drive my fist into the old chipped mosaic of Tirisero holding a snake. The pain seems distant, dull. It can't mitigate the anger that pulses through me. I march around the temple. A stone font sits in front of me, beneath the oculus, covered by a heavy lid. For a brief moment, awareness flickers through me. As if the font *sees* me, the way the stone circles in Eren seem to. As if some potent life lingers within it, and it recognizes me.

But when I tramp closer, the sensation ebbs. I study the font warily. The figures on this side seem to recall Tirisero's exploits— or his lack thereof. Words march beneath in archaic Idaean: THE SECRET FLAME.

It figures that I'm stuck here with the damned god of lost battles. I raise my hands to strike the font, but stop myself. Useless Tirisero doesn't deserve my anger, and even if he's a forgotten god, it's still blasphemy. I pace, instead. I should have gone back into the palace the moment I recognized the simulacrum. I could have saved her. I could have, but I didn't.

I work my hands through my hair, again, again. Tirisero smiles benignly at me from the font. "If you're going to take Elanna from me," I snarl at him, "at least let me save Eren."

The world knows I'm a sorcerer now. And even if it didn't, the emperor would never have acquiesced to my plan. He was always humoring me. He was always going to send the black ships, and Euan Dromahair.

All the gods, I am everything my father accused me of being, and more. A fool, begging the god of failure to help me.

Jahan. Madiya's voice. *Jahan!*

"No!" I shout. My voice rings, hollow, off the vaulted dome. "Leave me alone! Shut! Up!"

Jahan, she whispers.

"*No!*" I shout again, and then I *fling* the word at her across the tenuous connection we have. *No, Madiya.*

Jahan.

No.

I funnel all my anger at her, all my impotent fury, into an arrow. I pack it with all the power I can. Then I shoot it from my mind to hers. It scorches and burns. The very stuff of my mind seems to rip. I clasp my head, gasping. The burning lingers, an intangible pain.

But her voice is gone. Silenced—for the moment, at least.

A chunk of plaster falls from the ceiling and shatters two feet away from me. I back out into the noon glare of the sun. But the temple doesn't collapse.

When I look around, I see what's happened. The grass is singed to nothing, the wild poppies nothing more than charred husks. A mulberry tree is cracked and smoking, as if from fire. The juniper bushes have wilted.

I pulled power from everything I could. I've killed half the plants on this hill.

It's a good thing Elanna can't see this. I couldn't bear her sense of betrayal.

There's nothing I can do. No way to repair the damage. The font inside the temple, whatever it might be, can't hold the power of the stone circles in Eren and Caeris. If El saw me now, she'd know what I really am. A thief.

All the gods, what a fool I am! I'd rather have Elanna see this than lie in an unmarked grave, executed by the Saranons.

The fabric of my mind feels tender. Burned. But it doesn't do enough to placate the anger still inside me. I feel as though my veins are on fire. As though, if I tried, I could burn the whole city down.

But instead I pace beside the old parapet, staring down at the distant harbor. No plan comes to me. The ships are making ready to sail, but Elanna's past saving. I am left alone with the reality of what I have done, and the scar from a wound I don't remember receiving.

A CLATTER BRINGS me awake into a dim gray dawn. I'm off the rough pallet bed and onto my feet before I even come to my senses. I've hardly slept, starting awake at the slightest noises, when I wasn't whispering promises of revenge to Elanna or staring burning-eyed into the dark. Now I listen hard. Perhaps it's only a squirrel.

No—footsteps scuff. Someone's coming into the honeycomb of rooms behind the temple. I don't hear a bell, but it might be a particularly stealthy witch hunter. Or a watchman. Or even an ordinary thief.

I have no weapons—the most unprepared criminal who ever escaped the emperor. I press myself into the wall, trying to meld my skin and bones with its fabric.

The intruder curses. It sounds like he stubbed a toe.

And I recognize his voice. I separate myself from the wall and march toward him.

"I didn't know if you'd come back," I say. My mouth feels strange and crabbed. I'm trying to smile, I realize. Even though, at the same time, I want to shout at him.

He's here, though. Someone came back for me.

Pantoleon must have dropped a candle as well as stubbed his toe; he's crouched over, fumbling for it. He glances up. "There you are. You buried yourself deep in here."

He throws something at me: a loaf of bread wrapped in brown paper. I press my nose against it instinctively. It's still warm, but the smell turns my stomach. I don't remember when I last ate. I don't have any desire to eat now.

I give Pantoleon a hand onto his feet, and press the bread back at him. "You eat first. Were there witch hunters at your apartment?"

"My landlady let them up. They had a warrant. But they didn't find anything." He looks away, his mouth hard. "That didn't prevent Ida's chief of police from interrupting my lecture and interrogating me, however."

I feel sick. "You shouldn't be here. It's dangerous—"

"They let me go, Jahan." He gives me a mirthless smile. "I told them what I thought of you."

Nothing flattering, obviously. "They might still be watching your apartment."

"I know. That's why I stayed at T—at a friend's last night."

I look at him. So we're at the point where he won't even share the name of his lover with me. We used to dare each other to go talk to the girls we liked. The first time one took him home, he told me everything about it. But we were sixteen then. Callow. Even after what had happened to his father, even after what Madiya did to me, we still had a kind of innocence.

Now I seem to look at him across a gulf I can't bridge. A gulf of my own making.

"You needn't have risked yourself to bring me a loaf of bread," I say lightly. "I was fine starving."

But if anything, this seems to make him angry. "It didn't have to be like this, Jahan."

If I had come back looking for him, he means. "You could have contacted me. You could have told me what you were planning, instead of assuming I'd *intuit* it—"

He throws up his hands and strides away. I stalk after him through the dim rooms, out into a sunrise far more beautiful than it has any right to be. He stops by the stone wall. The sun is rising over the sea, a molten ball silhouetting the ships moored in Naval Harbor and the collision of roofs where the city spreads below us. Gulls cry and bells toll as the hour strikes six. Even the battlements of the Frourio, the distant prison, are limned by the morning light. All this glory seems wrong when El is gone.

But it's not only the beauty that catches my eye. Three ships are sailing into the harbor, reefing their sails. The sunrise catches their portholes in perfect silhouette. I can count forty on this side—an eighty-gun ship.

They're joining the black ships already gathered in the harbor. The imperial navy, preparing for war with Eren. Preparing to carry Euan Dromahair to the throne he's coveted for so long.

The idea steals over me, sudden. Inevitable. Perfect. A funnel for the anger in my gut. For revenge. "How many sorcerers are there in your underground society?"

He looks at me. "I have no idea. It's not as if we keep a roster."

That ought to rebuff me, but I have nothing more to lose. "A dozen? Two dozen? More?"

Pantoleon gives in. "Two dozen, perhaps. Why?"

"I want to meet them. Do they have much skill?"

"Whatever you're thinking, the answer is no."

"Not enough, you mean. But they've kept themselves hidden under the witch hunters' noses. They've survived. That takes a certain talent."

"Jahan, they don't respect you. They're not going to go along with whatever mad scheme you're concocting just because you're the Korakos—"

"I wasn't aware that infernal nickname had anything to do with this. Your sorcerers want a revolution—you keep telling me so."

Warily, he nods.

"And have they taken any steps to *achieve* it? Or have they simply given lectures about it?"

His stone-faced silence is answer enough.

"Then it's time for them to begin. For *us* to begin." I nod at the harbor. "That's the fleet Emperor Alakaseus is sending to Eren. We destroy it. With sorcery."

He blinks fast. "That would bring the witch hunters down on us."

"We can deal with the witch hunters. It's time to show the emperor we're not afraid of him, or them. It's time to tell him we want our rights. Tell him we want an alliance with Eren. Not war."

I watch him frown at the distant ships. He's thinking, mulling the plan over. The anger pulses in my head. It's hard to wait for Pantoleon to reply. If I've lost Elanna, then let it be for something. Let me fight in her memory. Let me do this one thing for her, even if she can't see it. Otherwise my anger is going to burn me into coals, and I think, after all Madiya's experiments on me, this is the thing that will send me mad.

"All right," he says at last, and the pulsing in my head eases. "But it's not for me or you to decide. It's Diodia. There's a meeting tonight. I'll present your plan to everyone."

I draw in a breath. The anger pulses through me, demanding I act. "Or I will."

He blinks at me.

"I'm not going to stay up here communing with the pigeons! It's my plan. I want to make sure you do it right."

"You would . . ." He cuts himself off, shaking his head. If I was expecting him to welcome this news with open arms, now that I'm doing what he's been demanding I do all along, I'd be disappointed. "I'll have to come back up here. I don't want to risk being seen . . ."

"I think I can manage to navigate the city alone," I say drily. "Tell me where to meet you, and when, and I'll be there."

CHAPTER FOURTEEN

I make my way through the dark city. I've had hours to rehearse my plan, and it still feels right. Necessary. The only way forward. Although Pantoleon's right—his friends have no reason to trust me—I'm determined to convince them without using even a whisper of persuasion. Any sorcerer worth his salt would recognize what I'm doing. And for once in my life, I'm seized with the inexplicable urge to be honest, as if somehow it will honor El's memory.

I'm going to help them. And they're going to help me destroy the fleet and save Eren. And then, together, we can bring this entire empire down.

Still, as I cut on silent feet through the neighborhood beneath Solivetos Hill, a tension lingers in my shoulders. It's not just wariness. Even with the rage burning in me, I feel as though I'm missing some essential warmth.

Elanna. Her death still doesn't feel real. But I'm doing this for her, for her people, for her memory.

I can't dwell on that, or the fury will overwhelm me. I walk faster yet, letting anger carry me. At least I've heard nothing from Madiya since I burned her out of my mind. Maybe I finally succeeded in silencing her entirely.

The spires of the university cut into the sky ahead of me. From two blocks away, I hear the raucous roar of the Den, busy even on Diodia. All the students come here to argue philosophical points and drink peasants' beer and feel generally subversive.

When I step inside, the racket deluges me after a night spent alone in an abandoned temple. I push through the high tables and crowded bar, where a server is explaining in a patiently exasperated voice that they've run out of prawns. The place smells of alcohol and armpits and ink, and somehow it's comforting, a piece of my youth I never wanted to leave behind. I pass unnoticed through the press of students and professors, climbing the steps to the back booths. Tucked behind the tied-back brocade curtains, some students play dice under the glow of tallow lamps; others argue over the distance between the earth and the sun. I feel a grin pushing up my mouth. This place makes me feel alive.

A narrow door is tucked between the last two booths. No one pays any attention as I open it and let myself through.

I'm at the top of steps, lit by a single lantern. A breath of cool, earthy air wafts up toward me. For a moment, I'm frozen, thrown back to huddling in a cave while someone's unknown footsteps came down toward me.

I shake off the fear clenching my heart and stride down the stairs.

At the bottom, racks of wine and barrels of beer thrust spikily out of the dark. I can just make out another door hidden between the shelves. Momentary uncertainty grips me. What if they don't listen? What if they reject my plan?

I won't let that happen. I stride up to the door and knock.

Pantoleon opens it. He just says, "There you are," but I hear both the unease and the hope warring in his tone.

"As promised," I say. "You didn't think I'd stand you up?"

He snorts and lets me in. The stone room is small, made comfortable by a dozen flickering candles oozing wax onto the table in the center. I suppose it shouldn't surprise me that there's a secret meeting room beneath the Den. But the two people sitting on the other side of the table *do* surprise me.

The young man, short and dark with a tasseled black cap, breaks into laughter. "Well, if it isn't our friend from the coffee shop!"

The woman, however, doesn't laugh. She's exchanged her scarlet turban for a dark-blue one, but I still recognize the person who shouldered past me in the coffee shop, declaring Jahan Korakides a sorcerer. Her gaze is assessing, and rather unimpressed.

I offer her a smile. "Tullea, was it? And you're Felix Tzemines. I'm afraid I never read the pamphlet."

"Oh, well," Felix says, still clearly delighted, "you already know it all anyway. Pantoleon, I must say this is a very good surprise! Well done!"

"I take it you already know each other," Pantoleon says drily. He exchanges a glance with Tullea—a rather more knowing glance than one usually gives one's colleagues. I look at her. She's far more formidable than Pantoleon's usual type, but perhaps she's his secret lover all the same.

"We merely made a passing acquaintance," I say. "Jahan Korakides, at your service."

"The Korakos," Felix says. He's shaking his head, still grinning.

"Felix is an assistant researcher to Lucius Argyros," Pantoleon explains. "And Tullea—Tullea Domitros—is a university lecturer. She specializes in the history of Paladius the First."

The shy smile he gives her tells me I'm right. They *are* lovers.

"Forgive me," I say, "but I was under the impression I was attending some sort of underground sorcerous coven. Isn't that why we're here?"

Pantoleon sighs, and Felix chuckles. "I'm the leader of the New Republic," he says.

You're a student, I think, but I don't say it. I turn to Tullea, only to find her watching me, her black eyes steady. She must be a few years older than Pantoleon and me, but she still has far too much gravitas for someone so young.

"You *are* meeting with the 'underground sorcerers,' Korakos," she says. "I manage them. Haven't you ever wondered who's been smuggling all those refugees to Eren?"

I can't say I expected it to be an extremely composed university lecturer, but looking at her, I have no doubts. "You must be a sorceress yourself, then."

She presses her lips together, then nods.

"And you?" I ask Felix.

"I wish!" he says with such idiotic fervor that I find myself laughing. Tullea snorts, and Pantoleon shakes his head.

"Only someone without a scrap of magic would *want* to be a sorcerer," I say.

Felix just shrugs. "It's always seemed to me that I should be a sorcerer—that it was my fate, but I've been cheated of it."

Well, this is a curious kind of madness. I feel my eyebrows lift.

"My colleagues and I help Tullea with her work," Felix adds. "We arrange passage on ships and so forth, to safely smuggle sorcerers out of Paladis."

Tullea clears her throat. She's sitting even straighter, ignoring the cup of beer in front of her, and I can only imagine how terrifying her students must find her. "The real question," she says, "is why *you* are here, Korakos."

"Yes!" Felix says, eager.

Pantoleon simply looks at me.

I feel myself flattened a bit beneath their eyes. But this is for Elanna. This is what she would want me to do; what I should have done for her all along. "I know I haven't stood beside Ida's sorcerers. I know that you have little reason to trust me. But know that I did take in those refugees you sent to Eren, Tullea. I did fight beside Elanna Valtai." There's a tightness in my throat at her name, and at what I'm going to say next. I've never spoken these words aloud to more than one person, and even though I'm ready to destroy the empire itself, it still feels strange. "I'm a sorcerer."

I breathe out, though sweat pools on my back. There. I spoke the truth aloud, in front of several strangers.

"Well, we knew that," Felix says, and laughs again.

Tullea drums her fingers on the table. "We knew that the emperor *claimed* it. I'm glad to hear it from you."

I force a smile. "I'm not only a sorcerer—I was raised to it from birth. From what Pantoleon has said, I imagine I know more than most of the sorcerers in Ida. So I have a proposal for you." I feel my smile turning into a manic grin. "I want to join you. But more than that, I want to offer my help. I want to train your sorcerers so they can actually take action without being cut down by the witch hunters like so much wheat."

Felix gasps with unfeigned excitement, but Tullea's gaze is far more calculating. "And what action do you propose we take?"

From her tone, I suspect she already knows; Pantoleon must have told her. This charade of ignorance is for Felix's benefit, perhaps— but also to test me. To force me to say the words myself.

I can play that game.

"I want to destroy the imperial navy," I say, and Felix chokes on his beer.

"Oh?" he says. "That's all? You just want to wander in and destroy the black ships, which have never been defeated?"

I grin and lean forward. Everything feels bright now. Possible. "We're sorcerers. They're not. The emperor's sending the fleet to Eren. But if we stop them, we stop the war with Eren. We ally with Queen Sophy. We let the whole world know that we won't let Alakaseus Saranon win."

Tullea watches me guardedly. "But with Elanna Valtai executed . . . The emperor could still attack Eren."

"But if we stop the emperor from even fighting," I say, "Eren wins. And then you—we—have an ally. A way to change everything."

Felix brightens at these words, and I feel my smile widen further. They're listening. Tullea taps her fingertips thoughtfully on the table. Maybe she recognizes that I'm not exactly operating in their best interests; maybe she sees that destroying the black ships doesn't completely benefit them. Maybe I am using them, just a bit, to get what I want.

But I *will* help them. And helping them makes Eren safe. It fulfills the promise I made Elanna, even if I can't bring her back.

"This is interesting." Tullea glances at Pantoleon, lifting an eyebrow. He simply looks tired.

Felix says, "Well, I—"

"*Felix.*" Tullea hooks her finger, and he leans close to her. She whispers heatedly at him, and I pour myself a cup of beer, pretending I couldn't simply magnify the sound of their voices if I wanted. At first, from the sound of things, I think Tullea isn't going to agree, that she's going to accuse me of being a mad, selfish bastard. But she nods when Felix turns around and says, "All right, Korakides. We're with you."

My chest feels warm. This is *happening.* "Excellent—"

"Though the final decision will be up to all of our sorcerers," Tullea says. She watches me, marking my every move. "I'll bring them up to Solivetos so they can meet you. So you can show them how to make magic."

"Ah." Some of the warmth drains out of me. "All right."

Tullea actually smiles. Maybe she didn't think I'd agree, when it came down to it.

"But"—Felix holds up a finger—"we need a demonstration of good faith. There's no point in destroying the fleet if no one knows who did it."

The point is to keep the fleet from sailing to Eren and destroying the hope I fought for, I think. But I don't say it. I offer Felix an interested smile instead.

It's Tullea who clears her throat and leans forward. "A revolution needs a leader, as you well know . . ."

"Felix is admirably energetic," I say.

She gives me a quelling look, even as Felix preens. "Felix is not a sorcerer. And after what you did in Eren, it's obvious to me that that's what the people need to latch on to. Someone who stirs their imaginations. Someone who already has a reputation."

"Elanna was a glorious figurehead," I say. *Was.* I nearly gag on the words. "We could fight in her memory."

Tullea blinks at me, and Pantoleon sighs. "Jahan, stop being so deliberately obtuse. It doesn't make anyone want to follow you."

Follow *me.* My hand has gone, unconsciously, to my scar. The old terror washes over me. Who would follow a man who has lied and deceived his way to the top? Someone who doesn't remember half his childhood? Who doesn't know the things he's done, or been made to do?

Who am I, to lead anything?

"You're the Korakos," Felix says eagerly, as if he heard my question. "The people already know you—they've written songs about you, by all the gods! Just think—*The sorcerer who was cast aside by Prince Leontius and led a rebellion against the Saranons and their witch hunters!* The people will love it. I love it."

"Glad to oblige," I say reflexively, but my mind seems to have stalled. I touch my scar. Leontius is my friend. I don't want to see him destroyed, or publicly humiliated and exiled like Loyce Eyrlai. He used to call me his only true friend. That Leontius, the one who let me into his life, is a person I like. A person I don't want to disappoint. I can't bear the thought that my truth has been revealed to him so harshly: that his only real friend never shared the greatest truth about himself.

Yet he did nothing to save me when the imperial guards arrested me. Nothing to save Elanna. He's cast his vote by inaction; it's obvious what he thinks of me. He's been angry with me since the moment I announced I was leaving for Eren. Furious since I returned. I still don't know why. I refuse to believe it's because he's just a Saranon like the rest of them.

The others are waiting for my response. I lower my hand.

This is it. The moment to declare myself not only a sorcerer, but an open enemy of the court where I struggled for so long to gain acceptance. The moment to tell the world the truth. And despite the anger concentrated in my chest, I want to hide. I want to persuade them that we don't need a leader, that their sorcerers don't need a public face.

But they do, and I know it.

What would El do, in my position? What would she want me to do?

"Well, I can't promise to be entirely satisfactory," I begin. "Some of those ballads about me are terrifically embellished."

Pantoleon rolls his eyes. Felix and Tullea exchange a glance.

"But you'll do it," Tullea says. "You'll claim responsibility for destroying the fleet, and all our future actions. We'll put it on posters and scatter it throughout the city."

"Your name will be our call to arms!" Felix says. "I'll have my people tell everyone they know. You know how fast gossip spreads in Ida. Especially," he adds, "about someone so famous."

Yes. Like wildfire. I close my eyes. This isn't what I thought I wanted.

Except I fought alongside the Caerisians and Ereni for this very thing: the freedom to practice our sorcery and to determine our own government. This is what I want. But I've been running from it, because I'm more comfortable in my disguise.

Yet I can't run anymore. There's nowhere else to go. The fire in me is burning too strong.

"Very well," I say, meeting Tullea's gaze. "Tell the world."

For Elanna's memory, and for the future of her people, I'll do whatever I must.

CHAPTER FIFTEEN

Tullea promised to bring her sorcerers up to Solivetos Hill, and the next night they arrive. They number ten or fifteen, but the darkness seems to magnify their presence. We've converted one of the abandoned chambers behind the dome into a makeshift council room and lit a fire in the old stone pit. For the first time, the barren rooms seem almost cozy, with everyone packed shoulder-to-shoulder. I sit between Pantoleon and Tullea—comfortable, I might say, or kept in place. At least I don't have to endure Madiya whispering into my head. Her voice seems to have vanished entirely.

The sorcerers come from all stations: One woman is a flower seller, one man a banker. There are several university students and two women who run a hat shop together. Most are young or middle-aged. The oldest sorcerers, Tullea tells me, have learned how to hide—if they're still alive and free—and don't need her help.

We make a circle around the fire, everyone's faces lit. They've brought food, and I've forced myself to eat a handful of pistachios and dried apricots, though they tasted like dust in my mouth. I've presented my proposal and outlined how we would achieve it, to a silence that seems generally willing.

But now one of the shopkeepers, Irene, says, "There's one thing we need to know, Korakos."

I smile. "What is that?"

She leans forward. "Are you a sorcerer, truly?"

The smile stiffens on my lips. I take in the deep coals within the fire. Then I force myself to look at their waiting faces, some eager, some bitter, some grim with the weight of too many years of struggle and too much false hope. They are ordinary people, or they look ordinary. But like me, they are something else inside their skin.

The fire pops. They're waiting for me to speak, and for once in my life, when a simple *yes* would suffice, it seems like too much to say, even though I've already confessed the truth to Tullea and Felix. Even though all of Ida knows it by now and, soon, will know that I've led our attack against the crown. There is a kind of thrumming in my chest; a heat in my palms.

I say, "I am a sorcerer. It's true. I was raised to it from birth."

No need to tell them more. No need to divulge all my secrets at once. The thrumming subsides. That wasn't so bad.

The banker says, "From birth?" and the flush moves over my body again.

I shouldn't have let that slip out. I don't know why I thought it would legitimize me. None of these people were raised to it; they've all struggled to suppress it, to hide it, to destroy the part of themselves that makes magic. Who has taught any one of these people to use their sorcery for anything other than to hide?

"Well," I say with a quick grin, "it might not have been the *cleverest* idea. But my father has strange ambitions."

I've said too much. But then again, who are these people going to tell? Besides, by now anyone might guess that my father is behind my sorcery. Especially if they had the sense to look at his library.

The sorcerers are exchanging glances. The other shopkeeper, Sabina, taps her fingertips together and looks at me.

"Show us," the banker, Nestor, says abruptly.

I'm so surprised that I find myself repeating him. "Show you my magic? I'm not here to entertain! Though if you'd like a game of it after, I can oblige."

He looks affronted.

Tullea says magisterially, "A demonstration might be in order."

Their wariness—their *offense*—chills the already cold air. Do they truly believe I would run from the law and hide myself up here, luring them after me, only to prey on their hope? Do they think I would *lie* to them?

Of course, I've lied so much, so publicly. To the emperor, to the court, to the city, to the entire empire.

I look around at their faces, lit orange by the fire. The demand hovers in the smoky air.

Fine. If they want a demonstration of magic, I'll show them what Madiya taught me. This time, instead of reaching for the earth's green power, I reach for the power of the fire itself.

Smother, I whisper. The flames flicker. They're resisting, because fire loves to burn. But I insist and, with a sudden pop, the fire goes out. My vision sparkles in the sudden darkness.

A voice comes, uncertain, out of the dark. "Did you do that, Korakos?"

"Yes. And now I'll bring it back to life."

I reach for the memory of fire, buried in the logs, still eager in the coals. The wood is willing to burn, desperate to destroy itself. *Light,* I whisper with my mind.

The coals kindle, and fire shoots up toward the ceiling. We all rock back. It settles after a moment into a more modest, if enthusiastic, blaze.

"Creating and destroying," I say to the sorcerers' baffled faces. They probably expected something more splendid, like Elanna's earth-moving sorcery, but my magic is more typically practical. They whisper among themselves, mouthing my words. *Creating and destroying?* They really don't know anything at all, I realize. I find myself breaking into an explanation, as if the words have been thirsty on my tongue. I've never tried to explain sorcery before, except once or twice to El. "Breaking and mending. Potentiality and reality. It's the basic tenet of sorcery: that any *potential* can be made manifest, no matter how unlikely. I can douse a fire because I can remind it what it felt like not to burn. I can bring it back to life because the memory of fire remains in the logs—the potential for flame. The potentiality principle is the same for a fire as it is for a human body. A gun. A ship." I pause. "A city."

All the gods, I sound like Madiya, or my father on one of his pedantic streaks. How proud they would be to find their wayward protégé parroting the knowledge they stuffed down his throat. I want to cringe.

"That's what you do?" Irene the shopkeeper says. She seems doubtful. "You see the . . . potential of things?"

"Yes. And I manipulate it. Anyone can, if they have the spark of magic." My face feels strange and I wonder if I was burned when the fire flared, but then I realize I've begun to smile. To smile, because even if I'm quoting Madiya and my father, the sorcery is still mine. The knowledge is mine, and I can share it. It doesn't make me their pawn, not anymore. After all, I burned Madiya out of my brain.

I can use the knowledge she gave me to destroy the fleet. I can teach these people, and together we can do almost anything.

I say to the sorcerers, "And I'm going to show you how to do it, too."

NONE OF THEM are particularly good. I suppose it shouldn't surprise me—they haven't been born to it, like Elanna was, or manipulated the way I have been. But we've spent half the night practicing the smallest magics, and few of them can manage the tasks. Nestor tries to relight a candle and burns himself instead. Irene tries to fade from our perception, insisting that she's not there, but instead we see her all the more clearly. Maybe if I hadn't tried to forget half the things Madiya taught me, or been made to, I could help them better. But after I've watched each of their attempts, I find myself at a loss as to how to help.

Only Tullea demonstrates a real aptitude—for illusion. She stands off to the side in dignified silence, weaving the particles in the air together to create whole scenes that flicker against the walls, a theater of her making within the temple's empty dome.

While the others take a rest, I walk over to her. She's spun a girl-figure out of shadows and is coaxing her to run against the temple's wall.

"You must be the envy of playwrights," I remark. "How did you learn?"

The girl-figure jumps high into the air. Tullea is smiling slightly—an expression I have not once seen on her face—but it falters now. The figure vanishes, the illusion unraveling. She's quiet for a long moment, and I think she's not going to answer. But then she does.

"It's what I did as a child," she says. "My grandmother often looked after me, because my mother worked as a tutor. Grandmother would spin figures out of the air to entertain me." She glances at me, as if assessing my degree of respect. "We created whole plays together. It was our secret. Once I mentioned it to my mother and got the worst spanking of my life—a good lesson for me, because the witch hunters would have been far, far crueler. I kept silent after that."

"It's lovely." And it is lovely—purely delightful, in the way it must have been for her as a child. It's the last thing I expected from Tullea Domitros. I eye her. "Your grandmother . . ."

Tullea lifts her chin. "She was never caught. She spent her life smuggling sorcerers to safety, using her illusions. She fought for us all."

The reproach in her tone is perfectly clear—*unlike you*—but I ignore it. This means Tullea must use her own talents for her underground movement. Which means . . . "So this isn't the only kind of illusion you spin?"

Her lips twitch. "Why, Korakides? Do you have a plan?"

I grin. "An idea. And if you can teach some of the others to help you . . ." I call to Irene; she comes over with a bashful look. "You haven't done anything wrong," I tell her. "It's just your magic works differently. When you try to hide your presence, you only insist that you're more real. But if you spin an illusion, that might be helpful—insisting that what's not there actually is there."

"Do you think so?" Irene says, looking back and forth from Tullea to me, her embarrassment forgotten.

This expression in her eyes, after all of the night's failure, is hope.

"Jahan makes a good point," Tullea replies. She looks speculatively at Irene. "Come, let's try it."

I leave them to it and drift out into the main temple. The sorcerers have paired off, whispering to each other and poring over purloined books. Sabina, Irene's companion, holds a plant in both hands—a type of oleander—but despite her furrowed brows, nothing in particular seems to be happening. The others cast me tired looks.

Pantoleon is crouched in front of the font, holding a candle close to the stone carvings. I crouch beside him. He taps a carven image of a man cradling what looks like a star, or a sunburst. "Tirisero," he pronounces, as if it means something.

"The god of failure," I mutter. "Maybe it's symbolic. There's a reason not even beggars come here, you know."

He squints at me, but his lips are pursed, his mind elsewhere. "I never studied theology. I never thought there was anything in it."

"Well . . ." I say, gesturing at the abandoned god's temple.

Pantoleon shakes his head. "Look at this." He taps the words carved into the rock. "THE SECRET FLAME . . ." He shuffles on his knees to the other side, where the phrase picks up. ". . . UNIFIED WITH . . ." We shuffle to the next side. ". . . THE DEEP WATER . . ." And the final side: "THE HEART OF TIRISERO."

"It's a pretty riddle," I say. "But aren't fire and water opposites according to the old philosophers?"

"That's what I always thought." He shakes his head. "It's probably nonsense."

Nestor comes up behind us. "We tried to get the lid off earlier. It won't budge. It's as if it's sealed."

I look at the old stone. Each short phrase is interrupted by images: the man with the star, the same man spreading arms that are wings, the man touching the chest of someone dead or ill, and finally, the man enveloped with flame, standing over rushing water.

Nonsense, indeed. But something about them tugs at me. The god of lost battles should, surely, be portrayed with a spear in his chest, or something equally dire. These images suggest something rather more mystical than I expected.

I look back at Nestor. His face is drawn with weariness. It's so deep into night it's nearly morning, and exhaustion tugs at my own bones. A sailor, Agapetos, has also come over, along with Sabina, still gripping the oleander.

Perhaps I don't need to teach them how to do grand things or draw on the earth for enormous power. With Tullea's illusions and my own magic, perhaps we only need to do something small. Simple. Because even the smallest thing can become great, if used correctly.

"Sit down." I gesture to them. "I'm going to teach you three things. One, to relight a candle. Two, to alter other people's perceptions. And three, to hear each other by speaking each other's names with intent." I glance at Pantoleon, who has spent years resisting my attempts to teach him. But even he seems to be listening, though his eyes keep straying to the font. "They're simple things. But if you can't do them all, at least master one. If you can manage one, then we can make our plan work."

More people have come to join us; in the other room, I hear Tullea and Irene talking about illusions. Maybe we can succeed yet. We have to. I'm not going to let Elanna down now, not even the memory of her. I gather myself, thinking of what she'd want, and begin.

I talk a long time and let them practice. Dawn creeps in without my notice. Most of the sorcerers look dead on their feet, but Nestor and Sabina are challenging each other to see who can make candlewicks burst into flame the fastest.

A noise outside startles me. Everyone goes silent and alert. But it's Felix Tzemines who trots, panting, into the temple, carrying a bundle of fresh bread and a jug of hot coffee. Everyone gathers around with grateful exclamations. Under the din, Felix edges over to me. "Word from Aexione." He jerks his chin toward the lee of the fallen ceiling tiles, and I follow. We have a modicum of privacy here, though Tullea sends us an accusatory glance.

I thicken the air around us to muffle our voices. "Don't tell me. The emperor's decided I'm dead and proposed a victory ball."

Felix snorts. "Not since we're spreading rumors of your survival."

I wince.

He hesitates, looking at me. Somewhat awkwardly, he says, "Emperor Alakaseus has given orders to the fleet commander. They're to depart for Eren in three days, on Atrydia."

I glance at our ragtag crew, exhausted from the long night's work. Whether they can succeed is anyone's guess, but what choice do we have? We have to try.

"Let's go the morning after next, then," I say. "The vessels should be unmanned."

Felix nods. "Will they be ready?"

"Necessity is a fast teacher. They'll have to be."

He nods again, and hesitates once more.

My brother, I think, my fists tightening. That must be Felix's other news. They've finally caught Rayka.

Felix clears his throat. "Since we let out word about you . . . the emperor's increased the price on your head to three thousand gold."

An incredulous noise escapes me. A sum like that could set a person up for the rest of their lives, quite comfortably. "Am I worth a man's life?"

"There's another thing." Felix glances at the sorcerers. "They changed the sentence for anyone caught harboring you or giving you aid." He laughs. "Quite a bunch of blackguards, aren't we? If any of us are caught, we'll be named a traitor to the crown and subject to the laws governing such."

He laughs, but there's nothing funny about this. We all know the punishment for such high treason: death.

A thrumming builds in my chest. If only I were more powerful—if only Madiya hadn't damaged me. I could take down the fleet myself, even if it cost my life. But instead I have to rely on the help of others. And in so doing, I put their very lives at risk.

Of course, if they're caught, it won't merely be the firing squad for them. If they're found performing sorcery, they will be hauled away by the witch hunters without a trial. I am asking them to chance their lives, but they understand the risk. Or I hope they do.

I turn back to Felix. "Then we ought to be more careful. You're certain you got up here unseen?"

He shrugs. "Being careful is dull, and you die either way. But no one followed me."

I smile. "Well, you may as well die knowing you did some good, rather than simply smuggling messages to renegade sorcerers."

"But that *is* something good." He spreads his arms. "This is my city. My people. If I have to die setting us free, I will."

I shake my head. Caution is too engrained in me. Still, I have to admire his courage, even if it borders on foolishness.

"Two mornings from now," he says, "we'll be there."

CHAPTER SIXTEEN

I'm a ghost on the water, the faint memory, already gone, of a small sailing boat passing between the great black-stained hulls of Paladis's warships. It's early morning on Enydia. The sorcerers have had two days to practice their illicit sorcery. We all have to hope it's enough. A fog creeps over Naval Harbor, hiding us. It's not even real, but an illusion cast by Tullea and Irene: It fits among the ships at awkward, unnatural angles, leaving the lower levels of the vessels exposed to our sight but completely muffling the decks. I wanted the sorcerers to unlock the potential in water particles, but they don't have the level of precision to do that work. Instead they've got the general appearance right, but not the details.

The other sorcerers are stationed throughout the streets and barracks, sowing confusion, misdirecting anyone bound for the harbor. I hope we trained enough, and that the early hour—and luck—are on our side. The illusion of fog isn't hard to maintain, but it needs to disguise a large area and fifty ships. None of us have the reach to set the ships on fire from shore. Even getting this close might not be enough, if we can't call upon enough power. We talked of burning them—the explosion would be impressive—but it would have required too much control and skill, which the other sorcerers don't yet possess.

No, ruining the fleet is up to me. The others simply must ensure that no one notices until it's too late. Then Felix's people will get to work, telling the world what I've done. If the emperor hated me before . . .

I focus on the matter at hand. If the fog falters, I can maintain it. I'll make it work. I'll have to.

I'm not going to let damned Alakaseus Saranon win this game.

The sailing boat continues to thread between the hulls. I wonder how many men are on these ships, if any. That was part of the reason for not burning them: We didn't want to cause loss of life if we didn't have to.

The harbor is sheltered enough. None of the sailors should drown. Elanna wouldn't want me to murder men who are merely doing their duty. Of course, *she* could have managed all of this alone, from shore. I can see how her eyes would have gone distant, luminous, as she called upon the power of wood and water. How the whole harbor would have shaken and transformed itself. How she'd have turned to me afterward, with that private smile she only ever seemed to give me. *There,* she'd say. *How did you like that?*

But now she's gone, and I must do this alone. Without her. For her. I swallow hard.

Beside me, Sabina drums her fingers on the gunwale. She's been tasked with persuading everyone that we're not here. Agapetos steers the boat. I need to focus on our plan. We have to account for the displacement of water and the difficulty of navigating our craft amid sinking ships. We've decided to start at the outer ring of ships and work our way in. As we approach the outermost vessel, I expand my mind to hold its shape, the weight of it in the water, its hulls and masts, the precision of nails and tar pulling the whole together.

It would be easiest, of course, to let it burst apart, an explosion of wood breaking at the seams, but that would draw attention. And if anyone is sleeping on the ships, it might kill them. Plus, I need to get Sabina and Agapetos out of here alive. It doesn't matter so much what happens to me.

So I murmur to the nails and tar. I draw on the elusive power of the water, and the hum of energy in my own body. This is going to leave me thin and hollowed out—but that doesn't matter. The boat seems to exhale as the tar softens and the nails begin to loosen and water creeps up through the cracks between the boards.

I release my hold on the nails. The ship will burst apart on its own now, sending hundreds of tons of ammunition to the bottom of the sea, without the ammunition needing to be lit. Sabina rubs her palms over her eyes.

"Only forty-nine more!" I whisper with a grin. Agapetos snorts, and Sabina rolls her eyes.

We move to the next, and the next. Such a careful process is impossible to hurry. The sky has begun to lighten, but the fog holds. The harbor remains quiet; only waves slop against the ships and a few gulls cry.

I've lost count—twenty or more down. Agapetos steers us to the next, working our way slowly back into the harbor, toward the quay. "We're nothing," Sabina chants under her breath. "Nothing, nothing, nothing."

It's a bit distracting, but I push her voice out of my mind. I loosen the nails. The ship begins to buckle as water slips in belowdecks.

A shout overhead. The echoing *thud* of feet running over the deck boards. A bell clangs.

"Damn," I mutter. Looks like we've found an occupied ship.

They can't see us, I remind myself. Sabina's taken care of that. Most likely they think some kind of accident is causing the ship to admit water. "Go," I whisper to Agapetos. If this one ship sinks more slowly than the others, if they rescue some gunpowder from it, it's not much of a loss.

We cut away toward the next ship, just as there's a whisper of sound behind us. I glance back. Where the awkward angle of the illusory fog ends, a man is peering out one of the starboard ports, straight at us.

He doesn't know what we're doing. We might be resupplying one of the other ships, for all he knows.

"Hey!" he calls.

Sabina sucks in a breath through her nostrils. "We're *nothing*!"

she whispers fiercely, but I can feel her insistence fraying as she stops believing it works herself. Agapetos hurls us toward the next ship, his muscles straining as he wrestles with the oars. I reach for the nails and tar, though my body already seems to be vibrating, like a string plucked too many times. But we have to hurry now. That man's going to sound an alarm.

But this ship is occupied, too. "Hello?" a voice calls overhead.

"We're nothing," Sabina whispers, but there are tears in her eyes.

"Agapetos, get us back to the quay!" I whisper. "Hurry!"

I gather all the remaining ships in my mind, but they overflow, too many objects gathered in my hands.

"Who's down there?" the man above us calls out.

I grab onto half the ships and yank the nails from the boards. With so many, it's impossible to be careful. A ship to our left *booms*, as loud as if we'd fired upon it. Another collapses in on itself, shocking a wave up through the water that kicks us back among the other vessels.

The fog is thinning to the consistency of milky glass, full of stranger angles and edges yet. Tullea and Irene must have been startled by the explosion; they're losing control. On a deck above us, two sailors stare down at our boat from an intact ship. Agapetos is desperately trying to correct, even as more ships pull apart and water slaps us back and forth, ramming our boat into the hull behind us. Overhead, the sailors begin to shout. But the boards are buckling, and I can no longer see them.

I take hold of our boat with my mind, the remaining ships be damned, and compress space. We're thrust closer to the quay, but another unexpected wave throws us off course.

The fog evaporates. Men are running onto the wharves, shouting, trying to man dinghies to get out to the fleet.

"They see us!" Sabina gasps, pointing.

A man at the end of a pier has run down, balancing a musket in his arms. He's aiming to shoot.

I compress space again just as the gun explodes. I yank the boat over to the other side of the harbor, the movement so forceful that we're shunted onto a gravel spit. Agapetos swears. Above the spit is an abandoned pier and the wall of the squat watchtower. But there's no time to free ourselves from the spit, even though we're still several feet from the shore, because people are shouting to our right, racing along the quay in every direction. We don't seem to have been spotted yet, but it's impossible to tell. Another gunshot explodes.

No—it's one of the magazines on the ships. I spare a glance behind me. Smoke towers from a ship into the air. A man is screaming. People are running.

Then another ship explodes, across the harbor. Alone. Spontaneous.

Who's doing this?

But I don't have time to stare. I fling myself overboard into the shallows, Agapetos and Sabina on my heels. The water surges into my shoes, dragging on my trousers, soaking them up to the thighs. I heave myself onto the pier and reach back to help the others up after me. Another ship explodes in a rush of smoke and fire. None of them have this much power—do they?

But then more gunfire erupts nearby. Tullea, Irene, the others. They better not have gotten captured.

Behind us, the harbor is a smoking chaos, fire catching from mast to mast. The other ships are breaking apart, their boards thrust open by the force of water. The few still intact are being rammed by debris. Several vessels have already been swallowed up to their masts; some planks drift, scattered like chaff on the choppy waves. Sailors are shouting, diving overboard. The fires burn and burn.

No one has yet reached our pier. The cannons on the watchtower above us can only shoot well over our heads.

There isn't a good way out, but I'm overcome by an idea. If I can compress space horizontally, why not vertically as well?

"Take my hands," I say to Sabina and Agapetos. They do, baffled but obedient. "And let's run!"

We race *toward* the wall. The moment my foot hits a bottom brick, I compress space. Gravity tugs us back toward the pier, their combined weight draws on my arms, but I *insist*.

And I stagger onto the top of the wall, falling over the crenellated battlements to the walk where guards patrol the harbor. I see only one man right now, some distance from us. The other guards seem to have all run down to the quays.

"I think I'm going to be sick," Sabina says. Agapetos just seems stunned.

"You'll have to do that later." I nod at the single guard, who has backed up and is now leveling his musket at us. "Go!"

We take off in the opposite direction from the guard. At the next tower, there are stairs down to the street. We run down them, back into the streets of Ida, and even though my lungs are burning, even though my feet squelch with each step, even though our plot didn't go quite according to plan and I don't yet know what's become of the others, I start laughing as I run. Because what was I born for, if not for this?

TULLEA AND IRENE aren't at Solivetos Hill, though the other sorcerers have all gathered, mostly unharmed. My drying trousers stick to my ankles, and the aftereffect of draining my own power makes me light-headed. But I find myself turning straight around and running back out into the street, Sabina and Nestor at my heels.

Somewhere, a lone bell tolls. Strange—it's alone. It's not on the hour; all the others rang out a few minutes ago.

I find myself running toward it, back the way we came, toward Naval Harbor. Pedestrians dodge out of my way. I've forgotten to even make myself unnoticed, and now it's too damned late. *Just a gust of wind,* I insist, but my mind is stupid with weariness. I don't know what power I'm even pulling on.

"Tullea," I call. "Irene!"

Neither of them answers.

Sabina catches up with me. "This is my fault!"

I shake my head, just as Tullea's voice pulses into my mind. *Jahan!*

I reach for the thread of her voice, letting it pull me down the street, narrowly missing a fruit seller and a boot shiner. The area near Naval Harbor is rougher, full of laundry blocking out the sky and women with wary eyes watching us from doorways and upper balconies. We're near the Frourio prison, and many men who live here work there as guards.

Through an alley. I emerge into another street—and I see them staggering toward us. Tullea's arms are covered in blood, but it's not hers. She's supporting Irene, whose steps are weak. Sagging. She's taken a shot in the gut.

But she lifts her face all the same, and sees us. "Sabina! Jahan!"

Sabina cries out. I'm running toward them.

Another bell tolls. Again, and again. Nearly overhead. Nestor gasps behind me.

Then more bells ring. Smaller ones, but no less demanding. They're nearby, drawing closer. Witch hunters.

I grab Irene bodily from Tullea and hoist her over my shoulder. She's limp, and the hand that clutches my collar is cold and clammy. Too cold, for someone who's been running hard.

But Tullea's looking over her shoulder. Her face is stricken with fear.

I look. Bells ring. Three witch hunters are striding through the streets, people shuffling out of their way.

"Go!" I shout at Sabina and Nestor. Tullea's already weaving some illusion, her hands busy, trying to create the image of us fleeing in the opposite direction. But the bells and witch stones must be working against her; the illusions shatter and break. She staggers as if in pain.

All the gods. I grab her arm, pushing her after the others, and swing to face the witch hunters, Irene heavy on my shoulder. One of them pauses and stares at me—a large man. It's Faverus.

It's only a moment's hesitation. But it must be enough.

One of his fellow witch hunters cries out. A tavern sign has catapulted from a wall and barreled into him, smashing him in the ribs. He crumples to the ground. Faverus swings back, wide-eyed, to crouch beside him. The other stares between his fallen comrade and us.

But I don't even see him. I'm staring at a doorway, where a boy is standing. Watching me. A thin, eighteen-year-old boy, with lank dark hair, a shabby coat, and my own pale eyes.

The other witch hunter lurches toward us, but the boy snaps his fingers. The cobblestones buckle in front of the man. He stumbles, and I hear the sick crunch as he breaks an ankle. He tries to push himself upright, but the cobblestones keep shifting under him, and he cries out. What is the fool trying to do, bury this man in the street?

Of course he is. And he wouldn't have any compunction about setting a gunpowder magazine alight and burning up an entire ship.

But he's here. He's free. Alive. *Safe.*

Someone grabs my arm: Tullea. "Jahan, *run!*"

"Yes—" I begin. But my brother . . .

But when I look back at the doorway, it's empty. He's gone.

Only the creeping vines covering the wall show evidence of his presence. They're blackened—charred to husks. The two witch hunters lie, their bodies ruined, in the street. He must have stolen their own power to work his magic against them. I can't tell if they still live.

I've hesitated too long. Irene is moaning softly on my shoulder. Faverus stares up at me from between the bodies of his fellows. Soon others will join them—not only witch hunters, but the city watch, the imperial guards.

I turn and run, pulling persuasion around me. *Nothing but the wind. A student running late to class.*

"What happened?" Tullea demands when I catch up to her on the next corner. "Was that you?"

I glance over my shoulder, awkwardly, feeling Irene's blood soaking into my shirt. Her fingers are tight in the back of my coat. But no lank-haired boys linger in the street behind us. ". . . Yes," I say slowly.

Tullea gives me a skeptical look.

But I don't respond to it, because I finally see—really see—what surrounds us. All the plants along the street have shriveled. A tree stands hollowed out. Two beggars have collapsed on the cobblestones. A woman crouches over them. "They're not breathing!" she says, her voice shrill with fear.

I drew on energy as I ran to make my magic, not even wondering what it was. Tullea drew on energy to create her illusions. And this is what we've done.

Realization hits her at the same time. She grabs my elbow. We exchange a single, terrified glance. We should help, somehow. We should fix this. But how do we fix what we've destroyed, without more destruction?

The woman in the street is pointing at us. "It was them!"

Tullea yanks on my arm, pulling me into motion. We run, Irene's weight heavy on my shoulder. I clamp persuasion around us, this time careful to use only my own power. My gut roils, from effort and guilt. Perhaps the beggars will yet survive. But I may never know.

Finally, the bulk of Solivetos Hill lurches up between the buildings before us. We duck inside, stopping at last.

My throat is tight. I've injured people in my own city—innocents— and now, once again, I've lost Rayka. I should have run for him when I had the chance. I wish he'd come to me. But I will lie for him, anyway. I will take the blame for all the deaths, the injuries, the damaged plants. I'll kept his secret, because that is the one thing I can do for my brothers, whether they know it or not.

I CARRY IRENE up into the heart of the temple, placing her carefully on a burlap sack beneath the dome. Sabina flings herself down beside her, gripping her hand tight, kissing her forehead. "It's going to be all right," she's whispering.

But Irene took a lead ball to the gut. It's not going to be all right. Her eyes stare, glassy, at the ceiling. Crimson blood is already soaking through the bandage wrapping her abdomen.

I rub my hands through my hair. All the gods. The woman needs a surgeon to save her, or laudanum to help her go.

"We need a physician," I tell Tullea.

She's already shaking her head. "We haven't had one among us since Leukos died. And to bring someone here . . ."

The streets will be crawling with witch hunters and militia by now. We needed to have taken precautions for medical help before launching our attack, not now. Not when it's almost too late. Not with the whole city out for my blood.

I look at the sweat slicking Irene's staring face. We all knew the risk we took. But it's different to see it claiming her. Difficult not to think of Finn, of the carnage on that battlefield in Caeris. Of the beggars in the street, and the witch hunters Rayka killed without remorse. Impossible not to think of Elanna, whose corpse I never even saw, who died without me. She would want me to save Irene. She would tell me to do something.

But in the end, there's nothing to do but crouch on Irene's other side. I take her hand. It's even clammier, the pulse weak in her wrist. But she grips back, ever so slightly.

Sabina looks at me. Tears stand out in her eyes. "We're in a holy place. The gods should lend their aid. I'm begging them, Jahan."

I swallow hard. She does know Tirisero is the god of lost battles, doesn't she? "Sometimes the gods are deaf."

Sabina looks away, and I see her throat work, swallowing down a sob.

Damn it all. Why did Madiya teach us to heal ourselves, but no one else? I remember the thin, useless magic I attempted on Finn. It was already too late. I have never been able to save anyone. Not even El.

And yet . . . my eye catches the stone carvings on the font. The god Tirisero presses his hand to a fallen woman's chest, and in the next panel, she rises, whole.

All the hairs rise on my arms. He's the god of losers. The god of cripples and the wounded in battle. The god of unanswered prayers. The god of wretchedness, of inexplicable cruelties, of unhealed af-flictions. The god of unfulfilled hopes.

The god whose worship was abandoned after Paladius the First's conquest of Ida. The god who, we're told, ruled the senate and lost battles, no longer necessary since Paladius was famously invincible.

But what if that's not the truth or even a fraction of it? Once again, I feel an awareness, similar to the stone circles in Caeris and Eren. What happens if I open the lid of the font?

Irene's breathing is shallow. Her lips move, but she can't speak. Sabina no longer troubles to hide her tears.

"We're sorcerers," she whispers. "Our magic ought to be able to do something, but . . ."

Maybe it can.

And if it doesn't, if its power somehow destroys me, then I'll have died trying. I'll have died sparing Eren from war, as much as I can, and trying to save at least one life.

I stand and approach the font. *The secret flame unified with the deep water, the heart of Tirisero.* Maybe it's a riddle about magic: the god who could transform into a bird, who could embody fire itself.

Pantoleon and Nestor couldn't shift the lid of the font; they said it was sealed. But maybe that's because they tried to open it the ordinary way.

Maybe they needed to use *magic*.

Open, I whisper with my mind, but the lid remains closed, hard and fast. I glance at Irene; she's breathing shallowly. I don't have much time. If it's a riddle about magic, then perhaps it's a clue as to how magic can open it.

Fire, first. I touch the font, the cool stone gritty under my fingers, and reach for the memory of fire contained in the stone. It seems unlikely—it's stone, after all, it's not flammable—but then I feel it, a sudden shift, a heat wrapping around the font's inner circle, underneath the lid.

Gritting my teeth against too much hope, I reach for water. It surges up. Of course—the font is a well, reaching deep, deep into the earth.

Fire and water. I hold them both in my mind, two opposites embodied in the font. Now for *the heart of Tirisero.* I touch the carven man's chest, but nothing happens. I don't sense a divine presence. There's just me and the fire and water ready for my command, and the woman dying on the floor behind me.

I try whispering the words aloud. *"The heart of Tirisero."* Nothing, again. I clench my hands at my chest, sagging with tiredness. Maybe it was a fool's hope. My ancestor could have opened the font—he would have known how. He would be ashamed of his legacy. Ashamed of my failure.

I lower my head. "I'm sorry, Mantius."

Sabina gasps behind me. My eyes fly open. The lid of the font has lifted upward on unseen hinges, leaving a palm-sized gap between it and the font's rim, where fire has burst to life.

Fire, and power. Power roars from the font, up through the depths of the well, funneled as strongly as any of the stone circles in Caeris and Eren. My mouth's open. But there's no time to stop and wonder. No time to question how I did it. This is something I can use. Or at least, I can try.

I drop back beside Irene, clasping her hand. Her eyelashes flutter. I reach for the power contained in the font, pulsing there, tangible now under the cracked mosaic, vibrating into the very walls around us. I am suddenly more awake than, it seems, I have ever been. Golden power rushes into me. I'm aware of my own body like a vessel into which gold light is being poured. I can feel my own beating heart, the roar of my own blood. I realize I can sense Irene's body, too, coiled like a mess of darkening crimson knots, and beyond it Sabina's, burdened with grief. Even in my inner vision, Irene's wound throbs, a steadily dimming light.

I reach for it. And I hear myself whisper aloud the words Madiya taught me long ago. "Knit together, nice and snug, smooth and strong, casting out all harm . . ."

Nothing happens. Sabina's head jerks up. She stares at me as if I've lost my mind. Perhaps I have, to recite something so childish aloud and imagine it might work, even with the power coursing through the very earth under my feet.

But then I feel it. The pulsing energy of the temple moves into me. It moves *through* me. Heat pours into my hands, radiating, brilliant.

I touch Irene's wound—or rather, the space just above it.

The power *erupts* through me—teeming into her, working and binding and scalding me. I hear a distant voice. It's mine; I'm shouting.

There's something ugly in the wound. Grimy. Wrong. The shot. I reach for it with a command. *Come out.* It's stubborn, but I insist. *Come now.*

It dissolves into powder and pours out of Irene's skin.

Still, power pours through me. My skin seems to be on fire; my insides are dissolving into pulsing light.

A hand on my wrist. "Jahan?"

I squint through tearing eyes. I didn't even know I'd closed them. Irene is sitting up—Irene, who was near death moments ago—looking at me with something between awe and terror. She's alert. The sweat has dried on her face.

"You're healed," I say. The power steadies in me, and then, inexplicably, it rushes out, and I pitch face-first into darkness.

CHAPTER SEVENTEEN

Someone keeps repeating my name.

"*No, Madiya,*" I say.

But there's a hand on my shoulder and I realize the voice is coming from outside myself, not within my own head.

"Sorry, Jahan," Pantoleon says. "We need you."

Every inch of my body aches. It's no use to whisper a healing spell: This is no physical wound, but pure, profound exhaustion. All the same, I force myself to sit up. I'm in the temple chamber, on my rough bed, but I have no memory of getting here. Pantoleon crouches beside me.

"We had to carry you in," he says. "Irene was sure you'd traded your life for hers—that you were dead."

I cough a laugh. "I feel as if I came close. But Irene—is she—?"

"She's fine." Pantoleon pauses. "More than fine. She says she feels better than she has in all her life."

I nod, even as my eyes start to close. I force them open. "That's good."

He looks at me, and even though it's Pantoleon—steady, dependable, unflappable—there is some of the fear and awe I worried I would see. If I explained to him that I don't even know what I did to open the font, he would surely not think it so extraordinary. "You were right," I try to say. "About the font."

"Yes, I see that." He shakes his head. "How did you *know,* Jahan?"

I rub my face. "I don't know. I'm not sure what the key was."

We look at each other, and then he sighs. "I didn't want to wake you, but we have a crisis."

I might have known I wouldn't get a decent night's sleep. "What now?"

He tilts his head. "Don't you hear it?"

"What—" I begin, and then I stop, listening hard. It itches the edges of my hearing.

Bells. A veritable roar of them, endless, ringing all around us. They must be ringing throughout the city, from every tower.

"Witch hunters," I say, and Pantoleon nods. I look at him. "It's not affecting you?"

He shakes his head. "None of us are affected—not here on the hill. But we got a message from Felix, demanding a meeting as soon as possible, away from the hill. He doesn't dare come all the way here. Agapetos went out to send an answer, and as soon as he left the lower gate, he went mad. He almost collapsed. Had to crawl back. He said it was as if the bells were trying to shatter his mind. He's safe now, but . . ."

"It affected him that quickly?"

Pantoleon shrugs, as if I shouldn't be so surprised. "He's resting."

"I'll take a look at him." But why are the rest of them unaffected? "Is the well of magic I opened protecting us?" I can still feel it pulsing through the stones beneath me, throbbing like intangible fire.

"Perhaps." Pantoleon hesitates. "When you opened it . . . *all* of us felt it. Like an explosion of light. You can feel it everywhere on the hill—even in the lower temple. It's as if it's so powerful, it blocks the bells."

I rub my face. "I don't understand it. Someone must have sealed the font and contained the power. I've never seen anything like it. Never *imagined* anything like it."

"Nor have I." Pantoleon eyes the ancient walls. "Whatever it is, at least it's protecting us. It's . . . immense. I feel half drunk with it."

I laugh. "It's cheaper than the Den. Now come, let's find Agapetos."

If I saved Irene's body, perhaps I can soothe Agapetos's mind. But how? I've never done such a thing, or I would have . . . I swallow hard. I touch the ugly ridged scar behind my ear. I would have healed my mother.

But the power here is unlike anything I've ever felt. It pulses in the walls, now, in the earth beneath our feet, insistent, seductive, immense. Maybe it can grant the ability I would once have sacrificed anything for.

"Agapetos is all right now," Pantoleon says gruffly. "It's Felix we need help with. We have a *different* crisis on our hands."

The realization sinks into me. "The witch hunters. The emperor has deployed them . . ."

"No one can get out. We're an island here." Pantoleon pauses. "And—even with our protections—they could still find us."

I rub my forehead. Someone has to venture into the city, to see what's come of our attack. The others are stuck here, but I'm immune to the bells. I can go.

We've emerged outside. It's night, and smoke from distant chimneys fogs the stars. The city seethes around us, alight. And for once in my life I feel a cold fear of going out into it. Of discovering what we've done. What action the emperor has taken in retribution.

I can't charm my way out of this. I have to face it. This is my city, there are my people; this is what we're fighting for.

"I'll go," I say to Pantoleon. "I'll check the defenses and meet with Felix."

He nods. "He's at the Den. Wants you there at ten." He pauses, as if to add more, but in the end merely clasps my shoulder. He swallows, and I pat his arm. It seems like I should say something, but no words are adequate. I'm grateful we're friends again. It sounds too simple, in light of all that's happening. Yet it's true.

I squeeze Pantoleon's shoulder and hope that, somehow, the gesture conveys everything I mean it to. Then I turn and slowly walk down the long steps, into the city.

EVEN IMMUNE TO their cruelty, the constant tolling of the bells sets me on edge. I ghost through the streets, a shadow among shadows— only my shadow has a pounding heartbeat and sweating palms. Exhaustion dogs me, especially after I strengthened the defenses at the lower temple, but I shove it back. Some of the energy from the font lingers in my sternum, a giddy spark warring with the grittiness of my eyes and the tension in my shoulders.

The streets hum with activity despite the late hour—and not only with activity, but with witch stones. The sound is so dense even ordinary people must feel the insistent racket. It's going to be a long walk to the Den.

Noise erupts on a street in front of me. I fling myself back against a wall. A man shouts. I creep forward.

A throng of imperial soldiers and city watch—and witch hunters— knot the street. They've surrounded someone; they're struggling to subdue him. In the jogging light, as they move, I glimpse a man with a sack over his head.

"I'm *not*!" he shouts, his voice muffled. "Ask anyone! I'm *not*—"

Someone socks him in the gut and he doubles over, silenced. They wrestle him into a waiting cart. Chains rattle as they secure irons around the man's wrists and ankles.

I stand frozen. Other people are already chained in the cart, sacks over their heads, irons clamping their wrists. Two women, another man.

I should have known Alakaseus Saranon would turn our rebellion into an excuse for a city-wide witch hunt. If he can't get my people, he's arresting anyone he can clamp hands on. Innocents, in all likelihood. No one will ever know whether these people are sorcerers or not; the witch hunters don't trouble to conduct public trials. Or any trials, so far as I know. Where are they taking them? The Frourio prison, here in Ida—or the Ochuroma, north of Aexione?

With the latest prisoner loaded, the convoy moves on. I need to go to the Den—I have to make the meeting with Felix—but I'm halted by my own cowardice. I'm willing to run and let these innocents suffer the blame for what *I've* done?

I flex my hands. I'm tired, and the magic isn't likely to come easy, even with the lingering spark of the font in my chest. If I make a show of force, they'll probably only crack down harder.

I stalk after the convoy, keeping to the shadows. They stop again, a few streets later, to roust a drunk from an alley. He fights hard, viciously, but they subdue him with a few swift clubs to the legs and gut. Then he's in the cart, the irons binding his limbs.

There's a lull. The guardsmen and witch hunters gather in a knot, arguing over where to go next. The people sit huddled in the cart.

My magic is such a tired, aching thing, after healing Irene and destroying the fleet. I can't take down all the witch hunters and guards, and the last thing I want is to make matters worse. Still. A small thing might be enough.

I slip past the men, holding my breath, though of course none of them notice me. I slide up beside the wagon and tug a woman's sleeve through the iron bars. "Don't run yet," I whisper. "Choose your moment."

Then I gather all their irons in my mind and break the fastenings. The clatter is lost beneath the echo of the tolling bells and the rattle of the small, tinkling ones the witch hunters carry.

I turn to run.

But there's a noise in the street—a newcomer—no, three of them, on horseback. A lantern flashes over their leader's face.

It's Alcibiades Doukas.

As if he feels my gaze, he glances up. He *sees* me.

Have I lost my mind as well as my grip on my sorcery? I bolt.

"Seize that man!" Alcibiades shouts behind me. Did the old bastard recognize me, even in the dark with my growing mess of a beard? Or did he simply see my shape and movement, and suspect?

It doesn't matter. I pound down an alley, struggling to compress space, but I'm only thrown forward a few feet, too drained to propel myself farther. I stagger gracelessly into a wall. There are torches and shouts behind me. I push myself through the fabric of the wall— slow, too slow—and stumble into someone's back garden. I charge through a door into the silent house. It's a useless struggle to muffle my footsteps. Out in the street—largely deserted—I sprint flat-out, a shadow flying among shadows. A beggar sits up to watch me pass.

I seem to have shaken my pursuit. Only distant shouts echo behind me. My lungs burn but I don't stop running until I see the lights of the Den.

And the party of militia outside it.

I slow. There's a witch hunter among them—I can tell by the infernal tinkling of bells—and, like the party I followed earlier, they have a cart filled with several people.

I rub a hand over my chin. Is Felix even here? Knowing him, this kind of danger would only seem a thrill, so I suppose he is. He's probably watching the witch hunters with a smirk from some place of safety.

Careful to keep the shadows about me, I retrace my steps to the nearby alley. I'll go into the Den by the back door—which, fortunately, is guarded only by the compost heap. I slip into the back of the tavern, then through the door to the cellar stairs, sagging in relief to find the cellar empty.

Voices murmur on the other side of the secret door. I let myself in.

"Jahan!" Felix jumps up from the table, his hat askew. "We didn't know if any of you would make it tonight. Did you run into the militia? The witch hunters are everywhere!"

"I made it," I say. Absently, because I'm staring at his companion.

"Jahan!" the man is saying. "What a relief! I should have brought—" But he catches himself and shakes his head, grinning. It's Bardas Triciphes, of all people. He looks impossibly clean, impossibly well groomed, in a black velvet suit. Rings wink on his fingers.

"We thought you were dead," he's saying, "or that you'd fled back to Eren. I admit I almost didn't recognize you beneath the beard. Felix, I can't believe you kept this secret from us!"

"What are you doing here?" I ask. "How do you know you're not under suspicion?"

He waves a hand. "His Imperial Majesty has never taken me seriously—my blood isn't blue enough. And he can't believe anyone—ah—*close* to him might be guilty of indiscretion."

The empress, he means. I suppose it's true, but we both know perfectly well that Augustus and Phaedra don't suffer any such shortsightedness where the Triciphes are concerned. They would relish the opportunity to destroy their stepmother.

Bardas is frowning at me, concerned. "Didn't the bells trouble you?"

I'm not about to confess my secret, so I just raise my eyebrows. I settle down at the table, reaching for the jug of beer. "Not *significantly*. But a little jot of madness is healthy in a person, don't you think?"

"Well, we must praise the gods we tracked you down at last," he says. "Thank you, Felix, for arranging this meeting."

"Since I'm here," I say, "how can I help you?"

Bardas taps his fingers on the scuffed table, a thinking gesture. "We can't risk the Saranons continuing on their current path. It was brave of you to destroy the ships—a bold statement. All of Ida's talking of you."

Felix grins at me—pleased with himself for spreading the news effectively—but I feel less warmth. I watch Bardas, and sip the beer.

"It was brave," he says again, "but now the witch hunters are rounding up people across the city. You encountered them, I'm sure. You've made yourselves targets—not only you, but anyone who seems mildly suspicious. You're going to get caught, and you'll be taken to the Frourio with the rest of them."

I must be staring. So they are keeping the prisoners in Ida. "That sounds a lot like a threat."

"It's a fact. The emperor has more men and more power, and your sorcerers are simply not powerful enough to stop him."

"We destroyed the fleet," I point out. "No one's discovered us yet."

He lifts an eyebrow. "They'll be looking much harder now. You need help."

I hear Felix draw in a breath. I'm thinking of Alcibiades Doukas on the streets with his men; of the people shackled in the wagons, their heads covered. Bardas is right, of course—it *could* be us. But even if Felix trusts him, I don't understand this.

"Why?" I say. "Why help? Why put yourselves at such risk?"

His gaze shifts back and forth before settling on mine. "Because we believe in reform, the same as you."

I'm sure he does. But I'd also bet my life that he's withholding some other secret.

"We're prepared to offer supplies. Food." He grins. "Razors. We can funnel you munitions, of a limited variety—"

I fling up a hand. "We're not starting a civil war!"

He looks incredulous. "Then what are you doing, Jahan? Do you think the emperor will simply come around to your point of view, after he tried to execute you and now you've destroyed his ships and killed his men?"

I stare down at my hands. The knuckles are still crusted with Irene's blood. "I will not condone the murder of innocent Idaeans."

Bardas looks at Felix, who doesn't offer help, then lets out an exasperated sigh. "We do agree on one thing, do we not? That the Saranons will never accept our reforms?"

Felix nods. But I think of Leontius, who talks more easily with common people than courtiers, who befriended a boy from the backwater Britemnos Isles. "Leontius . . ."

"Leontius Saranon has not spoken a single word in your defense since you left for Eren," Bardas says with increasing impatience. "If he's open to reform, he might have damned well let us know by now. Unless you know something I don't?"

"No." I can't point to any one thing. But I know Leontius isn't like Augustus and Phaedra, or like his father. There's a gentleness to him that he tries to hide beneath silence and disinterest. Even though he's rejected our friendship, I still can't shake the belief that if I could just talk to him, I could make him understand my point of view.

But there's no point arguing this with Bardas. He's saying, "Very well, then. We can also offer information—the emperor's orders, his plans. And"—he glances significantly at Felix—"we have ways to disseminate *your* information. We—"

He stops, his head cocked. "What do you—" Felix begins, but Bardas lifts a finger for silence.

I listen. At first all I hear are the other two shifting in their chairs. Their breathing. None of us speak.

Then I hear it. A rattle out in the cellar. A voice. "What do you keep down here?"

A bell clangs softly.

I'm out of my seat in a moment, moving silently to the door. There's no question they'll find it, if they're looking, but if they haven't seen it yet, I might still have time. I press my hands to the wood, dragging up energy from the pit of my stomach. *There's nothing here but a wall. Smooth blank stone.*

Even through the wood, I can feel the witch stones humming. They must have raided an entire quarry of the damned things.

Behind me, the others have risen to their feet. Bardas mouths, *Sorcery? Safe?* But I don't know what to tell him.

Footsteps scrape on the other side of the door. I *insist,* yet at the same time I feel it slipping, as if the witch stones are repelling my magic. Sweat trickles down my forehead. It would be foolish, and embarrassing, to be caught like this, like a rat in the basement of the Den. I'm not going to let these bastards take any of us again.

"There's a door here," a man's voice says on the other side. It's a voice I know, prim and overbearing. The witch hunter Quentin.

Felix comes up beside me. He makes a twisting motion with his hand.

I turn the latch on the door, muffling the sound with my magic. It still *snick*s faintly.

"Is someone in there?" Quentin demands. He rattles the doorknob. It holds. "Open this!"

I back away from the door, much good though it does me. There's no other exit. Once they force the door, we'll be trapped in here, sitting ducks for the witch hunters to claim. Won't they be pleased to get the Korakos, the leader of the New Republic, *and* the empress's troublesome cousin?

I turn to the others, but they're both looking at me. As if I have any better idea than they do how to save our skins.

In the cellar, someone says, "I'll have to find the key."

"Well, hurry!" Quentin retorts.

We have a little time, then. I study the cellar: stone walls, dirt floor. If we walk through the walls, we'll only end up in the earth, and I'm not sure how far I can transport myself and two others.

But if we go out a different way . . . The ceiling is also made of old damp-looking stone. "What's above us?" I whisper.

The other two also stare up. "The pantry, I think," Felix answers.

There shouldn't be any witch hunters in the pantry, unless they're keen to examine jam jars. And even if Felix is wrong, we'll be found out just the same as we would be here.

"I'll go first," I whisper. I climb up on the table. The ceiling is low; I can touch it without even extending my arms fully. Carefully, I nudge aside the particles that make up the cold stone. I push one hand through. Nothing happens—I feel only warm air—so I shove the other through, then work my elbows up onto the stone. I pull myself up, feeling the buzz in my head as I clear through the particles.

I'm in a dark room. It smells of spices. Nearby, someone's banging pots.

With a heave, I pull myself all the way up, then turn around to help the others through. I don't hear any witch stones, but the bells outside are still tolling. And if they're in the basement, they'll be elsewhere, too. I pull up Bardas first, then Felix. Just as his feet clear the floor, I hear the key rattling in the lock below. Felix bursts up with a gasp.

"Shh," I say, but Felix shakes his head.

"We can get out through the kitchen. Come on."

Without pausing to listen for witch hunters or guardsmen, he dashes out. I run after him. Someone's got to save Felix from himself.

Workers bustle in the kitchen. A boy turns to scold Felix but ends up simply gaping as Felix rushes past him. I pause, glancing back for Bardas. He's still in the pantry, hesitating. Felix bursts away out the back door. I look back and forth between the two of them. But Bardas is hiding a secret. I know it.

I turn back to the pantry. "Just going to my coach," Bardas says, eyeing the hubbub of the kitchen. People must be staring, though when I look back they pretend not to see me. "It's at the front—by the stable. Lend a hand?"

I collar the boy who stared at Felix. "Which wall lets onto the stable?"

He just points, still gaping. I gesture for Bardas to follow, and stride through the sink—the dishwoman exclaims—and the wall behind it. I nearly collide with the backside of a horse. It sidles, but I edge past, murmuring to it, softening it with persuasion. *Nothing to trouble you, just a friend here.*

Then we're in the stables, and Bardas lunges for an unmarked coach waiting outside. He waves at me in thanks, barking orders at the coachman. "Home! Now!"

I hesitate. I should get back to Solivetos Hill, but Bardas is hiding something; I know it like a whisper down the back of my neck. I just can't put my finger on what it is. Or maybe I just don't want to surrender to this niggling hope. I need to get back. I have to tell Tullea and the others what's happened.

Yet as the driver urges the horses out, I see that the back of the coach is empty. Bardas didn't bring a footman. I find myself charging forward. I hop lightly onto the back of the coach, clinging to the bar that runs across it. *Nothing more than a shadow. A loose cobblestone jolting from the coach.*

The vehicle picks up speed through the quiet streets. Wind streams through my hair. It feels a little like freedom. We rattle across the Middle Bridge, into Vileia. My hands have begun to ache from clenching the bar, but the Deos Deorum rises before us now, an edifice of shadowed galleries and darkened windows.

I hop down as the coach slows, coming through a back gate. *Nothing more than misplaced darkness.* I wait while Bardas disembarks and pauses to chat with the driver, and I begin to wonder if I shouldn't have come. Or, perhaps, if I should step out and greet him. Confess.

Before I can, he strides away into the house. I hurry after, following the shallow light of his taper into a small courtyard, then through an open doorway and up a flight of stairs. No servants appear, and the tension between my shoulder blades eases. He did come in secret, then; no one but his coachman seems to even know he left.

He stops at a door and lets himself through. I glimpse bookshelves and the warm glow of many candles before the door closes behind him. Cautiously, I approach.

On the other side of the door, voices rise. I press my ear against the wood, brushing aside the particles so I can hear clearly.

". . . left me here!"

A woman's voice. Light. Accented. An *Ereni* accent.

I must have misheard. I *must* have.

"I told you, it's too dangerous!" Bardas is saying. "If we were stopped, you'd have been recognized. Besides, you've been so unwell."

"We're allies. Allies don't trick each other. They don't leave the other one behind without even *telling* her where they're going."

I know that voice. I know it better than any sound on earth.

But this is impossible. She's dead.

I've fallen against the door, my hands bracing me up. A din is ringing in my ears, louder than any bells, but I can feel every dull thud of my heart.

". . . found them," Bardas is droning on, "and then witch hunters surprised us and we had to run. If they'd caught us, you'd be dead and so would I." He pauses. "I have some news you're going to like. About who came to the meeting."

No. I push myself upright. No, he doesn't get to tell her. That's my job.

I fumble my way through the fabric of the door, into the library's warmth. She's standing in front of the fire, a woman with tawny-brown skin and riotous chestnut hair, her hands on her hips. She's wearing a delicate mauve gown. It has *ruffles*.

A noise bursts from my throat. Laughter, I realize, only slightly hysterical. I seem so far from my body. They both turn, startled.

"I should have known," I'm saying, "that if you came to Ida, you'd find the latest fashions."

Because, of course, it's Elanna.

CHAPTER EIGHTEEN

"Jahan," she whispers. She's shaking. The ruffles quiver.

"El." This is no simulacrum. This is *her*, fierce, bright-eyed. *Alive*.

I start to step forward, but before I can cross to her, she runs to me. Her arms close around my neck. I hug her tight against me, not caring that Bardas Triciphes is here, not caring what he sees or what he thinks. She presses against me, whispering my name over and over. I bury my face in her hair, drinking in her warmth, the feel of her. She's alive. Somehow, she survived.

Here, in the Deos Deorum. With Bardas Triciphes. Who didn't so much as mention, in the conversation we just had, that he knew anything of her whereabouts. Or that she even lived.

Gently, reluctantly, I release her. She lets go of me at the same moment, as if the same realization has occurred to her. She's wearing a new necklace, I see, a thick silver choker. It looks heavy against the mauve gown. But she's *here*.

Bardas has closed his mouth. He's fiddling with his coat cuffs. "I suppose I shouldn't ask how you got in here . . ."

"*I* might ask why you didn't mention any of this," I retort. I feel out of breath. I can't believe she's standing before me. I want to touch her again, to reassure myself it's real. That she's real.

Bardas looks at the ceiling, as if it might offer him some excuse. "Maybe I hoped to avoid this scene," he mutters. "We had to think things through. Act carefully."

I can't believe this nonsense. "You mean you had to *lie* to me?"

"You claim we're allies!" Elanna rears up, hands back on her hips. "But you didn't tell Jahan they never executed me?"

Bardas winces in the face of our mutual anger. "It was an *omission,* not a lie . . ."

"We've spent days hoping he's alive!" Elanna gestures at me. "You know how much he matters to me. Didn't I tell you, if there was one thing you should do, it was to find Jahan and *let him know I lived*?"

"He didn't cooperate the first time," Bardas retorts. "He grabbed the simulacrum and ran off with it—"

"Because I thought you'd all been discovered!" I exclaim. "Pantoleon's people told me none of them did it! You said *midnight.* I waited. I wasn't going to leave El to rot. So I showed the entire world I'm a sorcerer, for the sake of a damned simulacrum. If you had just *told* me—"

Bardas throws up his hands. "We couldn't tell you more! What if someone had found the note?"

"They meant to rescue us both at midnight," El's saying at the same time. "Me first, then you. But my mind . . . I couldn't walk. Couldn't think, even to obey commands. They had to carry me out, keeping absolutely silent, then go all the way back for you—but it took too long. By the time they returned, with the simulacrum of you, the witch hunters had found you. I didn't know what had happened—I could hardly talk . . ." She stops, brushing a hand over the collar at her throat. Looks at me. Fiercely, she says, "Jahan, if I'd been in my right mind, this would never have happened."

"Your right mind?" I echo. Cold fear clamps the back of my neck.

"We saved your life," Bardas is pointing out. "Sylvia brought you back from the brink!"

I turn back to El. Lightly, I touch the collar at her throat. She looks at me, her nostrils flared, eyes wide. Brushing her skin makes my body burn.

But I focus on the collar. It's not the one I snapped off in the Hall of Glass. This collar has witch stones embedded in it, three of them at the front, like rough-cut jewels, but these are not for decoration. A faint hum echoes from them. The witch hunters would have had ample opportunity to produce this new collar, after they hauled her into the attic. The *bastards*. How is she functioning with it burrowing into her mind?

"That witch hunter—the grand inquisitor—he put this on me, after you broke the other one off. Said it would silence my tongue." Her voice catches. "I couldn't think. My mind went numb. It was as if it erased who I was. Everything I knew."

She shudders, and I can't hold back anymore. I grip her elbow. She fits her hands over mine, holding me close. "The inquisitor took the manacles off, at least. He said I wouldn't need them anymore." She draws in a breath. "And he was right. I don't know how the poor boy even carried me out."

"Boy?" I say.

She nods. "Sylvia—the sorceress who saved me—she has a boy apprentice who made the simulacrum. He's the one who got me out."

I blink. I don't know any sorceresses named Sylvia, much less ones with heroic boy apprentices. But then, I have closed myself off from Ida's sorcerers. A few days in their company doesn't mean I've learned about everyone.

Bardas coughs. "Yes, Sylvia. She's brilliant. Wonderful."

"I wouldn't be standing if not for her," El says simply. "She came with us back to Ida."

I shake my head, still dazed. "How did you get here? How did you get out of Aexione?"

Elanna and Bardas exchange a glance. "It wasn't easy," he says. "We've used the utmost discretion—bringing Lady Elanna here under cover of the Saranons' recent outing to the city. Oh, yes," he says, in response to my look of surprise, "there's a new play by Orovillo, and practically the entire court has come to see it. Even Prince Leontius is here. Of course, it's also Emperor Alakaseus's opportunity to demonstrate he doesn't fear us . . ."

I raise an eyebrow. "The attack on the harbor didn't send him running?"

"Not yet. But we don't have much time. He'll force Firmina back to Aexione soon, and limit our negotiations. That's why we must act now."

Elanna leans forward, holding my hands harder. "It's all working out, Jahan! I've already signed an agreement with Firmina, in Sophy's name."

I blink at her. An independent agreement with the empress? That means the Idaean Rose isn't simply helping Elanna out of the goodness of her heart. This isn't quite the game I expected Firmina Triciphes to play. And yet, I suppose, if anyone is to claim the crown, it might as well be her. I think of what she said to me in the gardens about her desire to change things—about her true reason for marrying the emperor.

"That's good," I say.

El nods. "It gives me hope. And then Bardas told me you destroyed the fleet . . ." She smiles brilliantly. "Eren's safe, for the moment."

"Have you been in touch with Sophy?"

A haunted look comes into her eyes. "Not yet."

"Lady Elanna has been quite unwell," Bardas reminds us. "She only began walking about yesterday."

Hope warms me. If this Sylvia person can help El, she can help all the sorcerers in the city. It gives us a chance. "Do you know what Sylvia did, to make your mind cope? Perhaps she could help—"

"Oh, Sylvia's quite keen to undermine the witch hunters." Bardas smiles. "I'm certain she'd be glad to proffer her advice, but—ah—perhaps tomorrow. She and the boy will be long asleep by now."

"Of course," I say. But for no reason I can identify, the hair prickles on the back of my neck. I tell myself all sorcerers are keen to undermine the witch hunters. It's not an ambition unique to Madiya and my father.

I turn to El. "You could come back with me. To our camp. That is—if you want to join me."

She smiles at me. It makes her nose wrinkle and her face soften, and warmth floods through me. "Or you could stay here tonight," she says, lifting an eyebrow. "With me."

"That is a tempting offer, madam . . ."

Bardas clears his throat. Elanna's eyes narrow, and I suppress a snicker. "Of course, Jahan, we'd be more than happy to accommodate you."

"Come along." Elanna pulls me along with her, pushing at a bookcase. It's a false door and, within, a narrow staircase twists upward. She pauses there, and slips her smallest finger around mine. She leans against me. Heat burns through me at the softness of her body. Heat—and relief. I thought I had lost her forever. But she's here, and she's whole, and I'm so damned glad I think my heart might burst out of my chest.

"El," I begin.

"Shh." She taps her finger to my lips.

We climb the stairs. Two doors face each other at the top. She points to one and mouths, *"Sylvia's."* The other, she opens. The bedchamber is small and the floor creaks, and I can't help glancing at the bed, swathed in green brocade curtains. A pile of books sits on the table. Windows overlook the dark Channel. It's a far more comfortable hiding place than mine has been.

We look at each other. Alone, at last.

I reach for her. "I'm sorry. I don't know how I could have imagined you were dead."

"I wondered the same about you." She looks up at me. "But I found you now, Jahan."

I raise an eyebrow. "I believe *I* found *you* . . ."

She laughs.

I touch the collar at her neck again, lightly. It's snug; it must be leaving welts. I reach for the fastening with my mind, trying to snap it, but the magic slides away, as if off a smooth surface. The witch stones must be blocking my power—as usual, it seems. I feel myself frowning.

"There's no use trying to break it off," she says. "We've been trying for days. If Sylvia's apprentice can't do it, no one can."

226 → CALLIE BATES

"Your magic," I begin, but she shakes her head.

"Let's not talk about that now. I just want to be here with you." She's smiling in a way I know well.

I lean into her. "Do you suppose Bardas is still below us? Can he hear anything?"

"I honestly don't care." She tugs herself up, wrapping her hands around the back of my neck. I feel for her hips under the folds of her gown and pull her close. Her mouth is hot on mine. Moist.

But her taste is wrong. So wrong I almost gag. It's bitter, yet sweet.

"Jahan? What's the matter?"

I've pulled back from her, a hand clamped over my mouth. Opium. She tastes like opium. "Someone drugged you."

"No," she says, bewildered. "Well, Sylvia has been giving me something. A tonic, to help with my head. I feel so much better after."

"It's opium," I burst out. I'm breathing hard. If I kiss her again, will it bring back the cravings, the ones I struggled to subdue after I came to Aunt Cyra?

Elanna's hand flies to her lips. "Are you sure?"

I nod my head. "I know that taste."

El, seeming to sense that the moment between us can't be regained, goes to the table and pours a glass of crimson wine. She hands it to me, frowning.

I drink. The wine burns the back of my throat. Guilt eats at me. El will think there's something wrong with her, some reason why I don't want to touch her, when the truth is that there's something wrong with me. But I can't find words to put around this fear that's building in my chest. I set down the wine and tear my fingers through my hair.

Fingers touch my elbow. El pulls my hands down and guides me to the bed. We sit together, our shoulders touching. She doesn't say anything. Gently, she pulls me down so that I'm laying my head in her lap.

I close my eyes. This is enough, I tell myself. It *is*. Elanna strokes my arm, and I hug her knees. At some point the dark comfort of sleep overtakes me.

A KNOCK AT the door brings me alert. I don't know how long I slept—minutes, perhaps, no more. El's hand has stilled on my arm. I sit so she can get up and go to the door. It must be Bardas. Couldn't he leave us alone for just a little longer?

The door scrapes. I squint through tired eyes. A boy's voice says, from outside, "We heard you up. She thought you might want a tonic."

I can't breathe. The cold in my legs seems to spike into my heart. I know that voice.

It can't be. There's no way my youngest brother followed me to Ida, but took refuge with Bardas Triciphes. It's a boy's voice, that's all. It's similar.

But I find myself pushing past Elanna and wrenching the door open. And there he is, Lathiel, slight and startled, holding up a guttering candle. We stare at each other. I can't seem to find words. I thought Father had poisoned his mind against me so much that he stayed home. But he's here—in the Deos Deorum?

"What are you doing here?" I say. "Why didn't you come to Aexione?"

Lathiel just looks up at me, wide-eyed. As if he's been caught.

There's a sound beyond him, from the door on the other side of the landing. Another light gleams. And before I even see the halo of her golden hair, or hear her call out, "What is it?" I know who it is. And I can't move. I can't breathe. I'm suffocating here, my heart ricocheting between my ribs.

This is where she is. This is where she's been, all this time.

This is why Lathiel came here—she must have called him, too. He must have stowed away on the *Celeritas*, and gone to find her.

What's she doing here? Does she think Bardas Triciphes will help her realize her ambitions? *Why?*

Then she comes into view, softer than I remembered, smaller, wrapped up in a dressing gown. She's been asleep like an ordinary person, not machinating plots or experimenting on hapless children.

Still, I can't seem to move, even to look at Elanna, who's touching my elbow. I can't look away from the woman approaching us. El's saying something, but I can't hear it over the pounding of my heart.

Then she's close enough to see my face. She lifts her candle. Her eyes are the same blue I remember, as cold as the winter sky.

"Jahan?" It's the voice that has pursued me all the way from Eren. The voice I burned out of my head.

I can't make my mouth form words. I can't make myself ask how she came to be here, or what Bardas thinks he's doing—or how he imagines she will help their cause. I can only whisper one thing.

"Madiya?"

She smiles. The woman who destroyed my mother, who ruined my childhood, who treated me and my brothers as nothing more than experiments, *smiles* at me. As if she's happy to see me. As if she's relieved.

"I knew you didn't mean to cut me from your mind," she says. "Though it was cruel of you. Painful. You should have listened to me sooner. After I helped Elanna—"

She helped Elanna? I finally tear my gaze to El, who's frowning. She tries to explain, "Jahan, this is Sylvia. She's the one who . . ." She stares at Madiya. "Who saved me."

Madiya interrupts. "Where's Rayka? He refuses to answer my summons!"

"No," I say. It seems like the only word that makes sense. I turn to El. "No. She's not your savior. She won't help us. She'll poison you—she'll destroy you. I won't—I can't—"

I grab Elanna's arm. I have to take her. How do I know Madiya hasn't already stolen her memories? How do I know she hasn't already begun to destroy this woman I love? I tug El, but she doesn't move.

"Jahan, we need to talk about this—we need to find Bardas and ask him . . ."

I hear the words come out of El's mouth, but they only rattle around in my head. It's happened already—Madiya has manipulated her. Worked holes in her mind. Maybe El no longer remembers the stories I told her about my childhood. Maybe she thinks that Madiya is trustworthy because she saved her, but Madiya would never do anything out of simple human generosity. No, she'll be using Elanna to further her plan. To destroy the witch hunters. It's all she's ever wanted.

"Come with me." The words seem to come from very far away, though they're mine. "She's going to destroy your mind."

"Jahan," El says, "we need to *talk*—"

"No." I stare from her to Madiya. To Lathiel, watching me with a steady gaze. Of course, Madiya doesn't have the power to create a simulacrum. She needed him to do it for her.

"Jahan." Madiya reaches out, and so does Elanna.

I bolt. She's going to come after. She'll push me down, dribble opium into my mouth. I'll wake up and I won't remember any of this. I'll forget who I am, why I'm here—

There's a staircase in front of me. I run down it, leaving everyone behind. I surge through the deserted halls. Through an empty courtyard. Out, my ears echoing, into the night.

CHAPTER NINETEEN

It's not until I stop at the Middle Bridge, panting, my chest heaving, that I realize what I've done. I abandoned Elanna. I left her there to be manipulated by Madiya. To have holes worked into her memory. To become a person I don't recognize.

Not only her, but Lathiel. I abandoned him once, for six long years; now I'm abandoning him again.

I could go back. I *should*. I pace across the empty street, making a complete circle, once, twice. Fear clutches me by the neck. I am such a coward. I can't face Madiya again. Not depleted, as I am. I need my strength back. I need a plan. If I go back to Solivetos Hill, perhaps I can take power from the Tirisero font. Perhaps that will be enough to save them both.

And if Elanna believes Madiya is her savior, then perhaps I've already lost her. Lost her even more completely than I did when I believed she'd been executed by Emperor Alakaseus.

"Hey! You there!"

I've wandered onto the bridge. A guard is shouting at me from up the street, his voice echoing over the water. Now the guards on the other side of the bridge are looking around.

I gather myself and run, hurtling across the bridge, toward the startled guards. At the last moment, I compress space. I pass through their bayonets and muskets, the scent of pipe smoke and the sturdy texture of their clothes. Then I'm pounding up the street, and they're shouting after me. I compress space again.

But my exhaustion catches up with me, or perhaps my fear. I stumble. If I keep on like this, I'm going to get caught. Already I feel hollow—more hollow than I have in years. And while it almost seems like it doesn't matter anymore, I can't abandon the sorcerers at Solivetos Hill. Madiya knows about them; Bardas will have told her everything. With his influence, it won't take much effort for her to find and suborn them.

I have to keep them safe. I draw the shadows around myself and trot down the street, ignoring the stitch in my side and the raggedness of my breathing.

I dodge two witch hunter patrols before, at last, the pillared temple rises before me. I pass through our defenses—*an empty, abandoned dome*—and stagger to a halt inside.

A figure moves out from an alcove, holding up a lantern. Tullea. Her face is drawn with lack of sleep. "Jahan? Did you see Pantoleon?"

"Pantoleon?" I say stupidly.

"He went back to his apartment. He said he had to get a book—he said he'd realized something. He wouldn't take no for an answer."

"Realized what?"

"I don't know!" She throws up her hands, nearly flinging the lantern at my head. "He just went out!"

"But the bells—they must have driven him mad—"

"You know what he's like, once he gets an idea in his head! He insisted he would be fine. I tried to follow him, but . . ." She swallows hard. "It felt as if the bells were bashing my head in. I couldn't do it, Jahan. Not even for him."

I can feel the weight of her shame—and her fear. She must hate how the bells render her powerless. I glance over my shoulder. Going back out into the street is the last thing I want to do. But I'm not losing Pantoleon now, not after I fought so hard to keep him as my friend. "I'll find him."

"Thank you," Tullea manages, and I can see how much it costs her pride to say the words.

I just nod and go back into the street.

*

IT'S SO LATE now that even the patrols seem to have ceased. The soft scuff of my footsteps is the only sound on the streets. Even the bells have slowed their incessant ringing, coming only on every quarter of an hour—more warning, now, than threat.

I can only guess at what route Pantoleon took back to his apartment. What could possibly have seemed so urgent that he left the safety of Solivetos Hill and braved the streets on this of all nights?

The doorways sit bare even of beggars. Alleys stand empty. I try to swallow down the fear rising in my throat. Why would Pantoleon take such a risk? I want to shake him, the careless bastard.

But it feels good to have something to do. Something beyond running in fear, terrified by the knowledge of Madiya's presence.

I've reached Wisteria Street, and there in the middle of the block is Pantoleon's house. Maybe he made it home and stayed there. It would be safer than risking a return through the streets.

I pass through the front door. I'm so weary it's a struggle to hold the wood particles apart. I creep up the stairs—*only a mouse*—and into my friend's rooms.

Even in near-darkness, I can tell the rooms are a disaster. They appear to have been ransacked. Books and pillows are strewn across the floor. My body thumps hot and cold; I fumble for a candle dropped on the carpet and pull the memory of flame out of its wick. My heart pounds. I'm terrified the light will show me Pantoleon collapsed on the floor, the life run out of him.

But the rooms are empty.

I don't have to guess what happened—the witch hunters found him. But is this a recent ransacking, or is it from days ago, when they first searched his apartment?

Brandy has soaked into the cloth binding several books. I mop it up with an already ruined throw pillow. The liquid's fresh. And Pantoleon, no matter how worried and distracted, would never leave a book to be ruined.

Which means . . .

There's a squeak on the stairs. Then the door flies open. Pantoleon's landlady stands there, brandishing a lantern and a club.

Instinctively, I fling my hands up.

"I'll scream," the landlady says. "I'll wake up the whole block. The watch will come."

"I'm a friend of Pantoleon's," I say, in my most soothing manner. "I'm looking for him."

"At four o'clock in the morning?" She tightens her grip on her club.

"Tell me where he is, and I'll leave you in peace," I say.

Her gaze shifts around the room, studying the fallen books and teacups, coming back to me.

"I'm unarmed," I add. "Although I have been known to slay people with my charm."

The woman's eyes narrow. "You're not a sorcerer. The bells would unhinge you."

Cold washes through my hands.

"Did you know he was a sorcerer?" she demands.

"No!" I force shock, disgust, horror into my tone.

The woman nods. "Yes. He came here all a disaster—I thought him sick with influenza or some such. But he couldn't think to answer the simplest questions. So I called the witch hunter patrol. They came once before, you know, to search his rooms. But he's a wily one—he outfoxed us all. I suspected him of something, though. Heard noises up here at all hours." Lowering her voice, she says in a dramatic whisper, "He's friends with *the Korakos*."

"Ah," I say. Thank the gods for my beard, or she would surely have known me on sight. "Well, that's enough to damn anyone."

"Exactly! This time, he couldn't hide the truth." She waves the club. "They took him, praise the gods. I can't believe I sheltered one such as him." And she spits as if to avert evil.

Pantoleon's own landlady betrayed him. I can't find the words to maintain my charade.

"I'm sorry to trouble you," I manage. "What terrible news."

She moves aside so I can precede her down the stairs, herding me with her lantern and club. "Student, are you? I've seen you before, I think."

"Yes. I've attended Pantoleon's lectures."

I let myself out the front door, in a normal fashion this time. The landlady pauses on the threshold behind me. "They're cleaning up the city," she says with approval. "It'll be safer now."

"Yes," I say. "You never really know your neighbors until something like this happens."

I didn't mean to say that. I start off, walking fast. But the landlady seems oblivious to my true meaning. She calls after me, "If you know of anyone looking for a room, send them to me."

I CAN'T BELIEVE they took Pantoleon. After I always urged him to be careful. After we finally reconciled.

Tullea doesn't even speak after I deliver the news. She simply stands, looking past me, sightless.

I'm the one who can't seem to stop talking. "They took him to the Frourio, at least, not the Ochuroma. As far as we know. He's in the city. He's prepared for this. He's strong . . ."

Eventually Tullea simply walks away from me. I stop, the words hanging out of my mouth. It seems impossible to have failed so much. First the realization that Elanna is still alive, then discovering I failed to save her—and Lathiel—from Madiya. Now this.

It seems like we should still be able to go back to Pantoleon's apartment, find him there, and bring him home.

I drop onto a stone ledge, running my hands through my hair. I need to warn Tullea about Bardas, and tell her that Elanna's alive, and somehow find the words to explain Madiya's presence and what it means and what she's done to me. But all I know is that El is in danger and I ran like a coward. The witch hunters are rounding up anyone they can find on the streets, including my oldest friend. And now Madiya knows where to find us. We must stop the witch hunters, and the emperor, and that's what she's always wanted. It's what she designed my brothers and me to do. It was her great plan, and we were her great work.

There is nothing I want more than to end their order. But still I balk at the idea of giving Madiya the satisfaction, at last, of doing what she's always wanted.

Yet what are they doing to Pantoleon now? How much of his mind have they already destroyed?

Bardas said she had some sort of plan—of course she does. She's been building it for twenty-five years.

"Rayka," I whisper, but as usual, my brother ignores me.

Maybe there's another way. A way to persuade the emperor to change his mind. If someone had the courage to oppose him, not merely in Ida, but in Aexione. In his own household . . .

Leontius is in Ida—he came down for the new Orovillo play. Bardas told me that Leontius has made no public appearances since my arrest. I know better than to assume it's out of some grief for me. More likely he's angrier than ever. But we spent two years being so close. I still can't believe his anger runs so deep that he wouldn't even hear me out, when I found him.

Besides, I still miss him. I want my friend back.

And though Leontius is not a wildly popular public figure, if he joins us it will add undeniable legitimacy to our cause. The emperor's own son and heir opposing him for sorcerous rebels. It will also give Bardas—and Firmina—second thoughts. Lees feels no particular love for his stepmother. I need to try one more time, to get him to hear me . . .

Of course, Alakaseus might simply disown Lees and name Augustus his heir. I push aside the thought. If it comes to that, public sentiment will be so riled up that the emperor's course of action will be far less clear.

I stand. My eyes are gritty with exhaustion, but I can't rest now. Not knowing that Madiya is in the city.

"I'm going to find help," I tell Tullea.

She just nods, but some of the life seems to come back into her. She shakes out her shoulders. "I'll keep Solivetos safe."

"Yes. And if Bardas Triciphes comes calling, turn him away."

"Bardas Triciphes?" she repeats, her eyebrows raised, once more the formidable Tullea I know. "He's helped us, you know. Smuggled us funds to relocate sorcerers."

"Bardas himself might be trustworthy, but I don't like one of his friends. A sorceress who's helping him. She doesn't have anyone's interests but her own at heart."

"Don't most of us?" Tullea says, but then she shrugs. "All right. I'll deny him, or them."

I'm touched that she trusts me. "You'll be glad you did."

"Just come back, Jahan. It's damned inconvenient, you running off all the time."

I flash her a grin and stride away into the streets.

CHAPTER TWENTY

The Old Palace lies on this side of the Channel—fortunately, since I don't much relish crossing one of the bridges again. It's so late—or early—that the bells are tolling only irregularly. The streets are quiet. I stick to the shadows until I come upon the bulk of the palace. All the entrances will be heavily guarded—the principal ones, at any rate, but perhaps not those less well known. I make my way to the lower gate, where I came through the "secret" tunnel with Quentin and Faverus. It seems months ago, though it's been little more than a week.

No witch hunters patrol this gate, and the guards must be watching from above. It's easy enough to slip through the bars—*only a shadow, a bird*—and run on silent feet into the tunnel. I pause, catching my breath, listening for pursuit. Nothing.

I creep through the dark, one hand on the rough stones. Somewhere, there should be an entrance leading up, at least according to the stories. I just hope they're true.

And that Leontius will listen to me this time.

I inch forward. The blackness seems complete, ready to swallow me whole. But this isn't the cave where Madiya experimented on me, and I force my breathing even. The most dangerous thing here, I tell myself, is me.

The wall vanishes under my hand. I've found the entrance. I turn in, blundering into a step, and bang my knee. At least no one seems to be guarding the place. I begin to climb. The steep stairs seem to have been cut for giants; after several turns, my breath is coming rough. But light is seeping in from above. The stairwell ends in a sunken garden, surrounded by the palace's high walls, and the arches of a colonnade.

The sky is gray. It must be nearly dawn, and Leontius is an early riser. I just have to find his rooms.

Through the colonnade, I find a hall. More stairs lead to a familiar corridor, though it's quieter than I've ever seen it. There's a distant rattle, a servant dropping firewood, perhaps. I stay close to the walls, ready to work persuasion if I must, but no one approaches. At last, around the next corner, I find the door to my friend's chambers. I draw in a breath. I shouldn't be nervous—we're *friends*—but then again, I suppose I am a disgraced favorite, the thing Aunt Cyra always warned me against becoming.

I walk through the fabric of the door.

The sitting room is warm. Wide windows overlook the harbor below. Leontius sits in a chair below them, intent on his reading. It's *The Journal of Botanical Studies*. I want to laugh. Elanna reads it with almost as much passion as he does.

Instead I clear my throat. I feel myself starting to smile.

His head comes up. He opens his mouth. For a moment, I think he's going to summon the guards. Then he lowers his head and his nostrils flare. "You."

So much loathing, compressed into a single word. I take a step backward despite myself. I've never seen Leontius so angry—and certainly not at me.

Maybe I shouldn't have come.

"How did you—" he begins, then cuts himself off. "No, I don't want to know how you got in. Tell me something." He draws in a breath. It quivers. I realize he's trembling, as if he's afraid and angry at the same time. As if *I've* frightened him.

I hold out my hands. "Lees—"

"The Getai," he bursts out. "Tell me. After they attacked us— I didn't hit my head, did I? That's not why I don't remember it."

I freeze, hands still open.

"And you," he says. "You didn't go berserk."

It's not a question, but I find myself nodding, though more than anything I want to disappear. Unravel this conversation. Make Leontius forget I ever came.

But I already made him forget, once. I did to him what I swore I would never let Madiya do to me again. When the Getai attacked, I acted without thought. I seized the power in all our bodies and compressed space so I stood in front of Leontius. The power drained some of the Getai; a few of our attackers collapsed. I flung persuasion at the rest of them—pure fear.

And I rammed my elbow into Leontius's ribs, shoving him onto the ground. It stunned him. In the chaos, everyone thought he'd suffered a concussion. They didn't think, when I cupped my hands around his head, that I was doing anything other than feeling for injuries.

"You stole my memories," Leontius whispers.

I look away, blinking at the flames in the fireplace. I should never have come. "I—"

"But there were *witnesses*," Leontius says. His hands curl and uncurl at his sides. "We wrote up *reports*. You must have stolen all their memories."

"No, no," I say, and my idiot tongue starts babbling, so relieved that this accusation, at least, I can deny. "I worked persuasion on them—so much persuasion—I made them think they'd just seen me go mad. It's not real sorcery, it's just a way of tricking the perception—"

I fall silent at his look of horror.

"You *tricked* them?" he whispers.

"It was easy to do—no one recognized what they saw—no one *expected* me to perform sorcery . . ."

"Is this what you always did?" he says, and with a gasp, "It *is*. You made the commander look the other way. Everyone. You did it to *everyone*—to my father . . ."

My hand reaches automatically for my scar. I shove it back down.

"Were we ever friends?" Leontius demands. "Or was that merely more *persuasion*?"

I stare at him. "No, Lees. The last thing I would ever have done is wanted—is persuaded—" I can't seem to say it without damning myself. "I never wanted the scrutiny of being your friend! No sorcerer wants that."

"You seemed to endure it well enough," he says coldly. He glances at the door. "I should summon the witch hunters. I should have you taken from here in chains."

"Why don't you?"

"Because you're my only friend!" he shouts at me, then stops, his chest heaving, flinching as if we've been discovered.

"No one heard," I say quietly. "I muffled the sound."

"What a convenience it must be, to do such things," he says bitterly. "Don't the bells and stones bother you?"

"No."

"Convenient," he mutters again.

We stare at each other for a long moment.

"Lees," I begin, "we *are* friends. I would never persuade anyone into friendship with me—don't you think I'd work sorcery on you now, if I were so unscrupulous? But we are true friends, and that is why I'm here."

Again, his nostrils flare with anger. "I've seen how you treat your friends."

I blink. What is he talking about? Pantoleon? Elanna? But he doesn't even know them.

"*Finn.*" Leontius flings the name at me. "Have you already forgotten him so quickly? He *died* for you."

"What are you *talking* about?"

"You dragged him off to Eren to be a hero! So you could find your sorceress or whatever she is! And he *died*. You killed him."

My grasp on reality seems to be spinning; I brace a hand on a chair. Carefully, I say, "Finn's father killed him, if anyone did. I certainly never forced him to go to Eren."

"But you *went*! You treated it as if it would be a grand adventure!

Then he *died,* and you—you—" He stops, covering his mouth with both hands.

I'm staring. I close my mouth. How blind have I been to this? *Finn* is why Leontius wouldn't speak to me? Finn Dromahair, of all people?

"I knew you were taking him into danger," he says softly. "But I couldn't stop you."

I rub my forehead. "Leontius, did Finn—did you—?"

He utters a sour laugh. "What do you think? Listen, you can't even say it."

"There's nothing wrong with it. Finn was charming. He—he would have been flattered, to know you regarded him with such affection."

"Flattered?" Leontius says. "You don't need to lie to me, Jahan. He preferred women."

"Why didn't you ever *tell* me?"

"Because I'm not pathetic," he retorts.

"Having . . . a regard . . . for someone isn't pathetic."

"It is if you know they'll never look back at you the same way." He glares at the window. "There! Have I humiliated myself enough for you?"

I shake my head. "You know that's not why I'm here."

He scoffs. "You just happened to be in the area, while running from the law, and thought you'd drop in. Am I right? Isn't that what Jahan Korakides would say?"

"Clearly you know me better than I know myself."

He gives me a sharp look. "You've become just like the rest of them. Or maybe you were always like them, and I didn't see it."

I wince.

"You *want* something," he spits. "And I bet I know what it is, too! You want me to intercede with Father on behalf of those criminals in the Frourio, don't you?"

"Most of them are innocents—"

"No one cares!" Leontius bellows. "No one cares whether they turned a damned elephant into a crocodile. It's all for show, the whole damned thing. I don't know why you think Father would listen to *me*. Maybe if I put on a mask and pretended to be Augustus, he would."

"But you're his son and heir! You will be emperor one day. This is your chance to stand up for a cause. To make your mark."

Leontius snorts. "And give Father the perfect opportunity to disinherit me? No. You *know* him. He would be thrilled. He's been looking for an excuse to get rid of me for years."

"If you allied with us, we would support you against him."

He stares at me, and I feel the opportunity—and our friendship—slipping out of my hands.

"He would haul me away in chains," Leontius says. "He would have me examined by witch hunters. He'd exile me, then, because no father wants his own son's blood on his hands, not even mine. And you know what? I'd do it. I'd go into exile. I could have a garden, and no one would ever trouble me. Except that would leave the empire to Phaedra and Augustus. And I won't do that to my people."

I don't know what to say.

He turns and picks up the journal. Over his shoulder, he says, "That will be all."

It's a dismissal, but I'm too stupid with shock to accept it. "Lees, at least let me know our friendship—"

"We were friends once," he says. "Or I thought we were. But we aren't anymore, and I won't be manipulated by anyone, not even you."

"Not even when your father is doing something utterly abhorrent?" I say.

"I'm playing the long game," he replies, "for all of Paladis, not just to make a onetime stand that will get me killed or exiled. You should go now. Or I'll be forced to summon the guards."

I look at his back. My friend, so shy, so retiring, now implacable. I want to touch his shoulder and ask how I can help him change this. I want to tell him he can't let his grief and anger harden his heart.

"I mean it, Jahan," he says.

So I go.

CHAPTER TWENTY-ONE

In the corridor, a man in fine clothes is striding toward me. Zollus Katabares. *No one to see here,* I insist. He frowns and blinks, but swerves past me and lets himself into Leontius's chamber with a soft knock.

It galls me that Lees will keep rigid, traditional Zollus by his side, but he won't listen to me. And it makes me feel far worse that, all this time, it was Finn he held a regard for. Maybe I would have done things differently if I'd known—maybe I would have tried harder to save him, or to at least let Leontius know what happened myself. But I can't walk back on the past. What's done is done.

I make my way back through the palace, more carefully now, and back out through the tunnel.

A voice whispers into my mind. *Jahan.*

It's Lathiel.

I almost answer him. Almost shout, *Lathiel!* But I hesitate. I may have burned Madiya out, but she can still force my little brother to contact me. Is he acting of his own accord, or as her pawn?

It galls me, but I can't answer. Not until I have a plan. But I don't know how I can make a plan, with only the sorcerers on Solivetos Hill to help me.

No, I have more resources than that. I have Elanna, if I can muster the courage to rescue her and find a way to break that damned collar off her neck.

And I have my brother Rayka. If I can find him.

Rayka. I draw on all the power in me, and the lingering spark from Tirisero's font. I make it a command. *Rayka.*

At first there's nothing. But then, like a reluctant spark, I *feel* him. He doesn't say my name. He doesn't even seem to be coming toward me; he's resisting, as usual. But it doesn't matter. Now that I sense him, I can find *him.*

I stride out, repeating his name, until the spark turns into a flame. It pulls me forward, across a square, to a temple whose graceful façade gleams in the sunlight angling over the rooftops behind me. I duck through the door, avoiding the beggars sleeping in the vestibule, and let the flame of Rayka's presence pull me through an atrium. There's a door here—locked—but that proves no impediment. I walk through, staggering as my feet hit stairs. I ease my way down. My outstretched hands hit a rusted gate. Somewhere on the other side, Rayka's presence flares brightly.

I pass through the rusted iron. The ground evens out. I seem to be alone in the dark. Somewhere, water drips. The sound raises the hairs on the back of my neck. I can hear my own breathing, too loud. I'm flung back to my childhood, to the steps leading down to Madiya's cave, to waking on the stone table, not knowing what had been taken from me—

But then a soft orange glow blooms over the pockmarked stone some distance from me.

I gulp in a breath. I'm not alone. I see my brother. I *hear* him. He's whispering, *There is nothing here to see.*

Rayka's persuasion has always been more like marching orders.

I step forward. Even though the old fear still trembles inside me, I'm smiling. He's here, and he's safe. Madiya didn't lure him back to her. "As usual, you're extremely subtle—"

I stop. The words freeze in my mouth. I'm stuck, unable to move, my limbs frozen in place.

My brother stalks toward me, sighting down the end of a musket. I can't even widen my eyes to glare at him.

Fortunately he has the foresight to look before he shoots. Then he rolls his eyes, lowering the musket. He looks an utter ruffian—his knee-length coat torn and grimed, his hair matted, a few weaselly wisps of dark beard clinging scruffily to his chin. He's shorter than me, a little slighter, but I can't imagine even the street thugs taking him on.

He swaggers toward me. "Enforced stasis," he pronounces. "Wherein one arrests matter so that it can't move. Easy to do with an object, hard to do with a living being." He smirks. "Unless it's your incompetent brother."

He snaps his fingers and I'm released.

"Maybe you should've done something else, then," I grumble, flexing my hands to bring feeling back into them. "How did you know it would work, if you didn't know it was me?"

He shrugs. "Usually it's enough to make someone lose feeling in a leg, or something. You'd know that, if you could do it."

We stare at each other for a long moment in the semi-dark. Rayka's lantern lights him from behind, making him look larger than he is.

"Where have you been?" I demand at last.

He eyes me. "I could ask the same of you. You never even answered when I called for you."

"When I was in Eren? You said my name *once* and disappeared! I thought you were captured. Or dead."

He scoffs. "You never thought I was dead. I'm not stupid."

Because apparently only stupid people die? I've been worried about my brother, desperate to make sure he's safe, but he's doing a good job of reminding me why I haven't really missed him. "I called you and called you—"

"I figured it out. I didn't need you."

He can't slither out of this so easily. "You said my name in a panic. You made me think Madiya had captured you. *Something* must have happened."

His gaze shifts around the stone chamber, and he fingers his musket. He must have stolen it—taken it from the military academy when he left, perhaps. It's obvious he doesn't want to answer me, but I stare him down.

"I answered her," he mutters at last. "Madiya. She keeps calling me. Every damned night for the last two months. You've heard her?"

I nod.

"I couldn't stand it anymore." He swallows. "So I answered. And she went off, you know how she does, how *glad* she was to hear from me, how we matter more to her than anything. The full works. And then she said we'd all be reunited soon—which made me think—" He stops, a muscle working in his jaw. He mutters, "It made me think she'd caught you."

I look at him. His shoulders have slumped forward, and his hair is lank. He must have been terrified these last two months, caught between the twin horrors of Madiya and the witch hunters. Terrified, and alone. I want to touch his arm, to reassure him, but I have the feeling he'd swing the musket at me if I tried.

"Well, she didn't," I say instead. "Though not for lack of effort."

One side of his mouth tugs up in a humorless smile.

I glance around at the damp walls. "Have you been scavenging about down here all this time? We could have been working together."

At that, he puffs up his chest. "Working together? I saved your life! I lit those gunpowder magazines!"

My sympathy snaps. "Which was *not* my intent—as you might have known if you'd bothered to find me."

"You're too soft, Jahan." But then he says, mulishly, "We were safer apart. So she couldn't get both of us at once."

I don't even try to argue this logic. "I found her, you know. She's holed up with Bardas Triciphes in the Deos Deorum. And . . ." And Elanna. But somehow I can't make myself confess this to my brother, even though he's the last person whose approval I want. Still, I don't want him to know how I abandoned El. He'd have real reason to scorn me then. I fold my arms. "That's why I tracked you down."

He folds his free arm over the musket, too, mirroring me. "What do you expect *me* to do?"

"Well, you could stop hiding in the cisterns, for one thing."

"I'm busy down here," he says defensively.

I look around. We seem to be in a kind of tunnel sloping toward an opening. Somewhere ahead of us, water still drips. I don't know how he can stand it. Doesn't it remind him of Madiya's cave? But then Rayka has always shoved his feelings aside more easily than me. "You're busy in the cisterns?"

He shifts. Of course he's busy: avoiding Madiya and the witch hunters. And me, apparently. The gods alone know why. Maybe being in the cisterns, the closest thing to Madiya's cave, actually makes him feel safe.

"I'm mapping the tunnels," he says. "The cisterns are connected. You can use them to cross under half the city—the oldest parts, anyway."

I sigh. This is exactly the sort of thing Rayka would do—tell himself he's accomplishing great things, when in fact he's simply slithering out of doing the right thing.

Although . . . we could use the tunnels.

"Do they connect to Solivetos Hill?" I ask. "What about the Frourio?"

He smirks. "I knew you'd be interested."

My mind is already spinning on ahead. This could change all our plans; it could *give* us a plan. "But the imperial army—does Captain-General Horatius know the tunnels connect?"

"It doesn't matter if he does," Rayka says. He's smug now. "I've been going to each entrance—and there are a lot—and putting a misdirect on it. It'll confuse people. Mess with their heads. They'll think they're going one direction, and they're really going the opposite. Even if they end up down here, they won't know which way to go."

"Unless the magic wears off," I begin.

"Right. So I've been going to the entrances *every day* and reinforcing the sorcery. I have a pattern. It works."

It's clever. If he's willing to help, it offers us a way to get off Solivetos. A way to stay in communication with Felix and the others—even Bardas, if we wanted to.

"This is good," I say.

"I knew you'd like it." He hoists the musket over his shoulder, pleased with himself now, forgetting to be annoyed with me. "Come on. I'll show you the way to the Frourio."

I start to protest—I need to return to Solivetos—but he's already snatched up his lantern and turned to go. Well, I'm not about to let him out of my sight now. And if I go back to Tullea with a plan to save the prisoners, or at least a route to get there, it's much better than news of my failure with Leontius.

With a sigh, I follow him. We're in a narrow kind of corridor, the stones cold and slightly damp. I can still hear water dripping nearby. I don't pretend I like it, but if Rayka can handle the eerie similarity to Madiya's cave, so can I. I've been in the cisterns before, like any university student worth his salt. Pantoleon and I came down here several times, blundering about with lanterns and rough maps; it seemed like a good place to find the forgotten tombs of sorcerers. And we did find them: a cave full of stacked skeletons brittle with age, covered by inadequate stones. But I've never come in this way, or this far. Rayka's candlelight shines off something sheer and smooth: a patch of quartz in the wall.

It's been cut—no, not cut; faceted. The stones have been formed into disks and fitted together, like a glittering mosaic. We've emerged into a large chamber, where a narrow walkway crosses over a pool of dark water. The ceiling is lost to the darkness, but it's much higher than the tunnel. Vaulted, if I had to guess.

"Is it a temple?" I wonder aloud.

Rayka shrugs. "Maybe the old Idaeans just liked to get their water out of fancy underground buildings. There are some inscriptions in the old alphabet, over there. I found a tomb hidden behind one of the tunnel walls, too. Lots of bones."

Part of me wants to find the inscriptions, but that's not why we're here. I keep walking. "There are more tombs, near the university side. You walk down directly into them."

He nods. "Some of the old Idaeans were driven in here after Paladius invaded. They hid down here forever. He never caught them all, because he could never map all the tunnels. There was a cave-in that trapped twenty of his men. They never got out."

I glance at my brother. "I never heard that." And I was the one who searched for such stories.

"That's because you never read Tertius's *Memoirs of the Conquest of Ida*. It's a firsthand account; he talks all about it."

I manage not to snort at what Rayka considers light reading. "Were they sorcerers?"

"Probably. Tertius thought they were involved in the plot to overthrow Paladius, but he wasn't sure because he never actually found them."

We've made our way through the quartz-lined chamber, now, and into a hall lined with columns, some collapsed. Water pools in the darkness beyond the columns. The hall ends in a round chamber with several archways; Rayka picks the one directly before us. "I got lost following the others," he admits. "Most of them end in rubble. I can walk through it, but some of the entrances have fallen in."

This passage takes us, eventually, to a long tunnel that slopes gradually upward. Rayka swings back to say, "The Frourio's right above—"

A deep groan cuts him off. We both stagger. Rayka's lantern swings against the wall, flickering madly. Another resounding *thud* echoes through the earth. I stumble to one knee. There's dust in my mouth, and my heart is knifing between my ribs. Mount Angelos must have woken. "Trust you to take us underground during an earthquake," I gasp at my brother.

Rayka's staring up the length of the tunnel. Clods of earth rain down from the ceiling above us. The place seems ready to collapse.

"Come on!" Rayka says, decisive. He runs ahead, up the shaking tunnel. I shove myself onto my feet and charge after him.

Behind us, there's a breathless crash. I stare back at a mound of rubble. The ceiling has collapsed where we just stood.

I sprint after Rayka. There's no way, after surviving a childhood in Madiya's cave, I'm about to let myself be smothered to death underground.

Ahead, an ancient, iron-banded door flickers into view. It must be the Frourio entrance. It seems pure madness that we're running *into* the prison, and Rayka laughs in front of me, as if he's just had the same thought. But we both burst through the door without hesitation.

We emerge into a small, cool room filled with sacks and barrels. The cellar. A narrow staircase leads up to another door—and the precious gap of daylight. Another resounding *thud* shakes the ground. Somewhere beyond the door, someone's screaming. It doesn't seem safe to stay down here, though I'm not sure how much safer it is to go up. More dust rains down on us from above.

"Let's go." Rayka starts for the steps.

I grab the back of his filthy coat. "We'll be seen!"

He snorts. "What kind of sorcerer are you? Come on. I'll make sure nobody spots you."

The condescending brat. I want to shake him, but I'm too desperate for open air. And he's already started up the stairs.

I follow. At the top, he pauses and puts a finger to his lips. I nod. We both listen. The building trembles around us. *Thud, thud, thud.* Outside, a man shouts.

It doesn't sound like an earthquake. It sounds more like cannons—thousands of them, so many they're shaking the old fortress down to its foundations. But that can't be right.

Rayka's heard it, too. We exchange a mystified glance.

Carefully, he lets himself through the fabric of the door. I do the same. We're in a cavernous, deserted kitchen. No one hides under the table at the center, as they would during an earthquake. Shouts echo from outside. Another rumble shakes the floor, and overhead the beams creak, as if the building is moving—as if we might be crushed. I sprint for the nearest exit, an open doorway leading to a wide courtyard. Rayka's behind me.

But in the doorway, I stop. My brother runs into me with a curse, but I can't even move.

A group of people—servants and guards—cluster together in the center of the courtyard. A large, square tower dominates the wall opposite us. To the left and right, two additional towers surmount the walls and battlements. Faces press against the upper windows. Prisoners. They're screaming. Hands reach out past the bars.

Because the walls—the ones to the right and left—are *moving*. Clambering outward through the earth, slow and sluggish, as if they're trying to walk. The ground trembles with each movement, and stones fall from the battlements, crashing down with a thunder like cannons. Bodies in imperial livery are strewn on the ground, crushed.

"It's *sorcery*," Rayka says.

I nod stupidly. There's nothing else it could be. But who's doing it? None of our people have this power. Any captive sorcerers would be overwhelmed by bells and stones.

The walls inch outward, and with a shaking gasp one splits apart. Daylight pours through the gap. In the towers, people are screaming. *"Help! Help!"*

"Those are the outside walls," Rayka's saying. "The exits for this courtyard. Some idiot must be trying to free everyone—"

"—by making the prison walk?" I finish.

We stare at each other. This isn't going to save anyone. We both lunge forward, by unspoken agreement, reaching for the walls on either side, grasping for power—

But it's too late. The right-hand wall *stumbles*. As we stare, helpless, every stone breaks apart. The wall collapses outward with a deafening roar, red blood scattering among the bricks. The men and women clustered in the middle of the courtyard are screaming, running toward the opposite wall.

Except it, too, is collapsing. It seems to shatter, breaking apart into a heap on the ground, the bodies of the prisoners tangled up in it.

In the sudden silence, my ears ring.

Pantoleon. Pantoleon was in here. He might have been in one of those towers. He might be dead.

Him, and the gods alone know how many others.

I'm clutching Rayka's arm. He's grabbing onto me. He seems to have lost his lantern, but he's clutching the musket to his chest. The early-morning light reveals him: wan and terrified. In the courtyard, people are shouting. Weeping. No one moves in either pile of bricks. Across from us, a few petrified faces peer down from the windows of the remaining tower, the one that never moved.

Some of the prisoners are still alive.

I start toward them instinctively. But just then a door at the base of the tower bursts open, and a dozen witch hunters run out into the courtyard, swinging bells.

"You're too late!" one of the surviving guards shouts at them.

"Cowards!" a servant screams.

The witch hunters must have run when the tremors started—to safety, perhaps, on the other side of the remaining tower. Now they're back. And they're blocking us from the prisoners.

"Jahan." Rayka's shaking my arm, whispering furiously. "We have to go."

"People are still in there!"

"I know, but we can't get to them now. We need a plan. We'll come back."

I hesitate, but one of the witch hunters has seen us. He's pointing. We've both forgotten to work persuasion.

My brother grabs the back of my coat and drags me into the kitchen. I want to protest, but he's right. We need a plan. We need a way to get the remaining prisoners away safely, not simply lead them into greater danger.

All the gods, was Pantoleon in one of those towers? How many more?

"Hurry!" Rayka heads for the cellar.

"But the ceiling collapsed in the tunnel."

He rolls his eyes. "You can walk through any matter, can't you? Come on!"

I cast a glance back at the ruined courtyard. Two witch hunters are striding toward us, pushing through the distraught crowd. Ray-ka's right. If we try to save them now, we'll only create further chaos. But it still burns. Reluctantly, I follow my brother back down into the cisterns, away from the disaster in the courtyard, and the prisoners crushed by fallen bricks.

CHAPTER TWENTY-TWO

I walk, numb, through the tunnels, Rayka leading the way. If the walls moved by sorcery, who did it? I don't know anyone with that much power—much less the motivation for such an act.

We emerge after several hours into a wide, echoing room, the ground littered with debris. Rayka crosses a narrow platform above a pool, to a large hole in the wall. He swings back to look for me. "Solivetos." He points at the hole.

I rub my hands over my face. This is the last news I want to take back to Tullea. But I don't have a choice, and we need to make a plan to save whoever's left. So I go after my brother. Through the hole—which is as tall as I am—stairs take us up at a nearly vertical angle. We emerge into a small room behind the lower temple. I can hear voices in the main chamber.

"—don't trust those I don't know." That's Tullea, her tone hard.

"We need your help. The people in the Frourio need your help! We're all sorcerers together, what difference does it make?"

My heart leaps. It's Elanna's voice. What's she doing here—how did she take the risk to cross the bridge back to the old city? How did she get away from Madiya? I stride through to the main chamber to find Nestor and Sabina flanking Tullea, while Elanna faces them, dressed in her customary trousers this time, with Bardas at her side. How did she persuade him to bring her here? El's gaze flickers to me, but Tullea doesn't notice my presence at first. She's too busy denying Bardas entry, just as I had instructed.

Madiya isn't here. I let out a breath. But if she's not here, where is she? And what is she doing?

"You say the walls of the prison walked," Tullea says. "But your sorcerer *friend* here failed to keep them intact. And now you've killed people we are sworn to protect. The emperor's men will think Jahan did it! Why should we trust someone who attempts something like that?"

Clearly the news has preceded us. I'm staring. Elanna, involved with the destruction at the Frourio? Has Madiya corrupted her mind that much?

"I didn't do it," El snaps. "I told you that in the first place!"

Tullea folds her arms. "Maybe not, but who did?"

Bardas intervenes. He looks exhausted, and I suspect he's not here of his own volition, but rather to clean up someone else's mess. "Another sorcerer. Someone who thought they could save the prisoners, and terrify the witch hunters and imperial militia into submission. But as we know, things did not go as planned. That's why we came, so we could explain there has been a mistake. And to warn you that the emperor is planning retribution."

I step forward, unable to suppress my horror. Tullea startles. "Jahan! Where did you come from?"

"The Frourio," I say briefly, "by a hidden route." I look at Bardas. "You gave Madiya back her sorcery? How?"

"It wasn't her," he says, wincing. "It was . . . someone else."

"How many sorcerers do you know?" I demand.

He glances around at all of us and mutters, "Too many."

Everyone is silent. Elanna looks at me and away, her mouth tight. Ashamed, I think, though this can't have been her doing.

"You were at the Frourio?" Tullea asks me. "Did you see who did it?"

I shake my head, but Tullea's gaze returns, accusatory, to Elanna.

"It wasn't me!" Elanna bursts out. "You have eyes! Look at this collar around my neck! *Look.*" She spreads her hands. "I can do nothing. *Not one thing.* The witch hunters took my sorcery from me. Besides, everyone thinks I'm dead. What good or ill can I possibly do any of you?"

There are tears in her eyes—tears of rage. I take an involuntary step toward her.

Her gaze fixes on me, warning me not to come too close. She's not angry at me, as I first thought. She's angry with herself. "Jahan should know that I would never condone such a thing. I would never attempt it. I would think of the lives inside, first."

"It was an accident," Bardas says tiredly.

"An *accident*?" Tullea draws herself up; she seems to grow a good three inches. "Who would ever imagine that might be a good idea?"

"It was an attempt to free the prisoners within," Bardas says. "It's not as foolish as you make it out to be."

"Perhaps your friend's intentions were good, but people are dead."

"Yes," Bardas says. He glances around at us, the unwilling messenger of worse news yet. He clears his throat. "Not only that, but the emperor has declared that all of the remaining 'sorcerers'—real or not—will be executed."

The floor seems to be falling out from under me. This happened too damned fast. "*All* of them?"

Bardas nods.

"When?"

He clears his throat. "Tomorrow morning. In Imperial Square, so everyone can see the fate that befalls sorcerers."

He's grim, but the earth seems to steady under my feet. "Then we have time to get them out."

"But how do we get in?" Nestor bursts out. "We don't have an army."

"Jahan can walk through walls," Sabina points out.

I utter a hollow laugh. "That would be a lot of people to bring out *through* the walls."

"If only we could . . . pick them up on a wind," she says, whimsical as ever. "Breathe them out of there."

Tullea glances at me, and I give a small shake of my head. I can move others through space, but only if I'm touching them, and I have no idea if I could move that many people at once.

"I don't think we have the power for such a feat," Tullea says evenly, but there's a tick in her jaw. She's surely thinking about Pantoleon, as I am, trapped in the fortress. "Perhaps, though, with Felix's help, we might distract the guards enough to walk through the necessary walls . . ."

But we all know that this is unlikely to work. Even with Felix's black-capped firebrands, the militia guarding the Frourio will outnumber us three to one. Not to mention that the witch hunters will negate everyone's magic. Whoever ruined the Frourio must have such immense power that they were able to work around the stones and bells.

Nestor says what we're all thinking. "There's no way."

No way—no good one, at least. But we have to at least make an attempt.

"Listen," I say. "Let me try. No matter the personal risk—"

A heavy sigh interrupts me. "There's no need to be so damned heroic, Jahan." Rayka has come to stand on the fringe of our circle, his hands in his pockets. He smirks around at us, smug and disreputable. "I have a way into the Frourio, if you're all so eager to go. I took Jahan there just now."

Everyone steps back in confusion. "Who are you?" Tullea demands, and Elanna stares from me to my brother.

I start to say, "This is my—"

"Call me Aquilius." Rayka smirks around at our circle, smug as a cat.

I roll my eyes. "And you accuse *me* of indulging in personal heroics?"

"So this is the brother who fled military school," Elanna says knowingly, and Rayka shoots her an affronted look.

"Tell us your plan, *Aquilius*," Tullea says.

Rayka's head swings back and forth; he's not sure whom he should glare at. But with a long-suffering sigh, he says, "The cisterns. I've been getting to know them. They're connected—"

"Only some of them," Nestor interrupts.

Rayka looks at him like he's insane. "Yes, *some* of the tunnels have caved in. But you're a *sorcerer.* You can figure out a way through a rock."

"Not everyone has your facility with rudimentary matter," I point out. My brother's sarcasm is already earning him a nasty stare from Nestor. "And you're forgetting that the bells bother almost everyone."

Rayka regards me with disdain. "Then they should stay here. You and I can take care of this ourselves. Unless," he adds, "you don't feel up to the challenge."

"Oh," I say, "you know I'm up to the challenge. As long as you don't feel the urge to blow the place up."

Rayka's chin comes up, but before he can retort, Elanna interrupts. "I'm coming as well."

I bite back the urge to tell her that she should stay here. Stay safe. But the *Caveadear* doesn't need me to protect her.

"You can't do anything," Rayka points out.

"Perhaps not sorcery, but at least this collar mutes the bells and stones, now. I can help the prisoners out through the tunnels once you've freed them." She pauses. "At least, I assume that's your plan?"

"Yes," Rayka says sulkily.

"We should wait for cover of darkness," I say. "Let the furor die down."

Rayka kicks at the dirt. "*Obviously.* I'm going to scout the tunnels. Make sure my misdirects are still intact."

"Good idea." El looks at me. "We need to talk."

I draw in a breath, but I can hardly disagree. We do need to talk. About her magic. About me. About Madiya. And so, as Rayka slips back down into the tunnels, I lead Elanna up the stairs to the height of Solivetos Hill, into the bright-blue day.

ABOVE THE TEMPLE, a forested ridge overlooks the city and the gleaming lip of the sea. Here, at least, are trees I didn't destroy when

I burned Madiya out of my head. Elanna seems to soften a little, now that we're surrounded by greenness, but I can't release my own tension. I feel sick. We sit on either side of a flat rock, not quite touching, not quite looking at each other. Behind us, Mount Ange-los looms, its snowcapped dome gleaming.

"I didn't know who she was," Elanna says softly. "I didn't know she was the sorceress who raised you."

"I know." The words taste hollow. Bitter.

"She saved me, Jahan. She made my mind whole again. I don't know how, but she did."

I can't bear to look at her. "And what did she take from you? Do you even know? Do you *remember*?"

"I remember *you*." El pauses. "She said nothing but kind things about you. It was . . . odd."

"Odd?" I want to laugh, or maybe throw up. I should have known, if she ever met Madiya, that Elanna wouldn't believe me. Madiya would twist everything around, make El think my stories about her couldn't possibly be true. Madiya's got her, and she must have erased the Elanna I knew. The woman I loved. This is almost worse than thinking she was dead.

I start to get up, but El grabs my hand and drags me back down. It takes all my strength not to push her away.

"Yes, odd," she says. "You can be quite impossible, you know. There should have been *something* for her to complain about."

I stare at her. Her lips are quirked, as if she's trying to smile but can't quite.

"It reminded me of Loyce Eyrlai and her lover," she says. "Some-times they'd say something kind first, to get you to listen to them. Then they'd go in for the kill. Slaughter you, and laugh. I was wait-ing for Madiya to do that to you, but she had only praise." El pauses. Her lips tighten. "I think it's because she wants me to bring you back to her. I think that's why she saved me in the first place, so she could pull you back in."

I swallow down bile. "And are you going to? Bring me to her?"

"All the gods, Jahan, no!" She blinks fast, pressing a hand to her mouth. "I came here to get away from her. To be with you. I talked Bardas into bringing me here so we could warn you about the emperor's retribution. I told him you wouldn't trust him without me. He and his friend meant that demonstration at the Frourio to prove their worth to you, I think, but it did just the opposite, and now he feels guilty for putting you in even more danger, and for causing all those deaths. And I do, too. But I came for *you*."

I can't seem to find any words.

El bites her lip, then continues on in a rush. "I—I can't believe I didn't know who Madiya was. I feel horrible for thinking so well of her."

"That's what she's like." I'm softening in relief so profound I feel tears prick my eyes. "She pulls you in until you can't get out."

Elanna reaches over and cradles my hands in hers, and this time I don't try to pull away. "I know. I remembered what you told me about her."

My chin drops. I can't quite look at her through the tears blurring my eyes. "I thought you might not believe me."

"I love you," she says. "I know you. Of course I believe you."

"I should have brought you out of the Deos Deorum," I whisper. "I left you there. I left you in Aexione—"

"It's all right, Jahan." She reaches up a tentative hand and brushes my hair. "It's all right. I don't need to be rescued. You don't need to do that for me. But Bardas felt guilty for failing to tell you I was alive, as well as for all the rest. So I got out."

"My brother Lathiel—I have to get him away from her."

"You will." She touches my chest. "*We* will. We'll do it together."

I reach out blindly and gather her against me. Her arms wrap around my neck, and the cool metal of the collar presses against the base of my throat. But she's *alive*. She's in my arms, and she believes me. She sees the truth about Madiya. There are no words to express how grateful I am.

She swallows hard, and when I pull back to look at her, I see she's weeping, too. "You were so angry," she says softly. "I thought I'd lost you."

"No, El. I'm yours. Always yours." It's such a relief to say those words. I hold her harder, and she hugs me back, fiercely.

Her lips touch my ear. "I made you a promise, Jahan. To love you, no matter what."

She remembers. Madiya didn't steal this from her; maybe Madiya didn't steal anything from her at all. Maybe Madiya's only seen her as a tool, because until now El hasn't resisted her. Tears blur my vision; my eyes ache. "And I promised the same."

"I'm glad you remember," she says, and I almost laugh at how she's echoed my thoughts. "I'm glad you didn't spurn me for some Idaean beauty. The empress, for instance."

"Firmina Triciphes has nothing on you." I kiss her neck, and taste the sourness of metal. I've accidentally licked her collar. I lean back to examine it. "I should get this off . . ."

"Madiya couldn't. Your little brother couldn't, either." She's digging at it now, leaving red streaks on her skin. "I can't work sorcery. I can't do anything. I can't go home like this—I've failed—"

She breaks off, tears flowing, and I cup my hands around hers, tugging them gently away from the collar. She's shaking her head, trying to say something, but all that comes out are broken words. I turn myself around and wrap my legs on either side of her, folding her up against me. She sobs into my shirt. I hug the warm, damp weight of her, cradling her body. When she finally draws a breath, I lower my forehead to hers. Our noses touch. Her tears dampen my own face. Tenderness pulls at me, so fierce I think it might consume us both. I stroke the hair back from her brow. She stares at me, eyes wide, chapped lips parted.

"What if I can't get it off?" she whispers, tugging at the collar again. "What if I take it off and—and my power—"

"You'll still be the *Caveadear*."

"Not the *Caveadear* my people want. Not the one they need." She lowers her voice. "What do I tell Sophy?"

I feel a crooked smile tug my mouth. "Tell her we'll find a way to break this thing off your neck. And then we'll teach a lesson to the bastards who did this."

She rubs her fists over her eyes, and some of the strength comes back into her. "I've been trying to be so strong. Not let Bardas and Firmina see how much this costs me." She leans against me with a long sigh. "I feel as if I always burst into tears around you and no one else. You're very tolerant."

"You endure my flaws . . ." And there are a good many more of those, I think, than hers. "Do the bells not trouble you now?"

"Not really. Madiya did something to them, I think. Changed them, somehow."

My neck stiffens, but I can't deny that, whatever Madiya did, in this instance it's a good thing. "We need to let the world know you're still alive. But you don't need your sorcery to terrify the emperor." I lean back, grinning at her. "You don't need to work any magic. They just need to learn you still live. That you're here, in Ida, ready to act."

She eyes me, suspicious.

"You have no idea how terrifying your reputation is. Besides, it's rather embarrassing when the sorceress you claim to have executed turns out to have slipped through your fingers. And . . ." I hesitate, feeling a fool, as I always do, when I confess something close to my heart. Quietly, unable to meet her eyes, I say, "It matters to me, having you here."

She's in front of me suddenly, her gaze fixed on me. Her breath touches my face, moist. "You're not angry with me?"

"*Angry* with you? For what, being captured? For Madiya trying to trick you? I thought you were angry with *me* . . ."

"Well," she says archly, "you do show a continual reluctance to say things you really mean." Her fingers brush my chin. "And I'm not fond of the beard."

I can't stop my grin. "Shall I conjure a razor?"

She pulls my head down. "Just kiss me, you fool."

So I do. Her lips are warm and the weight of her body intimately familiar. She twines her arms around my neck and murmurs in my ear, "Do you think anyone can see us up here?"

"Do you care if they do?" I ask drily, slipping my hands under her coat to feel the heat of her.

"Well, we don't need *all* of Ida to know we've reunited . . ."

We scoot backward into the shadow of the trees, tucked in among the rocks. No one should see us from below, but just in case, I draw a curtain of persuasion around us. *Nothing to see here.* Her mouth finds mine again. I bring her close; she starts tugging at my clothing. I pull off my coat, cushioning the rock beneath us, and she sighs as I unbutton her shirt. I lean into her body—so warm and familiar— and I feel as if I've come home.

Afterward, I curl against her on the rock and she tucks herself up against me. We fall asleep like that, on the rock overlooking all of Ida, the sun beating down on us.

I WAKE IN purple twilight with my head pillowed in El's lap. She shivers a little as I wake, coming alert herself. Somehow, she woke and dressed without waking me; her greatcoat cushions my ears. She looks down at me with deep satisfaction.

"Oh, dear," I say, feeling a smile spread across my face. "I've been caught by the *Caveadear* of Eren and Caeris."

"Yes, and she has you *exactly* where she wants you."

She bends over, the curtain of her hair falling around us, and I lean up to meet her kiss.

But bells toll the hour—seven o'clock. Almost time to find my brother and get moving through the cisterns. Reluctantly, I draw myself away and sit up, pulling on my trousers and shirt. Elanna rustles in a bag beside her, pulling out two oranges and a chunk of bread. "I went down earlier for food. You slept like the dead."

My stomach rumbles. I didn't realize how hungry I am—when did I last eat? I stuff the bread into my mouth and rip into the orange.

Elanna says she's already eaten. Instead, she worries at the ring on her finger. "Can you . . ." She hesitates. I stop eating; it's not like her. "Can you contact someone who isn't a sorcerer, through a mirror?"

"I can try. Who—" But I realize when she looks at me who she must mean. Worry makes her eyes stark. I reach for her knee and squeeze it. "Sophy?"

She nods and pulls a palm-sized shaving mirror from her pocket. I reach for it, but she curls her fingers around it, not letting go. "I have to tell her what's happened. She must think I'm dead, or captured. But I can't bear to tell her—" She swallows hard. "—I've lost my magic. I don't have the power she needs."

"But you're alive. That's what matters."

"And Rhia . . ." El rubs her eyes. "She was with me when I was captured. I saw her fall. I don't know what happened to her."

I reach over, gently uncurling her fingers from the mirror, and cup it between my hands. "We'll find out. Besides," I add drily, "it would take more than a couple of witch hunters to do in Rhia Knoll. You'd need an entire army."

El laughs at that, though there's a catch in her throat, and I turn my attention to the glass, reaching for a mental image of Sophy Dunbarron. *Sophy,* I call in my mind, letting the whisper arrow over Ida and the Middle Sea, all the way to Eren. If I can compress space physically, then my whisper can niggle Sophy's ear from anywhere in the world.

There's a long pause, and I whisper her name again. She might not be near a reflective surface. But I try once more, because Elanna is staring at me with stark eyes, and I can't bear to fail her in this.

And when I look down into the mirror, my own face has finally dissolved into one oval-shaped and milky-skinned, a wisp of blond hair falling over a pale eyebrow. She must have rushed to a mirror, though the light is too dim for me to make out the room surrounding her. Sophy looks exhausted and breathless, but her cheeks are flushed. And her mouth is open. *Jahan?*

"Is she there?" El asks. I nod, and she presses her hands to her mouth.

You bastard! I called and called for you.

Where—What's happened? Sophy is demanding. *Where* are *you?*

"Just a minute," I say. "There's someone who needs to talk to you more."

I pass the mirror over to Elanna, and Sophy shrieks so loudly I almost cover my ears, even though her voice is only audible in my head. *El. El, I thought—*

Elanna breaks in. "Is Rhia—is she—?"

She broke her arm. She was madder than a hornet. We practically had to tie her down to keep her from going after you. Sophy's voice turns indignant. *She called me a tyrant!*

El's grinning, even as tears stand out in her eyes. "She *would* say that."

I feel myself smiling, too. I might not have been among the Ereni and Caerisians for long, and the common people might have mistrusted me—but I miss them. Even Rhia Knoll, who's as sharp-edged as the blades she carries. Thank the gods she's all right.

What happened? Sophy's asking. *The emperor sent me this horrible, threatening letter—and then they were giving out that you were dead . . .*

"I was rescued." Her fingers flutter self-consciously to the collar at her neck. "Not everything is as it seems here. But tell me first what's going on at home. Have the Tinani . . . ?"

They quieted down for a while, after you flooded them out on the border. She pauses. *But people got word that you were dead, El. There have been protests all across Eren. There's this horrible man—Aristide Rambaud, the Duke of Essez—who says that sorcery is evil and vile, and that I must be pushed off the throne. He's allied with the Tinani. It's . . . ugly.*

"Then I need to come home," Elanna begins, but then she chokes up. "Except—oh, all the gods, Sophy—they took my sorcery from me. The witch hunters—they stole it."

Sophy is silent for a long minute. I can't see her expression, as Elanna has angled the mirror away. At last, Sophy says, *It's enough for me—for all of us—to know that you're alive. You're still our* Caveadear. *This is still your home. If you and Jahan can work against the emperor from the inside, I can hold out here a little longer.*

Elanna casts me a somewhat desperate glance. Maybe she thinks this is Sophy's way of telling her she shouldn't come home at all.

"We'll do what we can here," I say. "And then I promise I'll send El back to you."

Thank you, Jahan. There's no mistaking the relief in Sophy's voice, even in our heads.

"Jahan destroyed the emperor's fleet," Elanna says. "The one he was planning to send to Eren. There's hope, Sophy."

Sophy's eyes widen. *He did? Did the emperor—*

Abruptly, she looks over her shoulder, as if startled by some sound we can't hear. Her shoulders tense, and a look of stern resolve comes over her face. I'm reminded that we're speaking to the queen of Eren and Caeris. *I have to go now,* she whispers. *I'm sorry. Summon me again, please, as soon as you can. It is so wonderful to see you both. I—I'd begun to think I might not again.*

"I'll be back as soon as I can," Elanna says. "I promise."

I reclaim the mirror from her. "Take care, Sophy. Give Alistar our regards!"

Yes, yes, she says vaguely, and then she waves and disappears from the mirror. I close off the connection.

Elanna is looking at me. "You'll *send me* back to them?"

Have I said something wrong? "If that's what you want."

"Of course it is! I have to go home." She gets up, brushing down the back of her trousers impatiently. But it's with regret that she presses her lips together. Without quite looking at me, she says softly, "But you could come home with me, you know. You don't have to send me back to Eren like a package."

Turning, she strides away over the rocks. I scramble to my feet, protesting. "El!"

She swings around, her eyes lowered. "I'm sorry. This is your city. Your people. I shouldn't presume."

"No, I . . . I . . ." I'm stumbling over the words, because I don't know what the right ones are. How can Elanna just say things like that, so easily? How can she *know* with such certainty that she wants me with her? When I've told her I can't even marry her, because I'm so afraid of Madiya using her against me? Lamely, I say, "I want to be with you."

Her mouth tucks in, and I feel more than ever that I've somehow failed. But she holds out her hand. "We'll decide it when the time comes to leave."

This isn't the answer she wants, or deserves. Yet I don't know what to say. I don't belong in Eren and Caeris, and El doesn't belong here. How will we ever reconcile that?

All the same, I take her hand. She leans a little against me, and we go together down toward the temple.

CHAPTER TWENTY-THREE

Rayka's waiting for us, smirking. "Where have you been?"

"When you're older, we'll explain how it works between a man and a woman," I say drily, and Elanna laughs despite the tension between us just minutes ago. My brother glowers. I grin. I might not be good at love, but I feel better than I have in weeks.

Elanna tucks her arm around mine, dragging me toward the stairs. Tullea waits for us at the bottom. She presses a torch into my hand. She seems about to speak, but then simply nods at me. I don't know what there is to say. I can't promise that I'll find Pantoleon. We don't know the names of anyone who died in the collapse. I might find Pantoleon, or only the memory of him.

Rayka charges ahead of me, leading us down into the cisterns. El and I follow. The darkness seems to swallow us up, along with the faint *plink* of water. I shake off the old memories that threaten to swallow me. My brother moves quickly, his steps assured over the uncertain ground—the show-off.

We seem to walk for hours under the city. Eventually we arrive at the tunnel that slopes upward, and the collapsed rubble from the roof. I think my heart is thudding. Then I realize that it's not my heart, but noise above us. After a moment, it ceases. The kitchens must be in use. Rayka pauses outside the cobwebbed door. "Are you ready?"

"As ready as anyone can be," I reply. It makes me uneasy, though, leaving El here alone in the dark so like Madiya's cave.

She touches my cheek. "I'll be all right."

Rayka's fussing with the door, so I lean forward and kiss her swiftly. "If anyone comes through, blow out the torch and hide. Don't be brave."

She laughs. "That's heroic advice. I'll remember it."

"Well," I say with a grin, "our plan will work best if we *all* survive to see tomor—"

"All the gods, are you coming or not?" Rayka demands. "I don't want to do this on my own."

"Duty calls," I say, releasing Elanna. Her fingers linger on my elbow.

"Damned lovebirds," Rayka mutters.

I allow myself a last smile and a glance back at Elanna. She's leaning against the rough wall, chewing a strip of jerky. I wink at her. She smiles back, but there's a soreness in it, as if she's thinking about our conversation on Solivetos Hill. Or maybe she's just thinking about our possible, imminent demise.

There's no time to turn back to her. Instead I follow my brother through the door.

We emerge into the cellar. Rayka, sure-footed in the dark, trots up the staircase into the kitchen. He came back here this afternoon, moving unnoticed among the guards, to check the route to the remaining prisoners. I slip after him. *Nothing more than mice scratching.* A single kitchen maid slumps tiredly by the sink, washing out a large pot. She takes no notice as we creep through the still-open doors into the ruined courtyard. The piles of rubble loom to either side in the darkness. They must be searching for bodies still.

Rayka guides us around the rubble to the remaining tower. We slip through an entrance partially blocked by fallen bricks, and bolt up a narrow staircase to a close corridor. Somewhere ahead of us, a chain rattles. Someone coughs.

A light gleams. Two guards stand below a torch, talking. The jagged teeth of bayonets poke over their shoulders.

Looks like we've found the remaining prisoners—or some of them. I press my back against the wall, afraid even the slight sound of my breathing will give me away. Rayka hovers at my shoulder. I try not to inhale the rank odor of him.

No witch hunters here, at least—and no bells. Which tells me these prisoners are either not a threat or, more likely, aren't sorcerers at all.

Distracting the guards won't be the hard part. The hard part will be getting all the prisoners out unnoticed, past the *other* guards, down in the ruined courtyard.

Rayka's muttering. I elbow him—what if the guards hear?—but instead of shutting up, he grabs my arm and whispers in my ear.

I nod. It's a decent plan. "Don't kill them."

He rolls his eyes—a flicker of white in the darkness—and snaps his fingers, whispering persuasion to the muscles of the first guard's throat. *Tighten, tighten.* The guard chokes, scrabbling at his neck, before he collapses, unconscious. The other starts to exclaim. Rayka grunts and snaps his fingers again. The second guard gasps and also falls.

We wrestle them—blasted heavy since they're limp—into a corner. Rayka sets about stripping off their weapons and uniforms, while I approach the door they guarded. The men had no keys, but the lock presents little difficulty. I snap it like a gun and pull the door open.

Breathless silence awaits me on the other side. I walk in, holding the torch aloft, and flinch.

People are packed inside—twenty or thirty of them at least, their eyes gleaming in the torchlight. The place reeks of human sweat and waste. I feel sick. We should have come here sooner—not only this morning, but the moment we knew people were being taken here.

A man with broken spectacles limps forward. I gasp aloud at the sight of him.

"Professor Argyros," I begin. He's alive!

He looks at me, then peers closer. An astonished smile bursts over his face. "Jahan Korakides?"

A whisper passes around the room: "The Korakos."

I gesture the people forward, swallowing hard at the sight of their sunken faces and haunted eyes. They've endured so much. "Come quickly. And stay silent."

Rayka's waiting in the corridor, dressed in a guard's uniform. He thrusts the other one at me, but I shake my head and gesture to Argyros. "Give it to him. I don't need it. I'll go on to the next floor—there must be more people."

Rayka raises an eyebrow, but he beckons for the people to follow him, muffling their footsteps with silence. I catch Argyros's elbow. "Do you know if there are other people left? Pantoleon . . ."

"Pantoleon Chrysales? He's been captured?" Argyros shudders and clasps my shoulder. "I'm sorry, Jahan. I didn't know. There may be more prisoners, but I haven't seen them."

It's what I expected him to say, but disappointment hollows out my stomach. Pantoleon's survival seems almost impossible now. I release the professor, and he joins the others following Rayka down the corridor, back to Elanna.

I continue on, but the upper floor is empty. I pace past unoccupied cells, my breathing loud in my ears. There must be more prisoners, somewhere. Or maybe only their bodies remain, crushed in the rubble of the wall.

Ahead of me, a bell clangs. I hurry toward it, running out onto an open parapet. I'm above a large courtyard, undamaged by the morning's events. Below me, little more than shadows magnified by lanterns, I see witch hunters assembling prisoners in a single wagon, its bars liquid black in the yellow light. They seem to be preparing to leave—the driver climbs up on the wagon, and a boy leads out a second vehicle, a coach-and-four, stamped with the imperial crest.

Why are they taking away prisoners now, in the middle of the night? Unless these are actual sorcerers—being taken not to the place of execution, but to the Ochuroma . . .

Men emerge into the courtyard. Four of them, bells clattering on their bandoliers.

Maybe I'm right. My pulse is hammering in my ears. I look back for Rayka, but he hasn't followed me. He must still be getting the prisoners to safety.

The portcullis creaks as it's winched open. I have to act *now.*

So, like a graceless bird, I jump. As if I could fly. For a moment, as the air catches me, I imagine that I feel the rattle of wind through feathers. Like Mantius.

Then I land, my knees rattling with the impact, just in front of the wagon. The horses spook and buck. The driver shouts. I dodge around the horses.

A witch hunter surges in front of me, ringing a deep bell. I wave my hand, reaching for the bell's clapper, but my magic slides off. So I do what Rayka did—I pull power from the earth, and the paving stones shake. The man staggers. I compress space, coming up right before him and driving a fist into his chin. He falls.

Bells erupt around me, a cacophony. But I rattle the paving stones and compress space. It's like the Getai again, only this time I'm more confident of what I'm doing. I plow my fist into another witch hunt-er's face, seize a torch from another one and fling it at the coach. It misses but the horses buck and jostle in their traces, racing away through the courtyard. I hear more guards running. I grab the fire and drag it into a curtain of blazing orange, blocking myself and the two remaining witch hunters in, along with the wagon. The horses are dancing, the driver cursing furiously.

It takes only a moment to dispatch the last two witch hunters. I turn back to the wagon—

And a man walks through the flames. Unharmed. Light-haired. Bells gleam on his coat. With a flicker of his eyes, he takes in the fallen witch hunters, the spooked horses, me.

My mouth is open, my pulse too loud. How did Alcibiades Dou-kas just walk through fire? Did the witch stones protect him, or—

"You're too much damned trouble, Jahan Korakides," he says.

I compress space—so fast I don't see the pistol until it's too late. But I feel the reverberation in my body, the impact of the blow shat-tering my chest. The distant pain. The pistol smoking. Alcibiades watching me, his eyes hooded.

Then the fire erupts. It *whoosh*es into Alcibiades. He runs. As I waver, something strikes me in the side. I'm smashed at great speed across the courtyard. The flames have vanished but my eyes are still dazzled. I don't know what's happened. There's blood on my hands. A distant, burning pain in my chest.

My brother's holding me upright. He's dragging me, now, through the corridors, while somewhere guards shout. My impossible brother, the one who spent weeks—months—ignoring my summons, came back for me.

He's panting under my weight, with the effort of persuading everyone in the Frourio that there's nothing to see. I try to move my legs, but they seem to belong to someone else. My head swims. Red sparks dance in my eyes.

Someone shouts behind us, but Rayka compresses space and we lose them. He's gasping now, too, but he doesn't let me go. The stones seem to waver. I blink, and we're back in the kitchen, fumbling through the cellar, down into the cisterns, into sudden quiet. I blink, but my mind is too hazy to form coherent thoughts. Elanna should be here. Where is she?

"Damn it, Jahan," Rayka's saying. "You can't take down an entire prison by yourself!"

"Where's . . . El?" I manage, wheezing.

"She took the prisoners back! *She* did what she was supposed to, and didn't get attacked by the damned grand inquisitor himself—"

"Alcibiades . . ."

"The bugger got away—*with* the prisoners. What the hell were you thinking?"

We're limping together through the cisterns at full pace, and I can't find the breath to explain myself. I don't have an explanation, except that I acted without thinking. The walls seem to be squeezing in and out. I blink. Sweat drips into my eyes. Somehow, Rayka got a torch.

We walk and walk. For a time, delirious, I imagine we're clambering down into Madiya's cave, and I shout "No!" Rayka shakes me. Then we're crawling up the steps into Tirisero's temple, and

Elanna's grabbing my other arm, and I'm being hauled up the hill. The stars spin overhead. I try to grab El's hand, try to tell her something, but I don't know what to say.

The ground levels. I stumble. My head feels too wide. My brother's shouting at the sorcerers who have gathered around us, blank faces in the torchlight.

"Bring me anything!" he shouts. "He can take power from a rock if he has to. Though there won't be much green left in this place."

Elanna stares at me, horrified.

"I'm sorry," I whisper, but no sound comes out.

Then Irene is on my other side. "That didn't happen when he healed me."

"Since when are you an expert?" Rayka sneers.

El looks between Rayka and Irene, and whatever she sees there decides her. The world seems to fade and spin. "Take him inside the temple." I reach for her hand, but I can't lift my arms. Can't move my fingers. Then I'm on my back under the temple's high dome, feeling the power of Tirisero pulse around me, wild and dizzying. Elanna's hand is crushing mine, though normally my grip is stronger than hers. There's a cracked ceiling above me. Stars.

"What did you say?" El asks, a whisper.

"Vault . . . of the . . . heavens."

"That's a useless thing to waste your breath on. Heal yourself, Jahan."

The lid of the font is still open. I can feel the power pulsing in the walls. I whisper the words. *"The secret flame unified with the deep water, the heart of Tirisero."*

And the power sweeps into me, a roar like fire. Warm, too, like fire. It rushes over me, dizzying, overwhelming.

"Help," I whisper. I struggle to open my eyes.

And when I do, I'm not in the temple anymore. I seem to be in the heart of flame, pulsing around me, a gentle yet ferocious scarlet. The flames shift and coalesce into human form. A man—I struggle to sit upright, my chest heaving.

But the man pushes me gently back down. He touches his fingers to my wound. And I feel the flesh heal together in an explosion of white light.

I OPEN MY eyes. Someone has repainted the walls of the temple. The colors glow, vivid in the sunlight streaming through the oculus.

Without effort, I stand. My limbs feel light and easy. Strange.

A man and woman—no, a girl—stand before the font. The girl looks perhaps fifteen, her black hair tangled up in a matted braid, her feet bare. Her blue gown is rent and splattered with mud, but her eyes are bright and fierce.

And the man . . . he wears a cloak of black feathers. He's short, ugly. His nose looks as if it's been smashed in more than once.

My mind stutters. It can't be.

The girl's head jerks around, her gaze flashing toward the open door behind me. She doesn't seem to see me, however. I follow her gaze and, for the briefest moment, I hear what she does. A persistent *thud, thud,* echoing up from Naval Harbor.

"Now, you know how this works," the man is saying. "There's a cost to this. You won't be able to do everything you can now. No one will. Promise me you'll get on that boat to the west."

The girl flinches and shivers, as if at a new noise. "But I don't *want*—"

"This isn't about *want*. This is about *need*. You need to protect our power. Our knowledge." He shakes his head. "You're as soft as these damned Idaeans, girl. You know there is a cost to binding the power here."

She's still looking beyond me, out the door. "But *he* won't be able to use it?"

At first I think she means me. I touch my chest. I want to protest that I wouldn't hurt her.

"Paladius wouldn't know how to use magic if it punched him in the face," the man says. He throws off his cloak. Underneath it, he's a scrappy sort, in a jerkin and hose no better looking than the girl's. He puts both hands on the font and begins to chant. His low, resonant voice fills the room, swelling and bursting against the stones.

The girl watches, hugging his cloak to her chest, chewing on her lower lip. He casts her one last glance. I see all the affection in it. All the exasperation. All the hope and regret.

He keeps chanting, and light begins to spill from the font. I *feel* the power coalescing, circling, *demanding*. Being drawn out of the air around us, out of the walls of this very temple, being *pulled* into the font. The girl lifts the lid. The man nods to her, still chanting. The last of the light flees into the font, and she slams the lid down.

And the man disappears. He *shatters* into a thousand shining particles of light. They linger over the font, settling on it as delicate as dust.

The girl screams. "Mantius! Mantius!" Tears course down her cheeks. She tries to pry the lid off the font, but it won't come, so she beats her fists on it instead. "You lied to me! You *lied*!"

I want to shout, too. I lunge forward, as if I can help her lift up the lid of the font. As if we can bring him back together. One liar to another. My ancestor Mantius, with his cloak of black feathers. But I can't seem to grasp the stone lid. My hands pass through it.

The girl slumps against the font, her shoulders heaving. I take a step toward her. As if she senses my presence, she lifts her head. She frowns. Squints at the space before me, not really seeing me.

"Who are you?" I ask, and the girl jumps—

A swift twist of air. The girl disappears. And a small, sleek silver fox darts past me, out of the temple, racing into the brilliant day.

CHAPTER TWENTY-FOUR

I open my eyes. I'm panting. Morning light slants through the small square window above my pallet bed.

I sit, wiping the sweat off my forehead. I've never had a dream like that. El's asleep, her arms sprawled around her head, doubled over beside me as if she dozed off sitting up.

She comes awake, blinking. Then she throws her arms around me. "You're all right! I thought you'd—drained your power—or—or—"

"I'm all right." I realize, dazedly, that I am. I put her back gently, grasping her arm. "El. The sorceress in Caeris—the one you saw in Dalriada, who shapeshifted into a silver fox . . ."

"Tuah?"

"Yes. She had black hair, didn't she?" My skin still seems to be buzzing. I stand, pacing around the room, careless of the dried blood on my shirt.

"Yes . . ." El says.

"I had a dream—a *vision*—of her and this man." I swallow hard. I still can't believe it. After all these years, all the times I imagined him rescuing me, all these years of running from our family, I saw *him*. "Mantius. He's . . . my ancestor."

El's mouth opens.

"Tuah was just a girl," I say. "They were sealing the font—sealing all the power into it, so Paladius couldn't use it. They must have known his victory was inevitable." My throat works. "Mantius gave his *life* . . ."

And his son, Kyros, betrayed our people to the Paladisans.

"Tuah must have come to Caeris afterward," El says, her eyes wide. "Maybe she thought sorcery would be safe there, but then the Paladisans conquered it, too . . ."

"Yes." But I'm not seeing Tuah. I'm seeing Mantius dissolving into particles of light. That must be how I opened the font— I reached for the fire and water and spoke the words, yes. But I also spoke his name. Somehow, by conjuring his memory, I released the power he concentrated in the font. The thing he gave his life to protect.

If he gave his life for it, then it's my responsibility to protect it, too.

"Jahan . . ." Elanna's worrying at her seal ring. "What your brother said—about you draining the life out of things . . ."

All the gods. I forgot the fool spoke that secret aloud last night. I can't make myself meet El's eyes. "It's just my charming personality. Nothing can resist it." But she doesn't laugh, and I feel even more a fool. I try again, grasping for the right words. "We all have to draw our power from somewhere. For you, it's from the land. For most sorcerers . . . well, we have to use whatever we have access to. We can use any living force. Trees, plants, even the sea. All natural things have an energy, though it can be difficult to corral. In Caeris and Eren, it was easy for me, because the stone circles concentrated the power." I pause. "We can use our own life energy as well. Or if we're really unscrupulous, that of other people."

"You *drain* things," El says. "You kill them . . ."

I wince. "Not if there's an abundant enough supply. Here, in the temple, when I lifted the lid on the font—El, it's got so much power, you wouldn't believe it!"

She's still looking at me as if I'm a stranger. "I never thought we were so different."

I swallow hard, and sit back down on the pallet, beside her. "I should have told you. I—I'm sorry. It's not the way I want to be. It's just the way it works."

She nods, but I don't sense she's particularly pleased. "This . . . font. Where does its power come from?"

"I don't know. It's just there. It's *immense.*"

"And if you use it, you harm no one?"

I struggle not to grimace. "As far as I know."

Her forehead wrinkles, thoughtful. She seems about to speak, but just then footsteps scuff outside the door. Both of us turn.

Nestor bursts in, talking over his shoulder. "Here he is. He seemed to make himself better, but—Oh, Jahan! You look well."

But I can't spare a glance for him, or even a word of comfort. My mouth has gone dry. I can hear my pulse echoing in my head.

Because he's not alone. A woman has crowded into the room behind him. A woman smaller than I remember, with silver threading her golden hair. But still straight-backed. Still powerful. Still terrifying.

Madiya.

She marches straight over to me, ignoring Elanna, and squats beside the pallet. It takes every ounce of control for me not to scuttle backward like a crab, away from her. My escape is entirely blocked.

Behind her, in the corridor, I glimpse a slight boy with a flop of dark hair. Lathiel. She's brought him with her. If I can get past her—if I can grab my little brother—I can wrestle him away from her, at last.

If he'll let me save him. If she hasn't completely poisoned him against me.

"I heard you were injured," she's saying. "Someone shot you! I came immediately, but I was afraid—I thought I might be too late."

She presses her lips tight together. Her eyes seem bright. Tears? Madiya has *tears* in her eyes? For *me*?

I don't believe it. Not for a moment. "Get away from me." I start to get up, to aim for the corridor.

Madiya pushes me back down. Actually *pushes* me. And because

I'm at an awkward angle, I tumble backward. She's grabbing my arm. "You healed yourself? Is it the well—the font?"

I don't believe this. I wrench my arm out of her grasp, but she's still there, looming over me like the figure from my nightmares. I'm ten years old again, panting, my pulse ricocheting in my chest. She's going to push me down. Drip laudanum into my mouth. Rustle about in my head, reconfiguring the patterns of my mind to make me a sorcerer. I'll forget everything I ever knew. She'll make me like my mother, a mindless shell of a person.

"I never realized the Ida well was on Solivetos Hill. It's brilliant of you, Jahan. Did you . . ." She stops. My blank terror must register with her at last. Quietly, she says, "You look so much like your mother. Like Alia."

"You have no right to speak my mother's name." I feel as if I'm choking. *"Get away from me."*

She blinks. Even though she's kneeling, she seems to grow taller. "But I'm here to *help* you!"

I should strike her. But I laugh—far harder than I should. "Of course you are. That's what you always think you're doing. Helping Rayka and Lathiel. Helping Elanna. Helping Bardas and Empress Firmina. But look at what you've done—you helped kill dozens of innocent people!"

"I had nothing to do with that," Madiya says coldly. "I gave the ability, not the orders."

"And Lathiel." I look at my brother, still peering in from the corridor. I try to stand, but Madiya blocks me. "You've harmed him—"

"Harmed? I've never *harmed* anyone—least of all your brother!"

"What are your damned experiments, then? What were you doing when you ripped the memories from our heads? When you forced us to do magic that didn't come naturally to us, when you stole our mother's memories—"

"She betrayed us!" Madiya's on her feet now, her hands clenched at her sides. "She was going to . . . she would have let witch hunters take you to the Ochuroma! Her own children!"

"No, she wouldn't." Of course, Mother always said sorcery was a great evil. She screamed it at my father. She whispered it to me. But she didn't hate sorcery enough to send us to the Ochuroma. She didn't hate *us*. She would gladly have sent Madiya and Father to prison. But not her own children.

"You're lying." I clamber to my feet. Lathiel's right there in the corridor. I'll push past Madiya and get him. "You always lie. You want something from me, and now—"

"Who shot you, Jahan?" she interrupts. "Was it Alcibiades Doukas?"

I stop dead. How does she know?

"I knew it," she mutters to herself. Then she looks at me. "Do you remember the witch hunter who came to my cottage, when you were ten years old?"

I choke on a laugh. "Do I *remember*? Did you make me kill him? Or was it Rayka who did it?"

Madiya blinks. She glances at Elanna, who is watching us with narrowed eyes, silent. But I can tell from her tension that she's ready to act. To defend me, at a moment's notice. It gives me courage.

"*You* didn't try to kill anyone," Madiya says. "But your mother . . ."

I touch my scar, its ridge filled with a grief I've never really understood. But I know too well how Madiya tries to manipulate us. I glance at Lathiel. He watches me with wide eyes from the doorway. For him, I have to be strong.

"She was mad!" Madiya is saying. "You were children! What was I supposed to do?" There's a strange desperation in her—a kind of twisted grief. Or maybe it's *me* she's twisting, like she always has. "Was I supposed to let you go through your life knowing what she did? Was I supposed to let *her* try to do it again?"

"I don't know what you're talking about," I say coldly. "But you're obviously lying—"

"I *saved* you!" Madiya exclaims. "I spared you!"

"From *what*? Our own mother?"

She lunges forward, grabbing my jaw in both hands. I jerk back, but she just holds me harder. Elanna shouts, "Let him *go*!" But even though she hauls on Madiya's shoulders, even though I struggle, Madiya doesn't release me.

"It's all right, Jahan," she says, panting. "Here's the truth."

She presses her fingertips to my forehead, but there's nothing gentle about the gesture. An arrow seems to lance from her skin into my skull, digging through the fabric of my mind, pushing and twisting. As if from far away, I hear myself cry out. It hurts so damned much, I feel tears stinging my eyes. She has no right to grab me like this— I try to pull away, but she pinches me harder. I kick at her legs and she bellows in my ear.

"Hold still! I'm *showing* you."

"Let him go!" Elanna shouts again.

"No—" I begin.

But I stop, my mouth open. The inside of my head *burns*—as if she ripped open a scar. A spark rises out of it.

Not a spark—a memory. The one she stole.

It splits open.

I'm in the cave with my brothers, as if it's yesterday, as if it's now. I've run to the bottom of the steps. Footsteps echo down the stones. I look up. I'm smiling; it's my mother who emerges. She's safe. The witch hunter didn't hurt her. Maybe he hurt Father and Madiya instead. In her fine clothes, with her hair tidied up on her head, she seems more powerful than she ever has. Calm. She seems as if she could do anything. A knife flashes in her hand, bright and silver.

Boys! she calls. We run over, and Rayka shoves Lathiel back into my arms. He starts crying, but I'm too stupid to heed his warning. I just bob him up and down.

The witch hunters are here, Mother says. She's composed. Smiling. She holds the knife as if it's a friend. *They're going to take your father and that witch to the Ochuroma. But I won't let them find you, my dear, sweet boys. I won't let them take you away. Come here, Rayka.*

He goes to her, his eyes trusting. Docile. Hopeful.

She strokes the hair back from his forehead and kisses his cheeks. She murmurs something to him. His eyes grow a little bit wide. I think maybe he's going to cry out, but he never gets the chance. She pulls back her arm and plunges the knife into his chest.

He chokes. They're wrestling. I lunge toward them, trying to push Mother off, but I've got Lathiel in my other arm. He's screaming. I reach for Mother, but he bangs his forehead into my chin. My head snaps back. I feel a hand fisting the back of my shirt. Terror bursts through me; I try to run but Mother holds me tight. Her hair swings against my neck, falling loose from its knot. She's breathing hard in my ear. Something wet drips onto my shoulder—my brother's blood.

I have to break free. I have to save Lathiel—

Hold still, darling! Mother orders me in a singsong voice, but I don't hold still. I'm trying to break her grip. A stinging pain lances into the skin behind my ear. I catch a glimpse of Rayka's body crumpled on the ground. I'm screaming. *I missed,* Mother says petulantly. She tries to grab me tighter, but this time I break loose, bolting for the steps. But Mother charges after me, wrestling me to the ground. I lose Lathiel. He's crawling away. I try to push Mother back. Her eyebrows are knotted. She reaches for my cheek. *I'm trying to save you, darling.*

Shouts echo above us on the steps. My father barrels into us, knocking Mother down. She slashes at him with the knife. But I don't see the rest, because Madiya is there, terror white in her face, saying, *Jahan, are you all right?* And Mother, no longer calm, is screaming, *He's my son! I'm going to save him! You ruined his mind, and I'm going to get it out! I'm going to fix what you've done!*

Father slaps her. She starts to sob. Madiya is kneeling by Rayka, saying, *He'll survive, it's all right.* I watch, dazed, my chest aching. I've been crying. Madiya rushes over to her workstation, then comes back to me with a delicate bottle of laudanum. I open my mouth, numbly, to let her drop a tiny bit onto my tongue. The bitterness of the opium is a balm. I let it carry me away into darkness.

And the memory closes. I'm back in the small room behind the temple, sweat drenching my shirt, Madiya holding me upright, too close to her, Elanna digging her hands into Madiya's shoulders. I can't seem to find my breath. This is why she made us forget. This is why she thought she'd done my mother a mercy.

I gather myself, and this time, I shove Madiya away. She rocks backward into Elanna. Quietly, I say, "I did not give you permission to touch me."

Elanna nudges Madiya away from her. She staggers against the wall, but she's not shaken. She straightens her clothes. Her eyes have narrowed; she's not done with me yet. "Your mother loved you, I suppose," she says, each word weighted like a knife. "It was why she tried to murder you, in her madness."

"No," I say. Not denying it. The memory seemed too real. The grief, the terror of it, felt too right.

This isn't the answer I wanted. This isn't the truth I was hoping for.

But I'm not denying the truth. I'm simply denying Madiya the power over me. Denying her interpretation of this story. "But that's not the only memory you took from me. Every *day* you took memories. My mother didn't try to murder me that often."

Madiya's mouth compresses. Reluctantly, she says, "It was a corollary of changing how your minds work. Making room for sorcery . . . took away other things. It suppressed your other memories."

"Our memories of breakfast were sacrificed for walking through walls?" I say caustically.

"I didn't know it was happening at first," Madiya replies, her posture stiff. "Neither you nor Rayka told me. You acted as if I was deliberately punishing you. It was an *accident.*"

An accident—until she discovered what was happening and didn't stop doing it. Until she did it deliberately to my mother. To me. To Rayka. To Lathiel.

The truth, the real truth, hits me then like a horrible punch in the chest. "Why was our mother mad?"

Madiya stays very still. But her eyes dart back and forth. Behind her, Elanna stares at me, stricken. I can no longer see Lathiel in the doorway. I don't know if he's listening. I want to close his ears to this—but at the same time, I want him to listen. I want him to know.

"She wasn't always, was she?" I say, dragging the words up from a deep place. An ugly place. A place where, it seems, I've always known the truth. A place where I saw the laudanum bottle on my mother's vanity, and thought nothing of it. "You gave it to her, too—the opium. Once you realized you could destroy our memories, you tried to take hers. *You* sent her mad. Little by little. Every day."

Madiya just stares at me. This is not something she ever wanted me to guess. And now I suspect why she finally gave me back the memory of my mother trying to kill me—to make me more loyal to her. To make me, at last, stop mourning my mother.

But I never will.

"When did you do it?" I demand. "At night? She took the laudanum to help her sleep. Because she had nightmares. Did you come up to the villa then, and destroy pieces of her mind?"

"She was going to betray us!" Madiya bursts out. "She kept writing those damned letters to her sister! I don't know why Ghesar never took the pen and paper from her—"

I stand up, and Madiya shrinks back. "That," I say, "might be the only honest thing you've ever told me."

I stride out of the room, Elanna on my heels. Lathiel stands there in the corridor, his eyes large. He's trembling. Has she been giving him the laudanum? I reach out a hand, but he twists away from me and bolts, not even bothering to be invisible.

I start after him. "Lathiel!"

"Jahan, let him be." El grabs my elbow, slowing me. "Let him come around."

I stare at her. I want to break free and run after my brother, but maybe she's right. I turn back, one last time, to face Madiya. She's standing on the threshold of my chamber, more hesitant than I've ever seen her.

"What have you done to him?" I demand.

"Nothing!" she says, but guilt crosses her face, just for a moment.

I stalk back toward her. "He's frightened of the whole damned world. On Pira, he asked me if I knew how to kill a man without touching him!" I draw in a breath and say again, "What have you done to him?"

"It was just an experiment," she mutters. "Like any other."

I take another step toward her, and she must see, at last, that I'm not afraid of her. She begins to babble. "They were destined for hanging anyway. Convicts. I had him sneak us into the prison, make us invisible, muffle our sounds. There were two men in the cell. He had to drain the life energy from one to take the life from the other. The old theurges could kill people without touching them, by squeezing their hearts until they burst. So we tried it."

I swallow down my horror. She actually did what I always thought she did—made someone kill a man. But instead of Rayka or me, it was my littlest brother. No wonder his eyes are haunted. "You mean you forced him to try it."

She eyes me warily. "The boy's soft. He did it, weeping the whole time as if *he* was dying. He cried for two days straight afterward. I tried to take away the memory, but he hid from me. Your father tried to talk to him, to tell him it was something he needed to learn, but he wouldn't listen. I thought he was going as mad as your mother."

As mad as she *made* our mother, she means. "Why?" I demand. "Why does a twelve-year-old boy need to kill a man without touching him? Why does a twelve-year-old need to kill *anyone*?"

"The witch hunters," Madiya begins.

"It's always the damned witch hunters!" I shout. I lean toward her, lowering my voice. "If you ever touch him again, I will see you imprisoned for life. I will see your magic removed. You will never see daylight again. Do you understand?"

Her chin hardens. But when I lift my eyebrows, she nods minutely.

I put my back to her. El's waiting. She holds out a hand; her fingers twist around mine. I'm more grateful for her touch than I can say. Together, we leave Madiya behind, though my thoughts chase themselves around my head. She forced Lathiel to kill two men, and the horror of it overwhelmed him. Yet, instead of finding me at Aexione, he went to her. Her hold over him is that strong.

We emerge into the sunshine, and I spot him. He's huddled between the parapet and one of the burned-out trees, shaking. I release El's hand and approach him. His eyes, enormous, track my every movement.

I stop a few feet away. I don't want to force my presence on him, but I need him to know what I'm going to say.

"You never have to go back to her," I tell him. "You don't owe her anything. You don't belong to her. Your body is your own—your mind is your own. You never have to let her touch you again."

He blinks at me, wordless.

"And—" I swallow hard. "—I'm sorry. I'm sorry I left you there with her. I'm sorry I didn't take you with me when I left. I'm sorry I didn't go back for you."

I wait, but still, he doesn't speak. His shaking, though, has lessened. I want to hug him. Ruffle his hair. Give him all the reassurance I've withheld for six years. But his posture is still too wary, his eyes too frightened. So instead I just say, "I promise I'll be here for you now, if you want me. Always."

He just stares.

I sigh and, turning, go back to Elanna. She's waiting for me farther down the parapet. Below, I glimpse Rayka climbing up the steps from the lower temple, the sunlight shining off his hair.

Madiya ruined us more than I even imagined—she took away our mother, piece by piece, not all at once but over years and years. She stole Mother from us. And she stole our memories, too. Does that make us mad, like Mother?

No. Not exactly. But our minds have been changed. They're full of holes, and maybe we are, too, in the fabric of our being. The holes of grief we don't remember and can't even express. But even if those gaps can never be filled, even if our memories can never be returned, we can reconstruct the truth around them. We can survive. And maybe even, slowly, day by day, we can heal.

Elanna wraps an arm around me. I put mine around her. She doesn't speak, and neither do I. Yet her presence makes the old, ugly grief bearable. It makes it *seen*. We hold it between us, as we hold each other, and we breathe.

CHAPTER TWENTY-FIVE

We're still standing there when Rayka arrives at the top, minutes later. For a moment, I think relief eases his face. He strides over and grabs my arm, dragging me from Elanna. "Come on."

I let him pull me over to the wall overlooking the city. "I hear and obey . . ."

I stop. All thought of Madiya and our childhood flies out of my head. Metal winks below us in the streets; in the haze of shock, I didn't see it before. A river of muskets and bayonets, marching toward the lower temple. Bells ring. The earth groans as cannons are winched along.

"How," I begin, and then stop. Another man is coming up the steps, Tullea on his heels. He wears a jaunty black suit, but his familiar smile isn't there. Tullea looks grim.

"The militia followed him." Rayka spits, "And Madiya."

Bardas Triciphes strides over to us, breathing hard from the long walk up the stairs. "Jahan!" His gaze flickers behind me. "Lady Elanna. We've been found out. The damned Saranons suborned one of my servants, or . . ."

"You shouldn't have come through the streets," Rayka tells him, as if he's an idiot.

Elanna comes up beside me, brushing her hand unobtrusively down my arm. A steadying gesture. I'm grateful for it. "They followed you? What about Empress Firmina?"

He shrugs helplessly. "I don't know! They'll use it as an excuse to search her chambers. Maybe arrest her. We have to get her to Aexione."

"Aexione?" I repeat. "Why not just bring her here?"

Bardas shakes his head once, vigorously. "She needs to get to the emperor before anyone else does. Before Augustus and Phaedra."

Everyone seems to be looking at me. I hear myself say, "I'll gladly take a score against the Saranons," but I'm looking down at the guns winking in the city below. I can't leave everyone in the face of a siege—on top of a hill that doesn't have defenses.

More than that, I don't want to leave my brothers here, alone. With Madiya.

"My cousin has a plan," Bardas insists. "She can save us all, if she just gets to Aexione. She can stop this attack."

Do I believe him? I see the panic in his face. He's worried about Firmina, if nothing else. If she is imprisoned—or killed—we lose the one person in power who might help us.

El touches my arm again. Her face is fierce. She must have reached the same conclusion I have. "You go, Jahan." She looks at Tullea, who hesitates, then nods. "Tullea and I will manage. We'll let the entire city know that the Witch of Eren is here to defeat them. That'll put some fear into them."

"We need to close the lower temple," Tullea says. "Bring everyone up here."

Elanna glances at Mount Angelos looming in the distance. "If only I could make that mountain walk, we could scare them into surrender."

She needs her power back. I look at her, at the collar gleaming around her neck. Maybe with the power of Tirisero's font—Mantius's font, now that I know the truth—I can break it.

"Let me try something," I say. She turns to me, startled, as I touch the collar. Within the smooth metal, the witch stones hum, nudging me away. All the same, I feel with my mind for the metal itself, pulling all the power of the font into me, a stream of unseen fire. *Break,* I order the collar.

Elanna gasps. My eyes fly open. She's dropped to her knees, clutching her neck and hissing with pain. Tullea's run over, crouching beside her.

I drop down, too. "El, what's wrong? Did I injure you? Are you—"

"I'm fine," she manages, her voice choked. She opens her hands. The collar still clamps her neck, and now an ugly red flush stains her skin. "It's hot, that's all. I could feel it *thinning,* almost. I thought it was going to break."

But it hasn't, and I can't bear her disappointment. I reach for her hand.

"It's all right." She shakes me off and clambers to her feet, her chin set. "My name will have to be enough."

"But no one knows you're here," Tullea points out. "Or that you're even alive."

Elanna bares her teeth in a smile. "Then we will tell them. You have magic. All of you do. We'll proclaim it to the world. Jahan, we can manage without you. Go."

Only a fool ignores the *Caveadear,* but still I hesitate. There's a lot of metal glinting in the streets below. And Lathiel still huddles on the far side of the parapet, watching me now. "You can defend the steps. Destroy them if you have to."

Rayka shoulders forward. "I already have a plan for that."

Elanna and Tullea exchange a glance; they both seem prepared for battle already. They don't need Rayka's help, at least not yet. I shake my head. "You need to show me the route through the cisterns, to the Old Palace."

He sighs with disgust and stomps away down the stairs. I take a step after him, but pause. The troops are only getting in position now. If I go quickly, perhaps I can return before they attack.

"We need to strike at the head of the empire," Bardas says. "That's what you and Firmina must do."

"I suppose you're right." I glance back, though, at the rescued prisoners who are gathering behind us, Lucius Argyros among them. Madiya's come out of the temple. I give her a hard stare. She flinches.

I say to Elanna, "Don't let her anywhere near Lathiel, unless he asks for her. Even if he does . . ."

El grips my arm fiercely. "I won't. I'll talk to Lathiel."

I should talk to him myself—but the army approaching through the streets reminds me I have no time. My brother will have to wait. Irene and Sabina approach, passing me bread and cheese, and a cup of thin tea. I drink it quickly and pocket the food for the long walk through the cisterns. I don't like leaving, especially not with Madiya lurking here like a vulture, but my head is full of Bardas's argument. If Firmina can do some good in Aexione, it may make all the difference. And we can't afford to lose her.

I turn to El. "I'll put out the word," I say. "I'll tell the world the Witch of Eren is alive on top of Solivetos Hill, ready to make a stand."

She grabs me by the collar and pulls me in for a kiss, right there in front of everyone. Heat burns into my face, but all the gods, who cares if anyone sees us now? I kiss her back, hearing scattered laughter around us. When she draws back, she's grinning. "The Witch of Eren, and the Korakos."

"Yes," I say. I kiss her again, swiftly, and then I follow my brother down the hill.

THE CISTERNS BRING us to the secret tunnel burrowed beneath the Old Palace. Through a series of natural caves to our left, the sea thumps. I wonder if the Saranons still know they have this escape route—or secret entrance. The waist-high grate leading into the tunnel isn't guarded.

"Well, you can handle the rest on your own," Rayka says brusquely. He's been burning to get back to Solivetos Hill and enact his plan with the steps. He hardly spoke two words to me the entire way here. When I tried to talk to him about Madiya—tentatively, not even sure how to broach the subject—he just soldiered on ahead, silent. He doesn't remember what happened in the cave any more than I did, and he certainly doesn't want to hear about how he almost died at Mother's hand. He doesn't want to know that Madiya was slipping Mother's memories away all along, sending her to the place where, at last, she broke.

It's just as well. My bones ache with a kind of lifelong grief. I don't know if I can speak about it without breaking down.

"Keep an eye on Lathiel," I tell him as he turns to go.

"Right." But even though his tone is flat, I see his shoulders hitch upward. He might not be gentle with our little brother, but he'll keep Madiya away from him. I know that.

Rayka marches off, and I crawl through the grate, the buzzing particles of the iron bars cold inside my skin. The tunnel lies completely dark, except for the distant gaps of light at either end. I feel along the walls for the open staircase leading up. I'm befuddled in the dark, and it takes too long to find it. Finally, though, I climb up.

And stop, sucking in my breath. Voices echo at the top. Guards?

No, not guards. I slink up one step, another. They're in the sunken garden. Augustus never bothers to lower his voice; it echoes against the stones.

". . . never going to accept you," he's saying. "You might as well not exist."

My throat tightens. I grab at the stone wall, but it doesn't cool the anger rising in me.

"You wouldn't be the first to abdicate." A woman's voice, brittle and cold. Phaedra. "The son of Paladius the Second did. Where did he go? Omira? He lived on some little island in a beautiful villa. I'm sure he kept a garden. It could be just like home. You could even take Zollus Katabares with you."

"He's the only one who seems interested in your existence," Augustus quips. "Since you lost Korakides . . ."

"I have no intention of abdicating." That's Leontius, his voice so quiet I strain to hear it. "I wouldn't inflict that on my people."

"They would hardly miss you," Augustus says carelessly.

"I meant *you*," Leontius retorts. "I wouldn't inflict the two of *you* on the people."

There's a silence. I fight the urge to stride through into the garden and step in front of Leontius, my fists swinging. But he's made it abundantly clear he doesn't want my help or my friendship.

"I think you may wish to reconsider," Phaedra says, her tone falsely pleasant. "You can go of your own accord, or you can go whether you like it or not."

"I don't think either of us is such a bad catch," Augustus adds, sounding hurt. "The people adore us. We're always in the newspapers."

Not exactly a vote in his favor, I think. The newspapers love to mock him.

"So you plan to force me out." Leontius sounds tired. "I won't ask how, since I've never done a thing wrong. I'm sure you'll concoct some nonsense and spin it as the truth."

"Oh, that's where you're wrong," Phaedra says, with a smile in her voice. "We don't need to. We know what we've seen."

There's another silence. I take an involuntary step forward. What do they mean, they know what they've seen? What on earth has Leontius ever done? Most of the time he's digging in the garden, for the sake of all the gods. Not exactly execrable behavior.

"You can make all the claims you want," Leontius says, but his voice is unsteady. He must know what they're talking about. Why don't I? "You still have to get Father to believe them."

"Why wouldn't he?" Augustus says smugly. "Do you think he wants *you* to inherit? The one who begged him to stop 'the assault on our people'?"

He did? But Leontius told me he wouldn't take the risk . . .

"We all know most of the people rounded into the Frourio were innocents," Lees says, his voice clipped. "And now many of them are dead because Father wanted to make a point. It's weak. And abhorrent. I stand by what I said."

"Then you should also stand by your imminent departure," Phaedra replies. "Goodbye, older brother."

Augustus chuckles. "Goodbye!"

There's a rustle as they depart the garden. I'm left alone—shocked, in a way, but at the same time not surprised. It's always only been a matter of time before Leontius's siblings found a way to usurp his throne. What astonishes me more is the revelation that he stood up to Emperor Alakaseus.

Maybe I don't know my friend as well as I thought.

I edge forward, peering into the garden. He's standing underneath a myrtle bush. He doesn't seem to be doing anything.

I almost go forward. I almost go up to him and say I want to help. That we can work together.

But he doesn't want anything to do with me. And I need to find Firmina. She's proven she's willing to help us—and now she needs someone's help in return.

I've waited too long. Leontius is walking away now, weaving a little, bowled over by some emotion. I can just see his head disappear into the colonnade.

I go after him.

THE PALACE HALLS have erupted into chaos. Servants run in every direction with food and bags, and ahead of me Leontius is calling out orders for someone to ready him a coach to Aexione. We pass through an open courtyard, laced with mezzanines above us. Raised voices break out overhead. The servants slow, looking up. Leontius stares. I hang back—*nothing to see here*—and crane my neck back.

It's Firmina. I can see her silhouette, and hear her voice: "By *my* authority—"

Someone else rumbles a response, which echoes down into the courtyard. "You've been overruled by the Saranons, madam. My apologies."

Damn it. I'm too late.

I sprint for the stairs. Firmina's on the second floor, nose-to-nose with the captain of the guards. She's dressed in a blue redingote for travel, but he's gesturing her back into her chambers. "You're to wait here until a full guard is prepared to escort you, madam."

"But why am I being treated like this?" the empress exclaims. "I've done nothing to merit anyone's displeasure!"

The captain hesitates, but even from here I can tell Firmina has turned her most beseeching gaze upon him, and he's lost. "Of course not, madam—that is—your cousin Bardas has been discovered aiding and abetting the criminal sorcerers. Prince Augustus and Princess Phaedra believe you should remain with us, free from suspicion . . ."

"Oh, I see." Firmina's tone softens. It's marvelous acting; the captain leans forward as if she's hooked him with a line. "You are too kind, Captain. My cousin Bardas does the most ill-advised things— I am sorry to take responsibility for him. Do let me know when the guard is ready."

She retreats into the chambers and the captain, flustered, orders the guards to hurry their preparations. I wait until the mezzanine has cleared somewhat, then melt through the wall.

I don't see Firmina Triciphes at first. The room appears to be empty: just a collection of plush velvet furniture, a tea service, a fireplace filled with only coals. But before I can try one of the doors leading off the room, I hear a whisper.

You don't see me. You don't see me.

It's subtle. Persuasive to anyone without sorcery. But it's so well aligned with my own magic that I hear it.

And I see her, the way one glimpses a mirage, her arms braced on the table by the tea service. She seems somewhat insubstantial. I'm not sure she heard me come in.

The empress of Paladis is a *sorceress*? It seems impossible. Absurd. And yet there she is.

Bardas told me a sorceress was helping them . . .

"You're very close," I say. "I almost didn't notice you at all."

Firmina gasps. She turns, her hands up as if in self-defense. But then she sees me, and a brilliant smile bursts over her face. "Jahan! What are you doing here?"

"Bardas sent me," I say, though the simple delight in her face puzzles me. She's surrounded by guards and witch hunters. She ought to be afraid, but she's not. "He thought Augustus and Phaedra might have accused you—which it seems they have. I'm supposed to escort you out of the city, to Aexione."

She rolls her eyes. "I was going to manage that myself! But it is very chivalrous of you to come."

How skilled *is* she? "You might have had trouble once you were among people. Persuasion can be hard to maintain in a crowd."

"I suppose you would know," she says, with a smiling glance. "You've been brought up to practice sorcery, and I'm still learning."

Brought up to practice sorcery? How does she know? Unless Elanna told her, there's only one other person she could have heard that from. Madiya has been in the Deos Deorum—and before that, in Aexione. Elanna told me she'd met the empress and forged a treaty. Madiya must have been there, too. Bardas and Firmina have had her all this time and, I realize with a coldness running down my spine, I never asked why.

"I didn't realize you were a sorceress," I say. "You must have hidden it well . . ."

She grimaces slightly. "I inherited it from my poor father. He had some little magic—nothing much. Nothing the witch hunters could catch. But there's a kind of madness that comes over sorcerers when they can't perform their magic—have you seen it? It's a kind of melancholy, brought on by having to live a lie, I suppose. It killed him in the end." She looks thoughtful. "I learned a good deal from it."

"I'm sorry." I remember now that her father died the year before she caught the emperor's eye. But my mind is still spinning back to Madiya. Has she given Firmina the laudanum, too? Rearranged the patterns of her mind, to make her a better sorceress? "And you're . . . learning . . . from Madiya."

"Oh! Sylvia, you mean." Firmina tilts her head, apologetic. "I hope you don't mind that we dug through your correspondence."

"My *correspondence*?" I echo.

"I'm afraid so." She offers me a charming smile. "We suspected you of knowing sorcery, you see, Bardas and I. Little things you did. The way you manipulated some of the courtiers into accepting you.

And the story about how you saved Leontius's life . . . it sounded like magic to me."

I'm staring at her, my hands empty. I can feel my pulse at the back of my mouth. I should have known someone would see through the persuasion I worked on people, the lies I told about saving Leontius's life. But I didn't expect that person to be Firmina Triciphes.

"Then your brother came to court, and we realized he must be a sorcerer, too! Bardas heard some story about him setting off a musket without touching it." Firmina shrugs. "And everyone knows you've been in legal arguments with your father. So Bardas . . . looked into things. When Alakaseus banished him from court, he went to the Britemnos Isles. Found your father." She smiles. "Your father was very amenable to working with us, once he knew what we wanted. He introduced Bardas to Sylvia—to Madiya—and invited her to come here. She's been helping me do so many things. Work persuasion. Move walls. Then you came back. Things are working out awfully well, aren't they?"

But I can't answer. My mouth has gone dry, because the obvious has finally hit me. It was Firmina Triciphes who destroyed the Frourio and let me and my sorcerers take the blame. This woman in her elegant redingote, who's smiling at me.

"That was *you,*" I say stupidly. "*You* made the walls walk. You killed . . ."

"I didn't mean for it to happen as it did!" she protests, catching my hands in hers. "I meant to frighten the imperial militia, and let the sorcerers escape. I didn't mean—I didn't know—"

She killed Pantoleon when she made the Frourio collapse—unless he had already been evacuated to the Ochuroma by then, which was a death sentence all on its own. She killed so many people. I heard their screams. I saw their bodies crushed by the bricks. My throat burns. I want to shout at her.

But her regret is genuine. Her palms are damp. Tears stand out in her eyes.

"Trust me, Jahan," she whispers. "I would never have done it if I'd known."

I nod, mechanical. Wordless.

"But I had to try *something*," she says fiercely. "To have the power, and not use it to help . . . !"

I pull my hands free. "Madiya should have known it wouldn't work."

"She advised me against it." Firmina sighs. "But our time is running out, and I have to take risks." She glances at the door. "We should go now, Jahan."

"Yes." I shake myself alert. Later, perhaps, it will seem more possible that Empress Firmina has been a sorceress all her life. That she sent Bardas Triciphes to the Britemnos Isles to meet with my father. That he brought Madiya back with him. "We need to get you to Aexione."

"Indeed." She smiles slightly. "I must see my husband before my stepchildren find him first."

"Come with me."

She tucks her hand into mine, like a child—or a lover. When I look at her, she just gives me a winsome smile. I find myself thinking that if this woman is powerful enough to make walls walk—even if they end up collapsing—then I am not about to anger her in any way. Instead I pull her out the wall after me, into the servants' corridor. *No one to see here.* We hurry down, passing behind the kitchens. No one gives us a second glance.

"You're better at this than I am, Jahan," the empress says warmly.

We come into the stable yard. Men are readying a coach—for Leontius? I see him trotting out through the colonnade.

I tug the empress along. "You can go with Lees—"

"I'm afraid that may be too slow. We may get stopped. And my stepson . . ." She wrinkles her nose. Of course, Leontius isn't much fonder of her than Augustus and Phaedra are. I stifle a sigh. I'll get her through the city, then teach her how to compress space for herself on the road. I'm surprised Madiya hasn't taught her anything so practical—though if Firmina thinks she can move buildings, perhaps she's skipped the foundational steps and gone straight for spectacle.

Somewhere behind us, in the palace, a shout goes up. It sounds like Firmina's name.

"Oh, dear," she says. "We'd better hurry."

We run through the gate, dodging guards, and out into the street. It's packed. Militia are streaming across the Great Bridge, ranks and ranks of them. I almost stop dead.

"Are they all going to Solivetos Hill?" I ask.

The empress purses her lips. "Some may be going to quell other protests around the city."

The urge to run back to Solivetos is so strong I have to lock my legs in place. Elanna and Tullea can hold it, with the help of Rayka and the others. And if Firmina can persuade Alakaseus to treat with us, if she can counteract Augustus and Phaedra, then we all stand a greater chance of success. And survival.

So I tug her by the hand into the street. We'll be faster on foot, and more anonymous, blending into the stream of pedestrians angling past the marching militia and into Vileia. Once we reach the broad avenues, I look about for a coach we can steal.

"That one." The empress points to a bright-green phaeton, abandoned outside a mansion. It's the kind of thing a flashy court dandy would drive. Firmina climbs in while I unhobble the horses. *Nothing to see here.* The vehicle bobs when I hop in, and Firmina's already seized the reins. We charge forward through the streets. *Just some young nobles out driving too fast.*

We arrive quickly on the city's outskirts. Mount Angelos rises ahead, delicate clouds clinging to its crown. The empress slows the phaeton, so I can explain to her how to compress space.

A *boom* rattles through the earth. At first I think it's the mountain. But Firmina glances swiftly behind us.

It came from the city. From Solivetos Hill?

I'm swinging off the phaeton before I can even stop to think. "Can you manage without me? Even without compressing space, you should reach the palace before they do . . ."

She's watching me with concern. "What can you do against can-

nons, Jahan? Come to Aexione and we can deal with Alakaseus together."

Together? But I'm a criminal. The emperor will execute me long
before he listens to a word I say. Besides, Firmina Triciphes is the
most charming woman I've ever met. She doesn't need my help.

Another *boom* quivers through the ground. Elanna's back there,
in the city, without the full use of her magic. She, and Tullea, and
Rayka and Lathiel. Bardas. Even Madiya. And all the others. I need
to go back.

"I'm sorry," I say to the empress, and then I turn and run toward
the city.

CHAPTER TWENTY-SIX

The booming of the cannons doesn't let up as I make for the Middle Bridge, falling in among the ranks of militia. *Just another soldier.* Once I reach the university quarter, I dive for the nearest cistern entrance. Rayka's misdirect confuses even me. I stumble in two different directions before I finally let myself find it by touch rather than reason. Through the door, I fumble for an ancient torch on the wall, summoning fire out of it, and run down into the tunnels, to the steep stairs behind the pool.

But when I emerge into the lower temple, it's to a deafening thunder of cannons. A wall in front of me shakes and collapses. I sprint for the steps, blind with pure fear. But the steps no longer exist. They've been sliced clean away, as if someone cut them with a knife. It must have been my brother; he said he had a plan for the stairs.

Another cannonball bursts through the stones behind me. I bolt, flinging myself to the ground just in time. I reach for the cannons with my mind, trying to slam the vents closed, but only one attempt seems to succeed. Somewhere, bells are ringing. The witch hunters must be blocking my magic. Even with the cannons thundering, even with the lower temple destroyed, the energy of the font hums through the air. Maybe I can use it to pull myself up the steep, wooded hillside.

I climb over the empty threshold where the steps used to be, reaching for a mulberry tree. I use it to lever myself up. Compress space. My feet slide—dirt falls—but I dig my fingers into earth and tree roots and hang on. Pull myself up and compress space again. A spray of gunpowder narrowly misses me. I reach to break the guns, but again my magic slides off.

I climb, compressing space again, and again. The next time, my fingernails scrape stone. I've reached the ramparts. I drag myself up—

Into the snout of a musket.

It doesn't erupt in my face, even though I'm staring, frozen. Then the gun is flung aside, and hands grasp my forearms, hoisting me up. "What the hell do you think you're doing?" the woman shouts. It's Elanna, her face smeared with black powder.

I grin like an idiot, tumbling at last to safety. "It seemed like the best way to get back in."

The stones shake under another blast. El drags me to my feet, then seizes the musket. "They just attacked. No explanation. Just the mortar fire. None of the others can break their guns!"

I glance around, seeing Irene and Sabina loading their own muskets, and Tullea weaving an illusion on the other side of the temple. But it's shredded to nothing when it drifts close enough to the militia, and the endlessly ringing bells.

"It's the witch hunters," I begin, but then I stop. Elanna's staring down the hill, her face stiffening with horror.

I look, and my pulse pounds into my ears. A tall wooden structure is being winched upright below us. Another one follows it. Siege towers, three stories tall. They aren't as high as the hill, but once they're in place, the soldiers will be able to fire up at us from the shelter of the roof.

And hundreds of men crowd the streets—maybe thousands. Far more than there are of us. The emperor will see their lives as disposable, until ours are removed.

Cannons are being winched up into the towers. Maybe, at this near distance, I can break them. I don't see witch hunters. Cannons are harder to break than muskets, but by concentrating, I can pull out the lanyards and force the vents to collapse. I reach for the nearest one; the impact of its collapse rocks through me. The second one explodes in a gasp of black smoke and sparks. Shouts ring up from the siege towers.

Elanna's gripping the wall with one hand, the other clutching the collar around her neck. "This damned thing! I could make the whole hill walk and terrify them—I could make the mountain move—"

Behind us, another siege tower has risen up. A shot bursts out, skittering off the wall beside El's fingers. We both dive for safety. Another burst follows it.

I halt it in midair, and it crashes against the stones below us, sending up a plume of smoke. Sweat already soaks my shirt. If I have to stop every shot individually, this siege will last forever.

El's digging at her choker, and rage burns up in my throat. Rage that neither Alakaseus Saranon nor his ministers believe we constitute a threat, much less a voice that must be heard. I grab El's hands and pull her up. Maybe I couldn't break the collar before—but maybe I wasn't trying hard enough.

"I have an idea." We run back into the temple, and I stop right beside the font. Power rolls off it, intoxicating. Madiya told me I was brilliant to find it; she called it the Ida well. A *well,* not a font. Does that mean there are more? But I don't know where Madiya is, and I don't have time to ask these questions, even if I trusted her enough to believe her response.

I push my hand into the space between the lid and the font. Elanna crouches beside me, saying, "Jahan—"

But then her voice disappears into the roar of the font. Brilliant sparks pour into my hands, into my body. I'm alight. Electric. Vibrating. Light replacing the dull network of muscle and sinew. Is this safe? Am I going to burst apart like Mantius? But it feels good— warm, shocking, invigorating.

Someone grasps my elbow. Drags my arm backward. I gasp. Sparks dance across my vision. Through tearing eyes, I can just make out Elanna, clutching my arm tight.

"I thought you were going to *erupt,*" she begins.

The buzzing lingers in my hands. I lift them up and touch her choker. She gasps.

Break, I think. This time I hardly even have to insist.

The collar shatters under my palms. Clean shards that spray down Elanna's shirt and kick back into my face. She splutters. I wipe off my chin.

"It worked." The words feel awkward, too large, in my mouth. I'm grinning maniacally, I realize.

El's staring at me. Our eyes lock. For some reason, we both start to laugh.

"Who would have thought," I manage, "that all I needed to do was stick my hand in a magic spring—"

But Elanna cuts me off with a kiss, intent and ferocious. I lean into her, even though I hear the rattle of guns outside the temple. We need to go. But the power is humming in me, and I feel dazed to be back in the world.

Too soon, she breaks away, breathless. "You wonderful fool. Did you know that's what would happen?"

"Lucky guess." I'm still grinning, drunk on the buzzing in my skin.

A *crack* sounds outside. Both of us jump to our feet, running for the door.

"Where's Lathiel?" I ask.

She gestures back inside. "I put him with the prisoners, the ones who couldn't fight. They're in the back, keeping him safe. Madiya's here, somewhere, but I told them not to let her near him."

"Thank you."

Outside, our rebels have scattered back toward the safety of the temple walls. So we see him the moment we run out: my brother, standing on the parapet, his arms raised. He looks ready to dive over the edge like a bird. Like Mantius.

"*Rayka!*" I bellow, charging toward him.

He looks around. He's covered in black powder, and half his hair stands on end. The moment I see his face, the sweat on my spine freezes. What has he done?

"They had powder kegs," he says. There's a luminosity about him; several grubby reformers are looking up at him with awe.

"They were going to undermine the wall. Even without seeing, I could feel the fuses. Test the probable range of impact." He grins a little. "The same principles of warfare Vasilides taught us at the academy."

"Vasilides," I echo.

"I just had to spark the fuses so they exploded too soon. Well," he grins, "at just the right moment."

I step up to the parapet and stare down the hill. The siege towers have collapsed—not only collapsed, but *exploded.* A tangled mess of wood, metal, and the meaty red of bodies lies below us.

The top of my head seems to combust. "I told you to *defend* us! You were supposed to keep us *safe,* not massacre them!"

Rayka's jaw sets. He jumps down from the parapet. "It's *war.*"

"Those are *our own people.*"

"I won!"

"All the gods, Rayka, you didn't damned win! This isn't about *winning,* this is about everyone, in all of Ida, all of Paladis . . ." I see how he stares at me; I throw my hands up. "You know what? Never mind."

I swing back to the people watching us, who have largely busied themselves. Elanna's at the wall; she casts me a sick look. I don't know what to say. We need to strategize—decide whether we can attempt a truce—but right now, I'm so angry I can't even think. My brother is a sorcerer, just like me, only he's had more recent lessons. He has a finesse and control I don't. So there is no reasonable excuse for killing everyone in the siege towers and wounding who knows how many more below them.

There are other ways he could have done it—ways that aren't murder. And he knows it.

Nestor comes running up with a cup of water, clearly warring between triumph and fear. I take the cup and throw it over my head. The coldness shocks some of the rage from me. I can breathe again. Think again.

Rayka's right. This *is* war. The emperor is treating us as an incendiary faction that must be put down by an armed force. He won't use delaying tactics; he won't hesitate. He'll use every tactic of brutal efficiency to destroy us.

Except those are our own people, down there on the ground. The emperor might not have any compunction about firing on his subjects, but I don't have to operate by the same tactics.

The power of Mantius's font still hums in me. I know what I'm going to do.

Shaking the water from my eyes, I turn back to the wall. Elanna stands with her arms folded. We look at each other, and I can see she's had the same thought as me.

"Can you do this?" she says. "I know you can heal yourself, but . . ."

"I've done it for another before," I say. "I don't know if I can do it for so many. But I have to try. If nothing else—If nothing else, we can help."

She holds out her hand. Slowly, bursting through the earth, tree roots cobble together, making a kind of staircase we can climb downhill.

She scowls. "It's too damned sluggish."

"You can't always be instantaneously extraordinary." I smile at her, though my mouth feels heavy. Together, we climb down the hill.

Below, it's carnage, a mangled route of canvas, blood, and splintered wood. The wreckage of bodies is scattered back into the smashed stones and trees, torsos separated from legs, necks missing heads. On the other side of the lower temple, beyond the worst of the dead, soldiers and medics are pulling the wounded survivors toward safety. As we approach the ruined temple, a man limps toward us, holding up a piece of canvas stained with blood. The nearest thing to a white cloth he could find.

"Truce!" he calls, his voice hoarse. "We demand truce to care for our wounded, under the law of war."

I stop, holding up my hands. "You have it. We've come to help care for the wounded. One of our people was . . . was overcome with battle frenzy. It wasn't meant to go like this."

The man stares from me to Elanna and back again. "But aren't you the Korakos?"

"I'm Jahan Korakides. And this is Elanna Valtai." I pause. "And I'm Paladisan, just like you. I don't want to see our people die any more than you do, no matter what side they're on."

He blinks. There are tears in his eyes. He gestures us forward. "Then come help."

Beneath the siege towers, it's ugly. One man is missing a leg. Another his arm. One has taken lead shot in the gut; his forehead is slick with sweat, his hands clammy. The medics say he won't make it: "Best to give him opium and let nature work its course." But I kneel beside him, gripping his hand. He's panting, hoarse shallow breaths. His eyes are glazed; he doesn't really see me. They've already given him something strong from a flask.

The power of the font still pours down the hill. The witch hunters must have retreated following the destruction—or been injured in it. The bells have ceased. Gathering the power, I begin murmuring to the lead ball. It's fixed stubbornly in there amid the delicacy of his intestines. Closing my eyes, I whisper with my mind for it to work itself free. The man cries out, holding on to my hand hard.

And the ball slides from his body, onto the stretcher. He's shouting again, somewhere between triumph and terror and pain.

"You're doing well." I give him more liquid from the flask. The lead ball was the easy part. Now to mend his organs. To fuse his skin.

I put my hand over the opening in his gut. *As you were,* I tell the seeping intestines. *Knit together, as you were.*

It's slow work, but at last they begin to mend, the ripped organs reaching together, sealing up. Slowly, so slowly, a layer of muscle begins to climb over them, and the tenderness of new skin.

There's an exclamation over my head. I look up: One of the medics is staring down at the wounded man, who has, somehow, fallen asleep.

He kneels next to us. "How did you do this?" he demands. *"How?"*

"With my mind," I say. "With sorcery."

The medic gives me a long look. He glances at the patient, with the skin growing visibly, if slowly, over his wound. He looks back at me and jerks his chin. "A man over there is about to lose his leg. Unless you know a way to save it?"

I stand up. "I'll try."

I DON'T KNOW how many hours pass; I lose count of how many men I kneel over, of how many bodies I coax back into something near wholeness. The hum of power is gradually waning, leaving a headache and deadness in my limbs. The wounds are slower to heal now. I may heal all these men and leave myself dead with exhaustion. I'm helping to set a broken arm when there's a cough over me. I squint up through aching eyes. Lamps have been lit against the encroaching night; smoke smudges the tent. A man in a general's uniform, his coat riddled with medals, is looking down at me. His face is haggard.

Captain-General Horatius. I'm not sure whether I say his name aloud or not.

Two lackeys flank him. They're looking at me like hawks readying for the kill.

He's come to arrest me at last. I suppose it's inevitable. I'll have to run, faster than they can move. I'll have to find Elanna, whom I last saw tending to men with wounds less severe; her magic is still slow to come, but she can at least help others in ordinary ways. We'll have to get out.

But the captain-general doesn't arrest me. He holds out his hand, instead, to help me to my feet, careless of the dried gore that lingers on my fingers and palms. My body protests at standing upright. I've been kneeling so long.

"Korakos," he says. "I've come with word from His Imperial Highness, the emperor-apparent."

Emperor-apparent?

"Emperor Alakaseus suffered a pain in the chest this afternoon.

He's . . ." The captain-general pauses. "He's no longer among the living. The emperor-apparent has declared that hostilities here in Ida will cease and that sorcery is not to be considered a criminal activity. I'm to escort you up to Aexione at once."

My mind is still stuttering around his first statement. "The emperor collapsed—"

"It was sudden. Pray for his soul. That's all anyone can do." He nods at me. "Thank you for your work here. Now come."

He already turns, as if expecting me to follow, an obedient dog.

I don't. Firmina was going to Aexione—she was going to talk to Alakaseus . . . But Augustus and Phaedra were threatening Leontius earlier. "*Who* has demanded my presence in Aexione?"

Horatius stops and looks back at me, his exasperation plain in the sigh he exhales. The medics glance up from their work, not pretending they don't hear. "His Imperial Highness Leontius, the emperor-apparent, has sent me explicit instruction to bring you directly to Aexione. I am not even allowed the presence of a witch hunter."

I hesitate, but it's the irritation with which he says this last that convinces me. Only Leontius might have forbade the captain-general to bring a witch hunter.

"Very well," I say. "Give me a moment."

I don't wait for him to acquiesce. Striding away through the tent, I swing past stretchers and intent medics until I find Elanna, crouched in a corner wringing out bandages. Blood—not her own—streaks her cheekbone. She stands as I approach; I resist the urge to wipe the blood away with my thumb. Her eyes are dull with weariness.

"Come quickly." I grab her elbow and pull her from the tent, out into the night. One of Horatius's lackeys comes rushing after us: "Lord Jahan!"

I ignore him. "El, you need to get back up Solivetos Hill." I explain quickly that the emperor's heart gave out and that Leontius requires my presence. If I go, perhaps it means the end of all this. If Leontius has claimed the throne, if he's finally willing to reconcile, then we have all the hope in the world. Yet it's hard to believe it.

Elanna rubs her palms over her forehead. "What are we supposed to do?"

"I don't know. Horatius claims all hostilities have ceased, but . . ." I can't believe things have really ended, so quickly. "Let Tullea and the others know what's happened. I'll send word as soon as I can."

"Jahan." She grasps my arm. "How do you know they're not going to arrest you? I should come—"

"Horatius promised me safe conduct. You stay here. Keep our people safe."

Horatius's lackey has found us, his footsteps crunching in the gravel. Again, he calls, "Lord Jahan! Come at once or I'll be forced to take action!"

"They'd have arrested me by now if they wanted to." I reach for El's forehead, where the blood was smeared, and try to wipe it off. It's too dark to tell whether I got it.

She grabs my face and plants a kiss on my lips. *"Stay safe."*

"And you. Now go, before they decide to round you up, too."

Without another word, she turns and clambers over the ruined stones, making for the hill.

I swing back to Horatius's lackey, who is picking his way toward me with evident irritation. "There you are," I say pleasantly. "Ready to go yet?"

HORATIUS AND HIS officers bundle me into a plain coach-and-four. Inside, we all sit too close, four men occupying a too-cramped space. The officer beside me keeps reaching for his hip; he must have a pistol there. I can feel his distrusting glance leveled at my cheek, and the stare from the other officer sitting across from me, his knees almost bumping mine. They're wary, but they're also frightened. I suppose they've never been this close to a sorcerer before. And known it, anyway.

Maybe I shouldn't have conceded so quickly to the summons. But they haven't produced a witch hunter and, so far, that is enough to put me marginally at ease.

Of course, there are ways to harm a sorcerer without bells and stones. Fists and pistols might be just as effective, or more. Leontius might have sent for me—the gods alone know why, after what he said to me—but where is Alcibiades Doukas? Not to mention Augustus and Phaedra?

And where is Firmina?

No one speaks. It must be past midnight. The coach jolts over the cobblestones.

Somewhere nearby, a shout rises. The glow of torches gleams on the windowpanes.

"All the gods," Horatius mutters. "Not these lunatics again." He strikes the roof of the coach twice with his fist. The coach surges forward, the sudden burst of speed thrusting me back in the seat. But the torchlight still pursues us. The shouts echo over the squeak and thunder of the coach.

"Who's out there?" I ask.

None of them answer. Horatius is leaning his head out the window, trying to spot our pursuit. The officer sitting next to him pulls a club from the floor; the one sitting beside me produces the pistol he keeps fondling. I smell gunpowder as he loads the pan.

"No weapons," Horatius barks, leaning back in from the window. "The emperor-apparent has declared a cease-fire."

"As if that dolt knows what to do against these Idaean filth!" the officer exclaims.

"Hold your tongue!" Horatius says. "That is the emperor-apparent you're insulting. Do you want to be demoted?"

I feel the officer, stiff with anger, glance at me and away.

So Leontius's cease-fire—and his regency—are not popular among the imperial guard. Perhaps not among the entire court. It doesn't surprise me, but still unease tightens the back of my neck.

"The 'Idaean filth' are just as worthy of full citizenship as you are," I say quietly.

"They *attack* us!" the officer bursts out. "You—they—attack their own masters! You—they—you whine about your rights when you live in the most prosperous empire in the world!"

Horatius leans forward. "Marcos, that is enough, or you will be disciplined for speaking out of turn."

"Yes, sir. Sorry, sir."

"I would be interested in seeing your argument for why secondary citizens should not enjoy the rights of full citizenship," I say. Horatius isn't going to discipline *me*. "I can't imagine it occupies any solid moral ground."

"Lord Jahan . . ." the captain-general says.

"Another time." I gesture to the window. "Tell me who's out there."

Horatius is silent, and I think he isn't going to answer. The lights have finally faded into the distance, along with the shouting. Then he says, "A mob of one stripe or another. There's a man called Felix Tzemines who keeps shouting about the magnificence of the Glorious Republic. It'll be his crowd rioting. We've had to put them down with any means possible."

"You mean violence," I say flatly. It's been days since I saw Felix. I suppose it shouldn't surprise me, but there's a sick lurch in my stomach all the same.

"For the greater good of Ida and her citizens. Yes, I have had men shot. I have had them beaten. But it was my only recourse. I would never take action against any Paladisan, unless I were left with no choice."

"You could choose to listen to their demands."

"The demands of rabble, Lord Jahan? Why should I do that?"

I don't answer. Is this what he's said to Leontius, too? Is this how they all justify themselves, those men sitting up at Aexione?

Is this what Lees thinks? He's summoned me, and I came, docile as a cow, thinking only about our friendship. But I don't know what Leontius really believes. He certainly didn't want anything to do with me when I tried to ally with him. Maybe he'll attempt a truce, but he could equally have me thrown in irons. I think of how Augustus and Phaedra threatened him. Maybe he'll punish me, to demonstrate his own strength.

I suppose I'll find out soon enough.

*

WE REACH AEXIONE deep in the night. A faint, smokelike cloud clings to the crown of Mount Angelos. The town lies quiet, but inside the Grand Court torches are burning. The window muddies their light. Men shout outside. The coach stops with a hard rocking motion. It shivers as if someone's pushing bodily into it. The officers exchange glances, but Horatius's face just stays hard as flint. Does he know something we don't? I feel too hot. Panicked. Even before the door is flung open, I know we're not going to face a warm welcome.

Horatius clambers out before I can see anything but the glare of lanterns. Voices rumble. "—think you're doing—"

One of the officers pulls out his pistol. I edge forward, trying to push myself out of the coach, but Horatius blocks the door. He stands on the flagstones, his hands held up. "I was acting on Prince Leontius's orders! The emperor-apparent, I should—"

"Leontius Saranon is not your sovereign!" The speaker strikes Horatius across the face, and the old, battle-hardened general stumbles backward, into me.

I ease around him, blinking in the light. "If Leontius isn't the sovereign, then who is?"

But the words dry up in my mouth. A practical thicket of witch hunters and imperial guards surround us, weapons bristling. Bells ring and stones hum. In spite of myself, I take a step back. But they've surrounded the coach. There's no way out.

"Augustus Saranon is the rightful emperor of Paladis!" a guard shouts.

Behind me, Horatius bursts out, "Augustus? That viper? He's no more emperor than—"

Someone reaches past me and wrenches Horatius forward, striking his head against the flagstones. I push the assailant off, pulling the general up. Blood blackens his face. An idea hits me. Maybe if we can get back into the coach, I can compress space. I nudge him toward the door, trying to shove him back in—

"Arrest these men! Send them to the Ochuroma!"

I know that voice. I spin to face Alcibiades Doukas, cutting through the crowd with brisk authority. He smiles faintly when he sees me. "Jahan Korakides. We meet again."

Someone jostles behind him, pushing through the guards to the front. A man in military dress, its buttons so shiny they gleam in the dark. Augustus. Clearly he hasn't seen actual battle. He bursts out laughing when he spots me. "It *is* Korakides! My brother's a greater fool than I—"

I lunge for him. Two—three—four men seize me, but I don't need my hands to do this. I reach for the bandolier around Alcibiades's chest, urging it to clamp around his wrists like manacles. But without the power of the font, my magic slides off. Someone socks me in the gut. I double over, gasping, my vision blurring as I take a blow to the chin.

"The opium! Now!" Alcibiades barks.

Rough hands grasp the back of my head. I try to pass through, but it doesn't matter because more are there. A knee rams into my gut. I double over and am wrenched back. Fingers force my jaw open. I'm struggling, flailing. I haven't drunk opium since I was a boy, since Madiya burned holes in my memory. Since I staggered, half dead, to Aunt Cyra's door. I struggle and struggle, but the bitter liquid slides down my throat. The glass bottle clanks against my teeth. I gag. But more spills in, and more, and I'm forced to swallow or choke on it. The world is spinning. Stone presses, cool, against my cheek. I've fallen. I need to get up. I need to stop them. But my limbs won't obey me. The fog is creeping through my head, irresistible—

And then, like a candle, I wink out.

CHAPTER TWENTY-SEVEN

I wake gasping, in a feverish panic. My mouth tastes bitter. My head pounds. It feels like a feat of supreme strength to peel open my eyelids.

I'm curled on my side on a hard shelf that passes for a bed. Shackles clamp my wrists and ankles, clattering when I shift. My limbs are numb, trembling. There's a scrap of blanket under me. Dim light shines through a barred window set high in the wall. No idea what time it is, or how much time has passed. But I don't need anyone to tell me where I am.

The Ochuroma. Alcibiades Doukas sent me here. He knows the truth about me. Augustus and Phaedra have seized power. I'm separated from everyone I love.

I can't stop shivering. The shackles clank faintly.

I was dreaming about Madiya. I dreamed I was a boy and she gave me the opium, but I woke up in the middle of her operation and she was taking a scissors to my head, trying to cut out the parts she didn't like. Then I wrestled her off and looked into her face, and it was my mother. My mother, whispering, "It's for the best. It will keep you safe. I'll keep you safe. Shh." Then even as I screamed at her to stop, she plunged the shears into my skull.

The sob seems to wrench out of me. I can't stop it. Can't silence myself. I curl up, hugging my knees, and the low animal sounds rip out of my throat. My face is wet. I'm shaking and my stomach cramps, folding in on itself. The taste of opium lingers in the back of my throat. I want to shove it all away, into a deep part of me, but there's nowhere to shove it anymore, I am raw and all my secrets are exposed, even the ones Madiya hid from me. And here I am in prison, and I don't know what's happened to Elanna and Tullea and Rayka and Lathiel and everyone on Solivetos Hill. I don't know if they'll be able to make it to the cisterns, to escape the city somehow. But where would they go? Could they find a ship to take them to Eren? Or can they hold out longer against the imperial troops?

And what's become of Leontius? What did they do to him when they seized power?

I thought I'd failed when I couldn't maintain my lies at the imperial court. When I thought Elanna had been executed. But somehow this is worse. I am in the Ochuroma, and I feel as if I'm already broken.

My throat is raw. I can't sob anymore, though my damned eyes won't stop leaking. Sweat plasters my linen shirt to my back. I was down to my shirtsleeves at Solivetos, and the cell is cold. So damned cold. If I had more opium, I could endure this—

No. I bolt upright. My head swims and the cramps knead my stomach. Bile rises in my throat. I've been here before: the shaking, the sweating, the nausea. Wishing for a simple tincture of laudanum to dull my mind. Even after six years, now that I've had a taste of it again, my body demands more.

Metal scrapes, and I startle, my heart thudding. But it's only a bowl of runny porridge shoved through the bottom of the door. The idea of eating makes me want to vomit. Why should I try to, when I've failed so completely?

I fumble for the scar behind my ear. My knuckles, awkward in the manacles, bump over the ridge and I feel it as if for the first time. It's old and knotted—not a clean cut, as if my body couldn't bear to properly heal the wound. I reach for the memory Madiya took from me, the sight of Mother coming down those steps, the knife in her hand, the look on her face. Her calm; her composure. *I'm going to save you, darling,* she whispered to me, before she plunged the dagger into my head.

Perhaps it was a mercy that Madiya took those memories from us. Even if she did it for all the wrong reasons.

There's a rattle: a key in the lock. I swing my legs down, though tremors still rack them. Two witch hunters tramp in. One steps in the porridge bowl, stumbles and curses. Porridge splatters everywhere.

"You should eat your breakfast!" he thunders at me.

A second one approaches and I control a startle. It's Faverus. He looks drawn, almost careworn. He brushes past his companion to examine the witch stones embedded around my shelf. "Grand inquisitor said they didn't affect him," he mutters to his companion. "How's that possible?"

The other witch hunter eyes me warily. "Just get him up."

Faverus sighs and grabs at my shoulders. He won't meet my gaze. A sheen of sweat glazes his forehead, the way I remember. He's nervous again. "Come on, get up."

I almost ask him what he's so afraid of, but the other witch hunter is glaring at me. So I get up, stumbling as my numb feet hit the ground. The second witch hunter takes over, shoving me forward. I nearly go sprawling over the threshold. He yanks me up by the back of my shirt.

I shuffle down the hall, the metal clanking at my wrists and ankles. Can I break the shackles? I try to reach for a source of power, but there's nothing. Just the humming witch stones, which seem to bounce away my attempt.

Fear pulses through me. I already knew the witch stones somehow repulse my sorcery. Perhaps, out in the open, I'm immune to the stones and bells, and even here I don't feel any incipient madness. But perhaps the Ochuroma was designed to block a sorcerer from even using his power.

And I'm hollow from the opium. If they know about my old addiction, I have the feeling they could destroy me completely.

The witch hunters thrust me into a new chamber, empty except for a chair, a stool, and a lantern. They make a quick business of tying me to the chair. The rattle of chains is so loud I almost don't hear the new arrival come in.

Alcibiades Doukas has the nerve to smile at me, as if we've met pleasantly over the gaming tables in the Gold Salon. I don't return it. I note, with some satisfaction, that he looks exhausted. Dark marks lie under his eyes.

"Thank you, gentlemen," he says, and the others depart, Faverus sparing me a backward glance. Alcibiades takes up the stool and brings it in front of me so we sit almost eye-to-eye. It reminds me, of course, of our encounter at the palace. Only my mouth wasn't so dry then, and I wasn't so certain I'd lost everything.

"Break your chains," Alcibiades says.

I glare at him. He must know I can't obey this command.

Indeed, he smirks. "That's the remarkable thing about the Ochuroma's construction," he says. "Even if one is . . . immune . . . to the stones, this place still blocks magic. I've been studying it for years, trying to understand how it works."

"You must be a slow student, then," I say hoarsely.

He laughs. "You still speak well. Better than our other prisoners. Of course, most of them are slowly going insane. But you will simply rot here, your mind intact, until Emperor Augustus and Empress Phaedra order your execution."

"Are they marrying each other?" I ask. "That's disgusting."

"They are reigning *together*," he snaps, then closes his mouth. Looks at me. Smiles. "But you will never see the outside world again, so what is that to you?"

I shrug. "It's hardly my fault if Augustus and Phaedra want to breed stupid, incestuous babies who are even greater fools than the two of them."

Alcibiades studies me. "You have a remarkable tongue on you, for someone bound by chains."

"I have nothing left to lose."

"Oh," he says, "there's always something left to lose. Dignity. A limb." He raises an eyebrow when I don't flinch. "All right, then.

We certainly don't need to hurt *you*. I have a proposition." Rising, he unchains me from the chair with practiced ease. "Come along."

I shuffle after him down the corridor, even though every instinct in my body tells me to turn back, to convince him to harm me after all. They must have Elanna, though I don't know how they'd take her off Solivetos. It's the only explanation—they have her, and they're going to hurt her. They know I'll do anything to keep her safe.

Alcibiades stops in front of a door, thrusting open the wooden cover of the grille. He nods with satisfaction. "Go on, look inside."

I lean closer to the door, my blood pounding. If they harm a single hair on El's head . . .

I freeze. My eyes have finally made sense of the dimness, of the figure chained to the wall, his eyes wide, his face vacant.

I thrust myself back from the door. "Leontius isn't a sorcerer!"

"Really?" says Alcibiades, raising an eyebrow. "Then how did he make the Naiad Fountain erupt when we arrested him? He tried to drown us."

My mind stutters. "But he—he—"

"I thought for certain you would know this secret, Lord Jahan. Well, well. Now you do." He leans close. "Leontius Saranon is going to die. It's your choice how much he suffers before he does."

I swallow hard. I'm damned if I'll ask Alcibiades Doukas what he wants.

He sighs. "I require some information."

I just look at him.

"The emperor's death," he says. "It was . . . sudden. Unexpected, to say the least. Who killed him?"

I blink. "Sometimes men simply die, you know. Maybe his heart was rotten."

"Ah," Alcibiades says, "but we both know that it's possible to kill a man without touching him."

I stiffen. The hairs prickle on the back of my neck. Madiya told me that the ancient theurges could perform this magic. It doesn't mean Alcibiades knows about Madiya, and what she forced Lathiel to do.

"Or so I've read," he adds charmingly, and I relax a fraction. "If you didn't do it yourself, I suspect you know who could. Was it the prince? Did he decide he hated his father so much he must murder him?"

But I'm thinking of Firmina Triciphes, with her brilliant smile and her barely controlled sorcery and her determination to return to Aexione. I'm thinking of how she made a prison collapse. Of how Bardas argued that we must cut off the head of the state to control the body.

Would Firmina murder her own husband? Would she do it deliberately, or by accident? I just can't picture the Idaean Rose as a murderer.

But then, I didn't imagine she was the one who half destroyed the Frourio, either. Madiya's been experimenting on her. Perhaps this is why she forced Lathiel to kill those convicts. Perhaps it wasn't just to learn how to murder witch hunters.

Alcibiades is watching me, his eyebrows rising. Some of my thoughts must be visible on my face.

"Leontius wouldn't hurt anyone," I manage.

"Is that so?" He tilts his head, then shrugs. He snaps his fingers, and Faverus and the other witch hunter launch themselves from an alcove I hadn't noticed. "Cut off Leontius Saranon's right hand."

"No!" I cry out.

Alcibiades smirks.

"No one murdered the emperor," I say. Except I can't stop seeing Firmina Triciphes's composed face. She said she needed to get to Aexione before Augustus and Phaedra did. And now that I think about it, she never told me she was going to persuade the emperor to change his mind. She just said she needed to see him.

If she did kill him, is it wrong? Alakaseus Saranon would have destroyed us. But I can't shake the revulsion coiling in my gut.

Alcibiades is still watching me. I need to think—fast. I don't know what's become of Firmina. If she's at large, she's still an ally. And if she's willing to murder the emperor—possibly—she might be of great help.

"Very well," Alcibiades says. I've taken too long. He gestures to his men. "Do it."

"No," I begin, but Faverus is already unlocking the door to Leontius's cell. I can just see my friend lift his head. The other witch hunter is holding an instrument that looks like a meat cleaver.

Finally the solution hits me in the face. "What makes you think Augustus and Phaedra didn't do it themselves?"

Slowly, Alcibiades turns to me. He stares. "Murder their own father?"

"They're hungry for power. Why not suborn some sorcerer and force him to murder Emperor Alakaseus? It's convenient. They vehemently oppose sorcery; they denounce their own brother. So he takes the blame, along with me and my people."

Alcibiades has gone very still. His gaze crawls over me, and I realize I've said the wrong thing. The very wrong thing, indeed.

"Unfortunately," he says, with a strange false smile, "that is not the correct answer, Lord Jahan."

He snaps his fingers. Faverus is holding Leontius in place. The other witch hunter brings up his cleaver and swings it down, hacking my friend's hand off his wrist.

SOMEHOW I END up back in my cell. The door thuds heavily into place. The bolts slide home.

I'm numb. Stunned. I think I'm going to be sick. Alcibiades did it. He mutilated a Saranon—the emperor-apparent.

He hasn't hurt me. Hasn't given me more opium. Yet. He sent me back here with only a few brief orders, while they cauterized Leontius's arm. Before they do whatever torture they've planned next. Before they kill him.

I suppose it's only a matter of time before they do the same to me.

I shove at my shackles with my magic, but they don't give. The stones and bells must be blocking me. Finally I just yank at them, trying to pull them by brute force off my wrists. But it just leaves my skin scraped and bruised.

I need to get out of here. I need to save Lees. But even if I can heal a wound, I don't think I can give him back his hand. If they harm him further—if they push him to the brink—I can't bring him back from the dead. And I can't break the shackles or melt through walls. I can't do anything.

I slam my fists against the stones. It only leaves them aching. Everything in me aches. What are they doing to Leontius now? Will he survive the wound? I don't know if they will truly cauterize it, despite Alcibiades's claims, or if they'll do it properly. My friend could die from the infection. He could bleed out. They could torture him further, and then kill him.

And what's become of everyone in the city? Is everything over?

I refuse to believe it could be, but maybe I'm just deluding myself.

Finally I drop onto the shelf, running my hands over my face. The chain hits me in the nose. I'm a fool. I've lost.

No, there *has* to be a way out. A way to save Leontius, and myself.

Outside in the hall, voices carry and a door thumps. I jump up and shuffle to the grate in my door, trying to listen. But the wood is thick, and so are the walls. I can just hear someone say, "Aexione," and another reply, "Tomorrow morning." A loud scrape drowns out further words. I listen to the thuds of their feet, and chains rattling. A man is moaning. Weeping. I clench my fists. Is it Leontius?

Gradually the sounds fade. There's nothing but me and the stones and a growing sense of despair.

I can't give in to this. I pace the cell, though I can't do more than shuffle, and my limbs still tremble from the opium withdrawal. Beneath the floundering rage, something persistent niggles at the back of my mind. Something about the stones and bells. About the Ochuroma. Alcibiades said he'd been studying this place his whole career, trying to understand how it blocks magic.

How *does* it block magic? I stop pacing, startled by the revelation. We take for granted that the stones and bells send sorcerers mad and stop their magic, because they always have. Or at least, they have in recent memory, since the witch hunts began.

But Elanna's got a witch stone that she . . . transformed . . . somehow. She says she reminded it of its true nature. Which means that, of course, the stones and bells weren't always like this. Something's been done to them.

What can block magic . . . but magic itself?

There's a loose witch stone below the sleeping shelf. I pick it up. It hums in my hands, seeming to spit a little. I touch the walls. They, too, hum faintly. This whole place is made of witch stones.

At Solivetos Hill, I used the font's power to break the choker off Elanna's neck. I don't know if it broke whatever power lies in the witch stones in her collar. Madiya implied that there are other sources of power—other *wells* . . . The realization bursts over me. If the witch stones and bells rely on magic to work, if the Ochuroma's bricks are practically *made* of magic, then perhaps the prison itself is sitting on another well. If it is, perhaps I can use it.

I'm going to try it. Now. I sit, cupping the stone in my hands. I draw on the thin resources of my own power. If this exhausts me, so be it. But I need to know the answer.

Be as you were, I command the stone, with every ounce of strength I possess.

It *fizzes.* But then, quickly enough, it settles back to its usual hum. It's as if nothing happened.

Maybe I need different words. *Return to your true nature.* Again, it sparks, but nothing more. *You are only a stone.* Nothing.

I try more phrases, more insistence, but it's draining my own strength, not drinking from a deep well. I'm getting cold. The shivering starts again, and with it the bleak despair. Maybe there's some kind of magic in the stones—which would be scandalous, if true—but maybe I'm also just hoping too hard. And maybe, if there is a well, the magic in the Ochuroma's stones blocks me from using it.

Something rattles outside my cell. I sit up straight. It occurs to me that it's been a long time—an hour or two—since I last heard any movement in the hallway.

The door opens. Faverus comes in, carrying a bowl of porridge. I could launch myself at him, I think, and try to knock him unconscious with my chains. But my range of motion is too limited, and Faverus is a large man. Besides, my bones ache after worrying at the witch stone.

He sets the porridge down on the shelf beside me. "You should eat, this time."

I look at him. "What's going on? Are you playing nursemaid now?"

He pulls back, apparently wounded by this. It still perplexes me that a man so sensitive can be a witch hunter. Furtively, he glances over his shoulder. There's no sound in the corridor.

"I shouldn't tell you this," he says. "But . . . They took the prince to Aexione, to be executed."

I suck in my breath. "On what charge?"

He shrugs. "Not sure it matters, to be honest. Sorcery, for sure. Patricide, too, probably."

"But neither of those is true."

"Maybe he didn't murder the emperor." Faverus eyes me. "But if you'll pardon me, sir, I don't think you know all there is to know about Prince Leontius. He sure acted like a sorcerer when we brought him in."

"Maybe Alcibiades poisoned him," I say sourly, then realize I probably shouldn't have said that.

But Faverus doesn't seem to take offense. He shakes his head. "Inquisitor Doukas gets his orders from on high. From the emperor." He pauses. "Or maybe just his own mad self."

I stare at Faverus. He seems a bit uncomfortable. I knew some of his duties disgusted him, but it didn't occur to me that he might have opinions about his master. That he might dislike Alcibiades as much as anyone.

He's backing out the door now. "Good night."

"Wait!" I lurch up in a rattle of chains. "When is Leontius to be executed?"

He hesitates, glancing about, but it's only us and the humming stones. "In the morning, it sounded like. Before a crowd. They want to make a show of it."

Then, as if he's said too much, he slams the cell door. I'm left alone with the knowledge of my friend's impending death, and the fact that I have no way to save him.

IN THE END, I eat the porridge. It leaves my mind clearer. I take up the witch stone again, feeling it hum in my hand. If it *is* sorcery, perhaps I'm going about it wrong. Maybe it doesn't need to be commanded. I bring all of my awareness to it instead, letting the humming that I've resisted so long vibrate into my palms, until it feels like my blood and bones are quivering. The way they did when I plunged my hands into Mantius's font.

The magic feels . . . old. Stuck. Stagnant. But the stone itself, of course, is far older.

I let the humming consume me, even though my heart thuds dully and I wonder if this is my course straight to impending madness. But Madiya used to say that in order to understand sorcery, you have to become one with it.

I find myself humming along with the stone. A high, strange tone. It feels unnatural in my throat. But I hum as if my life depends on it, hardly stopping for breath. It's instinctive, not like the carefully planned sorcery Madiya taught me. I hum and hum.

At some point, I open my eyes. I realize I'm the only one humming now. The stone has ceased. I pass it from hand to hand, suspicious, feeling in it for the vibration I know must be there. But there's nothing, not even when I press it to my ear.

Whatever animated the stone is gone.

I stand, slightly dizzy, drunk from the humming. My skin seems to buzz. I've taken the stone's essence—whatever magic was placed on it—into myself. A deeper hum seems to echo up through the stones. The well, perhaps? The walls vibrate around me. I hum with them now, feeling more stones embedded below the sleeping shelf, at least a dozen of them, and a dozen more above. The buzzing rattles my bones, so deep it feels as if it could unmake me, but I stubbornly hum.

Finally, I stop. The stones have ceased humming, too. It's as if I'm standing in a small pocket of fresh air. I focus hard on the shackles around my wrists. If I remain in this circle, my head is just clear enough to force the irons off.

Break, I command, and they do. I stand there, staring at my bare arms, and start to laugh. All along, I could have done this?

Well, perhaps not. I feel almost too large for my skin, and now that I'm vibrating, I can feel the entire prison humming around me. It must be a well, a place where sorcery is concentrated, like Mantius's font. Only this has been twisted to work *against* sorcerers. It's not entirely unpleasant, but I don't know how long I can stand it.

I need to get moving. It takes quite a bit of concentration, but I break the shackles off my ankles, then, humming still more, force the locks on the door to retract. My larger magic still seems limited. When I try to walk through the wood, I just smack my nose into it.

With more care, I push the door open and creep out. The corridor lies deserted; a single lantern illuminates the dusty stones and ironbound doors. I wonder how many hide prisoners behind them. Of course, the emperor executed all the sorcerers he could in Ida; they can't have brought anyone here from the Frourio.

Yet I have the persistent feeling this place is less empty than it appears. The gods only know who could be hidden behind these doors, and how long they've been there.

Maybe I should save myself first. But I can't leave anyone else to rot in here. Not with Augustus and Phaedra in power, not with everything hanging so tenuously. So I grab the lantern from its hook and, steeling myself, stride to the nearest door. I peer through the grille. The door opens when I try the knob; the cell is empty.

With a shudder, I move to the next. Maybe they *are* all empty. The next holds nothing but dust. So does the one after. But then . . .

I stop. There's someone in this cell. A man, hunched over on the floor. His feet are bare.

Carefully, I push back the bolt. I open the door. The man doesn't move. I might have thought him dead, except his shoulders shift slightly as he breathes. With caution, I crouch before him.

He lifts his face. Just a little. It's vacant. There's no recognition in his eyes.

"Pantoleon," I whisper.

I had feared he was dead, crushed when the walls of the Frourio collapsed. But he must have been one of those evacuated after all. Perhaps he was even in that coach, the one I tried to stop.

He shifts at the sound of his name, like he knows he should know it.

My cheeks are cold. I'm weeping. I slam my palm against the ground. He doesn't even startle.

I don't know what they've done to him, but I'm getting him out of here.

I take his arms and tug him upright. He blinks slowly at me. He smells awful. His clothes are tattered. But when I pull him up, he stands, swaying slightly. "We're getting you out of here," I whisper, but tears prick my eyes again. Because even if I can get him out, can I save him? Can anyone? Can his mind come back?

I hug him. He brings one arm around me, hugging me back. Just for the briefest moment.

I let him go, wiping my eyes. There are witch stones embedded in the damned walls, drowning his sanity with their incessant humming, mirroring the vibration in my body. "I'm going to destroy the damned things," I mutter.

Pantoleon forms a whisper. His breath smells rank. "Ja . . . han?"

My mouth falls open. I'm so glad I think I might cry again.

He fumbles for my elbow. An intensity is coming into his gaze, a flicker of the man I knew. He hisses, "Sorcery." He points at the walls. At the stones. *"Sorcery."*

It takes me a moment, but I follow his meaning. The same discovery I just made myself. "They're magicked."

His eyes soften with relief. He nods.

"Someone took the energy in the stones and twisted it," I tell him. "They made them antithetical to magic, by *using* magic."

Again, he gives me a single nod.

"But the witch hunters aren't sorcerers," I say. "They can't have done this . . ."

Pantoleon shakes his head, then winces as if in pain. "Long . . . ago."

I grasp his meaning immediately. "Paladius the First. He forced some sorcerer to do this—to create magical objects the witch hunters could use . . ."

He's nodding, eyes closed.

"Pantoleon, you mad genius," I say, and his lips quirk in the faintest grin. I put his arm over my shoulders with a grunt—he's taller than me—and tug him toward the door. "Come on. I'm getting us both out of here."

But when we come out into the corridor, there's a whisper of sound. Footsteps. I halt. A lantern is swaying toward us, clutched in Faverus's hand.

He stops dead, staring. I stare back. If I were Rayka, I'd hurt him. Make him forget all this. But somehow I can't force myself to act.

"How?" Faverus asks. Just the one word.

I almost say, *Oh, a little sleight of hand . . .* But I stop myself. A significant part of me wants to tell this witch hunter the truth—so I do.

"Your bells and stones," I say. "Have you ever wondered how they work? Someone bespelled them. Long ago. You've been using magic all this time, to suppress sorcerers. This whole prison is sitting on top of a well of magic."

Faverus blinks. "But I'm not a sorcerer!"

"It doesn't matter. The bells and stones work no matter who uses them."

His chin tucks in. He's thinking about this. I grip Pantoleon tighter; now would be the time to run. But I'm curious. I want to see what Faverus does.

"We use sorcery to suppress sorcery," he says at last, slowly. "That's not what we're taught. They tell us that the stones and bells were created by the first witch hunters, under the supervision of the gods themselves."

I shrug. "Some kind of gods."

Faverus looks at me, and I'm surprised to see anger, of all things, in his face. "Then they've been lying to us, all this time. I knew it! I knew the . . ." He hesitates. Looks at us both. Then, more bravely, he says, "I knew the grand inquisitor couldn't be doing the work of the divine."

"Alcibiades Doukas's work mostly benefits himself," I remark.

He nods. "Come—this way. There's a back door that leads out."

FAVERUS WON'T COME with us, even though I point out that he's putting himself in danger by remaining here. He says there are other prisoners whom he wants to help escape. "And you," he says to me, "you're going to save the crown prince—the emperor, I mean."

"Yes," I reply, because I suppose I am, and being honest with Faverus has already led to good things.

"Godspeed, then."

He's brought us to the end of the corridor, where a secret right-hand door leads us down into a rough-hewn tunnel. Pantoleon is walking more steadily, but I keep a hand on his arm. The swinging lantern flashes off the gleaming eyes of a rat, and I wonder if I should have trusted Faverus so quickly.

But a few paces later, I smell fresh earth. A faint breeze creeps through the tunnel.

We emerge into a wide rectangle of scrubby grass. There's a single pine tree. Chunks of moonlit stone sit on the ground. I stop, and Pantoleon does, too. The smell of freshly turned earth comes from one of the stone chunks nearest us, its face blank.

We're in a cemetery. These are gravestones. And with the exception of the newest one, they're all carved with numbers. Some I can scarcely make out. 233. 162. The ones at the back are so faded I almost can't read them. 37. 29.

These aren't arbitrary numbers—they're *years*. The years sorcerers died. Not names. Not WIFE AND MOTHER, not A JUST CITIZEN. Just the year in which they were put in the ground.

Pantoleon pushes me away, stumbling to a stone nearby. I follow him. My heart seems to be squeezing in my chest. The year reads 268.

I can't seem to find words. What is there to say? It's almost ten years ago. His father could be under that stone, or any of these. Pantoleon makes a soft, choked noise. Then he says, his voice gritty, "Let's get out of here."

I nod. I still can't speak. There's a postern gate set in the wall, its latch long rusted. I don't bother to use magic; I kick it open. It feels good to hit something. The gate creaks but submits.

We walk out into the night. Free.

We're in a pine forest. The air smells high and clear; mountain air. Pantoleon wanders past me, staggers, almost falls. Then he *does* fall, collapsing to the earth, digging his fists into the soil. I drop beside him. Have we made things far worse by bringing him out?

But no—he's smiling. Weeping, at the same time.

"I thought . . ." he says hoarsely. "I thought I was going to die in there."

I find myself grinning at him. "Well, *I* thought you were already dead!"

We both begin to laugh. "Two dead men," Pantoleon wheezes. "You've got more lives than a cat."

I stare back at the bulk of the Ochuroma. It's more massive than it seemed from the inside: a hulk of stone that was once a fortress. I wonder how Madiya survived it for five years. No wonder she came out less than gentle, and bent on revenge.

"We're going to figure out the spells they used on the stones and bells," I promise Pantoleon. "And then take this place apart brick by brick."

He nods, resting his cheek against the earth. "That's . . . what I went . . . back for. To my . . . apartment. A reference . . . to the sorcerer . . . Paladius blackmailed . . . into creating this place. And the bells. Stones."

I stare at him. "You mad, brilliant bastard. *That's* what you risked your life for?"

"I thought . . . if we knew . . . construction of magic . . . we could . . . destroy bells. Defeat witch hunters."

I look down at him. Somehow, he's still smiling, the lunatic. "Did you know about the wells?" I ask. "The ones that concentrate magic in them?"

Excitement bursts over his face. He pushes himself onto his elbows. "*That's* what those references meant! I found stories about sorcerers going to wells—*dying* by wells. And then the wells couldn't be used, but it didn't lead to drought or any other consequence as far as I could tell . . ."

"It led to a *magical* drought," I say. "They're not necessarily water."

He stares at me, his mouth opening. "Jahan . . . if those stories are true, then there are wells everywhere. All over Ida—all over Paladis."

"And the sorcerers closed them." I shudder a little, thinking of Mantius and Tuah. "They gave their lives to seal them off—to keep Paladius the First from using them."

Pantoleon nods. "But you found a way to open them again—"

"One, anyway. And I think there's one beneath the Ochuroma . . ."

We stare at each other, then Pantoleon actually laughs. I'm grinning, too. "Well, this will be quite a change to the empire," I say. Pantoleon snorts. I look at him. I wish he'd waited to go back to his apartment; that he'd told me before he raced off. But here we are together, both of us alive, somehow, and I feel limp with gratitude. I squeeze his shoulder. He nods at me.

"We'll find all of the wells," I say. "We'll open each damned one."

He cracks a grin. "It'll be a new study. I'll specialize in sorcery. A new branch of inquiry at the university."

I chuckle and help him up. We have a long way to go—a long night of compressing space—and neither of us is at full strength. But we will reach Aexione by morning. We will find our prince. And then, if Leontius's abominable siblings don't capture us, we'll go on to Ida, to Solivetos Hill, to Elanna and the people who want change. We have an emperor to rescue, and a revolution to begin.

CHAPTER TWENTY-EIGHT

A crowd has already gathered in the Grand Court, surrounding a scaffold on which sits a single block. Common men might be hanged, but would-be emperors must be beheaded, it seems. I fight down nausea. It was hard enough seeing my friend lose his hand. I don't think I can endure this. We've walked all night, compressing space, avoiding twisting our ankles in potholes. I'm so parched my tongue sticks to the roof of my mouth. Pantoleon looks like a madman, with his dirty, rent clothes and his hair standing up in a thicket. I'm sure I appear no better. Already several people have mistaken us for beggars and tried to kick us or give us coin.

We hover outside the wrought-iron fence, watching the long line going inside. Neither Leontius nor his siblings have yet appeared; according to the conversations we've overheard, the execution isn't due to happen until noon. We have perhaps three hours.

I can get us inside the palace. But I'm not sure where to find Lees, or how well he's guarded—or, once we find him, how best to get him out. Besides that, I don't know what's happened to Empress Firmina, or to Elanna and Tullea at Solivetos Hill. We need information. And I'm too damned restless to wait here.

So rather than linger here with half of Aexione trying to give us bread, I tug on Pantoleon's sleeve and start off down the Avenue of Oranges. At this hour, Aunt Cyra is surely at home.

Away from the Grand Court, the town lies quiet under a tranquil blue sky. Pantoleon limps beside me—from exhaustion, as far as I can tell, not injury—as we approach Aunt Cyra's house. We slow outside it. Is she under watch? I don't see any guards. But maybe the larger question is whether she'll even still speak to me, now that I've revealed to the world I'm a sorcerer. Still, she's the woman who protected me for six years, who opened her house up to me and nursed me back to health. Surely we can overcome any of our differences.

So I guide us through the front door, using a weary burst of magic to soften our footsteps as we climb to the breakfast room. Sure enough, my aunt occupies the table, her morning gown an explosion of white ruffles. She's leaning intently over a letter.

"Good morning," I say, and she startles upright, jostling the table.

"*Jahan!*" She smacks the table, making the dishes rattle. I grin, though I'm not sure whether she's angry or pleased to see me; I don't think she knows, either. With a sharp sigh, she calls out, "I am not to be disturbed!" To Pantoleon, she says, "Shut the door."

He does. My aunt looks from me to him. "I suppose I should be glad you've returned at last, after I spent days persuading the emperor's men that I knew nothing about your sorcery. I'm lucky Empress Firmina vouched for me."

I wince. After everything she did for me, I left her here to endure that alone. "I'm sorry, Aunt. I don't mean to impose . . ."

"Nonsense. You *do* mean to impose. But—" She sighs. "—I would be offended if you didn't." She moves toward me, as if for an embrace, then pulls back. "Darling, you smell extraordinarily foul. And so does your friend." She peers at Pantoleon; her eyebrows rise. "It *is* Pantoleon Chrysales!"

"At your service." Pantoleon bows.

"You must have come from Ida," Aunt Cyra says. "Have you secured the city?"

"Ida, by way of the Ochuroma," I say drily, but then I pause, her words sinking in. "What do you mean, secured the city? I'm glad you have faith in me, Auntie, but that might be taking my skills a little far . . ."

She's gripping the table. "The *Ochuroma*? Jahan . . . ! Do you mean to tell me you've arrived here not only a criminal, but an es-caped prisoner?"

There doesn't seem much point in denying it. "Well, yes."

"I can't believe you let yourself get caught," she fumes. "Your sorceress has managed to take over half of Ida, and you look as if you've just crawled out of a hole!"

"Here I thought escaping the Ochuroma was rather an impressive feat," I remark. "What do you mean, my sorceress has taken over half of Ida?"

She waves her hands. "The Witch of Eren! Elanna Valtai! She made the trees *walk* down Solivetos Hill and surround the imperial troops. They tried to fight them. Can you imagine it—soldiers fight-ing trees! Needless to say, the trees won. Half the militia fled—deserted, according to Augustus Saranon. Your sorcerers have been pushing the other half back. Every tree in Ida is walking, if you be-lieve the stories." She pauses—my mouth seems to be hanging open—then adds, "I can't imagine it's good for the streets. The bricklayers will have quite a job repairing the damage those roots have done."

I drop into the seat across from her. My head is spinning, but at the same time, I'm smiling. Elanna's power must be returning—and perhaps she's figured out how to harness that of Mantius's font. I should have known the *Caveadear* wouldn't just huddle on Solive-tos Hill, waiting for my return. I snort a laugh. Maybe I should have handed full control over to her and Tullea long ago.

My aunt eyes me, but tactfully refrains from pointing out that my filthy trousers are ruining her silk upholstered chair. Then Pantoleon sits and her eyebrows truly fly up. But she just pours each of us a cup of coffee and pushes a fruit basket toward us.

"You didn't know," she remarks.

I'm still smiling, foolishly I'm sure. "No. Leontius—I thought, anyway—summoned me to Aexione." I explain how Augustus and Phaedra seized power, and I was taken to the Ochuroma.

"Hmm." My aunt rattles her fingers on the table. "So you're here to save Leontius, I suppose."

"And Captain-General Horatius, if I can." I hesitate. I don't know how much my aunt knows, or guesses, about Firmina and Bardas Triciphes. "Do you know what's become of Empress Firmina?"

"She's said to be in custody—in the Little Palace, I imagine." My aunt looks at both of us and sighs. "I don't suppose there's time to have you bathe before we go?"

"Auntie," I say, surprised, "you don't need to put yourself in danger—"

"Oh, I know you're perfectly capable of skulking into buildings, Jahan. But this time, I'm going to help you." She rises. "Bring that fruit basket, and we'll go."

THE GUARDS AT the Little Palace look bored. They examine the fruit basket, now stuffed with all manner of baked goods and other delectables, but no one troubles to really look at either my face or Pantoleon's. Aunt Cyra waits, wafting her fan, dressed now in a simple gown, a white plumed feather tucked into her hair. As she said earlier, no one truly sees footmen, even though we're now both shaved and moderately clean. And despite my aunt's scandalous connections—to me—it doesn't seem to occur to the guards that she might be doing anything more than solicitously bringing the empress some food.

All the same, disquiet touches the back of my neck. We're walking voluntarily into a heavily guarded palace. There are so many ways this could go wrong.

We're waved inside. A guard points us up a white marble staircase to the second floor, where more guards show us through to an airy salon. Again, no one seems to actually look at us. It's too easy. I want to elbow Pantoleon—I want to make my aunt turn around—but it's too late to back out. We would only raise further suspicions.

The salon is empty—and this time, the empress isn't merely trying to hide in plain sight. Pantoleon and I exchange a glance.

My aunt clears her throat. "Madam?"

A soft rustle comes from one of the other rooms facing the salon. There's a light step. I glance quickly around. Two tall sashed windows overlook the pond. I could plunge us through them, or try to, but the guards stationed outside might very well shoot at us.

The footsteps draw closer. Firmina Triciphes emerges, her hair loose and her lips parted. "Oh, Cyra!" she cries out, running across the room to my aunt and throwing her arms about her, girlish and fragile.

My suspicions are deepening—Firmina is neither girlish nor fragile.

Sure enough, when she glances at us over Aunt Cyra's shoulder, she catches sight of me and her eyes widen. She mouths, *Go* But then she carries on, her voice bright and prattling. "This *is* an unexpected pleasure. You're so kind to come. I've been all alone here for two days, mourning my poor dear Alakaseus."

I check the doors. We're alone still, but I still feel we're being watched. I want to set down the basket and run.

"I worried for you," Aunt Cyra begins.

But the second door clicks. My aunt falls silent. The door swings open with a tinkling of bells. I see Firmina grind her teeth, her eyes watering, just before three men step out from the other room. A witch hunter and two guards, their muskets cocked.

"Cyra Potazes," the witch hunter says, striding toward us, and with a start I recognize him. It's short, peremptory Quentin, the witch hunter who brought me to Ida. He looks as smug as ever. "An interesting choice of rescuer. Don't move, Lady Cyra. You're under arrest."

"How dull," my aunt drawls. "I can't recall doing anything wrong."

"Their Imperial Highnesses beg to differ," Quentin says primly. He casts a pointed look at Firmina. "You can't hide any longer behind Lady Triciphes. You sheltered Jahan Korakides. You can't tell me you didn't know he was a sorcerer."

Firmina intervenes, fluttering her eyelashes. "Cyra has the most generous heart. Please don't punish her for her kindness."

Quentin brandishes the bell. "We'll examine her for sorcery—and her servants, too."

I sigh. Pantoleon is wincing at the bell's incessant clattering. I reach into the sound, feeling for the point where the noise ends and the magic begins. I'm humming aloud, too, I realize. Everyone has turned to stare at me.

"Is your footman quite well?" Quentin asks, distaste curling his lip.

There it is. The magic leaches out of the bell. Pantoleon's face relaxes. I reach for the muskets the guards hold and, tugging on the guards' own power, snap the stocks. Both men exclaim in astonishment.

Quentin whirls toward them, then back to me. "Guards! Guards!"

But I've already muffled the room so the sound doesn't escape, though it taxes my tired mind. I grin all the same. "Hello, Quentin."

"Korakides?" He goes white. Then he starts ringing the bell even more frantically. "Korakides! I've got Jahan Korakides in here, damn it! Where is ev—"

He stops, swaying a little. Firmina is standing behind him, one hand outstretched, squeezing the air gently. He gasps. Struggles a little. But then his eyes roll up in his head and he falls to the floor. The guards, I realize, have already collapsed. Firmina just stands there, smiling.

"I didn't really need to be rescued," she says. "But it's sweet of you, Jahan."

I ignore her, dropping to my knees beside Quentin, feeling for the pulse in his neck. His face is slack, and there's a strange panic buzzing up inside me. I can't find a pulse. His skin is growing cold. Clammy.

I stare up at Firmina, who looks down at me with smiling innocence. "You killed him? You killed *all* of them?"

"I wasn't going to. But perhaps there's no need to be as careful as I have been." She shrugs. "Besides, he would have done the same to us."

So Madiya *was* researching it when she forced Lathiel to kill those men. Researching it for Firmina—so that she could murder without anyone knowing?

Well, I know how Alakaseus died, now.

I busy myself covering Quentin's face with my handkerchief. I don't want Firmina to see how badly she's shaken me. It's not as if I particularly liked Quentin, but this isn't the way I wanted to see him die, not to mention the two hapless guards.

"Oh, Jahan! You're so soft." Firmina is smiling at me. "He didn't feel any pain."

Aunt Cyra gestures at the doors; she looks a bit peaked herself. "Perhaps we should go, madam. Before anyone else discovers us . . ."

"Wise as ever, Cyra. Do come. We'll go out the back."

Pantoleon gives me a hand up. He mutters, *"That's* the Idaean Rose? Seems more like the Idaean Powder Keg."

I manage a smile. "At least she's on our side."

"I don't trust her, Jahan," he says.

I look after Firmina and my aunt, who are disappearing into the bedchamber. "It's Madiya's influence. Firmina and Bardas want the same things we do . . ."

Pantoleon is creeping not toward the bedchamber, but back to the doors we entered. Cautiously, he opens them. I hear him swallow. "Jahan."

I already know what I'm going to see. Yet it's still a shock to witness it: All four guards lie dead outside the salon, tumbled over one another on the marble floor. Is this how she got the power to kill the others? Did she drain all these lives to take the other lives? Who did she sacrifice for the emperor?

We ought to burn them. Bury them. But it will have to damned well wait until after we've freed Leontius and reclaimed Aexione from his siblings, and by then we may be known as murderers. I rub my forehead. Doesn't Firmina understand that these are her own people?

"Well, I suppose it makes our escape easier," I say, even though it makes me ill. Behind us, in the salon, Firmina is calling my name. "Come on."

We retreat through to the bedchamber, following Firmina and Cyra to a balcony where a frivolous stair winds down to the pond. The empress seems entirely too calm, while my aunt is gamely pretending she witnesses casual murder every day.

"Jahan will get us to Ida," Firmina is saying. "We'll join the rebels—"

I interrupt, unsure I like her volunteering my powers for everyone's use. "We need to set Leontius free first. We don't have much time. You and Aunt Cyra can make for Ida, and we'll join you there, as soon as we can." *If we survive this,* I think, but I don't say so aloud.

Firmina blinks. For a moment, I think she's going to disagree— drain the life from me, to get me to cooperate with her. But then her face softens. "Of course. Poor Leontius. I forgot they've decided to mete out the ultimate punishment to him."

I don't for a moment believe she forgot, but I have the sense not to question this. "He's the rightful emperor. We need him to be the figurehead of our rebels in Ida."

"Oh, yes! You're so wise, Jahan." Firmina smiles. "That will make Leontius quite the popular hero. The people will adore him as they never have before."

This seems quite a backhanded compliment, but it will have to suffice. "Then go. We'll be in Ida as soon as we can."

"Is it safe to let them go alone?" Pantoleon murmurs to me as we hurry down the stairs.

I shake my head. "Firmina can take care of herself. And woe to anyone who tries to cross my aunt."

He snorts. "True enough."

But all the same, after what Firmina has done, I wonder if he isn't right.

❊

EVEN FROM THE Naiad Pool, we can hear the drumbeats echoing up over the palace's roofs. My heart jerks. We've been strolling at a respectable speed, compressing space, but now I break into a run. Pantoleon swears and races after me. Are we too late? It didn't take so long to free the empress. I haven't heard the bells chime noon.

As we pass Astarea's Grotto, I feel a stirring, a pinprick of power, similar to that of the Tirisero font. But I don't have time to stop or investigate.

We run into the palace's familiar corridors, though they're less crowded than usual. Perhaps everyone has gone to see the execution— or been ordered to. It seems like something Augustus and Phaedra would do. I grab Pantoleon's arm, compressing space. I hurl us through the halls, until at last we stumble into the Grand Court.

Here's the crowd. People press shoulder-to-shoulder in the court-yard, filling the air with whispers and the reek of sweat. If I rise onto the balls of my feet, I can just see the scaffold, past a sea of tall hats and voluminous coiffures. A man is climbing onto it. White pure fear pulses through me, but then I realize it's not Leontius. It's a man dressed all in black, carrying a broadsword. The executioner.

Calls carry over the crowd. "There he is! They're coming out!"

At first I think they mean Leontius, but their gazes are fixed up-ward, on a balcony almost over my head. It's where Alakaseus used to, occasionally, make speeches. Pantoleon and I shoulder through the crowd until I can just make out a gold-trimmed sleeve above us. Augustus, of course. He's gesturing, though I can't quite see it.

My hands curl into fists. If I were Firmina, this would be the mo-ment I'd act. I'd take Augustus's sorry excuse for a heart and crush it with my hands.

But to do that, I would have to drain power from someone else. A life for a life. As Lathiel did. Even for Augustus Saranon, I'm not willing to make that sacrifice. No one deserves to die for him.

A collective gasp rustles through the crowd. "So beautiful!" Phae-dra must have arrived, and the people of Aexione are proving them-selves more interested in her fashionable gown than in my friend's life.

They're quieting now, and Augustus's voice lifts overhead. "Gracious subjects!" Pantoleon snorts. Of course this is how Augustus addresses the people he's assembled to witness Leontius's death—as if he's already been crowned. "This is a sorry occasion indeed. The revelation that my own brother conspired to murder our father— that all these years, he has been a sorcerer—has shaken us all to the core."

I swallow against the bile rising in my throat and turn my back to Augustus. I don't need to hear this. Augustus can pontificate all he wants, if it buys us time.

I push through the crowd, Pantoleon following me, winding a path toward the scaffold. It's still empty, except for the executioner. I scan the palace walls. A squadron of guards and witch hunters must be waiting to bring Leontius out, but I can't see them over the crowd.

Pantoleon, being taller, catches a glimpse. "The east wing. They're all in position."

"Damn," I mutter. We might be able to stop the execution itself, but how on earth are we going to get Lees out through this crowd?

Unless . . . I can compress space, and use persuasion. An idea begins to come together in my mind. Pantoleon starts weaving his way through the crowd. I follow, sunk in thought. We need a distraction.

Ahead of me, Pantoleon stops short. I almost bump into him. There's a man in front of us, reaching into the pocket of his coat. I glimpse the flash of the pistol just before Pantoleon grabs him in a stifling hug, pinning his arms to his sides. The man struggles, trying to butt Pantoleon in the chin with his head. I lunge forward and pull the man's head down. People in the crowd move away from us, leaving a small circle.

I'm panting. Staring. "Zollus Katabares?"

He recoils, and this time his head *does* connect with Pantoleon's chin. My friend grunts. Zollus is as impeccably dressed as ever, his cravat looped in precise folds, but there's a strange, wild glint in his eyes. "What are *you* doing here?" he whispers.

"I could ask the same of you." I jerk my chin at the pistol.

Zollus doesn't answer. But his gaze flickers from me to Augustus Saranon, still holding forth on the balcony.

I nearly bite my tongue. Zollus Katabares was planning to *assassinate* Augustus? He couldn't possibly guarantee he'd hit him from down here. "Isn't that taking your duty as Companion a little far?" I say. "What are you hoping for, a medal? They'll kill you, too, you fool."

He stares at me, his nostrils flaring. "I'm here for Leontius. I've stayed by his side through everything else."

Zollus Katabares has either lost his mind or gained a heart, or possibly both. I realize I'm just blinking at him. I feel somewhat poleaxed.

"*Jahan,*" Pantoleon whispers fiercely. He nods at the balcony. Augustus has finally ceased his monologue, and now Phaedra has stepped forward for "a few small words." We don't have much time.

"This is undoubtedly heroic, if incredibly stupid," I whisper to Zollus, "but how about helping us *save Leontius's life?*"

His mouth opens. He doesn't answer, which I take to be a yes. Pantoleon shoves him forward, and we push through the crowd once again, aiming for the east wing. I can see the guards now, in neat uniformed ranks, their bayonets tipped over their shoulders.

"Pantoleon," I whisper, "can you get back to the stables and snatch a carriage? I'll meet you there."

He eyes me doubtfully, but nods.

"Zollus, go with him." I pause. "But give me your gun."

He hesitates, looking me over. Maybe he reads some sincerity in my eyes. He reaches into his pocket and presses the pistol into my hand.

"Thank you." I gesture them on. It's my turn to be incredibly foolish, or possibly heroic, or simply, at bottom, desperate. If only we had gotten here sooner. If only Leontius had accepted my offer of help long before this. But here we are.

I cock the pistol. Slowly, giving Pantoleon and Zollus time to retreat through the palace, I lift my arm and aim well over people's heads, toward the distant balcony. My hand is shaking but it hardly matters. This shot won't harm anyone.

I pull the trigger.

The retort bursts through my arm. People are screaming. I swivel and compress space, diving through the crowd toward the east wing. Now people have begun to stampede, like cattle, drowning out Phaedra's speech. I risk a glance back at the balcony. Both imperial siblings have been rushed inside.

In the east wing colonnade, it's chaos. I glimpse Alcibiades Doukas ringing his bell. He's looking around. I compress space just before his gaze lands on me. Someone barks orders. The guard formation retreats, dragging Leontius backward into the palace. I can just glimpse him, a stocky figure smothered in chains, in the middle of the frantic guards.

Just another soldier, I insist, and push through the guards, letting their movement carry me into the palace and into the east wing. Orders fly back and forth. Somewhere, witch stones hum. We stop outside a room—I recognize it as the one Alcibiades used to interrogate me—and Leontius is shoved inside. The door hangs open for a moment while the guards argue over their orders, and I use the pause to slip inside.

My friend has backed up against the wall, chains wrapped around his torso and arms. He's closed his eyes. He looks defeated. Broken.

Finally, the door is slammed shut. We're alone. Leontius bites his lip. He tries to raise his one hand, but the irons barely permit him to move his arms. They must have wrapped him like this since Alcibiades cut off his hand. His face crumples as if he's going to weep. His pain is so intense and private I feel almost guilty witnessing it.

"Lees," I say softly.

His eyes fly open. He stares, shock haggard in his face, as if I am another surprise on top of so many more unbearable surprises.

"I'll get us out." I make quick work of his shackles, though I have to use my own energy to do it. Soon exhaustion is going to drag my whole body to the ground, but until that happens I'm not about to stop. Leontius rubs his elbows and wrists, red and raw from the irons. The stump of his arm looks ugly, as if it might break open and weep blood again. They did cauterize it, but it hasn't had time to heal.

Voices echo outside the door. "—bring the prince back—"

I grab Leontius's arm and drag him through the wall. We stumble into an office, empty except for stacked papers. Leontius looks dazed. Out in the hall, men are shouting. I pull him through the next wall.

Captain-General Horatius stares up at us from a chair. He's alone and, unlike Lees, only his wrists are shackled.

No time to break the irons. I drag the general up with my free hand. "Come on!" It's more of an effort to shove all three of us through the next wall, but I do and—

We're falling. We've run through the outside wall. I hit the ground and roll before I even have the wherewithal to gasp some magic. Rosebushes stab me. The general is groaning, and Leontius has staggered to his feet. I clamber upright. Everything aches dully, but I seem to be intact.

"Are you injured?" I ask the general.

He shakes his head. "Just . . . stunned."

I grin and give him a hand up. We've fallen no more than ten feet. "Then get your feet under you. Run!"

I lead them through the garden, toward the distant gate to the stables, working on breaking Horatius's shackles as we go. A carriage is waiting for us, Pantoleon sitting on the box. He waves to us. We bundle Leontius and Horatius inside, where Zollus waits. Pantoleon, as the only one unlikely to be recognized, drives. He snaps the reins and the horses charge forward. The road should be clear enough for us to reach Vileia, or at least the outskirts of Ida. I sink into the seat with relief.

Leontius is looking at Zollus with wonder. "You came!"

"I . . ." Zollus glances at me, then down at his hands. If I wasn't so sure Zollus doesn't have a heart, I might think he's suppressing tears. "I wouldn't leave you."

I snort. "He was going to murder your siblings for you. We dissuaded him."

Leontius startles, looking at me sidelong. I don't think he's ready to speak to me quite yet. It's unnerving that he's more comfortable around Zollus than me.

Zollus gestures at Leontius's missing hand. "They . . . did they . . . ?"

Lees just nods, and guilt swarms through my stomach. Alcibiades wouldn't have done it if I had cooperated—if I had given him the information he wanted. But then I would have betrayed Firmina.

"Let me look at it," I say, leaning forward. Leontius looks at me warily, but he inches his arm toward me. I take it in both hands, suppressing a wince at the sight of the angry, red cauterized stump. *Knit back together, as you were,* I whisper to his flesh, but I already know it's not going to work. I don't have enough power—I don't know how I would ever have enough power to re-create bone, flesh, and sinew out of nothing. This isn't like relighting a candle, or closing a wound. His hand is irreversibly gone. I've succeeded only in lessening the irritation, gentling the skin into a whitened scar. Softly, I say, "I'm sorry."

Leontius's mouth tightens, but he reclaims his arm, cradling the stump in his whole hand.

"What happened?" Zollus demands, ignoring me.

"I don't really remember," Leontius says. His voice is hoarse. Quiet. "The witch stones had me in such a state of . . . of . . ."

Beside me, Captain-General Horatius goes very still. "Your Imperial Highness, do you mean to say . . ." He stops and coughs. "Are you, in fact, a sorcerer?"

"N . . ." Leontius begins. But he glances at me. His shoulders hunch, as if he expects punishment. As if he expects us to strike him down. He draws in a breath. "After the Getai, I . . . I could sense water in the earth."

After the Getai? I realize I'm staring. My mouth has fallen open.

"You did something to me." Leontius is addressing *me,* now.

"No," I start to say. I halt. I took away his memories. I reached into his mind and shoved them down, deep, so he couldn't touch them anymore. But maybe, when I pushed them down, I pulled up something else instead. Madiya told me that's why we lost our memories, after all. That she took them accidentally, while she was manipulating our ability to do magic. Did I do the same thing, unwittingly?

Horatius has settled back in his seat, evidently relieved. "That's not such a terrible thing."

"Fairly useless, isn't it?" Leontius says bitterly. "Astarea's Grotto is always calling to me."

I'm so bewildered I find myself asking, "Because it's a spring?"

Leontius just stares at me. "I suppose so." He hesitates. Doesn't quite look at me. "You didn't do it to me deliberately."

"I wouldn't know how."

He seems to relent a bit at that. "I . . . I thought I heard you in the Ochuroma. Before they took my hand."

Now I'm the one who can't look at him. "You did."

Across from me, Zollus stiffens. I think he'd kill me with a glare if he could.

"Pantoleon and I were also captured." I pause. "Alcibiades Doukas was trying to use you to get information out of me. He wanted to accuse you of patricide. Turns out he didn't need my help to do that."

Leontius turns toward me, pressing his hand to his knee. He's suddenly intent. "Did someone kill my father?"

"Ah . . ." I hesitate. The carriage seems to be closing in around me; all three of them are staring me down. Do I name the empress? Leontius may not have much loved his father, but he's always been looking for an excuse to hate Firmina more. I find myself reaching for a lie. "That does seem to be the popular opinion."

"You know who did it," Leontius states flatly.

I should have realized he knows me well enough to recognize a lie. I draw in a breath. I'm not sure I trust Zollus or Horatius with this information—but we're all here together now. What choice do

I have? "Would you believe it if I told you that your stepmother was involved?"

Leontius's eyes widen, then he snorts. "That is the easiest thing in the world to believe."

But he's picking at his trousers now. Zollus shoots me another hostile look, as if I've betrayed the entire empire. He never used to be this protective of Leontius. Something's changed.

"Was Firmina at Aexione, too?" Leontius asks. "Today?"

I nod. "She went to Ida with my aunt Cyra."

His chin dips; he looks pensive. Zollus is watching him, looking worried, while Horatius occupies himself staring out the window. We're passing over a hilltop, and the bulky shoulder of Mount Angelos rises into view, veined with snow.

"It's odd," Leontius says quietly. "If she was able to do away with my father, she might have come to help me."

He's right, I suppose. "Well, she knows you never liked her . . ."

The carriage makes a sudden jolt, throwing me forward. Pantoleon's voice carries—"Whoa, there, whoa"—and we slow to a stop. I swing out the door just as the earth rumbles. The rocks under my feet shift and shiver; I almost fall. One of the horses whinnies. Pantoleon's holding the bridle, whispering soothing words to the creatures. I peer over the treetops to Mount Angelos, but it sits placid and white-crowned in the near distance. The breeze carries a strange, sour smell.

"The mountain's talking," Pantoleon says when I come up beside him. He's patting one of the horses' noses. "This fellow doesn't like it."

I rub the horse's warm cheek. "Steady on, friend." I can't help feeling sympathy; a tremor still runs through the ground, upsetting my own balance. "As long as no one's trying to make a prison walk, we'll be safe enough. Maybe Elanna's decided to make the mountain erupt after all."

Pantoleon gives me a look of horror. "And smother all of Ida? The Saranons would win for certain then."

"I'm sure she wouldn't, really," I say soothingly. The horse has calmed, the tremor ceased, though the peculiar smell lingers in the air.

"The road's practically deserted. Ride on the box with me?"

I'll gladly take Pantoleon's company to the awkward conversation in the carriage. "Definitely."

CHAPTER TWENTY-NINE

A mile later, another earthquake hits. Even from this distance, I think I can see rocks skittering down the slopes of Mount Angelos. The fearful horse bucks. When we slow, voices carry down the road behind us. Pantoleon and I exchange a glance. It could easily be a party of imperial guards pursuing us to Ida. He climbs back on the box and urges the team into a canter, and this time I compress space. Soon we've left our pursuit behind, and the sea lines the horizon with blue.

But as I compress space for a final time, we round a corner straight into a group of imperial militia. They stand across the road, blocking it.

Pantoleon reins in the team. Before either of us can react, a man's come forward to grasp the horses, while several more run up, surrounding the carriage. "You can't get into Ida today, fellows!" an officer calls to us. "Go back to Aexione!"

"We're here on the crown's business," I say. "We have special dispensation to go through."

The officer blinks at me. "The crown's closed the roads. No one in. It's too dangerous."

"Of course it's dangerous," Pantoleon says. "It's Ida."

The officer's eyes narrow, and several of his cohorts reach for their weapons. "We're blockading the city against the Witch of Eren. She's made all the trees—"

The ground rumbles, interrupting him, and our frightened horse bucks. The officer holding him stumbles back. Pantoleon jumps down to soothe the horse. I hop down, too. There's more than one way to get into Ida. The earth is quivering under my feet, and the strange odor makes the air foul. I open the carriage door and lean in. Leontius and Zollus have both pressed back in their seats, while Horatius is looking around, impatient.

"We've been stopped by a military blockade," I say. "Maybe one of you could persuade them to let us through?"

It takes a moment for my suggestion to sink in. Horatius's mouth opens, but he doesn't speak.

Leontius frowns; he knows me too well. "This has been your plan all along, hasn't it?"

I wink. "Only for the last few minutes."

Zollus is sputtering. "To *force* us to help you, as if Lees is your *puppet*—"

"It's all right," Leontius says, putting one hand to Zollus's knee, and Zollus stops dead, as if the contact has shocked the words out of him.

Horatius sighs. "I can speak with the men—"

"General, if you don't mind." Leontius sits forward, making to get out. A strength is coming into him. "*I'll* speak to the men. If you would back me up, it would be much appreciated."

The captain-general looks at my friend, and for a moment I think he's going to smile. Then he simply puts his hand to his heart. "Your Imperial Majesty."

Leontius blinks a little; even now, he doesn't expect such deference. But he nods and clambers out. I back up to give him room. In the late-afternoon light, he looks tired but somehow capable, cradling his empty wrist in his whole hand. He pauses beside me and mutters, "I hope to all the gods you know what you're doing, Jahan."

I just grin and execute a bow. "Your Imperial Majesty knows better than I."

"Hmph." But his mouth twitches as if he's suppressing a smile, and for a moment I almost feel we're friends again. Only maybe, this time, our friendship will be better than it used to be. More honest.

He steps past me. The officer has approached, saying, "I insist you gentlemen turn around—the crown's orders—"

"The crown orders you to let us through," Leontius says. His voice is mild, and the interruption gentle. But the officer halts all the same, looking Lees up and down, as if he knows he should recognize him. "Make way for us into Ida."

The officer begins to bluster again. "I need to see written orders—"

"Sir," I interrupt, "you have the honor of addressing the emperor himself. You might not want to contradict him."

The officer stares.

Behind us, Horatius is getting out of the carriage. "Titus!" he barks. "I thought I knew your voice. Are you talking back to His Imperial Majesty?"

Completely bewildered now, the officer stares among all of us. "Captain-General Horatius, sir? Emperor . . . Leontius? But they said you were to be ex—"

Horatius coughs loudly.

The officer swallows the rest of his words and throws himself onto his knees. "Your Imperial Majesty! I beg pardon. I didn't recognize you."

"Under all this dirt, I hardly recognize myself," Leontius replies. He's actually smiling. "Now let us through."

"But with all due respect, Your Imperial Majesty, the Witch and her sorcerers have taken over most of the city. We're holding on to Vileia by our fingertips. We've blockaded the bridges, but it's only a matter of time."

Leontius glances at me. "We quite appreciate the danger, Officer Titus. But we've come to parley with the witch and her sorcerers."

Titus gapes.

"You heard His Imperial Majesty," Horatius says gruffly. "Pass along the orders to let us through, now."

Titus gulps and bows. His gaze darts to me, and I know I've been recognized. I grin at him. "The world is changing, Titus. Instead of interrogating sorcerers, we converse with them! It's positively revolutionary."

"There's no need to terrify Titus, Jahan," Leontius says, but he's still smiling and again, despite all the months of silence and anger between us, I'm beginning to think he might actually forgive me. He nods at the officer. "Thank you for your service."

Lees climbs back into the carriage, while Horatius paces forward to have a few words with Titus. I hear the officer whispering frantically, "Sir, what about Prince Augustus and Princess Phaedra?" But the captain-general simply hushes him.

I hop back on the box beside Pantoleon. We'll be in trouble if pursuit catches us—but who will the officers believe if not Captain-General Horatius, who has stood by the emperor's side for more than two decades? Horatius is, I hope, warning Titus that Augustus and Phaedra will doubtless send more troops to wrest power back from us.

The ground trembles again. "The gods are speaking a *great deal,*" Pantoleon remarks, but we both cast doubtful looks toward the mountain. We both know the gods don't usually speak quite this much. I find myself thinking of Mantius's font and Elanna. Maybe she *has* harnessed its power to terrify the imperial army into withdrawing from most of Ida; the earth often trembled when she woke the land in Eren and Caeris. Yet something about this worries the back of my mind. According to the reports, El has made trees move, not mountains. She hasn't rerouted the entire Channel. The earth shouldn't be shaking this much.

But Horatius is coming back to us now. He gives me a nod, then swings into the carriage. Pantoleon flicks the reins. We roll forward, over the tremoring earth, toward Ida and Elanna.

OUR CARRIAGE MAKES its slow way through Vileia, edging around knots of soldiers hauling furniture out of the mansions to create blockades. Word carries as we pass, telling the militia to cease building walls against the rebels, and the men stare up at the carriage, their faces dirty and their mouths open, belatedly remembering to salute the new emperor.

I shift on the box, even as I smile and wave at the soldiers. Augustus and Phaedra must have figured out our plan by now. We have to secure Ida—and use Horatius's influence to bring the military over to our side—before they catch up to us.

The street curves, and the Great Bridge comes into view. Pantoleon gasps. Even I feel a thud of astonishment in my heart at the sight of what Elanna's done.

Trees have sprouted on the bridge, their roots curling over the stone sides. Dozens of them. Hundreds. They move slowly—far more slowly than they did in Caeris and Eren—each root curling ponderously forward to pull the tree itself along. But they've had the desired effect of terrifying Paladis's militia into retreat. The Great Bridge is now a forest and in the distance, where Solivetos Hill should be wooded, only bare rock gleams.

I'm grinning. El's magic is working again. On the far bank, more trees shift through the streets, flashes of green softening the stone. An impossible number of them. How did she recover so quickly?

We're halted at the base of the bridge. Horatius gets out to argue with the lieutenant on duty, and I hop down.

"No need to let us through," I say gamely. "We'd never make it through this woods in the carriage. Give me a white flag, and I'll walk over."

The lieutenant eyes me, skeptical, but a white flag is produced. I stride out onto the bridge just as another tremor shakes the earth, rattling the loose stones the trees have carried with them. Instinctively, I glance toward Mount Angelos. A dusty plume rises from its flank. Smoke, or the impact of falling rocks?

The trembling intensifies, juddering through the bridge beneath me. I break into a trot, leaping over the tree roots, toward the distant end. The bridge shakes again; I stagger into a tree. It feels as if the whole damned thing is going to collapse. I straighten and stumble forward again. To my right, the Channel sloshes wildly where it meets the sea. On the far end of the bridge, people move. They've seen me. They're shading their eyes.

"Elanna!" I shout. "Tullea!"

A tree sways in front of me and tumbles over. I scramble across it and break into a run. I've got to get there before Elanna destroys this entire bridge. It has to be her doing; she's going to make the mountain erupt in earnest. She probably thinks I'm dead.

A figure breaks loose from the ranks at the end of the bridge. *"Jahan?"*

It's El, her brown curls loose and wild. Relief pounds through my veins even though I was almost certain I'd find her. Another tremor throws me forward, but I regain my footing and race to her. "It's all right!" I'm shouting. "I've got Leontius! You can stop this!"

But she just grabs my arm. "Stop what?"

I gesture at the stones trembling below us, at Mount Angelos's shivering snow-crowned head. "The mountain!"

"I'm not doing it!" she says. "I'm not doing *any* of it. But it's not natural, either."

I stare behind her, looking for Rayka, but he's not there. Tullea's approaching, with Lucius Argyros at her shoulder. And—Madiya. She has her shoulders back, authoritative. I pretend I don't see her. The earth rumbles again beneath our feet. El and I both stagger, balancing against each other.

"My brothers . . ." I begin.

"None of us are causing the earthquakes," Elanna insists, divining my meaning. "We're trying to figure out a way to stop them." She's still gripping my arm. "What's happened? You saved Leontius?"

"Yes." I look at Tullea. "He and Pantoleon are on the other side."

Tullea's hand comes up to her mouth, but she's too strong to crumple. "He's *alive*?"

"I found him in the Ochuroma." I have to shout now over the creaking of the bridge. "I need some of you to come with me to the other side! We need a public alliance with Leontius. And we need to make a plan, arrange the military in Vileia to protect the bridges, before Augustus and Phaedra get here."

Madiya looks at me. With her hair swept up in a knot and her sleeves rolled to the elbow, she looks the way she did when she tormented me all my childhood. "Where's Alcibiades?"

"I have no idea." I put my back to her. "El, you should come. And Tullea—"

"I'm going." Tullea's already marching away from us, jumping over tree roots, nimble despite the shaking stones. I grasp Elanna's hand, and then we're running after her, back out onto the shaking bridge.

"Did Firmina find you?" I call over the noise.

"Firmina?" El looks surprised. "No."

Firmina isn't here—and neither is Aunt Cyra? Perhaps El simply hasn't been in contact with them . . . But my footing demands my attention. The water beneath us is quivering, too, now. The whole world seems to be trembling. I push myself forward by force of will, refusing to let go of Elanna's hand. A chunk of bridge falls into the Channel in front of us, leaving a tree suspended in midair by its roots. We edge carefully around the other side and then race for the far side of the bridge.

Leontius and Horatius stand beside the blockade, waiting for us. It looks like Pantoleon and Tullea have already found each other; they're locked in a tight, silent embrace, and I look away from their reunion, giving them what privacy I can.

"Gentlemen!" I call. "Has anyone worked out what the gods are saying yet?"

Behind me, there's a crash as another chunk of bridge falls into the Channel. The engineering must not have been quite as good as the Paladisans claim. Middle Bridge, visible in the distance, is still holding, even though it's older. If not Elanna, then who's doing this? Firmina? I don't know why she would try to destroy Ida.

"They're probably cursing your name," Leontius retorts, and I feel a grin burst across my face. He's joking with me again. Maybe he *has* finally forgiven me—or at least begun to.

"Lees," I say, "Horatius, I've brought our leaders. Over there with Pantoleon is Tullea Domitros. This is the *Caveadear* of Eren and Caeris, Elanna Valtai."

"A pleasure, despite the circumstances," El says, sweeping a curtsy in her trousers.

Even though he really shouldn't, after today's events, Horatius looks shocked. But Leontius steps forward, interest in his eyes. "Lady *Caveadear*, it is a pleasure. I'm Leontius Saranon."

"I would have guessed," El says guilelessly. "You look like an emperor."

Leontius blinks, nonplussed but pleased. And El is right—there is a new confidence in my friend's shoulders, a power in his stance. It's as if the desperation of our circumstances has given him the strength he never had before.

Horatius breaks in, though his gaze flickers behind me. "We should get His Imperial Majesty to safety. We've sent orders out through Vileia, but there doubtless will be confusion when Prince Augustus and Princess Phaedra's people get here."

A deafening *crack* sounds behind us, and I hear huge chunks of stone and plaster crash into the Channel. "Middle Bridge, perhaps?" I suggest.

Leontius looks at Elanna. "This is your doing, I assume?"

"No." El's voice is decisive. "It's not me."

"Then who? Unless the gods are speaking . . ."

A woman clears her throat behind us. I turn, and stare. Madiya has followed us across the bridge, and Lathiel has followed her. My little brother hangs back a few feet, watching her warily, as if he might spring on her at any moment—or she on him.

Rage burns up through me. Why won't she ever leave us alone? "Get *away* from us—"

"The gods aren't speaking," she interrupts. "Unless Alcibiades Doukas can channel their voices."

I huff with impatience. "*Alcibiades?* But he—"

"He's a sorcerer." Now, at last, Madiya has the decency to look discomfited. "I should know—I taught him."

I'm staring, my mouth falling open. How is this possible?

Elanna gestures at the quaking ground. "He has this kind of power?"

"Oh," Madiya says, "if he found one of the wells, he has a good deal more than th—"

An earsplitting roar interrupts her, bellowing through the air, deafening me. Elanna cries out, pointing. We all turn. The world is shaking, and so is Mount Angelos. And as we watch, the whole mountainside shifts. It seems, impossibly, to *melt*. A black cloud bursts from its crown, and the mountain slope rolls like a river.

Toward the city. Toward us, and our holdout against the Saranons.

CHAPTER THIRTY

People start shouting. Screaming. I'm standing, numb with shock, holding Elanna's hand. Tremors are ravaging the earth, more and more of them now. More chunks of the Great Bridge plunge into the Channel. Enormous plumes of smoke stack from the mountain into the sky. Ash is already beginning to fall. Soon we won't be able to see the mountain at all, or even the flashes of red fire from the spraying lava. We'll just feel the lava, instead, when it reaches Ida. If we can't stop it, we'll be subsumed by the fires. By the ash. By the surging water. Our whole rebellion will be extinguished, along with our lives.

But, I realize now, Alcibiades isn't only aiming to destroy us and Ida. He'll blame Elanna for what happened, because the magic looks like hers. Any survivors will think the *Caveadear* betrayed them all, though there's no logic behind it. But Alcibiades doesn't need logic: He just needs to frame her and convince the world to believe it. Then Augustus and Phaedra's grasp of power will be complete. No one will mourn us if they believe we destroyed this great city, and they will crack down even harder on the witch hunts. Sophy and the others in Eren won't stand a chance.

"There must be a way to stop it . . ." I begin. But how?

Madiya interrupts. "We need to stop *him*."

I stare at her. Of course, she thinks she knows best.

"No." Elanna's voice is flat. Certain. "We need to stop the eruption first, or it'll destroy the entire city."

Madiya shrugs, and I feel a stab of hatred. She looks so damned calm. Leontius is staring back and forth from El to me. He might be the emperor, but as far as sorcery goes, he's as educated as a small child.

"Can you do it?" I ask Elanna.

She draws in a breath. Her hands are fisted tight. "With the power of Mantius's font—perhaps." She looks at me. "And with your help."

I nod, even though I don't know how I can help her. I'm no steward of the land. But we have to try, so the Middle Bridge it is. We take off through the streets, leaving Horatius and Leontius, along with Tullea and Pantoleon, to get the militia to shelter—though if we can't stop the eruption, they'll suffocate to death no matter what happens.

Madiya follows us, my little brother trailing her. I swing back to face her. "We don't need your help. Leave Lathiel with me and go back."

"You're wrong, Jahan," Madiya says coolly. "You *do* need my help. And Lathiel's."

But Lathiel's shaking his head. His face is peaked, and I can see the tremor when he lifts his hand to touch her elbow.

"You haven't been giving him the laudanum, have you?" I say. "Do you even know why he's shaking?"

Madiya just pushes Lathiel behind her and lifts her chin. "He's going to be the greatest sorcerer the world has ever seen."

"Oh? And what about Rayka and me? It was going to be us when we were—"

"Jahan!" Elanna's shouting at us from the street ahead. "Come *on*! There's no time for arguments!"

Another quake rocks the earth. She's right. But still I hesitate, looking at Madiya and Lathiel. I don't know how to prevent her following us, short of physical violence. And I don't want Lathiel to see me punch her, even though it would be damned satisfying. At least, if she insists on coming, he seems to be pursuing her. Then I'll know where he is.

So I turn and run, compressing space to catch up with Elanna. When I look back, Madiya and Lathiel are on our heels.

We race across the Middle Bridge, dodging trees now swaying in the rising wind. The sky has turned pitch black and more ash is falling, sticking in our mouths and eyes, filtering into our lungs. All four of us are overtaken by coughing. Somewhere in the distance, despite the falling ash, I catch the red gleam of fire spewing from the mountain.

"Hurry." Elanna grasps my hand. Then we're running through the streets, past the university. Here, more trees crowd the cobblestones. But these have begun, strangely, to fray around the edges, like shadows exposed to light. El pants an explanation: "Tullea's illusions. She made trees to supplement my trees. I couldn't do enough alone. The ones on the bridge are real—they had to be, to frighten the imperial soldiers. But otherwise they're mostly illusion, with a few real ones mixed in."

No wonder they were able to terrify the city into submission. To all appearances, the trees not only marched like an advancing army, but multiplied beyond belief. I nearly laugh as we turn the final corner to find the bulk of Solivetos Hill before us. The steps have been put back into place—Rayka's doing, I suppose—and we pant up to the top and collapse in the upper temple. My limbs are shaking with exhaustion; I feel as though I could sink into the floor.

But then the power of the well pulses into me. It's like waking from a dream. My tired muscles feel bright with sudden life. My mind clears. Even the ash feels less sticky in my lungs.

I glance at Madiya. She's staring at the font, her hands open in front of her. Even she must feel its power.

"How is Alcibiades doing this?" I demand. If she's here, she might as well answer some questions. I want to ask how a sorcerer has gotten to be the grand inquisitor, but it will have to wait.

"He can't be a *Caveadear*," Elanna says. She looks a little ill at the thought.

"Oh," Madiya says, as if everyone knows this, "he doesn't need to be. You can create a similar effect with a knowledge of physics. That is," she corrects herself, "it is possible to make it *look* like the same thing, to the untrained eye. And all eyes in Ida are ignorant when it comes to sorcery."

"You never taught us how to do this," I say quietly. "I don't know how to make a volcano erupt."

"Well, *you* . . ." Then Madiya seems to think better of denigrating my abilities. She glances at Lathiel, but he's sunk to the ground beside the font. Shivering. "He can do it."

I stare at my little brother, whose enormous, hollowed eyes stare back up at me. "No," I say, "he can't. He's *sick.*"

"He'll be fine," Madiya says impatiently. "He's stronger than you ever were."

I stare at her. Lathiel is now her favorite, the one who will be the greatest sorcerer in the world, and this is how she treats him? As if he's a toy she can rewind and make perform again?

In two strides, I cross to my brother and pull off my coat. I kneel beside him and wrap it around his shoulders. I whisper to the linen, *Warm him.* His skin feels cool, clammy to my touch. When I clench his shoulders, he seems to struggle to focus on my face. "Stay right here," I whisper to him. "Hang on. I have to deal with this mountain, but I'm coming back for you. Don't let her take you anywhere."

He blinks dully at me. But then he nods, and my heart squeezes with relief.

I stand, folding my arms, facing her. Blocking her access to him. "You'll just have to deal with Elanna and me, I'm afraid. Tell us what to do—if you know."

Madiya's gaze shifts back and forth. She takes a step forward, as if she thinks I might let her touch Lathiel, but I hold fast and she sighs.

"It's simple enough, if one has the power," she says. "The mountain appears dormant, but there are always forces working within it. Igniting a lava flow is the same principle as lighting a candle, only on a grander scale. The volcano holds the *memory* of eruption. The *potentiality.* All one must do, in theory, is unlock it." She's got her professorial voice on, educating us with her usual alarming competence.

And I can see it. I can see how one might cause a volcano to erupt, the same way one might light a candle. If the candle has been lit before, it holds the memory of fire. A volcano that has erupted holds the memory of erupting. The potential to erupt again.

Elanna has bowed her head. Now she lifts it and strides over to the font. She puts her hands into the well; her back arches. A pulse of panic rises in me. But then she turns around, holding her hands up. Sparks of light seem to flare around them, there and gone.

"I'll try to soothe the earth," she says, "but I don't know if it will listen. It's so far gone, and I'm not the steward of this land."

Gathering herself, she walks out of the temple. With a last glance at Lathiel, I start to follow, but Madiya snags my sleeve.

"She can't do this," she says.

I stare at her; her eyes are level. Serious. "You don't know Elanna." I yank my arm out of her grasp. She has no right to touch me.

"Listen, Jahan. You can help her. It's the same principle as any fire, or anything that moves." Madiya's voice is stern, but there's something pleading in her manner. A hunch to her shoulders. "Take the power in the font, and *use it.*"

I study her. The woman who once, I thought, ruined my life. The woman who tried to shape me and my brothers into something we never asked to be. The woman who, when all things are considered, did the most to make me what I am. Not *who* I am—credit for that goes to Elanna, Aunt Cyra, the friends I've made in Paladis and Eren and Caeris, and most of all to myself. But Madiya is the one who made it possible for all of me to be standing here now. If not for her, would Ida even be welcoming reform, or legalizing sorcery? Would I be saving the city from Alcibiades and the Saranons?

Maybe not. But it doesn't excuse what she did to me. Or Rayka, or Lathiel, or my mother.

I hesitate. Wind bellows around the temple, and ash pours in through the cracked roof. I don't have time to waste.

So I decide to do what she says. Just this one time.

"Go out of the temple and don't touch Lathiel," I order her. "If you do, I'll know. And I'll make you regret it."

She actually flinches. But she does as I demand. I wait until she's retreated through the doors. Beside me, Lathiel still shivers, though less now that I've wrapped him in the coat. I can't stand leaving him here, but I have no choice. This time, I don't think Madiya will cross me.

I plunge my hands into the font, letting the power surge into me, the rich light buzzing in my skin. And then I walk outside to find Elanna.

SHE STANDS BY the wall in her greatcoat, barely visible through the spiraling ash and the vicious thrum of the wind. I fumble to her side, and when I brush her hand, the humming power inside me seems to recognize and mingle with that inside her. She turns to me, her eyes luminous.

"It's not enough," she says. "I can't call the eruption back. The ash . . ." She starts to cough.

I breathe in, feeling the ash drift into my lungs. Somehow, with Tirisero's power, I can spread my mind wide and feel what Elanna's already done. She's whispered to the land, trying to soothe it, but it won't be soothed. The land north of us is slowly shifting, redirecting the lava flows away from the city, but the lava itself is still flowing and the land is moving too slowly. And then there is the ash muffling the air, filtering into our throats. "Tell me what to do."

"The ash." She coughs again. "Move it out—bring in a wind."

So I reach for the wind itself, wild and high and fierce. I feel its potential, a strong and elusive thing. I tell the wind to sweep the ash in great gusts high into the atmosphere, away from Ida, but it's already blowing so strongly that at first it won't obey me. I dig my heels in, opening my arms wide, and let the well's power pour out of me. The wind jerks and snaps. Ash falls into my mouth and lands on my eyelids. My muscles are straining. The ash is smothering my nose; I can't breathe deeply enough. I don't know if I can do it.

But I pull more power into me, until I am as overspilling as the well itself, until my body hums. Away north of the city, where Aexione must be, I can feel another source of power, like a distant throb. It must be the well Alcibiades found. Its power runs like a river through the earth, up into Mount Angelos. Unstoppable.

Yet Alcibiades isn't trying to command the wind or the ash or the lava flows. He's poured all his power into the mountain itself and the fire within it. If we can contain its effects, we can fight back.

I reach again for the wind, and this time it obeys me. The first gusts are too low, nearly sweeping Elanna and me off the ledge. But they catch the ash, and I squint my eyes open to see it dance into a great black cloud. I'm more careful with the next, reaching for a higher layer of atmosphere, kicking the ash up and up, out to sea, up toward the lowering sun. The wind is cantankerous, difficult to hold, not particularly obedient.

But it does its job. The ash disperses slowly. It's lifted in great sheets off the top of the erupting mountain, piling high into the sky, away from Ida, away from us.

"Water!" Elanna gasps. "The sea!"

I can almost breathe now. I feel for the sea shoving up against the shore, the tension in the waves gathering, surging out from Ida. I reach for the potential in the water particles, but they slide away from me. Then I sense, strong and fierce, Elanna's power dart past my own into the waves. It's as if she's holding up the wall of water, letting it trickle slowly through her fingers. Beside me, she's gasping with the effort. Shaking. But she holds.

I don't know how to help and, besides, with so much of the ash lifted, I can see the spitting fires now on the mountain. The lava is still flowing down, spilling over the folds El has coaxed into the land. I stare at it, feeling the sweat cooling on the back of my neck. But Tirisero's power still thrums in me, and I find myself thinking, *What is lava but streams of molten rock?* If Alcibiades can make a mountain erupt by reminding it that it has the potential to do so, then I can make it cool by reminding it that the rock, though now liquefied, also has the potential to be solid.

But it's running—fast—and Alcibiades is still pouring his power into the core of the mountain itself. Perhaps, once again, I can slide past him. I draw in a breath—tasting the lingering ash in the air—and reach under the ground, to the pores in the earth through which the lava is seeping. I remind them that they have the potential to be solid. *Sealed up, solid rock, cool as marble.* I talk to the flowing lava, reminding it that it doesn't have to run: that it can grind, slowly, as rock, down to the sea. It is also reluctant, but again I *insist.*

And at last, it slows to a few rivulets of fire that seem to scald through my own body. Then even these trickle into nothing more than memory, into hardened, blackened rock.

The earth trembles, and subsides.

The mountain is still shivering, but Alcibiades's grip on it has slackened. Small tremors still run through the earth, but they're aftershocks, not the main event. Ash might still linger in the sky, but the wind is slowly blowing it away. Elanna soothes the rushing water and now releases a final stream away from Ida, out into the Middle Sea.

It's over.

I fall back into my body. I don't know how long we've been standing here. My feet are cold and numb. My hands feel hot, scorched, as if by fire.

Elanna sags against me. It's an effort to reach my arm around her waist. The power still hums inside me, irrepressible. My heart seems to beat too fast. But the mountain has quieted, though it will never be the same shape again. It's elongated now, a massive, square ridge rather than a dome. Through the dusty, darkening sky, evening stars seem to drift overhead, spun with the faintest ash.

Footsteps scrape the stones behind us. Rayka's running up the stairs. He's got a neckcloth wrapped around his nose and mouth, and for once he seems afraid rather than smug. When he sees us, he rips off the neckcloth. "You didn't help anyone!"

My head throbs, and shaping words with my mouth seems a foreign task. "What?"

"People, all over the city!" He gestures angrily, stabbing the air with his hands. "Ash in their lungs! Dogs! Cats! They're going to die from it!"

I push myself onto my feet, swaying. Elanna also stands. Madiya watches us from a short distance away, her arms folded. Lathiel's come out of the temple. I look between my brothers and the sorceress who raised us, and I understand what's wrong. I dispersed the majority of the ash, but I couldn't remove it all; some still dances in the air. And the wind could hardly sweep away what had already been inhaled by people and animals.

My brothers don't know how to heal anyone except themselves. Do I have the power to heal all the people in the city and the surrounding land? *Can* I do it, without touching them? Hundreds, thousands of people?

"Rayka, Lathiel," Madiya says, "give Jahan your power."

"*What?*" I say.

Rayka's chin comes up. "No!"

Lathiel just blinks.

"You two reach into the font, and let Jahan take the power through you," Madiya says, impatient. "It will work."

I stare from her to my brothers. Maybe she's right. Maybe it would work. But doing it—taking my brothers' power, at her orders—makes me no better than her.

Quietly, I say, "You have no right to force them to do such a thing. I'll do it myself."

I turn back to the parapet and stare over the city, feeling the power still buzzing in my hands. I draw in a breath. I don't know if I can do this alone, truly. I might save everyone, but drain myself. Most likely I will. But better me than all the thousands of people living in Ida and the peninsula. Better to lose myself than steal my brothers' power at Madiya's orders.

I gather myself. But just before I act, there's a light touch at my elbow.

Lathiel's looking at me, his gaze still somewhat unfocused, his hands still unsteady. But sparks shine in his hands. "I'm going to help."

"You're not well," I protest. I glance at Madiya, but she's retreated toward the temple, Elanna glaring at her. Did she put him up to this, somehow?

Lathiel shakes his head. "It's all right. She's not making me. I *want* to."

"You do?"

He nods.

A heavy sigh comes from my other side. "Let's get this over with."

I swing around to face Rayka. Light jumps in his hands, too. "You, too?"

"Why is that so hard to believe?" Rayka says crossly. "I don't want *everyone* to die. Just the people who deserve it."

I roll my eyes. "You're sure?"

"Yes," Lathiel says.

Rayka practically implodes. "All the gods, Jahan, just start already!"

I'm smiling, I realize. I reach out, gathering their hands in mine. It's the first time we've been together like this since I was fifteen.

"Kyros's shameful descendants, all gathered in one place," I say drily.

"And Mantius's," Lathiel says, and the hope in his voice makes my throat tighten.

I think of the vision I had of Mantius, sacrificing himself to seal the Tirisero font. My hero. *Our* hero. I want to be worthy of the man who gave himself to protect the city.

So I close my eyes, and I feel my brothers' power electric in their hands, pouring into me. I reach for it. I surrender into the power. The world seems to transform into flame. Into light, and the deep beat of water.

I reach for the nearest person—Elanna. I feel her familiar shape, and the ash coating her throat and lungs. She's still coughing. I whisper to the ash. *Release, come out.*

It's slow. Too slow, at first. But then I hear her gasp aloud, though I don't open my eyes, and I know the ash has seeped out through her very skin.

I reach for the next person. Rayka. The ash comes swiftly out of him. Lathiel's lungs are more reluctant to release it, but they do. Now, with them healthy, we can turn to the rest of the city. Many now, humans and animals alike. Time seems to have slowed; perhaps the god, or Mantius, is with me. I seem to sense a presence larger than my own or my brothers', though when I reach for it, it's not there. I stretch myself out into my city, to the poor and beggars crowding the streets, the university students, the shopkeepers and bankers, the rich huddled in their fine Vileia mansions, the militia and the rebels. The sheep and hens and cattle, the dogs and cats and birds. Every living thing. I feel them all, like thousands of shining lights dampened by the gray dimness of the ashes.

"Release," I whisper, "come out."

Power surges through me. It blinds me. Deafens me. Gold light envelops my eyes; I waver like a candle burning a flame it can barely control.

Then it *whoosh*es out. The command—the healing—passes through me. The power has passed through my brothers, and I'm afraid to take any more from them. So I pull away, my eyes watering, my vision still bleary with light.

But Lathiel and Rayka stay beside me: the three of us, together. The two of them, helping me. We're the descendants of Kyros, yes, but also of Mantius. And I think he might be proud of us.

There are hands on my shoulders. Elanna, holding me upright. I lean into her. She smells of burned grass, and somehow it's the most comforting scent in the world. There's a groan as Rayka drops to the ground, rubbing his face. Then Lathiel does, too. Only Madiya remains standing, watching from a distance.

My head seems to weigh as much as the temple. But I lift it and look at her. She's staring toward Mount Angelos. Toward Aexione. I can't feel the second well any longer, now that the power has drained from me, but I'm certain Alcibiades hasn't ceased using it.

Madiya still hasn't explained how she knows him—or how she supposedly taught him sorcery.

He's still out there, along with Augustus and Phaedra. And here in the city, Leontius is waiting for us somewhere, with Pantoleon and Tullea and all the others. But I only want to pillow my head in El's lap and sleep for ten years. I'm so exhausted I don't know whether I have any power left. If Alcibiades came after me right now, I'd probably just let him.

But we need to find Leontius. We need to claim the city, and then we need to claim Aexione.

So with a grunt, I drag myself to my feet. I offer El a hand up; she rubs her eyes. Lathiel scrambles up, and I reach toward him. When I put my arm around his shoulders, he leans into me. Rayka stands strong by my side.

We all look at Madiya, who still watches us. "You did well," she begins.

"You don't need to tell us," I interrupt. "We don't want to hear it."

Her lips thin. But she says nothing.

I point to the stairs. "After you."

CHAPTER THIRTY-ONE

We find Leontius and the others at the Deos Deorum. Its walls survived the earthquake, though one of the roofs has caved in. Strangely, Bardas isn't there. Elanna tells me she hasn't seen him since I left for Aexione. Our people have raided the larder, and there's a table full of fruits, breads, olives, wine, and everything else they could find—a good thing since my stomach feels ready to fold in like the roof.

Leontius embraces me. "You stopped the eruption!"

It's so good to have my friend back that I can't even find words. I just nod.

"You, and Lady Elanna." He smiles at El, even though a frown is still marking his brow. "Everyone!" he calls out. "Today my friends Jahan Korakides and Elanna Valtai have saved us all. A sorcerer connected to my brother and sister tried to make this mountain erupt and kill us. But they stopped him!"

A cheer runs through the room. Felix Tzemines whoops. Pantoleon comes over to whack my shoulder, and Tullea clasps first my hand, then El's. I congratulate Tullea on her tree illusions, and smile at Lucius Argyros and even Zollus Katabares, who still dogs Leontius's shadow.

Captain-General Horatius makes his way over. "No word from the palace. They sent guards in pursuit, but they were caught in the eruption, the same as us." He nods at Leontius, who nods back.

"We'll stay here the night, and send a messenger to Aexione come morning."

"We don't have time for that."

It's Madiya, of course. I sigh. Horatius draws back, affronted, but Leontius makes a face of polite interest.

"You don't understand Alcibiades," she says. "We have to go *now.*"

After seeing him cut my friend's hand off and then make a mountain erupt, I *do* feel I understand Alcibiades. I know Madiya's right, even though her orders are the last thing I want to take. And more than anything I want to lie down and sleep.

"I'm not risking my men, Madam . . . ?" Horatius says, bristling.

"You don't need to go," Madiya replies crisply, uninterested in introducing herself. "Jahan and I can manage. Come along in the morning."

Jahan and I?

"I didn't agree to go with you," I point out. "But—since it is probably wise—I will go. You can come if you like."

Madiya just blinks at me. She truly doesn't understand my meaning. And probably she never will. But at least now I can stand against her.

"I'm coming, too," Elanna says. She takes my hand in front of them all. I almost pull back, but then she glances at me, almost in challenge. What do I have to lose—and what do I care what these people think of us? I wrap my fingers around hers.

"Then let's go."

I pause to make sure Lathiel's safe beside a fireplace, tucked up in several blankets. I don't want to leave him, but at least Madiya's with me, so she can't hurt him. "Where are you going?" he asks, pushing himself upright. His eyes still look gray, his hands shaky.

"To finish things," I say. "It's all right to stay here. You'll be safe."

He hesitates, but nods.

I glance around but don't see Rayka. Well, it's not as if his presence could comfort Lathiel all that much. With a last reassuring smile at my little brother, I make for the door.

But this time Leontius follows me. "You should go on ahead," he says. "I'll get Horatius moving. We'll be behind as fast as we can—and bring everyone else with us, too."

I raise an eyebrow. "Bringing a mob to your father's palace? The court will hardly recognize you."

He actually grins. "I'll speak out, this time."

Elanna returns to tug me along; Madiya's already lost from sight. We make for the door while Nestor and Irene come running up with a basket of food for us to take. "Where is Bardas?" I ask them.

Irene shrugs. "Haven't see him in a while."

This worries me—especially since Firmina and Aunt Cyra apparently never made it to Ida, either. The empress has already proved herself willing to kill to get what she wants. But I have to put it out of my mind. I'll sort it out once we've dealt with Alcibiades, and Phaedra and Augustus.

Outside the Deos Deorum, Horatius rustles up a coach, and we're bundled inside. It's warm and close within, and despite the danger, I fight drowsiness. Elanna unpacks the food basket, and I look at Madiya in the dim light of the swinging lantern. It's strange to be here like this, so close. I can't say I like it, but at least I can tolerate it.

"Madiya . . . or is it Sylvia?" I ask. "You said you taught Alcibiades."

She flinches. The woman who experimented on us without pity or compassion actually flinches. "I . . ." She draws in a breath. "It is Sylvia, in fact. But I erased that name, Jahan. I left it behind in the Ochuroma. I couldn't be myself any longer, when the witch hunters were combing the empire for me."

"But you're using it again now."

A hesitation comes over her. I watch her decide to tell the truth; I recognize the effort of the decision, because I've made it so often myself. For the first time, uncomfortably, I realize maybe it's Madiya who taught me how to lie.

"I am, as a . . . a warning."

"To Alcibiades?"

She's quiet. Then, in a hard voice, she says, "They kept me in that cell for five years, Jahan. Experimented on me—new methods with their witch stones and bells, trying to see what would work. You see?" she says when I startle. "I know what it is to be experimented on."

"That doesn't excuse what you did," Elanna says. "You experimented on *children.*"

Madiya just looks at her. Uncomprehending. She really doesn't understand what she did wrong. I lace my fingers through El's, tightly. She squeezes back.

With a shrug, Madiya resumes her story. "I thought I would die there. No—I *knew* I would. But then a new guard came. He was the one who walked me back and forth from my cell to their workroom."

"Alcibiades," I say.

"Yes. He was a new recruit. Overzealous, because he was trying to hide the fact that he was a sorcerer. He had an ability I'd never seen before. He was . . . immune . . . to the stones and bells. They didn't send him mad, though they still inhibited his magic. His mother had done it to him, he claimed, when he was a child, as a way to keep him safe. As a sorcerer, he'd realized that the best place to hide would be in the Ochuroma itself—among the witch hunters' ranks. So he joined them." Her hands clench in the fabric of her skirt. "He wanted to help sorcerers, he told me. Save them from the inside. We struck a bargain. I'd teach him the magic I knew—which he could use outside the Ochuroma, away from the bells and stones—and he'd smuggle me out."

"Did he?" I ask.

She utters a cold laugh. "In a way. He brought me a pair of shoes and a bag of food and two silver pounds, and smuggled me out the back gate. I had to escape through the forest on my own, down through the heart of Paladis itself. I didn't even know where to go. I wanted to go home to Salesia but my parents had made it clear I wasn't welcome, not with my magic—that was why I left in the first place, you know. The witch hunters caught me trying to escape to the east." She pauses. "But I got to Manasi, on foot. It took days, and I was terrified the witch hunters were pursuing me. I wanted to go to the Occident, for they're rumored to have sorcerers, but I didn't have money for the passage and I needed to get out. Someone said that there was a safe haven for sorcerers on Pira in the Britemnos Isles. So I booked passage on the first ship I found. And when I got there, I met your father. He offered to help me."

"And so you stayed," I say. My voice sounds hollow, even to me.

She nods. "And when you were born a sorcerer, I realized I could give you the immunity that Alcibiades's mother had given him. That's how the experiments began. Of course, your mother ruined things from the start, interrupting me during that early experiment on you, making me damage the patterns in your mind. It's no wonder you've never been able to take in as much power as your brothers, or do any magic with ease. Your little mind was a mess of knots."

Elanna's grip tightens on my hand.

"Maybe you're wrong," I say, and Madiya looks at me, startled. She's not used to being contradicted. I go on, realizing it as I speak. "Maybe I could never take in power from other living things, like you wanted. But I can take in the power from the wells. From the stone circles in Eren and Caeris. Maybe you didn't damage me. Maybe I was just never built to work the way you wanted me to."

Madiya's chin comes up. She's getting annoyed now that I've pointed out my success has nothing to do with her. "Maybe," she says.

I shrug. "Maybe you never took the time to really understand me."

She gives me a baleful look, then sighs and shakes out her hair, as if she can so easily erase my criticism. "That day when you were ten. When your mother . . ."

"I know what day you mean." My voice is hard.

"Yes, well." She taps her fingers together. "A witch hunter came to my cottage, you remember. Your mother had contacted them . . ."

"I know." Though I didn't know whether to believe it at the time.

"Well," she says, "Alcibiades was the one who came."

I sit up straight. The man in the blue coat and the black hat—which, I now realize, covered his light hair. I never saw his face. I'd have known him immediately, otherwise, when I saw him again in Aexione.

Madiya nods, taking in my reaction. "He'd read Alia's letter, and he suspected it was me. So he came to Pira, looking for me. I had to put him off, and then your mother . . ." She shakes her head. "Alcibiades wanted to know what I was doing. He wanted help with some magic. He'd learned about the wells, and he thought I might be able to help him use them. But I'd heard how he'd been treating sorcerers. Torturing them harder than anyone else. There wasn't a single other sorcerer he smuggled out of that prison. I didn't want him to know about you boys—or find you. I threw him out of Pira, the bastard."

Elanna leans forward. "Why didn't he help any other sorcerers?"

Madiya shrugs. "Because he'd learned all he needed to know from me? He told me he regretted helping me escape. We could have done so much more *experimentation*, he said, if I'd remained in the Ochuroma."

A shiver runs up my back, and I suddenly wonder if there's a reason why Madiya's become what she has. If her time in the Ochuroma broke more than just her magic.

It still doesn't excuse what she's done. And I don't trust the pity I feel. This story may be true, but she's also using it to play on our sympathies. To get us back on her side, to do what she wants.

"He's very powerful." Madiya pauses. It's coming now, the real reason she told us this story. The thing she wants us to do. "There's no telling what he'll do now. That's why I left Rayka and Lathiel in Ida—in case we don't come back."

THE COACH STOPS abruptly soon after, still far from Aexione. The night sits dark outside, illuminated by only faint starlight, dusted

with lingering ash. The driver swings down. "There's some distur-
bance up ahead—trees down. Horses keep spooking."

"Stay here," I tell the driver, and I follow Elanna and Madiya out
into the night.

We leave the lanterns behind, and the darkness seems absolute. I
stumble over a fallen tree and stub my toe. Ahead, Madiya rips her
skirt. Even El can't seem to find her footing. "It's strange," she whispers to us, her voice disembodied in the night, "the ground seems to
have *buckled*."

It does. We're climbing a grainy slope—loose earth and debris
pushed upward recently. I can't see the road; it's disappeared into
rubble.

Madiya is a dim figure ahead of me. She takes a confident stride
forward—

And disappears. A sharp cry rises up. El and I scramble forward.
El tugs me to my knees, crawling, and in a moment I see why. The
road splits before us into a black chasm. Madiya lies just below us,
clinging to some tree roots, but I can hear pebbles and dirt rolling
when she shifts. Even her breathing is loud and harsh.

I stare down at her. The chasm makes a black mouth of indeter-
minable depth. Once I would have given anything for Madiya to be
swallowed by the earth. But seeing her like this . . .

I sigh heavily. The gods must be testing me.

"Hold on," I whisper to her. I call back to Elanna, telling her
what's happened. There's a long silence, and then the earth shakes.
Somewhere behind us, horses whinny. Madiya gasps.

"What are you doing?" I exclaim.

"Trying to close the chasm," Elanna grunts. "But it *won't*—"

The earth shakes again, and this time Madiya utters a short, sharp
scream. She's sliding. I try to scramble toward her, but the earth is
giving way under me, too. I dive back to safety. Madiya's slipping,
though. With another rumble, she'll fall in, and the earth will close
on her.

Another gasp. She slips again. I lunge—not with my body, but with my mind. I gather the shape of her and *heave*. She comes flying up out of the chasm, sprawling on the ground between El and me. The ground tremors again. We're rattling forward—toward the other side of the chasm. Elanna grunts. I edge over to Madiya. She's panting, but she shakes her head. She seems unharmed.

"Alcibiades is *resisting*," Elanna says. Tension pours off her. "Every time I try to close it, he pushes back . . ."

"I'll help you," I begin, but Madiya interrupts.

"We need to find *him*. Stop him, wherever he is."

And leave Elanna here, fighting against this opening chasm in the earth? I hesitate, though it makes a certain amount of sense. If she can close the chasm, then Leontius and the others can get across the road and meet us at Aexione.

"It's all right," El says. "I'll stay. I'll get it closed. Go!"

The earth lurches. The space across the chasm is too far to jump— but not too far to compress space. I grab Madiya's arm and take a running leap. We stagger onto the other side of the chasm, the ground trembling again. I let go of Madiya the moment I know our footing is secure.

She dusts her hands. "Where would he be?"

"I don't know—"

"He must be using a well. He doesn't have this much power on his own. Where is the nearest one?"

I start to say again, "I don't *know*," but then I pause. Leontius said something about sensing water in the palace gardens—in Astarea's Grotto. And I, too, felt a presence stirring there. "I think I can guess."

I lead us up the road, compressing space as I go. No further chasms await us, but we pass a party of militia blockading the road. *Nothing more than shadows in the night,* I insist as we pass. The guards watch, wide-eyed, from the fires. They're frightened, all of them. None of them have seen sorcery like this before.

For good measure, I snap all the guns I can. It's not all of the weapons, and I pay for it with an ache in my joints, but it'll make them think twice about stopping Leontius and the others from approaching Aexione.

At last we reach the town, silent in the depths of the night. The palace, too, sits quiet, though lanterns burn everywhere, and guards pace within the closed gates. *Nothing but shadows,* I insist as Madiya and I advance toward the bars.

But rather than passing unnoticed, the words blare loud into the night. I've shouted aloud, though I never intended to. "Nothing but shadows!"

Every gun within the palace gates swings up and trains on us.

Nothing to see, I insist, but again, the words echo into the night air, loud and idiotic. "Nothing to see!"

"Alcibiades," Madiya mutters.

"Who goes there?" a guard shouts.

I push Madiya backward. We can get to Astarea's Grotto another way, the long way along the Avenue of Oranges. But just then a gun explodes. Someone shouts. The spray of lead shot comes nowhere near us, but Madiya bursts into a run. I follow her. More guns erupt, and more guards shout in surprise. They must not be pulling the triggers themselves—Alcibiades must be doing it for them.

"I guess he knows we're here," I mutter.

Madiya snorts. "He knows a great deal more than is good for him. Here!"

We dive into the shadow between two great houses. The guns stop going off. I draw deeper into the shadows, trying to regain my breath. Madiya whirls around and clenches her fingers in my coat.

I stare down at her hand. She doesn't take the hint. So I grab her wrist and pull her hand forcibly away.

"Jahan," she says, and there's a strange note in her voice. A plea. A hope. "Alcibiades is powerful. You've seen how powerful he is. And you—you have healing magic. Like me."

"What?" I say. My lips feel numb.

"I could heal others," she says again, as if she thinks I might not have understood the first time. "The same way you can. It's how I managed to do the experiments—the little vestige of power left to me. But I never gave it to you boys. I never trained you to do it. You learned how to do it on your own, Jahan. You're brilliant. Clever. I never realized it."

I'm staring at her. After she insulted my abilities in the coach, now she's saying I'm *like* her? I'm not like Madiya, and I never will be.

"You and I can defeat Alcibiades together." She draws in a breath. Whispers, "Give me back my magic."

I reel backward, throwing her off me. She lured me in— complimented me, warned me of the danger with Alcibiades. But this is what she really wants.

"Please, Jahan," she says. *"Please."*

I look at her. Even in the dark, even filthy and reeking of ash and sweat, she exudes a kind of magnetism. Once, I would have tried to do this for her. I would have wanted to save her. To help her. So that she would praise me.

But I'm not a boy anymore. She no longer has that power over me.

"No," I say.

There's a pause, as if she can't believe what she just heard. "Jahan! I raised you—I taught you everything I know—I brought you up! And now you're being ungrateful, just the way you always have been—"

"And that," I say coldly, "is why I will never give you back your magic. Never."

Silence. She draws in a ragged breath, and I steel myself against another bout of her persuasion. She'll try another tactic this time. Guilt, probably. We don't have time for this—we need to go. Or I need to leave her here.

Before I can move, there's a whisper behind us. Footsteps. I whirl, bringing my fists up.

"*There* you are," a familiar voice says. "You morons."

I lower my fists. Two boys stand in the alley—both with ragged, lank dark hair and identical mulish stares. I never thought Rayka and Lathiel were much alike until this moment, but right now, there's no mistaking that they're brothers. I suppose I don't look much better.

"I told you to *stay*!" Madiya hisses.

"And leave you two to solve everything?" Rayka rolls his eyes.

Lathiel looks at Madiya. "You can't tell us what to do."

He's standing up to her? I'm staring. So is Rayka. And Madiya—she's pulled her shoulders back. Her mouth is open, but nothing has come out of it.

Rayka clears his throat. "So, uh. Where's Alcibiades?"

I'm only too glad to return to the matter at hand. "Astarea's Grotto, we think. Come on."

We take a back street this time, evading the guns. No guards patrol the perimeter of the imperial garden. We slip one by one through the gate and into the stillness of the shrubs and flowers. Ahead, the cypresses make tall shadows, clustering around the grotto. As we approach, I sense someone's presence within the trees.

Rayka grabs my arm, pulling me to a halt. We crouch behind a hedge. Madiya whispers, "Listen."

"Shut up," Rayka whispers back at her.

Footsteps crunch. Someone's come out of the grotto. Then Alcibiades's voice drifts, low and amused, over the plants. "Do I have company? Come and say hello."

Rayka stands, even as Lathiel and I try to yank him back down. "Hello, you bastard—"

He stops abruptly, choking. Flailing. He falls to the ground, heaving, gasping, his hands scrabbling at a hand that isn't there. It must be Alcibiades's magic—similar to how Rayka choked the guards at the Frourio, but Alcibiades isn't just trying to make my brother unconscious, he's trying to kill him. I grab for Rayka, trying to push Alcibiades away with my mind, but Madiya pulls me off him. "Go after Alcibiades—stop him—"

Lathiel is already running around the hedge, a silent shadow, obeying her out of habit. I plunge after him. He's running across the open space toward the grotto—

And then he's not. He's gone, invisible.

But I see Alcibiades. He stands on the grotto pathway, holding up a lantern. A discarded coat sits by his feet, along with the glinting shape of a pistol. He laughs at me. "Korakides? I might have known it was you. Is Sylvia with you? I'd like to pay my respects, one last time. Maybe she'll be more cooperative once I put her back in the Ochuroma."

"You won't," I snarl. "I know your secret, and the Ochuroma's—"

I stop, gagging. A fist has caught me around the throat. I flail, but there's no one there. No fist. Just a pressure. I'm choking. Black spots swarm in front of my eyes. I'm going to collapse—

Alcibiades grunts. The pressure eases and I heave in a breath, still on my knees. But now he's swinging around, reaching for someone who's not there. Someone invisible. Lathiel.

From the hedge, Madiya calls, "If you harm the boys, you'll never figure out what I did to make them great sorcerers!"

"I don't care about that, Sylvia," Alcibiades replies, laughing. "I don't need your help, and neither do Augustus and Phaedra. But it's been entertaining to play with you."

I crawl forward. One foot, one hand, then another. The folded coat and the pistol are so near. I compress space, but the motion catches Alcibiades's eye. He swings toward me, letting go of Lathiel, who drops to the ground, no longer invisible.

"We could have worked together, Sylvia," Alcibiades says over his shoulder. "But since you wanted to destroy the witch hunters, instead of using them to gain power in secret . . ." He shrugs, turns to me. Smiles. "We might have held all the magicians in the world under our sway, together. But I don't need anyone's help anymore. And unlike you, Korakides, I don't need the world to know I'm a sorcerer. If I have the witch hunters and the Saranons, I *control* the world."

The fist grabs my throat again. I'm gagging. But even as I try to get a grip on it, to break it, the fist shifts and tightens. I can hardly see Alcibiades now, or the garden, or Lathiel. He's sitting up behind Alcibiades, unnoticed. Maybe the grand inquisitor has discounted him because he's only a child.

But I can just see Lathiel stretch his fists up against his chin. See him squeeze them.

Do you know how to kill a man without touching him?

No. I refuse to let my little brother have another man's blood on his hands.

Alcibiades jerks. He staggers a little, fumbling at his left arm. Lathiel squeezes harder, but Alcibiades swivels and strikes him across the face. My little brother goes flying.

I'm gasping. Wheezing. But it's enough of a reprieve. I crawl forward and grab the pistol and the powder flask beside it. My hands aren't steady. Any moment Alcibiades is going to turn—he *does* turn—

There's a cry behind me: Madiya, running through the hedge. I spare a quick glance. She's carrying a stick, ready to strike Alcibiades with it.

But he merely snaps his fingers. A corresponding, sickening *snap* echoes up from Madiya. Her head jerks at a sharp, sick angle. Her body gives a single, violent shake. I can't look away as she falls, crashing to the earth, her neck broken.

Just like that, she's dead. Over. Done.

Alcibiades turns to me.

I've tipped the powder into the pan. I cock it. This is for Leontius, and for my brothers, and for all the sorcerers Alcibiades never freed from the Ochuroma, but tortured instead.

Alcibiades is staring down at me, laughing. "You're a sorcerer. You can do better than—"

I fire.

We're at close range. Alcibiades's head snaps back, though less sickeningly than Madiya's. Blood seeps, black, from the hole in his forehead. His arms jerk. The lantern tumbles from his hand. Then, gracelessly, he falls.

I climb to my feet. I wouldn't be surprised to find him still alive, ready to choke me with his dying breath, but his eyes are empty, the muscles of his face slack. He's dead, along with his ambitions to control the world—and all the sorcerers in it—from behind the imperial dais. I snatch up the lantern before it can burn a hole in the ground, and run for my youngest brother.

He's sitting up slowly. Alcibiades must have hit him with more than just the back of his hand. Blood drips from his nose. "I'm all right," he says thickly. Even his teeth are stained with blood. I rip a piece of my shirt off and stuff it against his nostrils. He manages, "Madiya?"

I shake my head, but Lathiel's already crawling onto his feet. So I grab his arm and together we cross back toward the woman who made us what we are.

She lies tumbled on the ground, her head turned at an impossible angle. Slowly, I kneel and feel for her neck, though touching her makes my skin crawl. But her flesh is cool and stiff. There's nothing there.

I look up at Lathiel. He's breathing hard, fast breaths, so loud I can hear them. It's over. Madiya can never touch him again. I reach up, and he grabs my hand. Neither of us can speak.

There's a groan from the hedge beyond us. Rayka comes crawling through, just visible since the sky has begun to lighten. He's bloody, bruised, as though he's been in a fight. "Is the bastard dead?"

"Yes," I say shortly, because I can't seem to put words around how damned glad I am to see him.

"She can't come back, can she?" Lathiel says, watching me with enormous eyes. "You can't bring her back?"

Rayka's come over to stand above us. Even he can't seem to speak.

"No," I say. I feel as if Lathiel's squeezing my heart as much as he tried to squeeze Alcibiades's. "No, she can't come back. I would never try anything like that."

Wordlessly, he nods. I hug him against me, and he hugs back. Rayka stands beside us, his arms folded. His shoulders quiver. I think he might be weeping. Not for Madiya, but for all the years she held us under her sway. For our mother. For ourselves.

My own eyes are burning. She'll never whisper into my head again. Never command me. Never cajole and manipulate me. Never keep my brothers from me, or try to win us back to her.

Birds are chattering in the cypresses. Dawn color touches the gardens, and it seems as if I can breathe again, more deeply than I have in years. My brothers are with me. They're safe. It's all I've ever wanted.

In the distance, a shout rises up over the palace roofs. A resounding din.

Elanna. I clamber to my feet. Elanna, and Leontius, and the mob. They must be here.

I turn back, reaching out my hand to Lathiel. He holds on to it. Together, Rayka leading the way, we run through the gardens, toward the palace and our people, and Leontius's siblings.

CHAPTER THIRTY-TWO

As we come around the corner toward the square facing the Grand Court, I see them, the rebels and even the militia from Ida, overflowing the square outside the palace gates. They're shouting, "Open the gates! Open the gates!" Behind the gates, the palace guard has retreated back toward the walls, well across the Grand Court. They're formed up in a defensive line. So far they haven't shot anything. Someone screams and points—my head jerks up. A green dragon swoops overhead, breathing fire. Illusion, I realize, and I laugh even though my heart's pounding perhaps faster than it should. In the crowd, Tullea waves at me, Pantoleon at her side. More magic weaves through the crowd—flashes of light, an ambling tree somehow mixed up in the crowd. Felix Tzemines throws his black hat in the air.

A woman is running toward us, shoving people aside. Elanna. Her face is smeared with dirt and scratches, but she's smiling. "Jahan!" She smashes against me, her hand tangling in mine, then stares at Lathiel and Rayka. "What happened?"

I try to explain, with interjections from Rayka. Lathiel just hangs on to me.

"The chasm closed," Elanna tells us, "almost of its own accord. It must have happened when Alcibiades was distracted." She glances over her shoulder. "Leontius is waiting for us. If you can, Jahan . . ."

Rayka takes over guarding Lathiel, and I push through the crowd with Elanna. Leontius occupies the center of the mob, perched on horseback. He casts me a wide-eyed look, but I wink at him and he puts his shoulders back.

"Korakos," he calls, "open the gates!"

I bow. "As you wish!"

I stride back through the crowd, which parts for me, until I reach the gates. With the energy of the grotto well still humming in my hands, even in my growing weariness, it's no trouble to murmur to the gate lock.

The gates fly open, and across the Grand Court, the palace guards bristle into tighter formation. I hold up my arms, keeping the crowd from surging through the gates.

"Aim!" a sergeant shouts, and the muskets pop as they're cocked.

I gather them all in my mind, with the humming brilliance of the grotto well, and, just before the sergeant can call *Fire,* I snap the locks and pinch out the sparks ready to ignite the gunpowder. Only one gun backfires, with a sickening *thud.* The others simply *crack.* Across the courtyard, the guards exclaim. Some throw down their weapons and run. Others struggle, trying to reload.

It doesn't matter—the guns are broken. And now we're pouring into the Grand Court, all the sorcerers in Ida, all the reformers, and at the heart of it all, Leontius Saranon.

A flash catches my eye. Someone is running off the balcony in the Inner Court.

Augustus. He's still up there. With any luck, he's barricading himself in the Salon of Meres.

"To me!" I shout, and there's a roar as we flood past the palace guards, through the colonnades, and into the palace itself. We're an unstoppable wave surging up the stairs. When I glance to my left, Elanna is there, fierce and battle-triumphant. I reach for her hand as we pour into the upper corridors, empty except for the staring eyes of marble statues.

The guards outside the Salon of Meres take one look at us and throw down their weapons.

I fling open the doors of the salon.

It's empty. Pieces of the diamond chandelier have shattered onto the floor, perhaps in the earthquakes yesterday. But no one occupies the room where Alakaseus Saranon let me know he would never allow us to win peace.

I run a hand through my hair. Augustus and Phaedra must have fled through one of the passages. Other people have crashed into the room—Leontius comes to a halt beside me, disheveled and angry. "Where are they?"

"They're either hiding, or planning to stab us in the back," I say. "Or both!"

Leontius rolls his eyes. "Their rooms, then." He leads the charge through the narrow hallway between salons, into the west wing. We burst into Phaedra's bedchamber. Clothes lie scattered; a perfume jar seeps oil onto the carpet. A terrified maid peers up from where she's hiding on the other side of the bed, and points to the passage connecting Phaedra's chambers to Augustus's.

His are not empty—shots ring out as we enter, from two guards wielding muskets. The bullets spray harmlessly into plaster. I break the guns, but the men don't have time to reload anyway. Leontius marches forward, Zollus right behind him.

"Stand down in the name of your emperor!" Zollus orders.

The guards glance at each other, then throw down their weapons. They both drop to their knees.

"Where is my brother?" Leontius asks in a dangerous voice.

"He-he fled, sir," one guard stammers. "With Princess Phaedra and a small retinue."

"What are their plans?" Leontius asks.

Both men shake their heads.

I push through to Lees. "I'll go."

I edge into the passage. No more guards here, but still I'm cautious winding down a staircase to a narrow door. I step through rather than push it open.

I'm in a small courtyard—I'm not sure I even knew this place existed. Fresh horse droppings litter the ash-flecked ground, and the tracks of carriage wheels disappear through the archway. I run out, following them. A small, deserted gatehouse; the gate itself stands open. I stare back and forth. Have they really fled, or just gone to ground at one of their distant holdings?

I can't see them from the air, like a bird—I need one of my brothers for that. I call to them: *Rayka! Lathiel!*

Footsteps scrape behind me, but it's Nestor who runs out of the palace. He's sweaty and grinning, and I can tell just by looking at him that he's ready to do something heroic. "I'll go after them, Jahan!"

"It's dangerous," I begin.

"This whole matter has been dangerous! It's all right, Jahan." He draws himself up. "I can manage alone."

"No, I'll come with you." I'm not about to let Nestor pursue these ruthless bastards on his own. "It's not—"

A shout interrupts me, in my head. *Jahan!* Not one of my brothers—Elanna. Then I hear, in the ordinary way, with my ears, a shout from the upper window: "Jahan!" There's a panicked edge to her voice. She's gesturing me up.

"Augustus and Phaedra?" I call.

"No . . ." She glances swiftly over her shoulder. "Come up! Hurry!"

I look around for Nestor, but he's already trotting into the gatehouse. Well, if he wants to go after the Saranons, it's his own skin he's risking. And to tell the truth, I'd just as soon not see either one of them ever again.

I climb back up the stairs. El's waiting for me at the top, rocking from foot to foot with impatience. She grabs my arm and tugs me back through the bedchambers, which are largely empty now, except for a few of our rebels admiring Phaedra's collection of porcelain shepherdesses. They seem happy, laughing together in triumph, a strange counterpoint to Elanna's urgency.

"The ministers are here," she says.

"The ministers?" I echo. I thought they'd fled into Aexione town, or the country, along with all the courtiers.

"Yes . . ." She shakes her head. "Firmina brought them—to approve the new emperor. She never left Aexione when you told her to.

She's been here all along. They're all in the Hall of Glass. Your aunt Cyra is there, too. I had to sneak out. I don't think she saw me."

A cold prickle runs down my back. There's something strange about this—something strange in El's manner, as well. "Won't they support Lees?"

Elanna presses her lips together. "You might say so . . ." We're nearing the grand staircase down to the Hall of Glass. She pulls me closer to her and whispers, "Jahan, I don't want to say this, because I like Firmina. But she never told us that she would stay in Aexione. She's never told us what her plan is, come to think of it. She never told us she intended to kill the emperor. And now she's brought the ministers to the Hall of Glass, and demanded Leontius come down."

"She wants what we do," I say slowly, "or at least, she's always claimed she does."

"She wants sorcery to be legalized. She wants constitutional reform." Elanna pauses. "But what *else* does she want?"

I'm staring at El, but I don't quite see her. I'm seeing Firmina Triciphes, the consummate actress. The woman who murdered the emperor, her husband, ostensibly to help our cause. Who killed Quentin and those guards, just because she could.

A hot thrumming has begun in my hands. Do we really know Firmina Triciphes at all?

Elanna pulls me down the stairs. The doors to the Hall of Glass sit tightly closed, and guards stand outside them. The *empress's* guards—their livery not purple and gold, but purple and white. Firmina not only brought the ministers, but also brought her own attendants—who are, presumably, loyal to her.

They recognize us. One opens a door and gestures us through.

We enter. Crystal beads shift under my feet; the earthquakes must have shattered several of the towering chandeliers. Only a few people occupy the far end of the cavernous room. Even from here, I can make out Firmina Triciphes, seated on the dais. Not on her usual stool, but on the emperor's gilded throne. Bardas stands at her left side, solemn.

Firmina looks up and sees us. "Ah, Jahan! Elanna! Welcome."

But I've stopped dead. Leontius is kneeling on the crimson carpet before her. No, it's not only the carpet that's red—it's blood pouring out of the healed wound at the end of his arm. He's slumped forward. He can't even seem to muster the strength to lift his head to see us. Zollus crouches beside him, whispering to him, but as I watch in horror, Lees falls farther forward.

"Leontius!" I'm running for him.

And then it's as if a great hand seizes me and jerks me back. I'm halted, struggling against the empty air.

"There's nothing any of us can do for him, Jahan." Firmina's voice is delicate with grief, and I stare up at her. The invisible hand around me tightens as she gently closes her fist. It feels as if the air is being slowly squeezed from my lungs. "He was too weak to rule. We always knew he would be."

To the left of the dais, the ministers are nodding. They all look mildly dazed. What has Firmina done to them? Some of our reformers have gathered on the dais's right side—Tullea, Felix, Lucius Argyros, Pantoleon. They, too, stare at us with dull eyes. And among them, a woman with a dirty white feather in her hair. My aunt, Cyra. She watches me with a tight little frown, as if it's a struggle to think. Her lips form a silent, questioning word—my name.

Firmina's taken them all. Everyone. Even Aunt Cyra, who did nothing but help her. She must be using the power of her guards—not only them, but the ministers and reformers themselves, draining them and persuading them at the same time.

A movement near the far wall catches my eye. Rayka, with Lathiel crouched behind him. They're fighting the persuasion, I can feel it, using the grotto well to try to push Firmina back. But so far, it's not enough. Rayka's sweating, and Lathiel's limbs shake with the effort.

Now Leontius falls to the floor with a soft gasp. I struggle to take another step forward, but the fist tightens about me and my breath gets even more shallow. Zollus is kneeling beside Lees, tugging on the prince's whole hand, weeping. I can't even turn my head to look for Elanna.

But I hear her. "Of course you're right!" she says with false cheer. El isn't half the actress Firmina is, and I know the empress is going to recognize it. But nevertheless, Elanna strides past me with confidence, approaching the throne. "I'm so glad we allied. Sophy will be delighted to join forces with a fellow female monarch."

A fellow monarch? But of course: Now I see the golden diadem encircling Firmina's brow. This must have been her plan all along—to destroy the Saranons one by one, then claim the throne for herself. She told me as much. She and Bardas both said the Saranons would never accept reform or change. At the time, I didn't recognize it for the warning it was.

Firmina smiles at El, distracted. Her fist loosens ever so slightly. I can hear the whisper of her persuasion wrapping around the ministers. *Firmina will be empress of Paladis. She will make an excellent empress. We want no one else.* The same words spin around the reformers, just loud enough for me to hear them. To recognize them.

If we can break her concentration, maybe we can break the persuasion as well.

"Paladis deserves a good empress," Firmina is saying. "Someone who listens to the needs of her people. Someone who has the power to take care of everyone in the empire, and protect them."

Beside her, Bardas nods. "It's all any of us have ever wanted," he says to me, pointedly.

Elanna's drawing closer to the throne. I wet my lips. The pressure has softened enough for me to speak. "Of course, that's what our great empire deserves," I say, and Firmina's gaze flashes to me. "Protection. The way you protected us from the Saranons."

If Firmina hears the dryness in my tone, she doesn't react to it. A particular smile warms her face. She leans forward, and I notice she's wearing a sleeveless silk-velvet robe over her gown—a coronation robe. She seems to have thought of everything. "The empress needs a consort to rule by her side," she says invitingly. "Someone who the people know and trust. Someone they revere as a hero."

I want to laugh—because if Firmina means me, then she's just made Elanna a great deal angrier than she was even to start with. But I swallow it. There's something about Firmina that makes me want to take her very seriously indeed. Perhaps it's the sight of Leontius bleeding to death on the floor.

And there's a hunger in her eyes that I recognize. I've seen this kind of desperation before, in my mother.

"You could heal the prince," I say. "He would abdicate the throne, if you asked."

Her lips pinch with disdain. "My dear stepson? He sees it as his duty to protect Paladis from my ambitions." She sighs a little. "Perhaps we should simply finish it."

She closes her fist. Leontius, whom I didn't think had any breath left to lose, draws in a ragged gasp. His eyes grow too large. She's done this to her husband. To the guards. And now she's doing it to my friend.

And in order to do it, she's drawing power from the ministers gathered around. From the guards, and from the reformers. From my aunt. The minister of state falls to his knees, his face gray, pressing his hands to his heart.

I lunge toward Firmina, breaking the last of the grip she had on me. Zollus is on my heels. I charge past Elanna to the throne, snatching for Firmina's hands. Guards shout at me to stand back. I hear muskets being cocked.

But Firmina's concentration breaks. She blinks at me, and laughs. "Dear Jahan, I wanted to spare you this. But if it's what you want . . ."

Pieces of tile shoot up from the floor, peppering me. I fling up my arms. One catches me across the face. My cheek stings. Someone's shouting—Elanna. Someone else slams into the empress—Zollus. But she casts him casually aside. His head cracks on the floor. The minister of state has crumpled now, along with two guardsmen. Another tile slams into my ribs. I double over, retching. Got to get up— got to help—

Crack.

Someone screams. I gasp in a breath. The wood of the dais is creaking—it's *moving*. Two great claws reach up from it, grasping toward the ceiling. A musket goes off. My ears are ringing.

Elanna stands below the dais, her hands thrust upward. The wood imitates her gesture, climbing and climbing into a cage that surrounds the empress. Firmina is struggling—one of the wooden bars breaks—but her concentration is slipping and now I see several ministers heave in breaths, and the reformers stirring from their trance.

"Arrest this woman!" the minister of finance is shouting. "Guards! Arrest her!"

"Down with the Triciphes!" Felix bellows.

Firmina breaks another bar, but she's realizing that she's lost her grip on the room. She seizes a piece of broken wood. It animates itself and strikes Elanna across the face. She falls. No, no, not El!

I'm running toward her, but Firmina stamps a foot and the floor shakes. I stumble and nearly fall. A crack runs down the marble steps of the dais. The cage splits in two. All the gods, she's going to get out—

Felix is pointing a pistol at the empress. "Stand down, or I'll shoot!"

Firmina flings up her arms. Felix collapses, the pistol flying from his hand, the energy yanked from his body. The ceiling quivers. I stare up, along with everyone else, as the ceiling *rises*. Pieces of plaster crumble down into the Hall of Glass, chips of chandelier striking people in the face, but Firmina has sliced the roof cleanly off the chamber. More people are falling, guards, reformers, ministers. The roof is lifting up, up . . .

It's going to fall. I see it the moment before it does, as all the rubble and chunks of parquet and plaster hang suspended there in the air.

I reach for the power of the grotto well and pour it into the ruined ceiling. I hold it up with all my might, grunting at the almost-physical weight of it. If it falls, it will crush us all. I try to gather all the pieces in my mind. And then I *push* them—letting them spill out into the garden, onto the lawn. It takes so much effort I seem to be

pushing pieces of myself, as well. My shoulders shake. Sweat slicks
my spine. But the ceiling moves and then, with an enormous thunder, it falls. Plaster and dust rain down. The open blue sky stares at
us overhead.

I drop back into myself. I'm gasping for breath, covered in sweat.
Many people lie upon the floor, drained. At least one of the ministers is dead, but Felix is crawling slowly onto his knees, thank all the
gods. Rayka seizes Felix's pistol and aims it at the empress. She's
holding her hands up, her gaze flitting wide-eyed over the room. It
fixes on me, desperate with hope. But I'm not Firmina Triciphes's
savior. I see Elanna sitting up, gingerly, to my left. Thank all the
gods. I thought Firmina might have ended her life.

"Arrest the empress," I tell Felix and the others, and then I turn
toward Elanna.

But just as I swivel, Firmina throws her arms up again. We all
flinch instinctively—but she doesn't reanimate the pieces of ceiling,
or make the walls fall in on us.

She *transforms*.

Her coronation robe falls. Her arms spread, growing long and
feathered. With a light hop, she leaps into the air—not a woman any
longer, but a swift, small falcon. She bobs a little, gaining her wings.

And as she gathers air, Bardas crumples to the floor, his arms out-
spread. His face is slack. Lifeless.

I'm staring. He helped Firmina in everything, and she used him.
She killed him.

A shot explodes. Rayka, aiming the pistol at the empress. But the
shot only sprays into the plaster. She's winging up into the sky. She's
gone.

I'm running after her. I reach for the grotto well, for all the power
harnessed there, but it doesn't feel like enough. It will never be
enough to stop Firmina Triciphes.

So I reach into myself. Into the part of me that dreamed it could
fly. Into the part of me that not only wanted comfort from Mantius,
but wanted to *be* Mantius.

And I'm running—*up* into the air. No, not running. I'm pumping my arms—my wings. My body is compressing and growing impossibly light at the same time. The air beats through my feathers. I'm the Korakos. A raven. Black-feathered as Mantius. I'm lifting high, high above the ruined Hall of Glass, up into the clear air, until the entire palace lies beneath me. Even though my wings are new, I'm gasping in this freedom, this new strength I dreamed of but never imagined I could possess.

And I see her—Firmina. I catch the scent of her passing. Power courses through me, both mine and the grotto well's. I compress space with an ease I never have before.

The impact of different air hits me. I tumble, flapping hard, and right myself. Firmina is closer, soaring upward on a current of warm air. Does she know I'm behind her?

I compress space again. This time the warm air lifts me up, a sudden bounce, and I'm soaring just below her. She's seen me, but she doesn't know who I am. I compress space within the warm air current, and she seems to recognize then what's going on. She flaps her wings, but I'm on top of her. I nip at the back of her head. She flips over, her claws digging into my stomach. But I bite her again, hard this time. She lets out a piercing cry. Her claws rake at me. I wrestle past them until I've got a grip on her.

We're tumbling now through the air, down from the stream of warmth, falling toward the distant ground. The sleek falcon struggles, but I grip her tighter. I nip at her neck. She flaps her wings, one last bid to escape, but the ground is spinning up close beneath us.

Her back strikes it, and, quick as that, she's human again, and naked. The impact must knock the wind out of her, but she's grabbed my wings now, in her human hands, ripping at them as if she can pull them off.

I tug at that part inside myself, somewhere in my gut, and then I'm human, too, taller than her and stronger. She's clawing at my arms, but I knee her in the stomach. She falls backward. This time her head hits the earth. I hesitate, bringing my hands up, but she just lies there. Her chest rises and falls. Her eyes stay open, blinking, full of the sky.

I crouch warily beside her. She's begun to cry—pathetic tears seeping through her eyelashes. As if some demonstration of fragility can move me, after what she's done. "Oh, Jahan—I'm so sorry— what if we—"

"I'm not bargaining with you." I shake her a little, and she goes limp. But I can feel something stirring—she's pulling on an energy. It pushes at my chest. Just a faint prod. But soon it will be stronger.

I know what I have to do. I'm not sure whether I can manage it— but I'm going to try.

"Hold very still," I breathe to the empress. "I'm going to help you. You've hurt yourself."

She gasps a little. "What do you mean?"

"You've hit your head. I'm going to heal it." I pat her hair, even though it sickens me a little to comfort this woman. "Then we'll make our plans together. How do you like that?"

More tears escape down her cheeks. Her hand scrabbles up, closing over mine. "Oh, Jahan. I knew you would understand."

Understand? I close my mouth. I don't have any words. Because I do understand; I know why she struggled against the Saranons and tried to overcome them all. Because my mother was like her, caged and desperate.

But that can't change what I need to do. I lean over her, putting my hands on either side of her face. She closes her eyes with a soft sigh. She trusts me, for the moment, though she shouldn't.

I reach into her mind. If I can heal others, if I can change Leontius's memories, perhaps I can do the opposite to Firmina. Madiya changed the way our minds work. She created patterns that were, before, only potential.

If those patterns can be created, they can be destroyed.

I reach into her mind. It is a chaos of bright sparks and long twisting lines. I swallow hard. I've never attempted this before—I'm not quite sure where to find the correct pathways that will affect her magic. But Madiya has experimented on Firmina. She's created new patterns—and these I can sense. They *feel* different—newer, almost raw, as if she stripped open too much, too quickly.

Close, I order them. The empress lies trustingly under my hands, and it almost pains me to give her hope, only to be taking everything away.

Almost. But what would this woman do, with access to her power?

I reach for the patterns again. *Close. Snug and tight. Sewn up, as if you were never there.*

Too slowly, they begin to shrink. To contract. Firmina's begun moaning. It must hurt. Maybe that's why Madiya always put us under when she performed her experiments. I focus harder, pulling the patterns tight. *Close, you bastards!*

When they are nothing more than nubs, barely open potential, I let her go.

Her face is blank, her eyes closed. She seems to have passed out.

I try to get up and sag instead onto the ground next to her. Everything hurts. My stomach is scored with bright-red scratches, and my muscles quiver at the faintest pressure. I can't stand; my feet can't seem to figure out whether or not they are actually talons. And I'm naked. I sag back on the ground, aching.

Firmina lies curled up on herself, her skin soft, her breathing shallow. She's naked. Vulnerable. My chest heaves. Have I ruined her mind? Made her like my mother? Am I like Madiya, then? Maybe killing her would have been more of a mercy. But I couldn't do that.

I rub my hands over my face. I did what I had to do. But it doesn't feel good inside me.

I need to find my brothers. And Elanna. Everyone.

I manage to crawl up to my knees. I flex my feet, trying to remind them that they know how to balance on the ground. But part of me is still convinced I should be flying.

A wild giddiness breaks out inside me. I transformed into a

raven—*me*, Jahan Korakides, the damaged one. Like my ancestor Mantius. The man whom my father wanted to model me after. The man whom I imagined comforting me as a child. Mantius, who gave himself up for the greater good. Now I've discovered what he worked so hard to hide. He, and all the other sorcerers who sacrificed themselves to hide the wells. I can find them, and I can change everything.

I'm standing, my arms open, the sun warming me. Still naked. Everyone's going to talk if I come back to Aexione like this. Part of me wants to dare them to.

But perhaps . . . One more time, I reach for the grotto well. Its power feels thin. Tired. It needs time to renew itself after first Alcibiades, then I, pulled so hard on it. But I make one last request, all the same. I can feel the weight of it in my mind. The shape.

Something rustles. My skin warms. When I open my eyes, I see a cloak has settled around my shoulders. It's made of black feathers, thickly sewn together.

I draw it tight. My eyes are prickling. I find myself looking around, as if there might be a specter of a sorcerer peering at me through the layers of the past, but we're alone in the garden. Bees drone in a flowered hedge. The sky gleams, impossibly clear.

Firmina is still unconscious. I sigh, but what else am I going to do? I'm not going to leave her here. I crouch beside her and lever her up into my arms, her weight surprisingly heavy for someone who tried to appear so delicate. I heave her onto my shoulder. She's still unclothed, but there's not much I can do about that. At least she's breathing. The well is tired, and so am I. And even if I could, I'm not conjuring a feathered cloak for *her*.

I make my way out into the garden, trying to get my bearings. We're well away from the palace—I can just make it out at a distance, beyond a wall of spearlike cypresses. To our left, past the shrubbery, a white wall presses through the softness of the garden. The Little Palace. Of course, it's Firmina's sanctuary—she must have intended to go there.

A shout carries up over the gardens. "Jahan!"

A woman's running toward me, past the reflecting pool, up the long path. Her hair is flying loose. I open up my free arm and Elanna catapults into me, hugging me tight against her. I breathe in the scent of her hair. The warmth and weight of her. Finally, I let myself feel the terror of seeing Firmina fling the wood at El in what could have been a killing blow. I hug her tighter.

She pulls back, taking in my cloak and the lack of garments under it. And Firmina, flung naked over my shoulder.

"I took away her magic." I explain, as best I can, what happened.

But when I finish, El still looks skeptical. "Where did *that* come from?"

She means my cape. I grin at her. "I conjured it. From the air. Like a real sorcerer."

"You conjured a *feathered cloak*?" She's snorting with laughter. "Not, say, a pair of trousers?"

Heat burns into my cheeks, but I find myself laughing, too. "My ancestor, Mantius, the one who transformed into a raven . . ."

"Oh, no, he didn't have a cloak of black feathers, did he? He *did*?" But she stops laughing and kisses me swiftly on the mouth. "It's quite a statement. Are you prepared for all the songs people are going to write now?"

"As long as they include you in them, I shall be quite content." I pause. "El . . . is Leontius . . . ?"

"He's living still. They—they managed to stanch the flow of blood." But her hesitation tells me he must be in danger yet. She shakes her head and gestures to Firmina. "He'll manage. We need to sort her out first."

"I'm not sure what to do with her yet." I nod at the Little Palace. "And I'm a bit frightened to see what's in there."

Elanna draws in a breath. "Then we had better get it over with."

We approach the Little Palace with caution, but it's unguarded. Firmina must have taken her retinue to the palace itself. Perhaps she left this place under magical safety, but it's evaporated now that I removed her powers. I lead the way inside, up the familiar staircase to the second-floor salon.

The door is locked. I reach for the smallest spurt of power from the grotto well and push the latch back. Together, we step inside.

Bile rises in my throat. The room is a disaster—furniture smashed and windows broken, drapes stripped from the windows. In the middle of the room, on the stained carpet, lies a pile of corpses. No telling how long they've been there. Flies buzz around them. They're men—guards, all of them, in imperial livery, except for one near the bottom with a pale-blue sleeve. A witch hunter. Quentin.

Elanna gags, ducking behind a settee to vomit. The stench is overwhelming. There must be fifteen bodies, at least. Firmina killed them all—drained them for power, and so that she could escape.

The empress's legs swing against my hip. Maybe I should have killed her when I had the chance.

But no. She'll live to face the consequences of what she's done. If she has any conscience at all—and I'm not convinced that she does—it will be a fate far worse than death.

I turn to El, who's pressed both hands over her mouth. Tears swim in her eyes.

"Let's go." I take her hand. "We'll send someone to identify the bodies. Give them a decent burial."

Together, we walk down the Little Palace stairs and out into the bright day.

"Jahan!"

A boy is shouting in the distance. Rayka. He comes into view, running down the path. There's a shape in his arms, long and limp, with a flop of dark hair.

I burst toward them. El races beside me. No. Not Lathiel, not after all this.

"He was trying to heal the people she drained!" Rayka's actually crying, his voice thick, his face splotched with tears. He thrusts Lathiel's body at me, shaking it as if our little brother weighs no more than air. "He took too much from the well. He just *collapsed*. I told him not to. The idiot . . ."

"Here." I gesture for Rayka to set Lathiel on the ground, and I heave Firmina down, propping her against a tree. Elanna, wincing, covers the empress's nakedness with her own coat.

I turn to my little brother, gathering him up, cradling him against me, his head lolling against my chest. The faintest breath touches my collarbone. He's alive, but I don't know how completely he drained himself. I don't know how to fix what's wrong with him. I don't know if I have enough strength left, or if the well does. But I have no choice.

Gently, I touch Lathiel's mind with my own. My body seems to creak; my head feels thick. But I can still reach into Lathiel. I can still feel a spark within him, though it's fading. The shallow beat of his heart pulses against mine. Too slow. Too weak.

I whisper to him. *Come back. Back together. Whole and healed.* I pour the energy of the grotto well into him, the way he poured the energy of Mantius's font into me.

It takes a long time. My head swims; even though I draw from the grotto well, my own energy seems to get mixed up in it. The well is tired, and so am I. I'm light-headed, as if I've been drained myself, and my mind is numb.

But when I open my eyes, Lathiel is gripping my arm. He's still pale. Still breathing too shallowly. But there's life in his eyes.

"I'm here," I say. "I'm here."

He curls around, blinking slowly, and buries his face in my feathered cloak. I pat his back. He's panting, hot breaths that stir the feathers. But I'm here for him, now, at last.

Something scrapes across from me. I look up blearily. Elanna and Rayka have been sitting across from us, watching. Waiting. Now El draws in a sharp breath. Rayka just stares, silent. His eyes are full of a nameless terror.

"It's all right," I say to him. "I brought him back."

"Oh," Rayka says, and he looks away, blinking fast.

Elanna's watching me. "Will *you* be all right?"

I nod. I will be all right. I don't quite trust myself to speak again, though. I know I need to get up. I have an emperor-apparent to find and an unconscious deposed empress to dispose of, along with the corpses of those she killed. I have an order of witch hunters to undo, and the bodies of Madiya and Alcibiades to bury.

But Elanna is murmuring to Rayka, and Lathiel is still clinging to me. So I stay where I am. For the moment, this is enough. I hold my little brother closer, and wait for his breathing to deepen.

CHAPTER THIRTY-THREE

Eventually, some palace guards find us. We leave them to identify the bodies in the Little Palace, and make our way slowly through the gardens to the palace. Lathiel seems reluctant to let me out of his sight. Rayka and Elanna scavenged some items from the Little Palace, and we've wrapped Firmina in a blanket, while I'm wearing a pair of trousers from the emperor's old bedchamber. It feels strange to wear the clothing of a dead man.

The palace is a kind of ordered chaos, full of returned servants and befuddled courtiers and reformers. Aunt Cyra stands, hands on her hips, directing the removal of the worst detritus. If her commandeering tone is anything to go by, she's survived unscathed. But before I can call to her, Sabina and Irene approach from the opposite direction.

"Jahan, come quickly!" Irene says. "I told the doctors you could help the emperor."

I swing Firmina Triciphes down from my shoulder. "We need to put the empress—the former empress, I mean—in custody."

"We'll see to it," Elanna says, gesturing for my brothers to stay with her. "You go to Leontius."

I follow Sabina down the corridor to Leontius's chambers. A cold dread has seized me, even though everyone tells me he still lives. At the door of his bedchamber, I stand rooted. I don't want to approach the bed. I don't want to see what's left of him, to find him as empty and dead as Finn.

But I approach. Because I must. Because he's my friend.

He seems shrunken in the massive bed, its golden canopy swallowing him up. Zollus Katabares sits beside him, his suit speckled in blood. He's staring me down. But I ignore him and approach Leontius. His face is pale. But his chest moves, ever so slightly, up and down, under the embroidered coverlet.

I crouch beside him. Distantly I'm aware that my cheeks are wet. He makes a wordless noise.

And then he opens his eyes. "Jahan," he whispers. He's weak. Exhausted. But he smiles.

"Lees." I'm gripping the coverlet. "I thought . . ."

A doctor has come up behind me. "Sir, you should move away—"

"It's the Korakos," Sabina raps at him.

"Oh, yes, with his magical remedy, I suppose. But really, my dear, you mustn't believe . . ."

I ignore him. "There's something I can try," I say to Leontius. He nods.

I reach for his arm. Elanna said they had stanched Leontius's wound, but it's still weeping from the cauterized end of his arm. It's pillowed in bandages. I peel them gently back. The wound seems to be a *rupture*—Firmina must have burst apart the barely healed fabric of Leontius's skin. We're fortunate, I suppose, that she attacked Leontius's old wound instead of creating a new one, or Lees might be dead by now.

I bend over the wound. I'm damned tired, and so is the poor drained grotto well. But I have just enough left to reach for his muscles, for his skin. Just enough to whisper to the pieces of Leontius to sew themselves back together, *Snug and neat, whole and healed.* Just the way I did for those soldiers after Rayka massacred them. Just as I did for myself.

But it's still not enough, even with the grotto well, to give him back his hand. The nerves and bone have been severed too long, and the pattern is impossible to re-create.

I open my eyes, and he's watching me. Perspiration lingers on his forehead, but his eyes are alert. I find myself smiling, even though guilt that I can't return his hand tugs at me.

"I feel the water," he says. "Under the palace."

My eyes ache. I pat his knee. "That's good."

"My father's dead."

"Yes."

"I have to be emperor now."

I look at him, not over my shoulder at the doctor or Zollus, who are staring, or Sabina, who looks proud.

I focus on my friend. He has a lingering fever I don't know how to shake, and the loss of blood has made him weak. But he's alive, and he'll become strong again. The prince who needed a friend, and who chose a boy who wanted to change the heart of this empire. And here we are.

"There's a lot of work to be done," I say. "The palace is chaos. The Hall of Glass is missing its entire roof."

He just looks at me.

"I don't know what trouble the reformers have gotten themselves into. And your ministers and court have had the wits scared out of them . . ."

Leontius is starting to laugh.

"Also," I add, "Firmina Triciphes tried to seize power. And Bardas is dead."

"Jahan Korakides." Leontius snorts. "When you're around, there's always work to be done. I just . . . I don't think I can get up quite yet."

"We'll have the servants bring some food and drink. I don't know how we'll explain . . . everything." I gesture at the palace around us, encompassing the missing roof and the empress.

Leontius shakes his head. "Did people witness what my stepmother did? The ministers were there, weren't they? Zollus said the minister of state is dead. So many people have seen . . . We can't hide the truth. They'll blame sorcery." His gaze slides to Zollus, and he bites his lip. Quietly, as if he's ashamed, he whispers, "*Our* sorcery."

"Our sorcery saved the day," I reply. "Everyone saw me turn into a damned raven."

The corner of Leontius's mouth crooks upward. "Is that why you're wearing a cloak of feathers?" He glances at Zollus and the doctor. "I think you had better tell me what happened."

Behind me, Zollus clears his throat. "Don't tire him, Korakides. Lees needs rest."

I start to point out that Lees asked me to talk with him, but before I can, Leontius smiles at Zollus. It's shy. Tentative. "Maybe you could have the servants bring me a hot tisane."

Zollus goes to attention, deeply serious. "Or a cup of broth?"

"Or brandy," Leontius says.

I laugh. "A *cup* of brandy?"

Zollus stares me down, apparently angry with me for making light of the situation, but Leontius sighs. "Oh, damn, yes. Make it a wagonload." But then he smiles again at Zollus, with a little more confidence. "Just the broth and tisane. Thank you."

"Anything for you," Zollus replies, so matter-of-fact I wonder if I heard correctly. He marches off into the hall, rapping orders at the servants. The doctor and Sabina follow him.

I feel my shoulders relax ever so slightly. At last, my friend and I are alone.

"Jahan . . ." Leontius lowers his voice. "What do you think of Zollus?"

I laugh, surprised. If only Zollus knew he'd been sent out so we could discuss him. Here I thought Lees wanted to go over sensitive affairs of state. "If you need to *ask* my opinion of Zollus Katabares, then we truly haven't spoken in a long time."

Leontius's face falls. He stares down at the coverlet.

Oh. *Oh.* All the gods, I am the biggest fool who ever set foot in Paladis! I scrounge for the merest semblance of tact. "He's changed, though, you know. I never thought he'd stick by you the way he has. It's . . ." *Completely astonishing* is *not* the right thing to say. "It makes him surprisingly likable."

"He's not what I always thought him, either. He's . . ." A slightly addled grin spreads over Leontius's face. "He's loyal. And fierce. And . . . protective."

And a much better choice for you than Finn, I think, but I have enough sense not to say it.

"But I'm emperor now," Leontius says. He's practically whispering. "I can't . . . I have to marry. Beget heirs. I can't just . . . *be with* whoever I choose."

"You can still be lovers."

He winces. "It's not the same, Jahan! I want to—to give myself *fully* to a person. I don't want to be like my father, who visited my mother's chambers once a year, out of duty. It's not fair. To me—or to Zollus, if he ever . . . if he . . ." He swallows and darts a glance toward the door. Zollus hasn't returned yet. "Or to my future wife. You know the things people will say. The songs they'll write." He pauses. "What is it?"

I must be staring. I shake my head. "Nothing. I . . ." It was just how much he sounded like me. How many times have I told Elanna I don't want to be like my father? But Leontius wants to commit himself fully—someday, anyway—to whoever he truly loves, and he can't.

Yet I could. I could, and I never have. Because I've always been too afraid.

I force myself back to the present conversation. "You don't have to marry. You could, I don't know, adopt."

Leontius snorts. "Oh, yes, I see the ministers agreeing with that! No, Paladis is going through enough upheaval. It will comfort the people to have a royal wedding." He sighs. "A royal heir . . ."

"But you don't have a bride yet," I say. "You have time, now, before you arrange marriage. Time to be with who you wish."

"And then," he says, "it would have to end."

"Yes." I swallow. "I suppose it would." I reach out and squeeze his knee. It's an inadequate gesture, but I think he knows I wish it could convey more. "I'm sorry."

"It's all right." He blinks and rubs at his eyes, but I'm not fooled by his insistence. Those are tears he blinked away. I wish this were something that I could change for him. Some law I or Pantoleon or Argyros could rewrite. He says, "If I had a child, when they're old enough, I could abdicate to live as I wish. With a garden, and whoever I love."

"Lees," I begin, but I don't know what to say. That would be more than twenty years away—more like thirty. Forty, even, if his sense of duty even allows him to step down. If he were anyone but the emperor of Paladis, he could live however he liked and no one would say a thing.

"It's all right, Jahan." He manages a smile. "I've made my peace with it."

But he hasn't. Who could make peace with decades of sacrificing one's personal desires for the empire? For the good of the people?

There's a noise at the door: Zollus, instructing one of the servants about the temperature of the broth they've brought for Leontius. Lees goes still, and despite everything there's a kind of desperate hope about him.

"I'll let you rest," I say, and rise. Cramps run through my legs, the aftereffect of the magic leaving my body.

He leans forward, capturing my arm. "Thank you, Jahan. For everything."

I shake my head. "I'm sorry," I say quietly. "I'm sorry I couldn't give you back your hand."

His eyebrows lift, surprised, as if the idea hadn't even occurred to him. "I'm alive, aren't I?" He frowns at his empty wrist, then nods. "There's nothing to apologize for. You saved my life—so many lives. This is what I am now. And it will remind people every day—it will remind *me* every day—of what we fought for."

My eyes sting. "You'll make a fine emperor, you know."

He goes quiet. "I hope so. But I've seen what happens when you rule."

There's little I can say to that, so I just squeeze his arm. I limp to the door just as Zollus comes in, carrying the tray of broth himself. I've never seen him do anything so solicitous. He pauses, out of politeness, to greet me, but his gaze keeps straying, concerned, to Leontius. Maybe he is worthy of my friend—or will be, given time.

I leave them to each other.

Out in the corridor, I feel almost dizzy with exhaustion. But Leontius's words linger in my mind—his desire to commit fully to a person. His desire not to be like his father.

There's something I need to do.

An hour later, coming back in from the Grand Court, I find Pantoleon and Tullea coming down the grand stair, both of them smeared with plaster dust. Pantoleon thumps my shoulder, wordlessly, and Tullea clasps my hands. "We tried to get Argyros and Felix to wait," she says, "but they're down in the cellars looking for champagne. Everyone wants to get drunk and celebrate."

And forget, I think. Everyone wants to forget the moment of terror when the entire ceiling lifted off the Hall of Glass, and Firmina Triciphes was ready to kill us all. I can't really blame Felix and Argyros.

"They're welcome to it," I reply. My eyes are so gritty; I feel as if I could curl up on the parquet and fall asleep. "The Saranons have been stockpiling it just for this occasion, I'm sure."

Pantoleon's studying me. "You look like hell."

I feel the side of my mouth crook up. "Better like hell than dead." I pause, looking at Tullea. She's thinking, I can tell, and probably not about me. "What happened to the ministers?"

She nods; this must have been her train of thought. "Some of the survivors ran off. Your aunt gave the others a talking-to before Felix and Argyros dragged them off."

"Getting them drunk might make them more amenable to sorcery?" I wonder.

Tullea winces, and Pantoleon laughs. "They're going to have to get a lot more amenable!" he says. "I'm going hunting for all the wells the old sorcerers covered up, once I find all the references in the texts. Soon all of Paladis will be fairly humming with magic."

"But will they legalize it?" Tullea says. She's looking at me.

I shrug, and then I find myself starting to laugh. "They will if their emperor is a sorcerer. And if we tell them the truth about the last grand inquisitor . . . that will be the end of the witch hunters."

"Good," Tullea says. She hesitates, then touches my arm. "I'd like to be involved."

If we put the ministers in a room alone with Tullea, they'd be bowing down to her within five minutes, I think. But I just nod. "Of course. We'll all work together. Perhaps Leontius will name you the minister of sorcery!"

She looks at me. "Or perhaps that's what he'll name *you*."

This could be a problem, I suppose. "I'll talk to him. But if anyone deserves the title, it's you, Tullea. You've been fighting your whole life for this. I've only come to it lately."

She smiles a little at that. "Will you come drink a toast with us, then?"

"Of course," I say, even though my entire body aches. "But I need to find Elanna, first. And my aunt."

Tullea points up the stairs. "They're in the Salon of Meres. El's drafting a treaty between Eren and Paladis."

Still working, even after all this. I smile. "I'll see you soon."

They go off, but before I can open the door, the sound of running footsteps interrupts me. I turn to find Nestor charging down the hall.

"Jahan! I tracked them down—Augustus and Phaedra."

I sigh. If I must pursue and confront them, it will just have to damned well wait. "Where?"

He grins. "Manasi!"

I stare at him. "What did they do, board a ship?"

"Yes, just before I got there." He's beaming now. "They're gone, Jahan. They exiled themselves."

"How convenient," I say, but relief is spreading through me, softening my shoulders. It might be too convenient, but I'll take it.

"Good work, Nestor. Consider yourself promoted to Saranon-exiler-in-chief."

He laughs and runs off to celebrate with the others. At last, I continue up the stairs.

In the long corridor, Aunt Cyra is just closing the filigreed doors of the Salon of Meres. She looks up as I approach. Her feathered plume is tattered, her gown splattered with blood and dirt, but she still looks as if she could sweep the entire palace into order with a flick of her wrist.

I run to her and gather her into a tight embrace. "I'm so sorry—so damned sorry—"

"Oh, Jahan." She hugs me back, briefly, too dignified for such sentiment even after all this. "You did exceptionally well."

Tears sting my eyes. "I left you in Firmina's hands. I should have known. She might have done anything to you."

To my astonishment, Aunt Cyra bursts out laughing. "Please, darling, give me more credit than that! Firmina wouldn't harm one of her most useful supporters—at least until their usefulness ran out, which I suppose poor Bardas's did in the end. I may not have sorcery at my disposal, but I know how to save my own skin. Besides, it was rather fun, being a revolutionary." She sobers. "Though I may not have succeeded in saving all the ministers."

"You helped her?" I'm shocked.

"Helping and harming were, in this case, two sides of the same coin. Why do you think Augustus and Phaedra escaped alive? And most of the ministers survived, in the end, not to mention your re-formers? She could have simply killed them all. But she wanted the appearance of legitimacy to her rule, and I encouraged that." Seeing my look, she explains, "After you rescued Leontius, we went around Aexione gathering the ministers to support us. Some came willingly; some, Firmina . . . persuaded. But better that, I thought, than murdering them the way she did her husband. We suspected that Augustus and Phaedra would never hold out against you, and we were right. I tried to convince Firmina to negotiate with your reformers. But her idea of negotiation was a bit different than mine."

I wince. "But she didn't harm you?"

"No. She wouldn't have succeeded with all the ministers without my help, not in time. She knew that." Aunt Cyra smiles faintly. "I only hoped I could delay her long enough for you to arrive. And you did."

I look at my aunt. She's one of the bravest people I know—courageous enough to shelter a sorcerer, and fierce enough to try to stop one from destroying her people and her country. Quietly, I say, "Thank you."

Her eyes soften. "Darling, thank *you*. You're the one who stopped her, when it came down to it."

I utter a self-conscious laugh. "And brought sorcery back to the empire."

"Well, without magic, life would be terrifically dull." Her lips quirk. "I always rather hoped you'd do it. Now you have, and look at you. You've grown into who you were meant to be, Jahan. You're not living the lie anymore. You're yourself now. It's good to see. So very good."

My throat has swollen so tight I can't speak.

Aunt Cyra gestures toward the door. "Not only that, but you've found a lovely, strong woman. I've been talking to Elanna. I like her."

"I'm glad," I manage, because I am. Aunt Cyra is the closest I have to a mother. It matters what she thinks of El.

She studies me, then takes my shoulders and plants a kiss on my forehead. "Go to her. She's writing a treaty for you."

"Thank you, Auntie. What you say means so much. I can't—"

She waves a hand. "Enough sentiment! Go in there. In the meantime, I shall go find some of the champagne we've been promised."

But she presses my shoulder before she leaves, the gesture holding all the warmth she can't convey in words. I touch her hand. We both know how much we've sacrificed to get here. We both know how much it matters, both of us standing here.

Then she sweeps away. I draw in a breath, and open the door into the Salon of Meres.

Elanna sits at the long table, writing intently, her hair tumbling over one shoulder and her lip tucked under her teeth. She barely glances up at me. "I want to get this written," she says. "Now, before anything else happens."

I raise an eyebrow. "How much more do you have to do?"

"Not much." She looks up, now, suspicious. "Why?"

I grin. "I have someone I want you to meet."

"Oh, Jahan." She groans, rubbing her hands over her face and flicking ink everywhere. "I don't think I can talk to anyone else today. I'm so damned tired. I don't want to make small talk, and explain what a *Caveadear* is, and . . ."

I reach across the table and pick the pen out of her hand, tucking it safely into its holder. She's splattered the document she's writing, too. "You won't have to make small talk. I promise. You should come. I think you'll like it."

She narrows her eyes but, grumbling, gets up and lets me lead her from the chamber. We descend the grand staircase. As I guide her out into the Grand Court and toward the gates, she stares about in surprise. "Where are we going? I thought you were taking me to have a toast with everyone else."

"Why don't you guess?" I suggest, grinning.

"If I could guess your mind, I'd know everything." As we emerge onto the Avenue of Oranges, its grand houses perfumed with climbing roses, a sigh unravels from her. "You brought me to see Aexione. It's beautiful."

"It is," I acknowledge, "but this isn't a sightseeing tour . . ."

Ahead, on our right, a gate stands open to the street. I'm relieved to see it's open, though I don't say so to El. I wasn't sure he'd actually come here, despite my urging.

I gesture for El to go in.

She balks, staring at the exotic ferns, and the bees droning in flowers from all corners of the earth. "Jahan . . ."

"This," I say, "is the *Kepeios Basiliskos*. The imperial botanical garden."

El presses her fist to her mouth. She can't seem to speak for a long moment, but at last she whispers, "I've been dreaming of this place for years. Since I was a girl."

I smile at her. "I know. You almost forsook your entire rebellion for it."

Without warning, she grabs me by the neck and pulls me in for a brief, burning kiss. "Thank you, Jahan." She rests her forehead against mine.

Footsteps crunch in the garden, and a man clears his throat. "Jahan?"

We spring apart. A man stands watching us, hands on his hips. He's tall and rangy and sun-browned, with a thatch of graying hair and spectacles swinging from a chain at his throat. He can't seem bothered to tie his neckcloth properly, or attend to the tear in his otherwise fine coat. Dirt is packed beneath his fingernails.

"I got out the latest samples from the Occident," he says, jerking his thumb over his shoulder. "The ones we got on our last expedition. You said it was urgent?"

"Yes," I say, smiling. "It is. Elanna . . ."

I turn to her. She's staring at the man, completely awestruck.

"El," I say, "this is Andras Markarades, the imperial botanist. Andras, may I introduce Elanna Valtai, the *Caveadear* of Eren and Caeris?"

El swallows and smooths back her hair, collecting herself. Her hands tremble slightly in the presence of her hero. "Sir, I am such a great admirer of your work. I can't tell you how much I look forward to every edition of *The Journal of Botanical Studies*. Your last monograph on the *Carica* genus in the Occident—"

Markarades snaps his fingers. "You're the one who woke the earth! The *Caveadear*!"

El blinks. "Yes? I mean, I am, but . . ."

"You speak to every plant! Rivers, and forests, and animals . . ." He draws in a breath, then looks meaningfully at us both. "Please come in. I have many questions for you."

"Oh," El says, "but I have so many questions for *you* . . ."

I let her go ahead of me, her eyes bright, her nerves already forgotten. The day is blue and brilliant and, despite my exhausted limbs, I feel a lightness lifting in my chest. Ahead, Markarades is saying, "We need to write a joint monograph, I feel, on the intersection of botanical study and sorcery," and Elanna is eagerly agreeing.

I smile. There's only one more thing I need to do.

AFTER THE MEETING with Markarades, and after we toast our victory at last with our friends, I take Elanna back to Aunt Cyra's house. My aunt sent the servants to safety in the country or with family earlier, and the building sits unusually quiet. I leave El to settle in while I check on my brothers—both of them asleep at the other end of the long hall. Lathiel lies curled in a ball, hugging a pillow to his chest, his eyelids flickering with dreams. Rayka snores. They're here. Safe.

Aunt Cyra rattles about below us, back now from the palace. I return down the hall to Elanna. In my absence, she's lit a fire in the grate and settled into the canopied bed.

"There you are," she says. "I thought I was going to have to send a search party."

I climb over the coverlet, not bothering to undress or even kick my shoes off. El's smiling, her hair a mess, the collar of her shirt open to reveal the notch in her collarbone. I'm so weary I think I might sleep on the spot, but there's also a strange energy coursing through me, bright and warm, the remnant of the power from the grotto well. I take her hand. She smells of the gardens and sunlight.

"Elanna Valtai," I say, and she bursts out laughing. "What?"

"I've never heard you say my name so seriously," she says, still quivering with laughter.

I grin. "Then perhaps you can guess what I'm going to say."

"If I could predict that, I could predict anything."

"Well . . . I don't have a ring. And it's difficult to kneel here . . ."

"Oh, I think you can manage," she says mischievously, but then my meaning must dawn on her. Her eyes grow enormous. "Jahan—"

"Will you marry me?" I blurt out, as green as any boy.

She laughs, but her hand goes to her mouth. "No—you swore you would never marry. And I told you I didn't mind."

"I know," I say, and I crack a grin. "All the gods, I didn't practice this speech. But El—I want—I don't know. I want something more permanent to hold us. I want—" I swallow hard. "—I want you to know, whatever happens, that I am yours. That my heart belongs to you."

Her gaze grows tender and somehow terribly sad. "And mine belongs to you," she says softly. "Even if we have to part again. If I have to . . . go home."

I swallow. I feel as nervous as a boy asking a girl to dance with him. "Yes. But I think marriage is also a promise. Because you must go home—I understand that—but I'm going to follow you there, Elanna Valtai. It may take months, until the city is settled, and the empire. Even years. But I will come to Eren and Caeris. And I *will* marry you. That is," I add, "if you want me to."

"*If* I want you!" she exclaims. "Jahan Korakides . . ."

Then she grabs my collar and kisses me. I wrap my arms around her. She fishes herself out of the covers and pulls herself in closer, wrapping her legs around my waist. "Madam," I murmur against her mouth, "you seem to have lost your trousers . . . or skirt . . ."

She gurgles a laugh. "And I finally found us a decent bed!"

"You didn't like the rocks up on Solivetos Hill?"

"Well, although I *am* the steward of the land, I do occasionally prefer down mattresses."

I run my hands up below her shirt. "Is this one of those occasions?"

She gives a delicious shiver. "Oh, yes." But she breaks away and grabs my collar again. She's smiling. "Jahan, I never said yes! *Yes!*"

Now I'm smiling, too. I lean in to kiss her again, and my hands tangle in her hair, and her weight settles against me, and my life has never felt so true and so right.

⁎

JAHAN.

It's a woman's voice, whispering into my mind. My heart thuds me awake, but it's not Madiya, because Madiya is dead. I'm safe—completely safe, at last. I'm tucked up against Elanna. The fire's gone out. Evening light filters in sleepy golden bars past the curtains.

Her whisper comes again. *Jahan!*

Elanna turns over drowsily. "What is it?"

"It's . . ." *Jahan!* she calls again, and the tenor of it finally registers, though I have no idea how the queen of Eren and Caeris is able to speak like a sorceress into my mind. "It's Sophy."

El sits straight up. "What? How?"

"I don't know." I fumble out of bed, hunting for a robe, but all my things have been packed away in trunks again. I wrap a blanket around myself and approach the mirror hanging on the far wall. Elanna rushes after me, trailing more blankets and, as if it will make her more prepared, her greatcoat. I touch my fingers to the cool glass and summon Sophy Dunbarron into my mind's eye. "Sophy!"

She appears immediately, haggard, her hair loose. She clasps her hands over her mouth at the sight of us, as if she might burst into tears. *Oh, thank all the gods!*

"What's wrong?" El demands.

Sophy rubs her hands through her hair. *Do you remember I told you there had been protests all across Eren, when everyone thought you were dead? Well, now the protestors are claiming*—She catches her breath, winces. *They're claiming a victory. Their leader made an attempt on my life—but I found proof—*

"We've won here," El says. "We've taken Aexione! That should be enough to dissuade them."

Tears are falling down Sophy's cheeks now, thick and fast. She shakes her head. Draws a deep breath. *That doesn't matter now, not to them. They say they've found a replacement ruler, that he's on his way to Eren.* She pauses. *He's coming to take my throne. To claim it's rightfully his.*

Elanna makes an impatient noise. "Who could possibly do that?"

Sophy swallows hard, and cold grips the back of my neck. I know what she will say even before she speaks.

Euan Dromahair. My natural father.

Even though I suspected, it's a shock to hear the words. Elanna is staring.

"But he has no right!" El protests at last. "And he has no support—no means—"

I must have gasped, because both women are staring at me. But I'm seeing that day in the Salon of Meres. How Princess Phaedra stood so close to Euan Dromahair. And this morning, Nestor followed them to Manasi. He said they'd set sail. I assumed they'd taken themselves into exile.

But maybe they just changed their base of operation.

"Sophy," I say. "What do people say about his supporters?"

That they're powerful and influential—all the usual things. She rolls her eyes. *Why?*

But El is staring at me, as if she knows what I've realized.

"Augustus and Phaedra Saranon," I say. I clear my throat. "Leontius's younger siblings—they wanted his throne. I have no proof. But Sophy, I would wager they are Euan's supporters, and they're headed to your shores, with him."

Sophy is staring. *The Saranons? But why would they come here?*

"Probably because they have nowhere else to go," El says grimly, "and for some reason they've allied with Euan Dromahair."

"They're opportunists," I add. "They see Eren's weak, and they want to take advantage."

El turns back to the mirror. "We're coming, Sophy. We'll be back in a few days. Just hold out a bit longer, if you can."

Sophy draws in another deep breath and nods. *I will.*

I CLOSE OUT the communication with Sophy. El's already flinging on her clothing. "How long will it take to reach Eren? Three days? Four? Perhaps we can conjure a wind—or compress space." But she pauses, her face falling. "I, I mean. I can speak to the water, somehow. I've never done it before, but there's a first time for everything . . ."

"El—" I begin.

"You need to stay here," she says fiercely, her shoulders taut. "Leontius needs you. Ida—all of Paladis—"

"No," I say, "well, perhaps they would *like* to have me. But Paladis doesn't need me." I reach for her hands. This isn't what I planned, but it's obvious, now, that it's what must be. "I didn't give you a ring, Elanna Valtai, so I'll have to stay with you until I find one."

She blinks hard. "I can't ask that of you."

"A ring? They're easy enough to come by. I just need the right design . . ."

"Jahan!" she exclaims, exasperated.

I grin and draw her close. "You're not asking it of me. I'm offering it to you. I want to be with you. And I'm not going to let Phaedra and Augustus Saranon set up stakes in your homeland."

She runs her fingertips down my arms, then looks up at me, almost shy. "It could become *our* homeland. If you stayed . . ."

Make a home in Eren and Caeris, away from the bright sun of Ida. Leave my friends, my fellow rebels. For Elanna. I look down into her brown eyes, the hope so tentative in them. A strong beat pulses through me. I want to hold her so close, every moment. I want to make her laugh. I want to wake up with her, and fall asleep beside her.

"We could build a—a school for sorcerers," she's saying. "For the refugees who've come to Eren and don't want to leave. And for the Ereni and Caerisians who want to learn magic. You could teach people what you know."

Like Madiya—only I would never experiment on people's minds. I could take everything I learned from Madiya, and all the knowledge stored in the mountains of Caeris, and bring it to people in a better way. A good way.

"Our sorcerers could take over the world," I say, and El laughs. I smile down at her. "I'll do anything, as long as I'm with you."

She hooks her hands around my neck and kisses me hard. When she releases me, we're both a little breathless. "Then let's go."

EPILOGUE

"If you're not going to be sorcerer imperial," Rayka says, "then that means the position's open, right?"

"Not to you." If such a position even exists. "That would be nepotism."

"Nepotism!" he splutters. "It would not! Just because you're acting like you own the whole damned world . . ."

I just grin. I don't *feel* as if I own the whole world, but it would be trite to tell him that I feel as if I've found my place in it. It was strange, coming through the rubbled streets of Ida to Imperial Harbor, to be greeted by people shouting my name. Strange to be seen for what I am, but I no longer feel so exposed.

"At least wait until you've taken your military exam," I say. "Then you can trouble Leontius all you like."

"Exam!" Rayka says crossly, blowing air out his mouth, but I can tell he's secretly pleased. "They don't need to test me. I'll do better than anyone ever has."

I roll my eyes, glancing back for Lathiel. He's trailing behind us, picking his way over the long earthquake crack in the quay. It's hard not to reach back for him; hard not to hold on too tight. He looks so slight in the overcoat we rustled up for him, and his eyes still seem hollow. There's still a tremor in his hands. But he's gripping a chest of belongings tight against his ribs. When I asked him what he wanted, whether he'd prefer to stay here with Aunt Cyra or come with me to Eren, he didn't hesitate for a moment. "I'm coming with you," he said, with a stubborn determination that made my chest contract. I'll keep him safe. I'll guide him through the withdrawal from the opium, and let him choose for himself what he wants to do with his sorcery and his life. But most of all, I'll keep him close to me. I won't leave him again.

Rayka and I stop, a few paces away from the great ship that will bear us to Eren. I look at him, even though his eyes slide away from mine. I know he can fend for himself. I know he'll be all right. But it's hard to leave him here.

I reach out and clasp his shoulder. He stiffens, but to my surprise he returns the gesture. My throat tightens. "You can always come to Eren, you know."

"Well, you can always come back here," he retorts, but his scowl doesn't fool me.

"Take care of yourself."

He shrugs a little, too uncomfortable to actually say goodbye, and swings away to talk to Lathiel. I let myself drink in the sight of both of them, together one last time. Safe.

There's a cough behind me: Leontius, approaching. He's giving us a royal farewell, with the imperial guard and the black ships at the ready to honor our departure—at least, as many as he could assemble on short notice. He's still weary from blood loss and walks slowly. On our way here, he was preoccupied with the question of where to imprison his stepmother. His bare wrist is covered in a cuff, and Nestor and Irene are scheming up designs for a false hand they might attach to it, powered by magic. Already he's despaired of pleasing everyone.

"Lees," I say, and reach out my hand. He clasps it. He can't seem to speak. I glance at Zollus, waiting patiently some distance behind. He nods at me, and I nod back. I don't know where he and Leontius stand. But I hope that my friend finds happiness, even if, in the end, it can't be all that he truly desires. "You'll make a great emperor. The emperor Paladis needs."

His head bows. "I don't know if I can do it without you, Jahan," he whispers.

"Nonsense. You have Pantoleon and Tullea, and even Zollus

might lend a hand." I wink at him. "And Eren isn't the whole world away. I can be here in a few days' time, if you need me."

Now he looks up at me, bright with relief. "Would you?"

"Well, once I've sent your beloved siblings packing." I smile at him and clasp his hand harder. "Yes, of course. You have only to speak my name, and I'll answer. I'll find a mirror. We can speak from anywhere."

His eyes grow moist, and mine itch a little, too. We smile at each other. It feels so damned good to be friends again.

Then Leontius glances to my left and I turn to find Elanna coming up beside me. Her shoulders are high and tight—she's impatient with these farewells—but she smiles at Leontius.

He bows to her. "Lady Elanna, I hope you know what an honor it has been to meet you."

El leans forward to kiss his cheek. "You'll do well," she tells him. "Remember that Eren is your friend, and so am I. And don't neglect your magic. Finding water beneath the earth will benefit your people more than you think."

Leontius smiles, too.

"Also," El adds, "I'm depending on you to send me *The Journal of Botanical Studies* by the swiftest post. We'll come back soon, you know. Markarades and I are collaborating on a monograph, and I need to discuss my findings with him."

Lees laughs, and I spread my hands. "You see?" I say, grinning. "We'll return."

He clasps my shoulder, then says conspiratorially to Elanna, "Write to me if Jahan starts giving you too much trouble."

"Oh, I'll do better than that," El says. "I'll bring him straight to Aexione for a reprimand."

I roll my eyes. "I'm standing right here, you know."

"I know, and I'm claiming you." El tucks her arm around mine. "It's time to go."

I smile one last time at Leontius, and gesture Lathiel to precede us onto the ship. But as we turn to follow him, Pantoleon and Tullea are waiting there by the gangway.

"I'll keep you updated by letter," Pantoleon says, "every time I find another well."

A lump tight in my throat, I thump his shoulder. I'll miss all the others, but no one more than my oldest friend. "Come to Eren," I manage. "When things have settled, I mean. There are plenty of sorcerers to study there."

"We'll both come," Tullea says, "if we can."

"We would all like that." I grin at Tullea, standing there regal in her crimson turban. Yes, Rayka's got stiff competition for sorcerer imperial.

Finally, I follow El up the gangway onto the ship. The day is bright and gulls wheel overhead; beyond the Old Palace, bells toll and hammers ring out on the Great Bridge, work having already begun to repair the damage done by trees and earthquakes. Ida goes on as it always has, and Mount Angelos towers over all, its shape forever distorted now. I look one last time at the people assembled on the wharves. If we survive whatever awaits us in Eren, we'll see them again. But it's still a struggle to swallow down the lump in my throat.

Overhead, the sails are unfurled. Sailors pull in the gangway. Slowly, the great ship slides from its mooring, out into the deep water of the Desporos Strait. Northwest, toward Eren and Caeris. Toward the land I thought I'd abandoned.

Ahead of me, Lathiel edges onto the forecastle deck. He leans up on his toes and inhales the smell of the wind, his eyes closed.

I swing around him and put my arm about Elanna. She's standing at the railing, facing forward into the wind, her hair falling out of its knot. She smells of the sea and springtime.

She leans against me. "I'm glad you're marrying me. If you weren't, I'd be worrying you'd started some new revolution, or some mad empress had kidnapped you, or you'd been imprisoned in a fortress . . ."

"Ah," I say, "but if I wasn't marrying *you*, I'd be afraid you'd woken an entire mountain range and made it stomp over the Tinani border to terrify King Alfred into submission. And then flooded all the lakes and rivers of Eren to drown the Saranons and Euan Droma-hair . . ."

She turns into my arms, laughing. "Perhaps that's what I *should* do! What do you think? And then you can turn into a raven and fly over it."

I lower my face to hers. "All I know is, this raven belongs to you."

And I kiss her, there in front of the entire ship, before the entire city of Ida, beneath the brilliant sun. She breaks away, smiling at me, and I feel impossibly light, as if I'm flying already.

We turn, then, to see the waters open on the other side of the strait, as the ship sails out into the glittering blue, toward Eren, and Sophy.

ACKNOWLEDGMENTS

Despite my daily mantra of "This doesn't have to be so hard," writing this book was challenging. And humbling. And on a personal level, it taught me a lot. As Elizabeth Gilbert writes in *Big Magic,* "Everything I have ever written has brought me into being . . . Creativity has hand-raised me and forged me." I didn't realize how true these words were until I wrote this book. (Although, I'm choosing a different mantra next time . . .)

Fortunately, many good people guided me through. First and foremost, thank you to my wise and generally amazing editor, Anne Groell, for unquestionably making this a better book. I'm also grateful to Tom Hoeler for great editorial feedback, and to my wonderful agent, Hannah Bowman, for guidance and insight on both writing and publishing.

A huge thank-you to the fantastic team at Del Rey Books, especially David Moench, Keith Clayton, Tricia Narwani, Julie Leung, Alex Coumbis, Scott Shannon, Stacey Witcraft, and Ryan Kearney. I'm so lucky to be taken care of by such great people! I'm grateful as well to copy editor Laura Jorstad. Thank you also to everyone at Hodder in the UK for doing wonderful work with this trilogy, especially Sam Bradbury, Oliver Johnson, Jenni Leech, and Sharan Matharu. I'm also grateful to the team at Hachette Australia for everything they've done! Finally, thank you to the wonderful people at Liza Dawson Associates.

I'm incredibly grateful for another stunning US cover and interior by the talented Ben Perini, Susan Schultz, Diane Hobbing, and Dave Stevenson. And in the UK, I'm thankful to Natalie Chen for creating another absolutely beautiful cover. You guys are making this author very happy indeed! Thank you, too, to Laura Hartman Maestro for bringing this world to life once again with not one but two completely gorgeous maps.

Thank you, retroactively, to Terry Brooks, Robin Hobb, Tamora Pierce, Charlaine Harris, and Scott Sigler for their generosity in blurbing the first book in this series. It means more than you know.

All my gratitude to my friend Licia for flying out to Seattle with me twice in twelve months and listening to me blather about volcanoes in view of Mount Rainier. Girl, you're the best, and the mountain in this book is for you. Thank you for always having my back!

So, so many thanks to my friend, soul sister, and critique partner Martha, for epic Skype sessions, code names, and giving me the key to the heart of this book, though I'm not sure you realized it at the time. I'm more grateful than I can say.

I'm also grateful to Emily for her generosity of time and effort, and for reading and commenting on an early version of the manuscript.

My family has, as always, been an incredible source of support. As ever, I'm profoundly grateful to my parents not only for reading and giving feedback and support, but also for enduring my vacant stares into the ethers. Thank you to Nancy for her constant belief and encouragement. And thank you to Eowyn for having a comic-con adventure with me and snickering wildly every time I take a selfie (#SealPeople).

Also, this book features one awesome aunt . . . so thank you to all my aunties, both adopted and biological! You make my life magical.

Finally, thank you to the readers, for holding this book in your hands.

Read on for a sneak peek at

The Soul of Power

BY CALLIE BATES

In the wake of *The Memory of Fire,* we're delighted to
give you a sneak peek at the third and final book in the
Waking Land series, *The Soul of Power,* releasing in
the summer of 2019. Enjoy!

PROLOGUE

The soldiers came early that morning. I woke in the chill before dawn to my mother's touch on my arm. "Sophy, get up. Put on your boots."

I rubbed my eyes. I wanted to go back to sleep. I was tired of running and being cold and hungry—though at first, when we had slipped out of our rooms in Barrody in the middle of the night, it had seemed like an adventure. The king of Eren's soldiers had not seemed like a real threat. I thought we'd go home to my grandmother with stories about our escapades, but we only kept running—and somehow more than a year passed. Food grew thin; my clothes did, too. Now I dreamed of real beds and a fire that actually kept me warm. I longed for my friends and the home I once had; those memories haunted me every day.

Ma stroked the hair back from my forehead. "Sweet girl, get up. I have a job for you."

I squinted open one eye. A job for *me*? I was almost eight and I was dying to prove myself as bold a rebel as my mother. All the same, I pretended nonchalance. "How much do I get paid?"

She managed the flicker of a smile, ghostly in the half-dark. "I need you to take a message to Duke Ruadan."

I bolted upright with a squeal. *"Me?"*

"Shh." Ma reached into the pocket of her waistcoat. She pressed a cool, hard object into my hand. Its metal chain trailed between my fingers; I felt instinctively for the clasp.

"I'm supposed to take him Pa's locket?"

My mother did not speak. She took my head in her hands and kissed me, once—resoundingly—on the forehead. Then she hugged me tight. I felt her heart pounding against my ear. The stifled noise in her throat. I knew then that whatever Ma wanted, it would not be an adventure. I knew it would leave an ache in the space beneath my breastbone—an ache I knew too well, by now.

"You're a strong girl, Sophy." Ma's voice was rough, huskier than usual. "Promise me you'll take this to the duke. You'll go all the way to Cerid Aven and not look back."

"How am I going to find you after?" I couldn't help the thin plea in my voice.

She paused. "I'll come after you."

"You promise?"

"Yes, sweetheart. I promise."

I hugged her tighter, and for a moment she returned my clasp. Then she pulled out of my arms, clambering down the ladder to the barn below, her boot heels ringing on the wood.

I swallowed hard and draped the necklace over my head. I had never worn it before, despite numerous pleas, and I marveled at how it settled into the hollow of my chest. A steadying weight, like my mother's touch—or my father's. The locket held a piece of his hair, a ruddy gold, tied up with a black ribbon. I knew, because I'd harassed my mother into showing it to me any number of times, since she refused to offer me his name or any further details about him. "I'll tell you when you're older," she'd say, and I'd roll my eyes and groan—not that it ever made any difference.

But now I was taking his locket to the duke—which must mean there was a secret message inside. Maybe the duke knew my father, and he was going to take me to him.

I put on my boots. I was already sleeping in my clothes—the same ones I'd been wearing for several months, since that woman in the hill town gave me the hand-me-downs that had once belonged to her son. The trousers were starting to get tight around my hips, but the coat sleeves still dangled, dirty, over my hands. Beneath me, in the lower part of the barn, a cow lowed, and the whispers of our rebel friends filtered through the dark. I clambered down the ladder, warming to the idea of carrying the locket. I was going to prove myself worthy. Then they wouldn't sing songs only about Mag Dunbarron, but about her daughter Sophy, too.

And maybe someone would give me a new change of clothes.

My mother and the other rebels were gathered in a circle toward the front of the barn. They'd opened the doors and fog seeped in, purling around their shoulders. They'd been talking quietly, but stopped as I approached.

"Ready to head out, Sophy?" Jock asked. His voice strained over the words.

They must all be afraid of sending me alone to Cerid Aven, where the duke lived. In truth, I was scared, too, but I wasn't about to let anyone see it—especially not my mother, who was the bravest person in the world. I widened my stance. "Of course I am!"

"Goodbye, then," he said. He kissed my forehead.

"Be careful, Sophy." That was Ethna. She, too, kissed my forehead.

The other rebels came forward one by one to kiss me and say goodbye—a dozen people with cold hands and sad eyes. My initial flush of pride began to shrink into something cold and scared. Maybe I wasn't being sent to be brave, but I didn't know why else I'd be sent away.

At last the goodbyes were done, and Ma led me out of the barn, into the fog, my hand tight in hers.

The last of my bravery slipped away. "I wish you could come with me," I whispered.

I heard her swallow. "I'll come after you, sweetheart. I promised, didn't I?"

We were silent, then, as we approached the edge of town, where small gaps showed through the wooden walls. The fog hid the soldiers' lights from us, but I smelled the smoke from their campfires, and heard an eerie jingle, like a horse's harness.

Ma paused beside the wall, her fingernails digging into my shoulder. "Once you reach the edge of camp, there's a path marked by a stone cairn. Follow it to the next cairn, and the next, and the next. You should reach Cerid Aven tomorrow, or the day after. You have hardtack?"

I nodded, waiting for her to give me a lecture about drinking only clean water. But she only said, "You'll make it."

I don't know if she really believed it, or only hoped.

"But how—" I began.

A creak sounded on the other side of the wall, shivering into the dark air. My heart surged. Ma hugged me tight—so tight I heard the sharp inhale and exhale of her breathing. She whispered, "Are you ready to be brave?"

The question she always asked me. The answer was always yes.

Although the truth was usually no.

"Yes," I whispered, even though fear tumbled liquid and hot through my limbs.

Something crunched on the other side of the wall, and I shuddered. There was a soft tap on the wood. My head jerked up, and my mother breathed against my cheek. "Go!"

I didn't want to go. I clung to her until she peeled my arms off and nudged me to the ground. My lips were trembling. Tears gathered in my eyes, but I had to be brave. My mother demanded it, and I couldn't let her down.

I crawled through the gap in the wall.

Rough hands grasped my wrists. The gap was low; I tasted dirt in my mouth. A man, little more than a silhouette in the fog, pulled me onto my feet. I caught the motion as he put a finger to his lips. Gestured to something behind him.

I stepped over to it, still shaking, numb with the shock of actually leaving my mother. My fingers met cold metal. A wheelbarrow. The man's hands closed on my waist, and I sucked in a panicked breath as he boosted me up. My shoe hit the metal with a resounding *ping,* bell-like in the fog. I jumped but the man didn't startle.

He settled me down in the bottom of the wheelbarrow, and I curled there with my knees tucked up to my chin. The man squeezed my shoulders, as if to reassure me. Then he unfurled a nubby blanket and threw it over me, and I was breathing hard in stuffy darkness, my heartbeat a crimson drum in my ears. I never got a good look at the man's face.

Several heavy objects settled on top of me. I smelled the pungent, sweet odor of new-cut wood. So he was pretending to gather fuel for their fires. The wheelbarrow tipped, jamming my feet below the rest of me, and we began to move.

At first I couldn't hear anything over the creaking wheels and the fear pulsing in my blood. Then there was a voice—in Ereni!—and white terror erupted through me, so bright I almost wet my too-tight trousers. But the man didn't stop. More voices passed overhead, a din of Ereni, and I shook in the bottom of the wheelbarrow, wondering if one of them belonged to the Butcher of Novarre.

The man kept on, and the voices faded. My chin jolted against my knees as we bumped over rough ground. Then suddenly I was lowered. The barrow stopped. The weights came off me, and the man ripped the blanket away.

He leaned over me. "You have two minutes. There's a trail at the base of the ridge. Get out and go!"

Then he was gone. I sat up in time to glimpse his retreating back.

I hauled myself out of the wheelbarrow, my legs shaking and buckling. I was going to be spotted by the Butcher of Novarre; I could feel it in my bones. I would be shot.

I forced myself to look around. The man had told me I had minutes, and I needed them. I wanted to live.

I was in a clearing beneath a forested ridge. A rock cairn marked the path between two trees. I forced my wobbling legs into motion and ran to the rock cairn that marked the narrow track. I charged uphill over roots and stones, my lungs burning. Near the top of the ridge, another cairn marked a turn deep into the woods. I looked back one last time, but I'd gone so far I could barely even see the Ereni camp. Only the faint whiff of smoke reminded me of what I'd left behind—that, and the locket pressing against my chest.

My MOTHER HAD trained me well. I could walk all day, with only short stops for water and a bite of hardtack. I'd learned to manage without much food. Even through a haze of exhaustion and fear, I knew how to keep going. At night, I knew not to light a fire but to make myself a bed out of dry pine needles.

I lay awake all night, all the same, touching my chest where the locket covered the empty hollow in my heart. Wondering why Ma had sent me away. Feeling small in the hugeness of the dark woods. I whispered words to comfort myself. The old poem about Wildegarde, the first steward of the land, and Aline, the queen of Caeris.

From the mountains beyond the moon, nursed by dragons, Wildegarde came—down to the court of Queen Aline. The queen did not know what to make of such a woman, her hands and legs covered in leaves as a tree is. She said, "Who are you? Why have you come?" and Wildegarde answered, "I am the breath of the mountains, the whisper of the waters, the swift passing of a bird, the hollows within the hills. I have come for you. I have come so we can make a song together."

I must be brave, I told myself. *Brave, like Aline. Like the queens of old.*

By dawn, I was ready to go again. The path clung to shadowy forests, only occasionally crossing farm fields and nearing towns, and I took care that no one noticed me. A second night passed much the same as the first, though exhaustion forced me to sleep. I began to wonder if I'd missed a turn; if I wasn't really headed for Cerid Aven but to Eren and all the dangers that lurked in the south.

When I ran out of hardtack around noon, I started to cry. Why had Ma sent me out like this? I wasn't brave. I was just a scared little girl, with aching feet and an empty stomach.

But scared as I was, I was still Mag Dunbarron's daughter. I made myself stop crying and walked on, passing the rocky shoulder of a high limestone hill that jutted far overhead. The forest had turned to a woods full of enormous old oaks, their trunks five times my size. I'd lost track of the rock cairns, and the path I was on seemed well trampled. I should get off it, find somewhere more secure. Except where was I supposed to go? I was so lost, and so frightened.

The edge of a pale-gray building came into sight ahead.

I slowed, my heart thudding in my hollow chest. The path had brought me here, but was this Cerid Aven, as my mother had promised? And how would I know? It wasn't as if there were a big sign out front, proclaiming my destination. Yet I had clearly arrived at a wealthy person's mansion. The building stretched into a series of fine, many-paned windows, and sculpted gardens cupped it, studied and elegant. If Duke Ruadan lived anywhere, it must be here.

I edged closer. There was a woman out in the gardens. She wore a blue coat over a pale-yellow gown, and her hair was piled up in a dark, lustrous mound atop her head, the way I remembered ladies in the city doing theirs. She was humming, patting her hand against her thigh in rhythm. Even though she was making music, something about her seemed unaccountably sad.

I tried not to make a sound, but she must have felt my gaze on her back. She turned and saw me.

For a moment, we both stared at each other, frozen.

"Who are you?" she demanded. The edge of an accent warmed her voice, and though it wasn't Ereni, I didn't know what it was. Maybe I had wandered off the very edge of the map.

"Is this Cerid Aven?" I asked, my voice high-pitched. If it wasn't, I'd run. I could run faster than this woman in her fine gown, I knew it.

"You're a girl," she said, and the sadness in her intensified. She held out her hand. "What are you doing out here, child?"

I asked my question again. "Is this Cerid Aven?"

She nodded.

Relief burst through me in huge, cartwheeling warmth. I actually swayed and almost fell onto my knees. The woman started toward me, her face worried. But I had a job to do. "I have a message for Duke Ruadan."

"A message? But you're barely . . ." She shook her head. "Caeri-sians." She took my arm, and I let her, because her touch was gentle and she looked so worried, the way my mother had looked when I'd fallen on that rock and sprained my ankle once. "I can take you to Ruadan. I'm his wife, Teofila."

"Oh," I said. That explained the accent—she came from Baedon, across the narrow strait. It also explained why she was sad. The king had taken away her daughter Elanna, who was only a little younger than me. "My name is Sophy Dunbarron."

As we went inside, I glimpsed my face in the windowpane. It was thin, with huge, staring eyes. My hair hung in dirty ropes beneath my hat. I looked like a beggar. A vagrant.

Teofila led me over fine carpets, past statues and paintings, calling out to well-dressed servants to bring tea and food and the duke. She took me to a big room full of cozy furniture the same yellow as her skirt and stood me in front of the fire. I had never felt anything so glorious. I thought I was going to melt into a puddle there on Duke Ruadan's soft wool rug.

Then I opened my eyes and a tall, sharp-eyed man was coming into the room. He gave Teofila a questioning look.

"This is Sophy," she said. "She—"

I widened my stance. I'd come all this way, and I had one job. I lifted my chin and addressed Duke Ruadan myself. "I have a message for you from Mag Dunbarron."

Ruadan looked startled. He exchanged a glance with Teofila. "Mag? Are you her daughter? Where is she?"

Duke Ruadan knew my mother by name? I wanted to melt again, though at the same time nothing seemed more natural. My mother was a force of nature; the queen of the rebels. Of course the duke who'd tried to lead a rebellion knew her. "She was in the village of Marose a few days ago."

"Marose," Ruadan repeated. Again, his gaze flicked to his wife.

I reached for my locket and pulled it over my head. "This is for you."

Wordlessly, he opened the locket. But only the single, inch-long strand of red-gold hair slipped from it, still bound tightly with a black ribbon. It fell to the carpet at my feet.

I stared at it. There was no message. No carefully folded paper with a secret missive from my mother. "It's my father's," I said.

Teofila crouched beside me. She handed the hair to Ruadan, and touched my cheek. "Sophy, are you sure your mother was in Marose?"

I nodded. I couldn't escape the feeling I'd been cheated.

She drew in a breath. Ruadan was watching us, but Teofila didn't take her eyes off me. "It's just that we've had some terrible news from Marose this morning. The Butcher of Novarre had the town surrounded."

"I know! I had to escape in a wheelbarrow."

Teofila gripped my hands. "So you were there when it burned?"

My mouth dropped open. The hope that had been fluttering in me stilled and died. I whispered, "Burned?"

"Yes." She held me harder, but did not spare me the truth. "Your mother must have sent you to safety. The whole village was burned to the ground, along with everyone in it. I'm sorry. I'm so, so sorry."

Air whined in my ears. I was more numb than I had been when I climbed from the wheelbarrow. I couldn't comprehend it. Everyone, dead? The rebels, the villagers? *The cows?*

The duke crouched beside Teofila. He reached out, touching his fingers to my chin. I looked up at him, and I knew then that he'd known my mother, because there was winter in his eyes the way there was winter in my heart. But there was also something else. Hope.

"You don't have a message," he said. "*You* are the message."

Teofila looked at him sharply.

"She's the future of Caeris," he told her. "Sophy," he said to me, with an urgency I didn't understand, "did Mag ever tell you who your father was?"

I shook my head.

The duke gripped my shoulder. He held the locket out to me. "This hair belongs to Euan Dromahair, the rightful king of Caeris. He's your natural father, Sophy."

I glanced uncertainly at Teofila. Her lips were pressed together, but she nodded at me. It wasn't entirely reassuring. My father, the man who should be king? It didn't make sense. And yet, knowing my mother, I believed it.

"And if he doesn't come to Caeris to claim his throne," the duke continued, "or if his son doesn't, do you know who will?"

"Who?" I whispered.

Ruadan Valtai looked into my eyes, searchingly, as if he were trying to find the backbone of a queen. "You."

And I knew then that I must be brave, alone.

CHAPTER ONE

Ruadan is gone now, executed on the steps of the Tower in Laon, and all I am left with, in the cold light of dawn, is memories. And a creeping doubt about whether I can possibly become the queen he raised me to be.

There's a soft noise outside my tent. The mountain women who form my queen's guard shift on the other side of the flap but don't seem alarmed, so I guess who it must be.

I throw on my riding habit and step out just as Elanna goes by, a slight figure bundled in an overlarge greatcoat, curls of chestnut hair escaping over its worn collar. As usual, she seems oblivious to my presence. I follow her out into the gray-green dawn. Light softens the rough tents that make up our rundown camp above the river Ard, near a town called Tavistock. Across the wide, rocky water, mingling with the fog, smoke drifts from the Tinani camp where King Alfred's troops are waking to begin their latest offensive. They should have no idea that the Butcher of Novarre is here, along with Elanna and myself—or at least, I hope they don't. The Butcher keeps claiming our ranks are littered with spies loyal to the Ereni nobles who fled the kingdom after our rebellion, and who now have the ears of King Alfred of Tinan. I've heard no rumors that they wish to reinstate Loyce Eyrlai, so maybe they're simply working against us out of spite. Given the narrow-minded thinking of some of my ministers, I wouldn't be surprised.

The guards on the edge of camp acknowledge El, but—as usual—no one seems to take much notice of me. Despite my greater height and brilliant red coat, the people only have eyes for their *Caveadear.* I might as well be invisible.

We leave the guards behind, though. El doesn't want anyone to witness her weakness.

At the top of the bluff, overlooking the river, she pauses, and I step up beside her. Softly, I say, "Can I help?"

She casts me a tight, skeptical look. She's been angry with me ever since I encouraged Jahan to go to Ida and argue our case before the emperor of Paladis, but now she simply seems condescending. "No, Sophy. There's nothing you can do."

I swallow down a pulse of frustration. As if she needs to remind me, again, that she possesses sorcery and I don't. That she is the real leader of Eren and Caeris, the one they truly respect, and I am not. That *she* is Ruadan's real daughter, and I am merely the one he replaced her with. As soon as she returned to Caeris, our rebellion and our lives became all about her. She is the *Caveadear,* the steward of the land, the future of Eren and Caeris. She's the hope of the kingdom, the symbol of magic reemerging throughout the world.

I am the backup. A would-be Aline to her earth-shaking Wildegarde. The second choice—the girl who took her father's throne when her dead half brother could not, and whose father has never once acknowledged her existence. Who took the throne, in some ways, because she knew her mother would expect it, encourage it, if she still lived.

I'm not proud of how I feel. I remind myself that I love El like a sister. But like a sister, I wish she would learn how to share. And take me seriously.

She's already descending the steep trail down to the river—a spot she picked out yesterday, when the Butcher insisted a display of her magic would put the terror of the gods into the Tinani and destroy their current offensive.

I'm more worried about it destroying El.

There's a scrape behind me. Rhia Knoll hops up through the fog,

alert despite the tiredness pinching her eyes. I can feel my own exhaustion mirroring hers. As usual, a frown puckers her black eyebrows, belying her delicate features. She tugs the collar of her
dark-blue coat up to her ears. The wind is sweeping down from the
north, bringing the coldness of the still-snow-capped mountains in
the Tail Ridge, though we're in the north of Eren, several days'
travel from the peaks.

Rhia peers toward the foggy river. "Is she down there?"

I gesture with my chin. El has reached a rocky shelf above the
water. She's just visible through the fog, her old greatcoat rendering
her shapeless.

Even though she frustrates me, I'm worried about her. Rhia and I
might be tired, but Elanna's exhaustion seems so deep it runs into
the marrow of her bones—and into the land itself. The Butcher
wanted her to perform this feat of magic at high noon, for the world
to see, as if she could merely snap her fingers and burst the dam
upstream that will flood the Ard. And perhaps, in the days after she
woke the land, she could. Now, though, her magic is tired and so is
she. I'm afraid she won't be able to swamp the Tinani camp, and if
we have to fight this battle with guns and men and horses, we're
going to lose. Tinan's being supplied by the empire of Paladis; they
have more manpower and more guns. And it's not been our forces
that have stopped the Tinani crossing the river, despite the Butcher's
attempts to impress his superior generalship upon everyone. Elanna's
the one who has stopped them, time and again.

She needs help. A respite. Something. Yet I'm too afraid to suggest she rest. We all are.

"Are you feeling better?" Rhia asks me.

I inadvertently touch my fingertips to my stomach, then stuff my
hands into the pockets of my coat. "I don't know what you mean."

She eyes me. "Don't be cagey with me, Dunbarron. You looked
green all last month. Father thought someone was poisoning you."

"Oh, that." I attempt nonchalance. "Something I picked up in
Laon—stomach sickness. Everyone had it."

Rhia raises an eyebrow but shrugs. I slowly release my breath.

Rhia remained on the border the last time I went to the capital, so how would she know I'm lying? Besides, for all I know, people have been ill; it's that time of year.

All the same, the temptation to tell her the truth presses against the back of my throat. We're alone on the bluff—or as alone as we're going to get—and the weight of this secret is pulling me down. I feel the need to confess like a hand between my shoulder blades. But I know what Rhia Knoll will say. She'll tell me I'm being a fool in more ways than one. There's only one solution for this problem, and Rhia won't have any trouble telling me what it is.

Am I being a fool?

Of course I am. I know it, but I have no other choice. At least, not one that will let me sleep at night. Ruadan used to say that we are defined by the decisions we make, and that the larger the choice, the more we must face it head-on, clear-eyed. I made this choice; I can't pretend, even to myself, that it was an accident.

But sometimes I wish Ruadan had said something else. That we are more than the sum of our decisions.

I fold my arms, unable to confess, and neither of us says much. The fog's beginning to burn away as Elanna sits motionless on the shelf below us, giving no indication she's aware of our presence. The cold seeps into my bones.

"Queen Sophy!"

I turn. A runner is coming up the hillside from our camp. "You have a visitor," he pants.

I look past him, toward the rough, fraying tents the Butcher insisted on using, trying to disguise the fact that not only is he here, but El, Rhia, and I are, too. Our intelligence intercepted the Tinani plan to cross here north of Tavistock, and now we can only hope that information was accurate. I wonder if the two new arrivals who have appeared outside the command tent—two men, from the looks of it, on black horses, though I can't make out their faces from here—have anything to do with that. The Butcher's come out to greet them; I recognize his bandy-legged silhouette.

"There'll be hot coffee down there," Rhia says. She's been obsessed with the stuff since she first had it in Laon a few months ago. Now, true to form, she charges off toward camp. The messenger hesitates between her and me.

I glance down the slope, toward El. She's still unmoving. To all appearances, she's unaware that we're even up here.

With a sigh, I follow the messenger and Rhia toward the command tent.

The men have gone inside by the time I arrive, along with Rhia, who's standing in front of a silver coffeepot with a look of sweet bliss on her usually ornery face. "Here, Sophy." She thrusts a cup at me. "It'll do you wonders."

One of the new arrivals swings around. "Soph! I mean . . . Your Majesty," he corrects himself, doubling over into a low bow.

I smile down at the top of his head. "Alistar." For once, his hair isn't pomaded into spikes, but lies flat in soft brown waves. My fingers twitch.

He looks up at me, and his eyes spark in a familiar way. "You look well."

I claim the cup of coffee from Rhia and smirk at him over the rim. But then out the corner of my eye, I catch sight of the Butcher's disapproving scowl and sigh. Some people—Rhia, for instance—don't care that Alistar and I are together, but I know from past conversations that the Butcher considers my relationship with Alistar a disgrace to my crown. Maybe this is just because he hates to see other people having feelings, not to mention affection, but enough other people seem to agree with him that I've become self-conscious. I can already feel the weight of his stare.

I give Alistar a stern glance. "What are you doing here?" I ask, striving to sound businesslike and not as if his knowing smile is unraveling me. "I thought you were evacuating the people from Tavistock."

It's the other new arrival who speaks, his light voice Ereni-accented. "I'm afraid I interrupted Master Connell's work." He bows. "Your Majesty."

I finally look beyond Alistar and startle. His companion is a young man with cropped auburn hair and a fox's clever face. Philippe Manceau, the minister of public works.

"Lord Philippe," I say, and though I know my tone is starved of warmth, I can't change it. "What are *you* doing here?"

Again, he bows—an insistence on etiquette that sets my teeth on edge. "The ministers wished me to observe the *Caveadear's* use of magic in person. I prevailed on Master Connell to guide me here."

"I was coming this way anyhow," Alistar says gruffly. I can tell the *Master Connell*ing is putting his back up.

I study Philippe Manceau, the Count of Lylan. He's the only man in the tent—in the entire camp—not in uniform or at least wearing a sash to show his allegiance to Eren and Caeris. Instead he's in dark, somber colors, like a banker who's gotten lost on his way to examine an investment. I don't need to ask which ministers decided, independently, that they needed to send a representative to check up on me. The Ereni are always doing things like this, to quietly remind me that, as far as they're concerned, I'm still on probation.

Philippe gestures toward the river. "Who can resist an opportunity to see the steward of the land in action?"

"I can think of a few," I remark. Half of the people in my Ereni cabinet openly distrust magic—and, by extension, Elanna. They were elected, so I can't simply throw them out, but we all know they bought those votes. We may have brought elections to Eren, but even though most commoners seem to approve of my rule, the wealthy still control their lands—and, thus, many people's choices.

And some of those nobles are still angry that we overthrew the Eyrlais. Philippe, I suspect, is one of them, though he's never said anything overtly against me.

The Butcher of Novarre intervenes. "You'll see, Lord Philippe. If all goes according to plan, the Tinani will no longer pose much of a threat to Eren at all."

"Let us pray to the gods that this is the case," Philippe says.

"Who needs gods when we have the *Caveadear*?" Rhia says. She's drunk a second cup of coffee and seems to be vibrating slightly.

I exchange a glance with Alistar. "Let's go down to the river."

᪲

DOWN BY THE shore, Elanna raises her arms. We all fall silent, watching her. She looks so small down there. A hush lifts from her, so strange and tremulous even I can feel it. My skin itches. I rub the back of my neck. I may not be a sorceress, but sometimes—often, lately—my body reacts when magic is performed nearby.

Philippe turns his head toward me, and I force myself still. At least Rhia and Alistar are also here. A loud clatter echoes from the Tinani camp, then all falls into silence like an indrawn breath. It extends and extends. The sunlight glimmers on the water. The weight of it tugs through the reeds along the shore. On the other side, some Tinani have come down and are staring across at us, gesturing.

Pressure pulses behind my eyelids. There's a rushing in my ears. I stumble, my body flushing with heat, my head swimming and my stomach churning—

Philippe catches me against his arm. "Are you ill?"

"I—"

Water erupts down the river. A surge of it, swelling and overflowing the reeds on the banks. Shouts rise from the Tinani camp. They're on a curve, and the river is naturally pouring into their camp—but I can hardly hear them over the roaring in my ears. My coat seems to be strangling me. I fling out a hand—someone grasps it—but I'm blinded, my ears filled with a sweep of verdant sound—a kind of music that rises, trembling, through the layers and fissures of the land, caught on the current of the great black river. It splits through the earth's inertia, a driving green force that transforms everything in its wake. I'm shaking, dizzy—

My knees fetch up against a rock. An arm cups my back. Alistar is hugging me to his chest; his face blurs, and then my eyes focus. His eyebrows are pinched. With worry?

"You're ill, Soph," he says.

I shake my head. "I'm fine."

I've never *felt* Elanna's magic before. Not like that. I've *seen* it, and felt the tremble of tree roots skimming the earth, but I've never *heard* it in my own body, as if it were a part of me. As if it were a song so powerful it mingled with my very blood.

I'm still light-headed. Rhia and Philippe are hovering anxiously behind Alistar's shoulders. When Rhia says, "Put your head between your knees," I do.

Or at least I try. My stomach bulks up, in my way. I jerk back, glancing down at the overlarge twill waistcoat—once Ruadan's, for he was taller than me—that I've been wearing for weeks over my increasingly muddy riding skirt. Its plain brown buttons seem to stare back at me, innocent.

Alistar crouches beside me. "Sophy, breathe. It's all right. What happened?"

"I'm fine. Don't let anyone else see."

"No one's watching but us. Are you all right? Should I call a doctor?"

"No—"

Above us, Rhia tenses. She screams. *"Elanna!"*

I lift my head, but another wave of nausea rolls through me. This shouldn't be happening. The nausea left me weeks ago. All the same, my stomach feels as if it's doubling over on itself. I press my hands to my cheeks. My face feels cold and clammy.

"Where's El?" I manage.

Philippe has also tensed, rocking up onto his toes. He shouts. *"Caveadear!"*

Rhia sprints away, leaping over the lip of rock onto the narrow path. I force myself upright. Alistar's leaning forward, past Philippe. He sucks in a breath. Swears. Whatever he sees galvanizes him, too. "Elanna!" He leaps up, then pauses. He points at me. "Stay here, Soph."

He charges down the steep trail, Philippe at his heels. I crawl forward on my hands and knees. The nausea is passing. My ears are clearing.

A bell rings over the water—a quivering, grasping sound.

Witch hunters. My whole body jolts with sudden, white fear.

They found us—they found El. I stare across the water, willing them to come into view. But the fog, rather than clearing, is gathering more densely over the river. I can only just make out movement on the opposite bank.

There's a noise below me—a grunt. I look down, and I see her. I see *them.*

Below me, a man is running down along the bank's edge. He wears simple, dark clothes—they're wet, I realize, as if he got caught in the flooding water. Another man hurries behind him. My heart turns over. These aren't our men; they must be Tinani. But how did they even *get* here over the flooding river?

Unless they knew El was going to be here. They could have crossed over, somewhere upstream where the river narrows, before dawn.

Or they could have been here much longer. They could have been put into place long before we arrived; they could have been waiting for this moment. And the intelligence the Butcher intercepted, about the Tinani being here . . .

The first man jumps over a rock. He's almost reached her. *"El!"* I scream. Alistar and Philippe are still too high up. Rhia has had to slow on the steep bank, still more than a man's height above El. One of the assailants reaches for El's arm—she dodges him, but the other is coming up, and—

She slips. The rushing water catches her. She's swept off her feet. Her hat falls off. Black water billows up her greatcoat.

Then the water sweeps Elanna under. Downstream.

The men race after her along the bank. Behind them, Rhia takes a flying leap and dives into the water after El.

I'm running. Running after Alistar and Philippe, down to the shore. "El!" I scream.

The land loves her. She can control the flood and where the river's sweeping her. Can't she?

Downstream, her head pops back up, wet and sleek as a seal. The current is driving her toward the opposite bank. She thrashes, but it makes no difference. She doesn't know how to swim. Rhia seems to—she's making headway toward El, at any rate—but now the roaring river's caught them both. They're sweeping away from us at impossible speed.

And the assailants are still running along the bank—downstream to the ford, no doubt. Shouts echo from the opposite bank, still shrouded in fog, over the roaring water. We're all being followed.

Ahead, Alistar's flinging off his coat as he runs. Philippe pumps his arms. I manage not to trip on the rock scree. "Downstream!" I shout as I barrel between the men. "Go downstream!"

We're all running together now, along the marshy shore, my feet catching in pots of mud and moss-slimed rocks. El's and Rhia's heads flash above the black water. The next moment, El disappears again. Rhia shouts, for all the good that does. The two men have vanished around the curve in the river.

We charge through the marsh, past drowning trees, onto a rock spit of land jutting into the river. Water surges over my shoes, drenching my stockings, weighing down my skirts and the heavy wool of my coat.

An arm reaches out of the water far ahead of us, just visible through the dense fog, on the opposite bank. El's head follows. She drags herself up through the muck, a small, distant figure. Rhia swirls past her with an echoing cry, thrashing toward the shore.

"I'm going after them." Alistar tugs off his boots.

"So am I," Philippe begins.

There's a shout behind us—the Butcher charging through the trees toward us, shouting for us to stay back. He points toward the opposite bank.

I turn, squinting. The fog is still too thick, but again I hear shouts.

I'm defenseless. Weaponless. The queen of Eren and Caeris, standing bareheaded on the riverbank.

And the *Caveadear* and the daughter of the warden of the mountains are trapped in enemy territory.

But I was the girl who slipped under the Butcher's nose.

Alistar's already splashing deep into the water. He knows how to swim; we used to challenge each other to see who could hold their breath longest in the clear, cold pool beneath the Sentry Rock at Cerid Aven. He flings himself forward with sure strokes.

On the opposite bank, El's clambered up, staggering as she vanishes through the fog into marsh grass. She seems to be heading for Rhia, who's also made it to shore, though much farther downstream.

The fog, rather than lifting, drifts more thickly from the river. Elanna's disappeared completely into it now. As I watch, it swallows Alistar, too. Maybe it's El's doing—to hide us, to save herself.

The thought galvanizes me. I grab Philippe's elbow; he's hesitant to get in the water. Maybe he can't swim. "This way!" I say. We run along the bank, staggering over downed trees and the long grass hiding soft, watery holes. Mist gathers around our ankles, growing thicker and thicker over the river. We are swaddled in white. There's little noise but my breathing in my ears and the rush of Philippe's and my footsteps. Behind and to our right, soft whistles fly through the woods—the Butcher and his men communicating our location. He must be heading for the ford half a mile downstream, and so are El, Alistar, and Rhia.

And the men who sneaked onto the bank.

The Butcher may be able to deal with them—if Philippe and I can distract the Tinani, even for just a few minutes.

"We need a diversion," I tell Philippe between gasps for breath. "We need to make them think El went the opposite way."

What would my mother do? What *did* she do, when I was a child?

The fog twines thick around us. White, muffling. Disorienting, even on land, but especially on water.

"How far can you throw?" I ask Philippe.

"A rock?" He fishes one out of the shallows. His silhouette is melting into the fog; his breath billows, white.

He turns and with his whole body, throws the rock back upstream. It splashes loudly.

I nod. "Another. Farther, if you can."

He tries again. This one makes a smaller splash, closer to shore. The fog chokes the water, so thick now I've no idea where Alistar is, much less Elanna and Rhia.

Philippe throws another rock, and I crouch and do the same, making as much racket as we can. My arm starts to ache. Philippe looks at me, ghostly in the gloom. "It's not—"

"Shh," I whisper.

A voice echoes across the river. A Tinani voice. I know enough Tinani—the language is sort of an amalgamation of Caerisian and Ereni—to pick out the words *here* and *watch* and *nothing.*

"Come on," I breathe in Philippe's ear, tugging him back upstream. I fumble for another rock and throw it, farther up.

The Tinani go silent, then their voices rumble again.

We throw more rocks. A Tinani soldier barks an order, somewhere nearby.

The fog has fully swallowed us now. Moisture condenses, cold on my face. I crouch, listening hard, gripping Philippe's arm to still him. The Tinani voices are drawing away from us—upstream.

By silent consent, Philippe and I rise and begin to make our way back downstream along the marshy riverbank. The trip seems to take longer than it should. In the white, it's impossible to see our soldiers, but my ears catch a murmur of voices. There's a sharp whistle.

"It's me," I say as the soldiers appear through the fog.

"Milady." They relax their guard. We've arrived at the ford, as far as I can tell; the ground has firmed to solid sand.

The Butcher pushes through the throng of soldiers. "We thought we'd lost you two."

"We were diverting the Tinani," I say. "But Alistar crossed the river."

The Butcher swears. He looks drawn. Cross. "So we've three to find. Do I have a volunteer to take a party across?"

"No," I blurt out, before I think better of contradicting Gilbert Moriens in front of his men. Tension thickens the foggy air. "I mean, let's wait a little longer. If we've successfully drawn the Tinani off, El and the others can cross back here. We don't want to draw more attention. You know Alistar and Rhia can handle most anything. I don't want to put anyone else at risk unnecessarily . . ."

I'm babbling, but my point must have been taken because Lord Gilbert gives a curt nod. The men relax fractionally.

"We wait here," the Butcher says.

Philippe touches my arm. "I'll escort you back to camp, my lady."

"I'm staying to wait for my friends. You can go back."

He holds my gaze. I don't look away. It's as if he wants to communicate something—as if he really does want me to go with him—and while this makes me wonder, I also don't entirely trust him.

At last, he sighs. "Fine. We stay here."

There wasn't a *we*, but I let this go. I stamp my feet to keep warm and blow on my hands. The fog gathers around us—a cold and inescapable embrace. I listen and listen, but I hear nothing. Nothing but the men around me breathing and sighing, shifting their feet. They must be as exhausted as I feel. My back aches. I try to beat back the worry creeping through me. If we lose El—Rhia—if we lose Alistar . . .

A sound.

A bell, ringing.

"Damn the gods," Philippe whispers.

The witch hunters have followed us downstream—or maybe they were waiting here all along. A shudder runs through me.

Another bell rings. A shout goes up. Across the river, a woman screams. I startle forward instinctively.

"Henri, Laurence, take your men and go!" the Butcher barks.

I start to move past him, but he grabs my arm. "Your Majesty, you have to *stay here*."

I gather my breath to shout at him, except he's right. If it's an ambush, we can't afford to lose El, Rhia, Alistar, *and* me. Someone has to stay here.

And it has to be me.

Angry tears burn my eyes, but I hold myself back. The Butcher gives me an approving look; I want to smack him. El has an admirable tolerance for the man, but I can never even look at him without remembering his past—what he did not only to me, but to so many others in Caeris and Eren alike. It galls me that he has the nerve to act superior—because while he may be a good tactician, he has never been an admirable man.

We wait. The Butcher on my left, Philippe on my right. The fog muffles their faces and I start to panic. What if Alistar's dead or captured? And I never told him?

Finally, a grunt carries over the water. Feet splash. I suck in my breath. A man's voice—in Ereni. Our people.

They come into view—their faces weary, their bodies silhouettes in the fog. As I stare, they part. Alistar staggers forward, carrying Rhia's limp body. Alistar's face is haggard. And Rhia . . .

Alistar sees me, and relief eases his face. "Sophy!"

"Where's El?" I whisper.

He shakes his head. Droops close to me, so I smell his sweat and the brackish water, and I see Rhia's eyelids twitching as she fumbles toward consciousness.

"They took her, Soph," he says. "The witch hunters. They have Elanna."

ABOUT THE AUTHOR

CALLIE BATES is a writer, harpist and certified harp thera-
pist, sometime artist, and nature nerd. When she's not
creating, she's hitting the trails or streets and exploring
new places. She lives in the Upper Midwest. *The Memory
of Fire* is the sequel to *The Waking Land,* her debut fantasy novel.

calliebates.com
Facebook.com/calliebywords
@calliebywords

ABOUT THE TYPE

THIS BOOK WAS SET IN SABON, a typeface designed by the well-known German typographer Jan Tschichold (1902–74). Sabon's design is based upon the original letter forms of sixteenth-century French type designer Claude Garamond and was created specifically to be used for three sources: foundry type for hand composition, Linotype, and Monotype. Tschichold named his typeface for the famous Frankfurt typefounder Jacques Sabon (c. 1520–80).

EXPLORE THE WORLDS
OF DEL REY BOOKS

Read excerpts from hot new titles.

Stay up-to-date on your favorite authors.

Find out about exclusive giveaways and sweepstakes.

Connect with us online!

Follow us on social media
 Facebook.com/DelReyBooks
 @DelReyBooks

Visit us at UnboundWorlds.com
Facebook.com/UnboundWorlds
@unboundworlds

DEL REY

Printed in the United States
by Baker & Taylor Publisher Services

He nods, resting his cheek against the earth. "That's . . . what I went . . . back for. To my . . . apartment. A reference . . . to the sorcerer . . . Paladius blackmailed . . . into creating this place. And the bells. Stones."

I stare at him. "You mad, brilliant bastard. *That's* what you risked your life for?"

"I thought . . . if we knew . . . construction of magic . . . we could . . . destroy bells. Defeat witch hunters."

I look down at him. Somehow, he's still smiling, the lunatic. "Did you know about the wells?" I ask. "The ones that concentrate magic in them?"

Excitement bursts over his face. He pushes himself onto his elbows. "*That's* what those references meant! I found stories about sorcerers going to wells—*dying* by wells. And then the wells couldn't be used, but it didn't lead to drought or any other consequence as far as I could tell . . ."

"It led to a *magical* drought," I say. "They're not necessarily water."

He stares at me, his mouth opening. "Jahan . . . if those stories are true, then there are wells everywhere. All over Ida—all over Paladis."

"And the sorcerers closed them." I shudder a little, thinking of Mantius and Tuah. "They gave their lives to seal them off—to keep Paladius the First from using them."

Pantoleon nods. "But you found a way to open them again—"

"One, anyway. And I think there's one beneath the Ochuroma . . ."

We stare at each other, then Pantoleon actually laughs. I'm grinning, too. "Well, this will be quite a change to the empire," I say. Pantoleon snorts. I look at him. I wish he'd waited to go back to his apartment; that he'd told me before he raced off. But here we are together, both of us alive, somehow, and I feel limp with gratitude. I squeeze his shoulder. He nods at me.

"We'll find all of the wells," I say. "We'll open each damned one."